PENGUIN CLASSICS

FOUR STORIES BY AMERICAN WOMEN

CYNTHIA GRIFFIN WOLFF received an undergraduate degree from Radcliffe; after spending a year at Harvard Medical School, she withdrew to return to the English Department, where she received a Ph.D. in Literature from Harvard University. She has published essays on a wide diversity of subjects, including Henry Fielding, the English and American Gothic traditions, Jane Austen, Kate Chopin, Mark Twain, and Babe Ruth. She has authored three books: *Samuel Richardson and the Eighteenth Century Puritan Character* (1972); *A Feast of Words: The Triumph of Edith Wharton* (1977); and *Emily Dickinson* (1986). In addition, she has edited many volumes of American literature. She teaches nineteenth- and early twentieth-century American literature and culture at the Massachusetts Institute of Technology, where she holds The Class of 1922 Professorship of the Humanities.

Four Stories by American Women

Life in the Iron Mills,
by Rebecca Harding Davis

The Yellow Wallpaper,
by Charlotte Perkins Gilman

The Country of the Pointed Firs,
by Sarah Orne Jewett

Souls Belated,
by Edith Wharton

EDITED AND WITH AN INTRODUCTION BY
Cynthia Griffin Wolff

AND WITH NOTES BY
Sarah Higginson Begley
and
Monica L. Kearney

PENGUIN BOOKS

PENGUIN BOOKS

Published by the Penguin Group

Penguin Group (USA) Inc., 375 Hudson Street, New York, New York 10014, U.S.A.

Penguin Group (Canada), 90 Eglinton Avenue East, Suite 700, Toronto,
Ontario, Canada M4P 2Y3 (a division of Pearson Penguin Canada Inc.)

Penguin Books Ltd, 80 Strand, London WC2R 0RL, England

Penguin Ireland, 25 St Stephen's Green, Dublin 2, Ireland (a division of Penguin Books Ltd)

Penguin Group (Australia), 250 Camberwell Road, Camberwell,
Victoria 3124, Australia (a division of Pearson Australia Group Pty Ltd)

Penguin Books India Pvt Ltd, 11 Community Centre, Panchsheel Park, New Delhi – 110 017, India

Penguin Group (NZ), cnr Airborne and Rosedale Roads,
Albany, Auckland 1310, New Zealand (a division of Pearson New Zealand Ltd)

Penguin Books (South Africa) (Pty) Ltd, 24 Sturdee Avenue,
Rosebank, Johannesburg 2196, South Africa

Penguin Books Ltd, Registered Offices: 80 Strand, London WC2R 0RL, England

This collection first published in Penguin Books 1990

20 19 18 17 16

Introduction and notes copyright
© Cynthia Griffin Wolff, 1990
All rights reserved

"Life in the Iron Mills" was first published in 1861.
"The Yellow Wallpaper" was first published in 1892.
"The Country of the Pointed Firs"
was first published in 1896.
"Souls Belated" was first published in 1899.

LIBRARY OF CONGRESS CATALOGING IN PUBLICATION DATA

Four stories by American women/edited and with an introduction by
Cynthia Griffin Wolff; and with notes by Sarah Higginson Begley.
p.   cm. — (Penguin classics)
Includes bibliographical references.
Contents: Life in the iron mills/by Rebecca Harding Davis—The
yellow wallpaper/by Charlotte Perkins Gilman—The country of the
pointed firs/by Sarah Orne Jewett—Souls belated/by Edith
Wharton.
ISBN 0 14 03.9076 6
1. American fiction—Women authors.   2. Women—Fiction.
I. Wolff, Cynthia Griffin.   II. Series.
PS647.W6F68   1990
813.008'09287—dc20   90-7360

Printed in the United States of America
Set in Garamond No. 3

Contents

Introduction

From the beginning of the American fictional tradition, there has consistently been a wealth of productive women authors: indeed, two of the works that may be said to have inaugurated that tradition were written by women—*Charlotte Temple* (1794), by Susanna Rowson, and *The Coquette* (1797), by Hannah Foster. By the 1820s, Catherine Maria Sedgwick, Lydia Maria Child, Margaret Bayard Smith, and others like them had become active in the profession of novel-writing. And by midcentury such women were successful enough to perturb even that great and justly admired craftsman Nathaniel Hawthorne, who wrote in irritation to his editor about the "damned mob of scribbling women" and worried about the possible effects of their influence upon American literature. When *Uncle Tom's Cabin* was published in book form (1852), its sales were so phenomenal (300,000 copies in the first year) that it set a standard for "best-sellers" that would not be surpassed for many decades. Harriet Beecher Stowe continued to write fiction after her explosive appearance into American life—one of an ever-expanding field of widely read women novelists during the later nineteenth century.

Indeed, there were so many female writers of fiction before the First World War that there is a certain peculiarity in having to urge the proposition that they existed. And yet one must. With some exceptions, the work of these women has achieved neither the enduring popularity nor the continued praise that has been accorded male authors, and it has fallen into an obscurity that has all but erased it from the memory of a once enthusiastic general public.

There can be no doubt that some of these novels ceased to be read or even recollected primarily because their literary quality was inferior. Overwhelmingly domestic in their focus, they tended to be doggedly sentimental, even lachrymose: their plots were often predictable and formulaic, and the language could become florid, melodramatic, or embarrassingly graceless. Such shortcomings are not surprising. Until very late—perhaps until the last two decades of the nineteenth century—women who wrote fiction almost never thought of themselves as artists. *Nor were they in any way encouraged to do so.* Instead, they were expected to address limited subjects, using only those novelistic devices that would make no strenuous demands upon the reader. Too often, then, the result was mediocrity.

When present-day scholars began to reexamine this body of work they often found strikingly suggestive plot patterns; sometimes, they made powerful inferences from the relatively stereotyped delineations of character. Thus there has been a resurgence of interest in this body of fiction; however, it has more often been expressed in scholarly writing than in classroom teaching.

Perhaps the most important insight to emerge from all of the recent study of this area is a growing awareness of the shaping, selecting, sometimes stifling influence of ideology upon the process of writing and reifying literature.

The web that has been woven by the exercise of ideology is so complex that only its most obvious elements can be identified in this brief context. As an initial step, we might observe that the regulations governing "appropriate" subject matter (women were expected to write only about the domestic, personal realm) were an expression of the implicit ideology concerning the real-life roles that American women were expected to play. Hence these regulations were confirmed by limitations upon behavior that were rigidly enforced by society: until after the Civil War, no "decent" woman in a town of any size could be a salesclerk or a stenographer or a nurse (medical schools, of course, generally did not admit them); in 1913, when Edith Wharton published her masterful study of buccaneering capitalism, *The Custom of the Country,* no woman was allowed on the floor of the Stock Exchange on Wall Street (hence no woman novelist could obtain firsthand data from that mighty arena). Second, we might note that the language of "propriety" was little more than a thinly disguised vernacular of power: it was somehow "right" that men could hold public office and that women, if they held power at all, could exercise it in none but circumscribed and indirect ways—that men in general could earn money and women in general could not. Finally, this language of power reflected an unstated but nonetheless sovereign value of American cultural standards. The supremely interesting and admirable enterprises of human endeavor were held to be those that pertained to the exercise of individualism and conquest; by comparison, the virtues of compassion, charity, amity—the capacity to forge and sustain communal bonds—were held to be only of the second order. By extension, then, even if women became *very great artists within the realms that had been delimited as "appropriate,"* they would nonetheless run the almost certain risk of being consigned to some second order of aesthetic existence—having "failed" to address the "epic" potentialities of the American wilderness. (And to complete the impossible paradigm, should any woman novelist have the temerity to address the "inappropriate" subjects of big business or epic conquest, editors and reviewers might be inclined to draw back in horror at this violation of sacred propriety.)

These are the baffling constraints that have traditionally restricted American women writers at all times; however, perhaps no group of women writers experienced the conflicting demands of this ideology more painfully than those women who wrote fiction during the fifty or sixty years following the beginning of the Civil War. This was a period of widespread social change. It was also the period when, for the first time, the women fiction writers of this country could begin to think of themselves as artists—working not merely (or even primarily) for the pleasure of some current reading public, but for the enlightenment of generations. Such women were pioneers, and they were obliged to invent their own new modes of fiction, not entirely ignoring the domestic inheritance of the women writers who had been their immediate predecessors, but not being limited by it either. Of course, they were not always fully successful; yet even some of their imperfect efforts have great interest and merit. And sometimes they created works of superb subtlety and strength—works that have been, until recently, undervalued because they did not satisfy that clamoring American demand for an affirmation of adventure, conquest, and the assertion of naked individualism.

Perhaps no work brings together the many forces abroad during this tumultuous period better than Rebecca Harding Davis's remarkable short story "Life in the Iron Mills," which was published by the *Atlantic Monthly* in April 1861—almost simultaneously with the fall of Fort Sumter and the beginning of the Civil War. The story was an oddity—an innovation—a bold indictment of the dark satanic mills. Indebted, perhaps, to Dickens (to his portrayals of that city of dreadful night in *Bleak House*) or to Mrs. Gaskell (who wrote fictions like *Mary Barton,* urging the fact that even the poorest British workers treasure their own domestic pieties as deeply as the well-to-do), "Life in the Iron Mills" was an entirely new kind of *American* fiction. It anticipated the future, looked fifty years ahead toward the work of Norris and Dreiser and Upton Sinclair. Yet it did not lean, as so many of those later works of social protest did, upon gloomy, philosophical abstractions concerning the animalistic elements of human nature. Instead, it took the insights of Harriet Beecher Stowe one step further. In *Uncle Tom's Cabin,* Stowe had eloquently urged the essential humanity of black people—the indefensible *inhumanity* of their enslavement—and the imperative of making political reforms. Her mode of "argumentation" had been "domestic": these feel and love just as you do; understand them as you understand yourself and the members of your own family, and grant them full and equal membership in the "family" of America. What Rebecca Harding Davis argued, through the medium of her compelling short tale, was that slavery is not essentially a matter of color, that "slavery" is a socially constructed category, and that the white millworkers of western Virginia are perhaps as brutally "enslaved" as their unfortunate black brothers and sisters of the Deep South.

One way of describing Davis's work is to observe that she introjected the "woman's realm" and its network of moral values into the specifically public world of economic competition. Even more daringly than Stowe, whose work was consistent with the abolition movement's attitudes, Davis invaded territory that had been reserved entirely for men in this country—territory that was unquestioningly consigned to their supervision—the realm of business and manufacture and money. "Life in the Iron Mills" demands that this squalid realm (dominated by the ethics of conquest) yield to the virtues of compassion and amity (hitherto consigned to the lesser realm of women).

The revolutionary proposal is announced by the very format of the story. It opens within the home, narrated in the first person by a speaker whose gender is never specifically identified but whose value system would have seemed to contemporary readers irrefutably "feminine." Yet this narrator cannot endure even one full paragraph thus confined: "The air is thick, clammy with the breath of crowded human beings. It stifles me. I open the window, and, looking out, can scarcely see through the rain the grocer's shop opposite. . . ." Initially looking out of a series of windows, the speaker soon exits the home, issuing an invitation to the reader that is a challenge as well. "I am going to be honest. This is what I want you to do. I want you to hide your disgust, take no heed to your clean clothes, and come right down with me,—here, into the thickest of the fog and mud and foul effluvia. . . . There is a secret down here, in this nightmare fog . . . I want to make it a real thing to you. You, Egoist, or Pantheist, or Arminian, busy in making straight paths for your feet on the hills, do not see it clearly,— this terrible question which men here have gone mad and died trying to answer."

The men of power within the fiction are those who manipulate money: professional men like "the doctor" and businessmen like "the factory owner," Mr. Kirby. And if not all seem equally callous, their varying degrees of avarice and passivity merely constitute different forms of acquiescence to the fundamental notion that an individualistic pursuit of money and success is possible without the intrusion of troubling moral doubts. " 'What has the man who pays them money to do with their souls' concerns, more than the grocer or butcher who takes it?' " Mr. Kirby inquires with irritation.

Will YOU be equally complaisant? the narrator asks the reader as the story moves agonizingly toward its conclusion.

Despite the untimeliness of its initial appearance, "Life in the Iron Mills" won immediate recognition. When James T. Fields accepted it for publication, he welcomed the unknown thirty-one-year-old author with enthusiasm, paying her generously and requesting the exclusive rights to everything she wrote. Distinguished older au-

thors recognized the power of this work, and Nathaniel Hawthorne, who was in Washington, D.C., at the time, wrote to ask
whether he might pay a call on her home in Wheeling, then still
in Virginia. Not surprisingly, the accelerating hostilities between
the North and South made this visit impossible; however, fourteen
months later Davis was able to spend many hours with Hawthorne—as well as with many other New England notables—when
she went to Massachusetts to be the houseguest of her publishers,
James and Annie Fields. Their brief friendship (Hawthorne died
two years later, only sixty years of age) was immensely reassuring
and rewarding to her. Unlike the more "philosophical" writers such
as Bronson Alcott (Louisa May Alcott's father) and Ralph Waldo
Emerson, Hawthorne understood the harsh realities of the human
struggle for survival; and like Rebecca Harding Davis, he admired
fiction that refused to sentimentalize this struggle.

Rebecca Harding Davis continued to write fiction; in fact, she
was relatively prolific. Her early novels like *Margaret Howth* (1862)
and *Waiting for the Verdict* (1869) continued the examination of
America's two forms of slavery—the wage slavery of factory workers and the conditions of enslavement faced by blacks even after
the Emancipation Proclamation. Yet none of her subsequent work
realized the promise that "Life in the Iron Mills" had given; instead,
it seemed to repeat the awkward elements of the tale. And her
last work drifted into the very sentimentalism that she had so long
decried. When she died, in 1910, few remembered the vigor of
that first, phenomenal story, and it soon passed into total obscurity.

There is an almost macabre irony in the pattern of Rebecca
Davis's literary reputation. Her son, Richard Harding Davis, also
became a professional writer. He was a skilled reporter and editor
for *Harper's Weekly,* particularly known for the vivid, factual quality
of his journalism. For many years—until "Life in the Iron Mills"
was "rediscovered" in 1972—Rebecca Harding Davis was remembered chiefly as the mother of Richard Harding Davis. Now the
roles have become reversed.

As we turn to Charlotte Perkins Gilman, it would be gratifying
to be able to trace a strong, continuous development of the possibilities for women and art that were initially explored by Rebecca
Davis, but we cannot. American women writers, however profes-
sionally successful they might become, were still not encouraged

to be "artists," and Gilman was no exception to this generality. In fairness, it must be added that, alone of the authors collected here, she did not aspire to Art. An important social activist, an early and influential proponent of women's rights, Gilman wrote profusely; her principal writings were explicitly political (the most important: *Women and Economics,* 1896), and her fiction and poetry tended always to have a pronounced polemical intent. "The Yellow Wallpaper" is an exception to her general work—not because it is such a brilliant piece (for much of Gilman's writing displays the same clear, penetrating intelligence that has crafted this story), but because it lodges her most ardent political convictions with unique force in a piece of fiction. Although it is by no means an account of some personal experience, the story has intimate roots in some of the most painful events of Gilman's adult life; and we may perhaps take the measure of her creative skill by observing her capacity to detach herself from the *particularities* of her own case while still managing to draw upon its harrowing effects in order to make a fictional statement about the *general* case of American women.

In 1886 after the birth of her daughter, Charlotte Perkins Gilman suffered an intensification of the "nervous prostration" that had plagued her from the earliest months of her marriage. After more than a year of frustrating attempts to recover the health she had known earlier, Gilman was forced to conclude that the immediate cause of her debilitation was the physical and emotional burden of marriage and motherhood—for during two long trips away from her husband, she found herself without significant symptoms, and these symptoms returned nearly as soon as she rejoined him. Thus in 1887, with great reluctance on both sides, she and her husband agreed to divorce (an extraordinary measure in the late nineteenth century).

There is no reason to suppose that Gilman's husband, Charles Walter Stetson, bore any resemblance to the husband in "The Yellow Wallpaper." Gilman consistently recollected him with love and respect. "There was no quarrel, no blame for either one, never an unkind word between us, unbroken mutual affection," she wrote in her autobiography. "Our suffering was mutual . . . his unbroken devotion, his manifold cares and labors in tending a sick wife, his adoring pride in the best of babies, all coming to naught, ending in utter failure—we sympathized with each other but faced a bitter necessity. The separation must come as soon as possible." However, for the *doctor* who had treated her during the deepest moments of her mental distress, S. Weir Mitchell, Gilman had nothing but residual rage.

S. Weir Mitchell was a distinguished Philadelphia physician; he was one of the earliest medical doctors in America to address the mental illnesses about which Sigmund Freud had begun to write. Many of Mitchell's patients were women (Edith Wharton was successfully treated at his clinic in 1898), and many of them responded favorably to the "rest-cure" that he often devised. In Gilman's case, however, though the month's stay at his clinic was restorative, Weir Mitchell's subsequent prescription outlined what proved to be a disastrous course.

> "Live as domestic a life as possible. Have your child with you all the time." (Be it remarked that if I did but dress the baby it left me shaking and crying—certainly far from a healthy companionship for her, to say nothing of the effect on me.) "Lie down an hour after each meal. Have but two hours' intellectual life a day. And never touch pen, brush or pencil as long as you live."
>
> I went home, followed those directions rigidly for months, and came periously near to losing my mind. The mental agony grew so unbearable that I would sit blankly moving my head from side to side—to get out from under the pain. Not physical pain, not the least "headache" even, just mental torment, and so heavy in its nightmare gloom that it seemed real enough to dodge.

Above all, it was the prohibition forbidding work that enraged Gilman—the enforced passivity and the assumption that in order to achieve "health" a woman's best course was to become "childlike." The most optimistic prediction for any adult who has been counseled into such behavior is indolence and vanity and selfishness. And of course the most terrible eventuality is madness.

The madness may be all too literal. An active, nervous temperament that is isolated and then forbidden to engage in useful mental activity may, indeed, drift into insanity. However, "madness" becomes a metaphor as well, a way of categorizing the regulations of a society that regularly consigns all of its women into roles of dependency and passivity: hypnotic, obsessive, frighteningly alive—the extremity of the speaker in Gilman's story stands for some element in the lives of *all* the "pampered," middle-class American women of the time. The central episode of "The Yellow Wallpaper" draws on Gilman's experience during her own sickness; the more general insight concerning American women also had personal roots, but these were spread more widely. For the generalized "madness" of America's social mores that had affected the author had affected her mother as well—and her mother's mother. Some of the story's urgency undoubtedly derived from Gilman's conviction that until the nation stopped treating fully half of its population in these mutilating ways, the tragic legacy of "madness" could only perpetuate itself.

Gilman was descended on her father's side from Lyman Beecher; and she was justly proud of the lineage of strength in her kinswomen. In her autobiography she recollects, "Harriet Beecher Stowe is best known, but Catherine Beecher, who so scandalized the German theologian by her answer to 'Edwards on the Will,' is still honored in the Middle West for her wide influence in promoting the higher education of women; and Isabella Beecher Hooker was one of the able leaders in the demand for equal suffrage." It was an honorable tradition, and one of Gilman's sorest wounds was that the father who had bequeathed this heritage vanished soon after her birth. "The doctor said that if my mother had another baby she would die. Presently my father left home. . . . He made no official separation, said his work kept him elsewhere. No word of criticism did I ever hear; Mother held him up to us as a great and admirable character. But he was a stranger, distant and little known." This desertion is so dramatic an event that one might expect Gilman to have focused upon it as a cause for her own subsequent unhappiness and as a talisman of men's insensitivity to women. In fact, she does neither. Her overriding reaction is an awareness of misery on both sides.

Insofar as there is "blame" for the situations that inflicted this tragedy upon her childhood, Gilman finds its root in her mother's *background*—in the life and training that had instilled in her none of the sustaining strengths that could be found in the Beecher

women. Her mother's own mother had married very young, no
more than a "child of fifteen. . . . At seventeen she had a baby,
which died, and another at eighteen . . . my mother." Gilman's
mother grew up in an atmosphere that quickly became an extreme
variant of the inculcation of "feminine" docility: she was praised,
pampered, spoiled; delicate in health, she was cosseted in every
way. It is perhaps not surprising that despite numerous, persistent
beaux, she remained unmarried until her thirtieth year—in those
days, the edge of confirmed spinsterhood—for there is no indication of her disposition to take on the burdens of a family, and
every indication that her parents were prepared indefinitely to
sustain her in a pleasing state of extended girlhood.

Subsequently, then, when her marriage failed, she was entirely
without the emotional resources that were necessary to handle the
responsibilities she had been left with. "After her idolized youth,
she was left neglected. After her flood of lovers, she became a
deserted wife." It was a grotesque caricature of the possibilities
awaiting any women who unquestioningly accepted the dependent
role that attended marriage in the nineteenth century. Little wonder, then, that the daughter of such a marriage would despise the
vulnerability that emotional dependency must bring, and as if circumstances alone would not have been enough to terrify the child,
her mother drove the lesson home like a brand. "Suffering for a
lack of a husband's love, she heroically determined that her baby
daughter should not so suffer if she could help it. Her method was
to deny the child [Charlotte Perkins Gilman] all expression of
affection as far as possible, so that she should not be used to it or
long for it."

The lesson was well learned. Yet out of this skein of misery,
Gilman nonetheless found the strength to work for the happiness
of others; she turned her energies outward. "This world seemed
to be suffering from many needless evils, evils for which some
remedies seemed clear. . . . I was deeply impressed with the in-
justices under which women suffered, and still more with the ill
effects upon all mankind of this injustice." The theme that consistently invigorates Gilman's political work is a confidence in the
value of an active life—physical activity (she campaigned for wom-
en's gymnasiums and protested the mutilating restrictions of wom-
en's clothing), emotional activity (she was outspoken about

women's sexual needs), and intellectual activity. She was in all ways committed to the value of personal and communal growth. "The business of mankind [is] to carry out the evolution of the human race, according to the laws of nature, adding the conscious direction, the telic force, proper to our kind. . . . [We can] replenish our individual powers by application to the reservoir; and the best way to get more power [is] to use what one has." To be sure, Gilman urged each one to develop the full talents of self; nonetheless, it was implicit to her creed that adequate *self-development* always took the larger good of the community as its ultimate goal. This was no continuation of the old theme of epic conquest and egoism. Instead, it was a plea for sanity and sense in the definition of roles. Women, like men, must be encouraged to make their own happiness: they must be educated, given responsibility, rewarded for achievement. This is the only antidote for the kind of madness Gilman has depicted so well, and most of her adult energy was devoted to providing such an antidote to her society.

"The Yellow Wallpaper" stands alone in the manner of its focus upon the communal "illness." Readers have always found it a disturbing experience ("The story was meant to be dreadful, and succeeded," Gilman remarked). Yet from the beginning, legions have admired it. After its publication, physicians wrote the author averring that they had changed their methods of treating "nervous prostration" in women after encountering this narrative. W. D. Howells, the noted novelist and editor, praised it and asked permission to reprint it in a collection he was putting together, *Masterpieces of American Fiction.* Gilman agreed, but shrugged off the honor of having written a "masterpiece." Having made her statement, she was eager to get on with her political activity; a brief and brilliant meteor of American literature, she left only this little tale to dazzle us.

In some ways, the many parts of Gilman's life and work testified to the growing complexity of the part women played in American communities. On the one hand, women in general were still consigned to passive roles—excluded from the professions and dismissed as potential artists. On the other hand, activists (like Charlotte Perkins Gilman) were ever more successfully challenging this pattern. What is more, the work of some women writers was beginning to be taken seriously as "American literature." One can find evidence of this complexity in the fictions of both Sarah Orne Jewett and Edith Wharton.

Of all the authors in this volume, Sarah Orne Jewett had the most benign and supportive circumstances in which to write. Born in Maine near Bowdoin College, the daughter of a prosperous physician and his well-educated wife, Jewett and her two sisters were encouraged to take a lively interest in literature and the arts. Jewett never married (and was thus never hindered from writing by the press of domestic duties), and she inherited an ample enough income from her family so that she could live very comfortably without worrying about money. How she would occupy her time, then, became largely a matter of choice.

At first, Jewett wanted to pursue the practice of medicine. Frail as a child, she had become more and more robust by spending a good deal of time in the open air, much of it traveling with her father as he went his rounds attending the sick. A conscientious, intelligent man, Dr. Jewett instilled the fine grain of New England consciousness into his favorite daughter; neither self-flagellating nor obsessed with some spectral divinity who legislates our lives, Dr. Jewett pursued his devout Christianity through his practice as a country doctor. Here he exercised forbearance and compassion, ministering to his patients' emotional needs as well as to their bodily disabilities. He found everyone interesting, and he savoured the significance of apparently trivial events, the salience of the smallest details. He marked the seasons' passage by minute changes in wild flowers and cultivated fields, and he studied the configurations of houses and the relationships of their occupants as closely as he studied the symptoms of his patients. There was a well-considered moral attitude behind this behavior—and one that was transmitted to his daughter. However, both father and daughter shunned the role of reformer or propagandist, seeking instead to act in a useful and meaningful way in the immediate community in which they found themselves—Berwick, Maine, at the conclusion of the nineteenth century.

If Sarah Orne Jewett had pursued her original desire to become a doctor, perhaps she would have been obliged to embrace the *theory* of reform more fully, for women were still almost entirely excluded from the medical profession in the years just following the Civil War when she would have had to seek professional training. After consideration, however, she recognized that despite her hard-won health, the general weakness of her constitution (she suffered severe bouts of arthritis) rendered her unfit for the exhausting practice of medicine. Writing fiction became not a second-best compromise, but a significant alternative, for she had been writing for years under her father's supervision. Nor did the meticulously crafted fictions she constructed as an adult differ in essential ways from her juvenile writing: both exhibit an abiding confidence in the overriding importance of commonplace events and minute details.

Jewett represents an important link in a *succession* of women writers: the way in which she pursued her passion for regional life and the depth of her devotion to the vocation of chronicling the New England world, particularly as it provided a life for women, were both deeply indebted to the work of Harriet Beecher Stowe, whose novels after 1860 initiated an exploration of rural New England life (especially that of Maine). Like Stowe, Jewett was a close friend of Annie Fields, for James Fields was her editor as well as Stowe's, and Mrs. Fields became a friend and patron of both authors.

In her later years, Jewett would offer the same kind of example and support for Willa Cather, who was to expand the tradition of meticulous regional chronicling to the Midwest and the great Southwest. Cather and Jewett corresponded, and Jewett once wrote to Cather: "The thing that teases the mind over and over for years, and at last gets itself put down rightly on paper—whether little or great, it belongs to Literature." Such a sentiment is suggestive in many ways; however, it marks one milestone of overriding importance. Without apparent hesitancy, Jewett addresses the realm that had been denied for so long to American women writers—"literature"—and she defines it in ways that clearly diverge from the path of epic conquest and the American devotion to individualism.

Jewett wrote from the conviction that the things that are most real, most significant, and in many ways most beautiful are essentially simple: the poignant moments of human experience that every reader will understand and with which many will empathize—the details that italicize character. Jewett crafted her prose with painstaking care, stripping excesses to leave only the sparest and most eloquent necessities of language. She studied the speech patterns of New England carefully in order to render the idiosyncracies of verbal parsimony with accuracy: very often dialogue is combined with a significantly revealing gesture, so that the balletic pairing of utterance and movement combine to render complex, sometimes indirect habits of communication. And underlying the entire fictional process is, perhaps, the quiet perception of a paradox: those things that seem most personal, most intimate, and most important in life are often the very things that virtually every human being experiences—the commonalities of loving and birthing and dying. Thus in understanding the people of Dunnet's Landing, a reader will experience the recognition of self as well.

The world that unfolds within *The Country of the Pointed Firs* is "framed" in several ways: it is conveyed into the fiction through a summer visitor who acts as narrator—a citizen from the larger scene of American life. This visitor, herself an artist, has her own intermediary within the fiction, the herbalist-healer, Mrs. Todd, from whom she is renting a room for the summer. Something of a physician and something of a mystic, Mrs. Todd provides insights into human experience, patient strength, and tolerant endurance; these combine to endow her with great wisdom. In her presence, even the most common events begin to reveal momentous import. For example, Mrs. Todd was widowed early; and her unaffected description of this grief and of her regret in another, earlier, lost love becomes the vehicle for gaining a glimpse of the tragic possibilities in all human life.

"I always liked Nathan [her husband], and he never knew [about her earlier, true love]. But this pennyr'yal always reminded me, as I'd sit and gather it and hear him talkin'—it always would remind me of—the other one."

She looked away from me, and presently rose and went on by herself. There was something lonely and solitary about her great determined shape. She might have been Antigone alone on the Theban plain. It is not often given in a noisy world to come to the places of great grief and silence. And absolute, archaic grief possessed this countrywoman; she seemed like a renewal of some historic soul, with her sorrows and the remoteness of a daily life busied with rustic simplicities and the scents of primeval herbs.

No author need appeal to epic conquest, Jewett suggests, in order to discover a subject of profound importance.

Repeatedly, *The Country of the Pointed Firs* reiterates the end of New England's age of heroic conquest: the novel is populated by retired ships' captains and widows. " 'Shipping is a very great loss,' " elderly Captain Littlepage observes regretfully. " 'There was hardly a man of any standing who didn't interest 'imself in some way in navigation. It always gave credit to a town. I call it a low-water mark now here in Dunnet.' " However, Jewett is less doleful than some of her characters about this loss.

In a measured, almost symmetrical way, the grand sweep of adventure and exploration in literature is replaced by exactitudes of perception. Without the distraction that could come from a rapid kaleidoscope of events, the residents of Mrs. Todd's world can meditate upon their emotions and give direct, unpretentious expression of them; taken together, these country-dwellers become a rich chorus of many moods. Mrs. Todd serves as guide—the pathfinder in a subtle landscape of experience and the chronicler who often remembers more about her neighbors' lives than they remember themselves. If Mrs. Todd is our conductor, the narrator becomes our principal interpreter—putting the insights from Dunnet's Landing into the perspective of a more cosmopolitan experience, for she can identify the things that make this fictive world so surprisingly significant for the residents of the outside world.

More than any of the other works of fiction in this volume, perhaps, Jewett's novel has unchanging value. It shares its timeless quality with her other writing, which was not keyed to particular social problems nor to the possibilities that have been offered by unique historical moments. Jewett's work probes the calm center of human experience, and its superb quality was acknowledged almost from the first years of her publication. W. D. Howells, who also recognized the haunting quality of "The Yellow Wallpaper," was the one to suggest that she should collect the early short stories into a volume; and it was he, too, who saw that, despite the relative weakness of plot in her fictions, Jewett was an artist of the first order.

With Edith Wharton, women novelists finally achieved the position that had always been available to their male counterparts. Wharton took her writing seriously as "literature," and she thought of herself as an "artist" who wrote not merely for the contemporary reading public, but for the ages. At the same time, however, she was thoroughly professional: she was ambitious, she made money from her fiction (in fact, a lot of money), and she could be a tough businesswoman in dealing with her editors. Wharton understood that the American traditions of epic conquest and individualism were not (in their most usual formulations) accessible to a woman writer; nonetheless, she found ways to avail herself of these traditions when she wished to do so—through brilliantly oblique inventions of social satire and through agonizing portraits of society's victims, those who were the incidental casualties of a system that valued "success" on almost any terms. Since she lived to be seventy-five years of age and since she wrote prolifically, the range of her fiction is very large. However, her most consistent concern is the plight of women—often brilliant, sensitive, honorable, but always largely powerless—women who must somehow find a way to live meaningfully in a world that has restricted their behavior and limited their options. Indeed, Edith Wharton may have had no equal in analyzing America's infatuation with power as it had impacted upon the *"woman's realm"*—the domestic world that had been so unrealistically idealized as a paradise of comfort and bland tranquillity. Furthermore, Wharton was uniquely conscious of the difficulties that confronted women in the area of sexuality. Her appreciation of the effects of repression and the suffocating patterns of denial is so acute that even her earliest stories (which date from the final years of the nineteenth century) still seem poignantly "modern." Such is certainly the case with "Souls Belated."

Wharton did not attain her triumphs as an author easily. Only fifteen years younger than Jewett, she was born into a world that still did not encourage (or in many cases even *permit*) the sustained expression of artistic talent in a young woman. Ironically, perhaps, the rural world of Jewett's Maine in the decades just before and after the Civil War was generally somewhat more permissive in its attitude toward the deportment of young ladies than was the fashionable world of post-Civil War New York City inhabited by Edith

Wharton and her family. "My parents and their group, though they held literature in great esteem, stood in nervous dread of those who produced it," Wharton recollected many years later in her autobiography. "Washington Irving, Fitz-Greene Hallack and William Dana were the only representatives of the disquieting art who were deemed uncontaminated by it; though Longfellow, they admitted, if a popular poet, was nevertheless a gentleman. . . . I cannot hope to render the tone in which my mother pronounced the name of . . . Mrs. Beecher Stowe, who was so 'common' yet so successful. On the whole, my mother doubtless thought it would be simpler if people one might be exposed to meeting would refrain from meddling with literature." Wharton went on to describe a complex system. In the tightly knit, old-fashioned world of her parents and their friends, any kind of "artistic" creativity was questionable: it indicated the possibility of associating with people who were not very "nice"—people who might dress peculiarly or live in dubious sections of town, people whose manners were unpredictable and whose sexual behavior might be scandalous. Even a *son* would have been roundly disapproved of for pursuing a life in which he consorted with such people. In the case of a daughter, actually entering upon such a life as an active participant was unimaginable. It was almost as shocking as the notion that a young woman might have sexual desires.

During the last four decades of the nineteenth century, a heavy "Victorian" morality pervaded much of America, and few places were so marked by its rigidities as the world of "Old New York," in which Edith Wharton had grown to maturity. Girls and young women were expected to feel no sexual urgings; when they married, they were expected to "submit" to the desires of their husbands only because it was their wifely duty. Boys and young men were expected to "sow wild oats"; sexuality in them was tolerable, even amusing (so long as it was pursued discreetly—"elsewhere"). In women, however, such attitudes were beyond the pale; and this rigid, punitive double standard affected society's attitude toward marriage as well.

Married men sometimes had a mistress and sometimes were known to be engaged in dalliances with women who would never be "received" by their friends and family. Thus if a married man found himself unhappy at home, he might make additional domestic arrangements by way of compensation. Or he might choose to devote himself to business—staying at work or traveling, thereby seldom having the need to spend time with his wife. These accommodations were all available to men, but none of them was available to women. Divorce was deemed shameful, and *anyone* who had been divorced was regarded as somehow having fallen beyond the range of acceptable behavior; yet even in this matter, society's lethal censure fell more heavily upon women than upon men. A divorced man was a curiosity, perhaps; maybe something of a rogue. Still, if the marriage had failed for what was generally perceived to be no fault of *his,* little by little he would be accepted back into the social scheme of things; eventually, he might even seem a "catch" for a marriageable daughter. A divorced woman, on the other hand, was a pariah: usually (if she had enough money to do so), she was expected to live elsewhere—to go to Europe or to the wilds of California; if she stayed in the cosmopolitan East, she became a shadowy figure in the family circle, relegated to the periphery, for no one would be expected to include her in public occasions. Her status as one fit to be seen in society *might* be regained if she remarried (especially if she remarried "well"); however, even in this case, it was generally deemed tactful to spend some penitential time elsewhere and then to return, almost as if reincarnated in a new and once-more-acceptable domestic form.

This is precisely the kind of mortal isolation that confronts Lydia in "Souls Belated"; fully to appreciate her plight, however, a modern reader must realize one additional fact about women's lives. It was not the case that divorced women, or women who had never been married, could live as self-respecting, independent people. Women were still excluded from the professions and from the business world; if they ventured to go into public places without an escort in the evening, they might be taken for a prostitute, or at least for a "loose" woman. Society expected every decent woman to be married, and females were effectively prohibited from all meaningful alternatives. Unfortunately, instead of uniting to protest these intolerable restrictions, women themselves sometimes became the sternest and cruelest enforcers of them. Thus just as Wharton could discern the misery of all women who had to live under such constraints, she could also perceive that the victims all too often vented their rage upon each other. Prohibited from exercising "power" in the larger world of commerce or intellect, women turned their thwarted energies into the domestic realm, where they ruled tyrannically over dinner tables, opera parties, or even remote European resort communities.

"Souls Belated" is a deceptively simple story, elegant and spare, but set forth with a surgical precision that ultimately emphasizes the complexity of the lovers' dilemma. The principal focus is upon Lydia, of course, who seems fated to be entrapped by *some* system of repression no matter where she turns. The marriage from which she fled had seemed to offer two kinds of slow torture: the slow starvation of her husband's obtuse emotional withdrawal and the suffocation that was everywhere represented by her mother-in-law's house. At first, a romantic elopement with Gannett had seemed to redress both forms of anguish. It is only little by little that Lydia has begun to wonder whether this relationship, too, must be characterized by a baffling maze of hesitations, half-truths, and dead ends.

One issue in the tale is the authenticity of Gannett's feelings for Lydia: does he love her and desire her still, or does he merely feel a decent sense of obligation or (what would be even worse) pity? Even more problematic: is it *possible,* given the circumstances under which they must exist, for Lydia *or even Gannett himself* to *know* the full complexity of his true feelings for her? And what of her feelings for him? The story seems to inquire but little in this direction; nonetheless, a careful reader must take note of the many times Gannett expresses his own fears, his own need for explicit and emphatic reassurance. Indeed, in a social environment where the free and open expression of feelings has been so generally prohibited, is it ever possible adequately to ascertain a mutuality of passion?

The ultimate question raised by this tantalizingly unresolved narrative is to what extent we all unwittingly affirm the very prohibitions from which we seem to suffer. To what extent are society's "rules" outside of us, and to what extent have we each internalized the norms that we are so prepared to criticize? Lydia had chaffed under her mother-in-law's narrowness; does she not simply recreate her mother-in-law's attitudes even at this distance from the source? Has Lydia *really* struck out for freedom? Is she *capable* of being "free"? Indeed, what *is* "freedom"? Could *any* human being tolerate complete freedom, or would such a state be tantamount to madness?

At one level, the story is about these two particular lovers; at another, it is about the complex and profoundly imperfect social system within which they must make their lives. Ultimately, however, it is about all men and women: about the paradoxes of commitment and liberty, love and power, pity and cruelty. That *something* is wrong here is beyond dispute; yet Edith Wharton challenges each reader to locate a *correctable* source of difficulty. In suggesting this challenge, Wharton asks us to define the strengths and limitations not only in the world of "Old New York" but of our own world as well. Customs change. Human needs and motivations change a good deal less.

Though each of the four pieces of fiction in this volume deals with some timely social problem or situation, all assume the same truth: that the essential elements of human emotion remain much the same from century to century. Probably the authors of these four fictions would welcome the notion that the tradition of women novelists to which they contributed so richly was less an *alternative* to the male tradition of epic conquest that had excluded them than it was an *addition* to it. Taken together, these two traditions provide insights from which all readers may profit and upon which all future writers may build.

—Cynthia Griffin Wolff
Massachusetts Institute of Technology

Suggestions for Further Reading

BOOKS ABOUT WOMEN WRITERS

Baym, Nina, *Woman's Fiction: A Guide to Novels By and About Women in America,* 1820–1870. Ithaca, New York, and London: Cornell University Press, 1978.

Davidson, Cathy N., *Revolution and the Word: The Rise of the Novel in America.* New York: Oxford University Press, 1986.

Douglas, Ann, *The Feminization of American Culture.* New York: Knopf, 1977.

Tompkins, Jane, *Sensational Designs: The Cultural Work of American Fiction.* New York: Oxford University Press, 1985.

REBECCA HARDING DAVIS

Harris, Sharon M., "Rebecca Harding Davis: From Romanticism to Realism." In *American Literary Realism, 1870–1910,* Albuquerque, New Mexico, Winter 1989, 21(2): 4–20.

Olsen, Tillie, ed., *Life in the Iron Mills and Other Stories.* Old Westbury, New York: Feminist Press, 1985.

Pfaelzer, Jean, "Rebecca Harding Davis: Domesticity, Social Order, and the Industrial Novel." In *International Journal of Women's Studies,* Montreal, Quebec, Canada: May–June 1981, 4(3): 234–244.

CHARLOTTE PERKINS GILMAN

Fetterley, Judith, E. Flynn, and P. Schweickart (eds.), "Reading About Reading: 'A Jury of Her Peers,' 'The Murders in the Rue Morgue,' and 'The Yellow Wallpaper.'" In *Gender and Reading: Essays on Readers, Texts, and Contexts.* Baltimore, Johns Hopkins University Press, 1986.

Fleenor, Julian, "The Gothic Prism: Charlotte Perkins Gilman's Gothic Stories and Her Autobiography." In *The Female Gothic,* Julian Fleenor, ed. Montreal: Eden Press, 1983.

Kennard, Jean, "Convention Coverage or How to Read Your Own Life." In *New Literary History: A Journal of Theory and Interpretation*. Charlottesville, Virginia, Autumn 1981, *8*(1): 69–88.

SARAH ORNE JEWETT

Ammons, Elizabeth, "Going in Circles: The Female Geography of Jewett's *Country of the Pointed Firs*." In *Studies in the Literary Imagination*, Atlanta, Georgia: Fall 1983, *16*(2): 83–92.

Colby Library Quarterly, Waterville, Maine: *9*, iv, 1970 (Special Issue on Sarah Orne Jewett):

Cary, Richard, "Violet Paget to Sarah Orne Jewett," pp. 235–243.

Parsons, Helen, "The Tory Lover, Oliver Wiswell, and Richard Carvel," pp. 220–231.

Stouck, David, "*The Country of the Pointed Firs:* A Pastoral of Innocence," pp. 213–220.

VanDerBeets, R., and J. Bowen, "Miss Jewett, Mrs. Turner, and the Chautauqua Circle," pp. 233–234.

Voelker, Paul, "*The Country of the Pointed Firs:* A Novel by Sarah Orne Jewett" pp. 201–213.

Hirsh, John, "The Non-Narrative Structure of *The Country of the Pointed Firs*." In *American Literary Realism*, 1870–1910. Arlington, Texas: Autumn 1981, *14*(2): 286–288.

Holstein, Michael, "Writing as a Healing Art in Sarah Orne Jewett's *The Country of the Pointed Firs*." In *Studies in American Fiction*, Boston, Massachusetts: Spring 1988, *16*(1): 39–49.

Sherman, Sarah Way, *Sarah Orne Jewett, an American Persephone*. Hanover, New Hampshire: University Press of New England, 1989.

Zagarell, Sandra, "Narrative of Community: The Identification of a Genre." In *Signs: Journal of Women in Culture and Society*, Durham, North Carolina: Spring 1988, *13*(3), 498–527.

EDITH WHARTON

Ammons, Elizabeth, *Edith Wharton's Argument with America*. Athens, Georgia: University of Georgia Press, 1980.

Bloom, Harold, ed., *Edith Wharton* (Modern Critical Views Series). New York: Chelsea House, 1986.

Fryer, Judith, *Felicitous Space: The Imaginative Structures of Edith Wharton and Willa Cather*. Chapel Hill: University of North Carolina Press, 1986.

Leach, William. *Edith Wharton* (American Women of Achievement Series). New York: Chelsea House, 1988.

Lewis, R. W. B., *Edith Wharton: A Biography*. New York: Harper and Row, 1975.

Nevius, Blake, *Edith Wharton: A Study of Her Fiction*. Berkeley: University of California Press, 1953.

Walton, Geoffrey, *Edith Wharton: A Critical Interpretation*. Cranbury, New Jersey: Fairleigh Dickinson University Press, 1982.

Wolff, Cynthia Griffin, *A Feast of Words: The Triumph of Edith Wharton*. New York: Oxford University Press, 1977.

Life in the Iron Mills
by *Rebecca Harding Davis*

> *"Is this the end?*
> *O Life, as futile, then, as frail!*
> *What hope of answer of redress?"*

A cloudy day: do you know what that is in a town of iron-works?
The sky sank down before dawn, muddy, flat, immovable. The air
is thick, clammy with the breath of crowded human beings. It stifles
me. I open the window, and, looking out, can scarcely see through
the rain the grocer's shop opposite, where a crowd of drunken
Irishmen are puffing Lynchburg tobacco in their pipes. I can detect
the scent through all the foul smells ranging loose in the air.

The idiosyncrasy of this town is smoke. It rolls sullenly in slow
folds from the great chimneys of the iron-foundries, and settles
down in black, slimy pools on the muddy streets. Smoke on the
wharves, smoke on the dingy boats, on the yellow river,—clinging
in a coating of greasy soot to the house-front, the two faded poplars,
the faces of the passers-by. The long train of mules, dragging masses
of pig-iron through the narrow street, have a foul vapor hanging
to their reeking sides. Here, inside, is a little broken figure of an
angel pointing upward from the mantel-shelf; but even its wings
are covered with smoke, clotted and black. Smoke everywhere! A
dirty canary chirps desolately in a cage beside me. Its dream of
green fields and sunshine is a very old dream,—almost worn out,
I think.

From the back-window I can see a narrow brick-yard sloping

down to the river-side, strewed with rain-butts and tubs. The river, dull and tawny-colored, *(la belle rivière!)* drags itself sluggishly along, tired of the heavy weight of boats and coal-barges. What wonder? When I was a child, I used to fancy a look of weary, dumb appeal upon the face of the negro-like river slavishly bearing its burden day after day. Something of the same idle notion comes to me to-day, when from the street-window I look on the slow stream of human life creeping past, night and morning, to the great mills. Masses of men, with dull, besotted faces bent to the ground, sharpened here and there by pain or cunning; skin and muscle and flesh begrimed with smoke and ashes; stooping all night over boiling caldrons of metal, laired by day in dens of drunkenness and infamy; breathing from infancy to death an air saturated with fog and grease and soot, vileness for soul and body. What do you make of a case like that, amateur psychologist? You call it an altogether serious thing to be alive: to these men it is a drunken jest, a joke,—horrible to angels perhaps, to them commonplace enough. My fancy about the river was an idle one: it is no type of such a life. What if it be stagnant and slimy here? It knows that beyond there waits for it odorous sunlight,—quaint old gardens, dusky with soft, green foliage of apple-trees, and flushing crimson with roses,—air, and fields, and mountains. The future of the Welsh puddler passing just now is not so pleasant. To be stowed away, after his grimy work is done, in a hole in the muddy graveyard, and after that,— *not* air, nor green fields, nor curious roses.

Can you see how foggy the day is? As I stand here, idly tapping the window-pane, and looking out through the rain at the dirty back-yard and the coal-boats below, fragments of an old story float up before me,—a story of this old house into which I happened to come to-day. You may think it a tiresome story enough, as foggy as the day, sharpened by no sudden flashes of pain or pleasure.— I know: only the outline of a dull life, that long since, with thousands of dull lives like its own, was vainly lived and lost: thousands of them,—massed, vile, slimy lives, like those of the torpid lizards in yonder stagnant water-butt.—Lost? There is a curious point for you to settle, my friend, who study psychology in a lazy, *dilettante* way. Stop a moment. I am going to be honest. This is what I want you to do. I want you to hide your disgust, take no heed to your clean clothes, and come right down with me,—here, into the thickest of the fog and mud and foul effluvia. I want you to hear this story. There is a secret down here, in this nightmare fog, that has lain dumb for centuries: I want to make it a real thing to you. You, Egoist, or Pantheist, or Arminian, busy in making straight paths for your feet on the hills, do not see it clearly,—this terrible question which men here have gone mad and died trying to answer. I dare not put this secret into words. I told you it was dumb. These men, going by with drunken faces and brains full of unawakened power, do not ask it of Society or of God. Their lives ask it; their deaths ask it. There is no reply. I will tell you plainly that I have a great hope; and I bring it to you to be tested. It is this: that this terrible dumb question is its own reply; that it is not the sentence of death we think it, but, from the very extremity of its darkness, the most solemn prophecy which the world has known of the Hope to come. I dare make my meaning no clearer, but will only tell my story. It will, perhaps, seem to you as foul and dark as this thick vapor about us, and as pregnant with death; but if your eyes are free as mine are to look deeper, no perfume-tinted dawn will be so fair with promise of the day that shall surely come.

My story is very simple,—only what I remember of the life of one of these men,—a furnace-tender in one of Kirby & John's rolling-mills,—Hugh Wolfe. You know the mills? They took the great order for the Lower Virginia railroads there last winter; run usually with about a thousand men. I cannot tell why I choose the half-forgotten story of this Wolfe more than that of myriads of these furnace-hands. Perhaps because there is a secret underlying sympathy between that story and this day with its impure fog and thwarted sunshine,—or perhaps simply for the reason that this house is the one where the Wolfes lived. There were the father and son,—both hands, as I said, in one of Kirby & John's mills for making railroad-iron,—and Deborah, their cousin, a picker in some of the cotton-mills. The house was rented then to half a dozen families. The Wolfes had two of the cellar-rooms. The old man, like many of the puddlers and feeders of the mills, was Welsh,—had spent half of his life in the Cornish tin-mines. You may pick the Welsh emigrants, Cornish miners, out of the throng passing the windows, any day. They are a trifle more filthy; their muscles are not so brawny; they stoop more. When they are drunk, they neither yell, nor shout, nor stagger, but skulk along

like beaten hounds. A pure, unmixed blood, I fancy: shows itself in the slight angular bodies and sharply-cut facial lines. It is
nearly thirty years since the Wolfes lived here. Their lives were
like those of their class: incessant labor, sleeping in kennel-like
rooms, eating rank pork and molasses, drinking—God and the
distillers only know what; with an occasional night in jail, to atone
for some drunken excess. Is that all of their lives?—of the portion given to them and these their duplicates swarming the streets
to-day?—nothing beneath?—all? So many a political reformer
will tell you,—and many a private reformer, too, who has gone
among them with a heart tender with Christ's charity, and come
out outraged, hardened.

One rainy night, about eleven o'clock, a crowd of half-clothed
women stopped outside of the cellar-door. They were going home
from the cotton-mill.

"Good-night, Deb," said one, a mulatto, steadying herself against
the gas-post. She needed the post to steady her. So did more than
one of them.

"Dah's a ball to Miss Potts' to-night. Ye'd best come."

"Inteet, Deb, if hur'll come, hur'll hef fun," said a shrill Welsh
voice in the crowd.

Two or three dirty hands were thrust out to catch the gown of
the woman, who was groping for the latch of the door.

"No."

"No? Where's Kit Small, then?"

"Begorra! on the spools. Alleys behint, though we helped her,
we dud. An wid ye! Let Deb alone! It's ondacent frettin' a quite
body. Be the powers, an' we'll have a night of it! there'll be lashin's
o' drink, the Vargent be blessed and praised for 't!"

They went on, the mulatto inclining for a moment to show fight,
and drag the woman Wolfe off with them; but, being pacified, she
staggered away.

Deborah groped her way into the cellar, and, after considerable
stumbling, kindled a match, and lighted a tallow dip, that sent a
yellow glimmer over the room. It was low, damp,—the earthen
floor covered with a green, slimy moss,—a fetid air smothering
the breath. Old Wolfe lay asleep on a heap of straw, wrapped in
a torn horse-blanket. He was a pale, meek little man, with a white
face and red rabbit-eyes. The woman Deborah was like him; only

her face was even more ghastly, her lips bluer, her eyes more watery. She wore a faded cotton gown and a slouching bonnet. When she walked, one could see that she was deformed, almost a hunchback. She trod softly, so as not to waken him, and went through into the room beyond. There she found by the half-extinguished fire an iron saucepan filled with cold boiled potatoes, which she put upon a broken chair with a pint-cup of ale. Placing the old candlestick beside this dainty repast, she untied her bonnet, which hung limp and wet over her face, and prepared to eat her supper. It was the first food that had touched her lips since morning. There was enough of it, however: there is not always. She was hungry,—one could see that easily enough,—and not drunk, as most of her companions would have been found at this hour. She did not drink, this woman,—her face told that, too,—nothing stronger than ale. Perhaps the weak, flaccid wretch had some stimulant in her pale life to keep her up,—some love or hope, it might be, or urgent need. When that stimulant was gone, she would take to whiskey. Man cannot live by work alone. While she was skinning the potatoes, and munching them, a noise behind her made her stop.

"Janey!" she called, lifting the candle and peering into the darkness. "Janey, are you there?"

A heap of ragged coats was heaved up, and the face of a young girl emerged, staring sleepily at the woman.

"Deborah," she said, at last, "I'm here the night."

"Yes, child. Hur's welcome," she said, quietly eating on.

The girl's face was haggard and sickly; her eyes were heavy with sleep and hunger: real Milesian eyes they were, dark, delicate blue, glooming out from black shadows with a pitiful fright.

"I was alone," she said, timidly.

"Where's the father?" asked Deborah, holding out a potato, which the girl greedily seized.

"He's beyant,—wid Haley,—in the stone house." (Did you ever hear the word *jail* from an Irish mouth?) "I came here. Hugh told me never to stay me-lone."

"Hugh?"

"Yes."

A vexed frown crossed her face. The girl saw it, and added quickly,—

"I have not seen Hugh the day, Deb. The old man says his watch lasts till the mornin'."

The woman sprang up, and hastily began to arrange some bread and flitch in a tin pail, and to pour her own measure of ale into a bottle. Tying on her bonnet, she blew out the candle.

"Lay ye down, Janey dear," she said, gently, covering her with the old rags. "Hur can eat the potatoes, if hur's hungry."

"Where are ye goin', Deb? The rain's sharp."

"To the mill, with Hugh's supper."

"Let him bide till th' morn. Sit ye down."

"No, no,"—sharply pushing her off. "The boy'll starve."

She hurried from the cellar, while the child wearily coiled herself up for sleep. The rain was falling heavily, as the woman, pail in hand, emerged from the mouth of the alley, and turned down the narrow street, that stretched out, long and black, miles before her. Here and there a flicker of gas lighted an uncertain space of muddy footwalk and gutter; the long rows of houses, except an occasional lager-bier shop, were closed; now and then she met a band of mill-hands skulking to or from their work.

Not many even of the inhabitants of a manufacturing town know the vast machinery of system by which the bodies of workmen are governed, that goes on unceasingly from year to year. The hands of each mill are divided into watches that relieve each other as regularly as the sentinels of an army. By night and day the work goes on, the unsleeping engines groan and shriek, the fiery pools of metal boil and surge. Only for a day in the week, in half-courtesy to public censure, the fires are partially veiled; but as soon as the clock strikes midnight, the great furnaces break forth with renewed fury, the clamor begins with fresh, breathless vigor, the engines sob and shriek like "gods in pain."

As Deborah hurried down through the heavy rain, the noise of these thousand engines sounded through the sleep and shadow of the city like far-off thunder. The mill to which she was going lay on the river, a mile below the city-limits. It was far, and she was weak, aching from standing twelve hours at the spools. Yet it was her almost nightly walk to take this man his supper, though at every square she sat down to rest, and she knew she should receive small word of thanks.

Perhaps, if she had possessed an artist's eye, the picturesque oddity of the scene might have made her step stagger less, and the path seem shorter; but to her the mills were only "summat deilish to look at by night."

The road leading to the mills had been quarried from the solid rock, which rose abrupt and bare on one side of the cinder-covered road, while the river, sluggish and black, crept past on the other. The mills for rolling iron are simply immense tent-like roofs, covering acres of ground, open on every side. Beneath these roofs Deborah looked in on a city of fires, that burned hot and fiercely in the night. Fire in every horrible form: pits of flame waving in the wind; liquid metal-flames writhing in tortuous streams through the sand; wide caldrons filled with boiling fire, over which bent ghastly wretches stirring the strange brewing; and through all, crowds of half-clad men, looking like revengeful ghosts in the red light, hurried, throwing masses of glittering fire. It was like a street in Hell. Even Deborah muttered, as she crept through, " 'T looks like t' Devil's place!" It did,—in more ways than one.

She found the man she was looking for, at last, heaping coal on a furnace. He had not time to eat his supper; so she went behind the furnace, and waited. Only a few men were with him, and they noticed her only by a "Hyur comes t' hunchback, Wolfe."

Deborah was stupid with sleep; her back pained her sharply; and her teeth chattered with cold, with the rain that soaked her clothes and dripped from her at every step. She stood, however, patiently holding the pail, and waiting.

"Hout, woman! ye look like a drowned cat. Come near to the fire,"—said one of the men, approaching to scrape away the ashes.

She shook her head. Wolfe had forgotten her. He turned, hearing the man, and came closer.

"I did no' think; gi' me my supper, woman."

She watched him eat with a painful eagerness. With a woman's quick instinct, she saw that he was not hungry,—was eating to please her. Her pale, watery eyes began to gather a strange light.

"Is't good, Hugh? T'ale was a bit sour, I feared."

"No, good enough." He hesitated a moment. "Ye're tired, poor lass! Bide here till I go. Lay down there on that heap of ash, and go to sleep."

He threw her an old coat for a pillow, and turned to his work.

The heap was the refuse of the burnt iron, and was not a hard bed; the half-smothered warmth, too, penetrated her limbs, dulling their pain and cold shiver.

Miserable enough she looked, lying there on the ashes like a limp, dirty rag,—yet not an unfitting figure to crown the scene of hopeless discomfort and veiled crime: more fitting, if one looked deeper into the heart of things,—at her thwarted woman's form, her colorless life, her waking stupor that smothered pain and hunger,—even more fit to be a type of her class. Deeper yet if one could look, was there nothing worth reading in this wet, faded thing, half-covered with ashes? no story of a soul filled with groping passionate love, heroic unselfishness, fierce jealousy? of years of weary trying to please the one human being whom she loved, to gain one look of real heart-kindness from him? If anything like this were hidden beneath the pale, bleared eyes, and dull, washed-out-looking face, no one had ever taken the trouble to read its faint signs: not the half-clothed furnace-tender, Wolfe, certainly. Yet he was kind to her: it was his nature to be kind, even to the very rats that swarmed in the cellar; kind to her in just the same way. She knew that. And it might be that very knowledge had given to her face its apathy and vacancy more than her low, torpid life. One sees that dead, vacant look steal sometimes over the rarest, finest of women's faces,—in the very midst, it may be, of their warmest summer's day; and then one can guess at the secret of intolerable solitude that lies hid beneath the delicate laces and brilliant smile. There was no warmth, no brilliancy, no summer for this woman; so the stupor and vacancy had time to gnaw into her face perpetually. She was young, too, though no one guessed it; so the gnawing was the fiercer.

She lay quiet in the dark corner, listening, through the monotonous din and uncertain glare of the works, to the dull plash of the rain in the far distance,—shrinking back whenever the man Wolfe happened to look towards her. She knew, in spite of all his kindness, that there was that in her face and form which made him loathe the sight of her. She felt by instinct, although she could not comprehend it, the finer nature of the man, which made him among his fellow-workmen something unique, set apart. She knew, that, down under all the vileness and coarseness of his life, there was a groping passion for whatever was beautiful and pure,—that his soul sickened with disgust at her deformity, even when his words were kindest. Through this dull consciousness, which never left her, came, like a sting, the recollection of the dark blue eyes and lithe figure of the little Irish girl she had left in the cellar. The recollection struck through even her stupid intellect with a vivid glow of beauty and of grace. Little Janey, timid, helpless, clinging to Hugh as her only friend: that was the sharp thought, the bitter thought, that drove into the glazed eyes a fierce light of pain. You laugh at it? Are pain and jealousy less savage realities down here in this place I am taking you to than in your own house or your own heart,—your heart, which they clutch at sometimes? The note is the same, I fancy, be the octave high or low.

If you could go into this mill where Deborah lay, and drag out from the hearts of these men the terrible tragedy of their lives, taking it as a symptom of the disease of their class, no ghost Horror would terrify you more. A reality of soul-starvation, of living death, that meets you every day under the besotted faces on the street,— I can paint nothing of this, only give you the outside outlines of a night, a crisis in the life of one man: whatever muddy depth of soul-history lies beneath you can read according to the eyes God has given you.

Wolfe, while Deborah watched him as a spaniel its master, bent over the furnace with his iron pole, unconscious of her scrutiny, only stopping to receive orders. Physically, Nature had promised the man but little. He had already lost the strength and instinct vigor of a man, his muscles were thin, his nerves weak, his face (a meek, woman's face) haggard, yellow with consumption. In the mill he was known as one of the girl-men: "Molly Wolfe" was his *sobriquet*. He was never seen in the cockpit, did not own a terrier, drank but seldom; when he did, desperately. He fought sometimes, but was always thrashed, pommelled to a jelly. The man was game enough, when his blood was up: but he was no favorite in the mill; he had the taint of school-learning on him,—not to a dangerous extent, only a quarter or so in the free-school in fact, but enough to ruin him as a good hand in a fight.

For other reasons, too, he was not popular. Not one of themselves, they felt that, though outwardly as filthy and ash-covered; silent, with foreign thoughts and longings breaking out through his quietness in innumerable curious ways: this one, for instance.

In the neighboring furnace-buildings lay great heaps of the refuse from the ore after the pig-metal is run. *Korl* we call it here: a light, porous substance, of a delicate, waxen, flesh-colored tinge. Out of the blocks of this korl, Wolfe, in his off-hours from the furnace, had a habit of chipping and moulding figures,—hideous, fantastic enough, but sometimes strangely beautiful: even the mill-men saw that, while they jeered at him. It was a curious fancy in the man, almost a passion. The few hours for rest he spent hewing and hacking with his blunt knife, never speaking, until his watch came again,—working at one figure for months, and, when it was finished, breaking it to pieces perhaps, in a fit of disappointment. A morbid, gloomy man, untaught, unled, left to feed his soul in grossness and crime, and hard, grinding labor.

I want you to come down and look at this Wolfe, standing there among the lowest of his kind, and see him just as he is, that you may judge him justly when you hear the story of this night. I want you to look back, as he does every day, at his birth in vice, his starved infancy; to remember the heavy years he has groped through as boy and man,—the slow, heavy years of constant, hot work. So long ago he began, that he thinks sometimes he has worked there for ages. There is no hope that it will ever end. Think that God put into this man's soul a fierce thirst for beauty,—to know it, to create it; to *be*—something, he knows not what,—other than he is. There are moments when a passing cloud, the sun glinting on the purple thistles, a kindly smile, a child's face, will rouse him to a passion of pain,—when his nature starts up with a mad cry of rage against God, man, whoever it is that has forced this vile, slimy life upon him. With all this groping, this mad desire, a great blind intellect stumbling through wrong, a loving poet's heart, the man was by habit only a coarse, vulgar laborer, familiar with sights and words you would blush to name. Be just: when I tell you about this night, see him as he is. Be just,—not like man's law, which seizes on one isolated fact, but like God's judging angel, whose clear, sad eye saw all the countless cankering days of this man's life, all the countless nights, when, sick with starving, his soul fainted in him, before it judged him for this night, the saddest of all.

I called this night the crisis of his life. If it was, it stole on him unawares. These great turning-days of life cast no shadow before,

slip by unconsciously. Only a trifle, a little turn of the rudder, and
the ship goes to heaven or hell.

Wolfe, while Deborah watched him, dug into the furnace of
melting iron with his pole, dully thinking only how many rails the
lump would yield. It was late,—nearly Sunday morning; another
hour, and the heavy work would be done,—only the furnaces to
replenish and cover for the next day. The workmen were growing
more noisy, shouting, as they had to do, to be heard over the deep
clamor of the mills. Suddenly they grew less boisterous,—at the
far end, entirely silent. Something unusual had happened. After a
moment, the silence came nearer; the men stopped their jeers and
drunken choruses. Deborah, stupidly lifting up her head, saw the
cause of the quiet. A group of five or six men were slowly approaching, stopping to examine each furnace as they came. Visitors
often came to see the mills after night: except by growing less
noisy, the men took no notice of them. The furnace where Wolfe
worked was near the bounds of the works; they halted there hot
and tired: a walk over one of these great foundries is no trifling
task. The woman, drawing out of sight, turned over to sleep. Wolfe,
seeing them stop, suddenly roused from his indifferent stupor, and
watched them keenly. He knew some of them: the overseer,
Clarke,—a son of Kirby, one of the mill-owners,—and a Doctor
May, one of the town-physicians. The other two were strangers.
Wolfe came closer. He seized eagerly every chance that brought
him into contact with this mysterious class that shone down on
him perpetually with the glamour of another order of being. What
made the difference between them? That was the mystery of his
life. He had a vague notion that perhaps to-night he could find it
out. One of the strangers sat down on a pile of bricks, and beckoned
young Kirby to his side.

"This *is* hot, with a vengeance. A match, please?"—lighting his
cigar. "But the walk is worth the trouble. If it were not that you
must have heard it so often, Kirby, I would tell you that your works
look like Dante's Inferno."

Kirby laughed.

"Yes. Yonder is Farinata himself in the burning tomb,"—pointing to some figure in the shimmering shadows.

"Judging from some of the faces of your men," said the other,
"they bid fair to try the reality of Dante's vision, some day."

Young Kirby looked curiously around, as if seeing the faces of his hands for the first time.

"They're bad enough, that's true. A desperate set, I fancy. Eh, Clarke?"

The overseer did not hear him. He was talking of net profits just then,—giving, in fact, a schedule of the annual business of the firm to a sharp peering little Yankee, who jotted down notes on a paper laid on the crown of his hat: a reporter for one of the city-papers, getting up a series of reviews of the leading manufactories. The other gentlemen had accompanied them merely for amusement. They were silent until the notes were finished, drying their feet at the furnaces, and sheltering their faces from the intolerable heat. At last the overseer concluded with—

"I believe that is a pretty fair estimate, Captain."

"Here, some of you men!" said Kirby, "bring up those boards. We may as well sit down, gentlemen, until the rain is over. It cannot last much longer at this rate."

"Pig-metal,"—mumbled the reporter,—"um!—coal facilities,—um!—hands employed, twelve hundred,—bitumen,—um!—all right, I believe, Mr. Clarke;—sinking-fund,—what did you say was your sinking-fund?"

"Twelve hundred hands?" said the stranger, the young man who had first spoken. "Do you control their votes, Kirby?"

"Control? No." The young man smiled complacently. "But my father brought seven hundred votes to the polls for his candidate last November. No force-work, you understand,—only a speech or two, a hint to form themselves into a society, and a bit of red and blue bunting to make them a flag. The Invincible Roughs,—I believe that is their name. I forget the motto: 'Our country's hope,' I think."

There was a laugh. The young man talking to Kirby sat with an amused light in his cool gray eye, surveying critically the half-clothed figures of the puddlers, and the slow swing of their brawny muscles. He was a stranger in the city,—spending a couple of months in the borders of a Slave State, to study the institutions of the South,—a brother-in-law of Kirby's,—Mitchell. He was an amateur gymnast,—hence his anatomical eye; a patron, in a *blasé* way, of the prize-ring; a man who sucked the essence out of a science or philosophy in an indifferent, gentlemanly way; who took

Kant, Novalis, Humboldt, for what they were worth in his own scales; accepting all, despising nothing, in heaven, earth, or hell, but one-idead men; with a temper yielding and brilliant as summer water, until his Self was touched, when it was ice, though brilliant still. Such men are not rare in the States.

As he knocked the ashes from his cigar, Wolfe caught with a quick pleasure the contour of the white hand, the blood-glow of a red ring he wore. His voice, too, and that of Kirby's touched him like music,—low, even, with chording cadences. About this man Mitchell hung the impalpable atmosphere belonging to the thoroughbred gentleman. Wolfe, scraping away the ashes beside him, was conscious of it, did obeisance to it with his artist sense, unconscious that he did so.

The rain did not cease. Clark and the reporter left the mills; the others, comfortably seated near the furnace, lingered, smoking and talking in a desultory way. Greek would not have been more unintelligible to the furnace-tenders, whose presence they soon forgot entirely. Kirby drew out a newspaper from his pocket and read aloud some article, which they discussed eagerly. At every sentence, Wolfe listened more and more like a dumb, hopeless animal, with a duller, more stolid look creeping over his face, glancing now and then at Mitchell, marking acutely every smallest sign of refinement, then back to himself, seeing as in a mirror his filthy body, his more stained soul.

Never! He had no words for such a thought, but he knew now, in all the sharpness of the bitter certainty, that between them there was a great gulf never to be passed. Never!

The bells of the mills rang for midnight. Sunday morning had dawned. Whatever hidden message lay in the tolling bells floated past these men unknown. Yet it was there. Veiled in the solemn music ushering the risen saviour was a key-note to solve the darkest secrets of a world gone wrong,—even this social riddle which the brain of the grimy puddler grappled with madly to-night.

The men began to withdraw the metal from the caldrons. The mills were deserted on Sundays, except by the hands who fed the fires, and those who had no lodgings and slept usually on the ash-heaps. The three strangers sat still during the next hour, watching the men cover the furnaces, laughing now and then at some jest of Kirby's.

"Do you know," said Mitchell, "I like this view of the works better than when the glare was fiercest? These heavy shadows and the amphitheatre of smothered fires are ghostly, unreal. One could fancy these red smouldering lights to be the half-shut eyes of wild beasts, and the spectral figures their victims in the den."

Kirby laughed. "You are fanciful. Come, let us get out of the den. The spectral figures, as you call them, are a little too real for me to fancy a close proximity in the darkness,—unarmed, too."

The others rose, buttoning their over-coats, and lighting cigars.

"Raining, still," said Doctor May, "and hard. Where did we leave the coach, Mitchell?"

"At the other side of the works.—Kirby, what's that?"

Mitchell started back, half-frightened, as, suddenly turning a corner, the white figure of a woman faced him in the darkness,— a woman, white, of giant proportions, crouching on the ground, her arms flung out in some wild gesture of warning.

"Stop! Make that fire burn there!" cried Kirby, stopping short.

The flame burst out, flashing the gaunt figure into bold relief.

Mitchell drew a long breath.

"I thought it was alive," he said, going up curiously.

The others followed.

"Not marble, eh?" asked Kirby, touching it.

One of the lower overseers stopped.

"Korl, Sir."

"Who did it?"

"Can't say. Some of the hands; chipped it out in off-hours."

"Chipped to some purpose, I should say. What a flesh-tint the stuff has! Do you see, Mitchell?"

"I see."

He had stepped aside where the light fell boldest on the figure, looking at it in silence. There was not one line of beauty or grace in it: a nude woman's form, muscular, grown coarse with labor, the powerful limbs instinct with some one poignant longing. One idea: there it was in the tense, rigid muscles, the clutching hands, the wild, eager face, like that of a starving wolf's. Kirby and Doctor May walked around it, critical, curious. Mitchell stood aloof, silent. The figure touched him strangely.

"Not badly done," said Doctor May. "Where did the fellow learn that sweep of the muscles in the arm and hand? Look at them!

They are groping,—do you see?—clutching: the peculiar action of a man dying of thirst."

"They have ample facilities for studying anatomy," sneered Kirby, glancing at the half-naked figures.

"Look," continued the Doctor, "at this bony wrist, and the strained sinews of the instep! A working woman,—the very type of her class."

"God forbid!" muttered Mitchell.

"Why?" demanded May. "What does that fellow intend by the figure? I cannot catch the meaning."

"Ask him," said the other, dryly. "There he stands,"—pointing to Wolfe, who stood with a group of men, leaning on his ash-rake.

The Doctor beckoned him with the affable smile which kind-hearted men put on, when talking with these people.

"Mr. Mitchell has picked you out as the man who did this,— I'm sure I don't know why. But what did you mean by it?"

"She be hungry."

Wolfe's eyes answered Mitchell, not the Doctor.

"Oh-h! But what a mistake you have made, my fine fellow! You have given no sign of starvation to the body. It is strong,—terribly strong. It has the mad, half-despairing gesture of drowning."

Wolfe stammered, glanced appealingly at Mitchell, who saw the soul of the thing, he knew. But the cool, probing eyes were turned on himself now,—mocking, cruel, relentless.

"Not hungry for meat," the furnace-tender said at last.

"What then? Whiskey?" jeered Kirby, with a coarse laugh.

Wolfe was silent a moment, thinking.

"I dunno," he said, with a bewildered look. "It mebbe. Summat to make her live, I think,—like you. Whiskey ull do it, in a way."

The young man laughed again. Mitchell flashed a look of disgust somewhere,—not at Wolfe.

"May," he broke out impatiently, "are you blind? Look at that woman's face! It asks questions of God, and says, 'I have a right to know.' Good God, how hungry it is!"

They looked a moment; then May turned to the mill-owner:—

"Have you many such hands as this? What are you going to do with them? Keep them at puddling iron?"

Kirby shrugged his shoulders. Mitchell's look had irritated him.

"Ce n'est pas mon affaire. I have no fancy for nursing infant ge-

niuses. I suppose there are some stray gleams of mind and soul among these wretches. The Lord will take care of his own; or else they can work out their own salvation. I have heard you call our American system a ladder which any man can scale. Do you doubt it? Or perhaps you want to banish all social ladders, and put us all on a flat table-land,—eh, May?"

The Doctor looked vexed, puzzled. Some terrible problem lay hid in this woman's face, and troubled these men. Kirby waited for an answer, and, receiving none, went on, warming with his subject.

"I tell you, there's something wrong that no talk of *'Liberté'* or *'Egalité'* will do away. If I had the making of men, these men who do the lower part of the world's work should be machines,—nothing more,—hands. It would be kindness. God help them! What are taste, reason, to creatures who must live such lives as that?" He pointed to Deborah, sleeping on the ash-heap. "So many nerves to sting them to pain. What if God had put your brain, with all its agony of touch, into your fingers, and bid you work and strike with that?"

"You think you could govern the world better?" laughed the Doctor.

"I do not think at all."

"That is true philosophy. Drift with the stream, because you cannot dive deep enough to find bottom, eh?"

"Exactly," rejoined Kirby. "I do not think. I wash my hands of all social problems,—slavery, caste, white or black. My duty to my operatives has a narrow limit,—the pay-hour on Saturday night. Outside of that, if they cut korl, or cut each other's throats, (the more popular amusement of the two,) I am not responsible."

The Doctor sighed,—a good honest sigh, from the depths of his stomach.

"God help us! Who is responsible?"

"Not I, I tell you," said Kirby, testily. "What has the man who pays them money to do with their souls' concerns, more than the grocer or butcher who takes it?"

"And yet," said Mitchell's cynical voice, "look at her! How hungry she is!"

Kirby tapped his boot with his cane. No one spoke. Only the dumb face of the rough image looking into their faces with the awful question, "What shall we do to be saved?" Only Wolfe's face, with its heavy weight of brain, its weak, uncertain mouth, its desperate eyes, out of which looked the soul of his class,—only Wolfe's face turned towards Kirby's. Mitchell laughed,—a cool, musical laugh.

"Money has spoken!" he said, seating himself lightly on a stone with the air of an amused spectator at a play. "Are you answered?"—turning to Wolfe his clear, magnetic face.

Bright and deep and cold as Arctic air, the soul of the man lay tranquil beneath. He looked at the furnace-tender as he had looked at a rare mosaic in the morning; only the man was the more amusing study of the two.

"Are you answered? Why, May, look at him! *'De profundis clamavi.'* Or, to quote in English, 'Hungry and thirsty, his soul faints in him.' And so Money sends back its answer into the depths through you, Kirby! Very clear the answer, too!—I think I remember reading the same words somewhere:—washing your hands in Eau de Cologne, and saying, 'I am innocent of the blood of this man. See ye to it!'"

Kirby flushed angrily.

"You quote Scripture freely."

"Do I not quote correctly? I think I remember another line, which may amend my meaning: 'Inasmuch as ye did it unto one of the least of these, ye did it unto me.' Deist? Bless you, man, I was raised on the milk of the Word. Now, Doctor, the pocket of the world having uttered its voice, what has the heart to say? You are a philanthropist, in a small way,—*n'est ce pas?* Here, boy, this gentleman can show you how to cut korl better,—or your destiny. Go on, May!"

"I think a mocking devil possesses you to-night," rejoined the Doctor, seriously.

He went to Wolfe and put his hand kindly on his arm. Something of a vague idea possessed the Doctor's brain that much good was to be done here by a friendly word or two: a latent genius to be warmed into life by a waited-for sun-beam. Here it was: he had brought it. So he went on complacently:—

"Do you know, boy, you have it in you to be a great sculptor, a great man?—do you understand?" (talking down to the capacity of his hearer: it is a way people have with children, and men like

Wolfe,)—"to live a better, stronger life than I, or Mr. Kirby here?
A man may make himself anything he chooses. God has given you
stronger powers than many men,—me, for instance."

May stopped, heated, glowing with his own magnanimity. And
it was magnanimous. The puddler had drunk in every word, looking
through the Doctor's flurry, and generous heat, and self-approval,
into his will, with those slow, absorbing eyes of his.

"Make yourself what you will. It is your right."

"I know," quietly. "Will you help me?"

Mitchell laughed again. The Doctor turned now, in a passion,—

"You know, Mitchell, I have not the means. You know, if I had,
it is in my heart to take this boy and educate him for"—

"The glory of God, and the glory of John May."

May did not speak for a moment; then, controlled, he said,—

"Why should one be raised, when myriads are left?—I have not
the money, boy," to Wolfe, shortly.

"Money?" He said it over slowly, as one repeats the guessed
answer to a riddle, doubtfully. "That is it? Money?"

"Yes, money,—that is it," said Mitchell, rising, and drawing his
furred coat about him. "You've found the cure for all the world's
diseases.—Come, May, find your good-humor, and come home.
This damp wind chills my very bones. Come and preach your Saint-
Simonian doctrines to-morrow to Kirby's hands. Let them have a
clear idea of the rights of the soul, and I'll venture next week they'll
strike for higher wages. That will be the end of it."

"Will you send the coach-driver to this side of the mills?" asked
Kirby, turning to Wolfe.

He spoke kindly: it was his habit to do so. Deborah, seeing the
puddler go, crept after him. The three men waited outside. Doctor
May walked up and down, chafed. Suddenly he stopped.

"Go back, Mitchell! You say the pocket and the heart of the
world speak without meaning to these people. What has its head
to say? Taste, culture, refinement? Go!"

Mitchell was leaning against a brick wall. He turned his head
indolently, and looked into the mills. There hung about the place
a thick, unclean odor. The slightest motion of his hand marked
that he perceived it, and his insufferable disgust. That was all. May
said nothing, only quickened his angry tramp.

"Besides," added Mitchell, giving a corollary to his answer, "it would be of no use. I am not one of them."

"You do not mean"—said May, facing him.

"Yes, I mean just that. Reform is born of need, not pity. No vital movement of the people's has worked down, for good or evil; fermented, instead, carried up the heaving, cloggy mass. Think back through history, and you will know it. What will this lowest deep—thieves, Magdalens, negroes—do with the light filtered through ponderous Church creeds, Baconian theories, Goethe schemes? Some day, out of their bitter need will be thrown up their own light-bringer,—their Jean Paul, their Cromwell, their Messiah."

"Bah!" was the Doctor's inward criticism. However, in practice, he adopted the theory; for, when, night and morning, afterwards, he prayed that power might be given these degraded souls to rise, he glowed at heart, recognizing an accomplished duty.

Wolfe and the woman had stood in the shadow of the works as the coach drove off. The Doctor had held out his hand in a frank, generous way, telling him to "take care of himself, and to remember it was his right to rise." Mitchell had simply touched his hat, as to an equal, with a quiet look of thorough recognition. Kirby had thrown Deborah some money, which she found, and clutched eagerly enough. They were gone now, all of them. The man sat down on the cinder-road, looking up into the murky sky.

" 'T be late, Hugh. Wunnot hur come?"

He shook his head doggedly, and the woman crouched out of his sight against the wall. Do you remember rare moments when a sudden light flashed over yourself, your world, God? when you stood on a mountain-peak, seeing your life as it might have been, as it is? one quick instant, when custom lost its force and every-day usage? when your friend, wife, brother, stood in a new light? your soul was bared, and the grave,—a foretaste of the nakedness of the Judgment-Day? So it came before him, his life, that night. The slow tides of pain he had borne gathered themselves up and surged against his soul. His squalid daily life, the brutal coarseness eating into his brain, as the ashes into his skin: before, these things had been a dull aching into his consciousness; to-night, they were reality. He gripped the filthy red shirt that clung, stiff with soot,

about him, and tore it savagely from his arm. The flesh beneath
was muddy with grease and ashes,—and the heart beneath that!
And the soul? God knows.

Then flashed before his vivid poetic sense the man who had left
him,—the pure face, the delicate, sinewy limbs, in harmony with
all he knew of beauty or truth. In his cloudy fancy he had pictured
a Something like this. He had found it in this Mitchell, even when
he idly scoffed at his pain: a Man all-knowing, all-seeing, crowned
by Nature, reigning,—the keen glance of his eye falling like a
sceptre on other men. And yet his instinct taught him that he too—
He! He looked at himself with sudden loathing, sick, wrung his
hands with a cry, and then was silent. With all the phantoms of his
heated, ignorant fancy, Wolfe had not been vague in his ambitions.
They were practical, slowly built up before him out of his knowledge of what he could do. Through years he had day by day made
this hope a real thing to himself,—a clear, projected figure of
himself, as he might become.

Able to speak, to know what was best, to raise these men and
women working at his side up with him: sometimes he forgot this
defined hope in the frantic anguish to escape,—only to escape,—
out of the wet, the pain, the ashes, somewhere, anywhere,—only
for one moment of free air on a hill-side, to lie down and let his
sick soul throb itself out in the sunshine. But to-night he panted
for life. The savage strength of his nature was roused; his cry was
fierce to God for justice.

"Look at me!" he said to Deborah, with a low, bitter laugh,
striking his puny chest savagely. "What am I worth, Deb? Is it my
fault that I am no better? My fault? My fault?"

He stopped, stung with a sudden remorse, seeing her hunchback
shape writhing with sobs. For Deborah was crying thankless tears,
according to the fashion of women.

"God forgi' me, woman! Things go harder wi' you nor me. It's
a worse share."

He got up and helped her to rise; and they went doggedly down
the muddy street, side by side.

"It's all wrong," he muttered, slowly,—"all wrong! I dunnot
understan'. But it'll end some day."

"Come home, Hugh!" she said, coaxingly; for he had stopped,
looking around bewildered.

"Home,—and back to the mill!" He went on saying this over to himself, as if he would mutter down every pain in this dull despair.

She followed him through the fog, her blue lips chattering with cold. They reached the cellar at last. Old Wolfe had been drinking since she went out, and had crept nearer the door. The girl Janey slept heavily in the corner. He went up to her, touching softly the worn white arm with his fingers. Some bitterer thought stung him, as he stood there. He wiped the drops from his forehead, and went into the room beyond, livid, trembling. A hope, trifling, perhaps, but very dear, had died just then out of the poor puddler's life, as he looked at the sleeping, innocent girl,—some plan for the future, in which she had borne a part. He gave it up that moment, then and forever. Only a trifle, perhaps, to us: his face grew a shade paler,—that was all. But, somehow, the man's soul, as God and the angels looked down on it, never was the same afterwards.

Deborah followed him into the inner room. She carried a candle, which she placed on the floor, closing the door after her. She had seen the look on his face, as he turned away: her own grew deadly. Yet, as she came up to him her eyes glowed. He was seated on an old chest, quiet, holding his face in his hands.

"Hugh!" she said, softly.

He did not speak.

"Hugh, did hur hear what the man said,—him with the clear voice? Did hur hear? Money, money, that it wud do all?"

He pushed her away,—gently, but he was worn out; her rasping tone fretted him.

"Hugh!"

The candle flared a pale yellow light over the cobwebbed brick walls, and the woman standing there. He looked at her. She was young, in deadly earnest; her faded eyes, and wet, ragged figure caught from their frantic eagerness a power akin to beauty.

"Hugh, it is true! Money ull do it! Oh, Hugh, boy, listen till me! He said it true! It is money!"

"I know. Go back! I do not want you here."

"Hugh, it is t' last time. I'll never worrit hur again."

There were tears in her voice now, but she choked them back.

"Hear till me only to-night! If one of t' witch people wud come, them we heard of t' home, and gif hur all hur wants, what then? Say, Hugh!"

"What do you mean?"

"I mean money."

Her whisper shrilled through his brain.

"If one of t' witch dwarfs wud come from t' lane moors to-night, and gif hur money, to go out,—*out,* I say,—out, lad, where t' sun shines, and t' heath grows, and t' ladies walk in silken gownds, and God stays all t' time,—where t' man lives that talked to us to-night,—Hugh knows,—Hugh could walk there like a king!"

He thought the woman mad, tried to check her, but she went on, fierce in her eager haste.

"If *I* were t' witch dwarf, if I had t' money, wud hur thank me? Wud hur take me out o' this place wid hur and Janey? I wud not come into the gran' house hur wud build, to vex hur wid t' hunch,—only at night, when t' shadows were dark, stand far off to see hur."

Mad? Yes! Are many of us mad in this way?

"Poor Deb! poor Deb!" he said, soothingly.

"It is here," she said, suddenly jerking into his hand a small roll. "I took it! I did it! Me, me!—not hur! I shall be hanged, I shall be burnt in hell, if anybody knows I took it! Out of his pocket, as he leaned against t' bricks. Hur knows?"

She thrust it into his hand, and then, her errand done, began to gather chips together to make a fire, choking down hysteric sobs.

"Has it come to this?"

That was all he said. The Welsh Wolfe blood was honest. The roll was a small green pocket-book containing one or two gold pieces, and a check for an incredible amount, as it seemed to the poor puddler. He laid it down, hiding his face again in his hands.

"Hugh, don't be angry wud me! It's only poor Deb,—hur knows?"

He took the long skinny fingers kindly in his.

"Angry? God help me, no! Let me sleep. I am tired."

He threw himself heavily down on the wooden bench, stunned with pain and weariness. She brought some old rags to cover him.

It was late on Sunday evening before he awoke. I tell God's truth, when I say he had then no thought of keeping this money. Deborah had hid it in his pocket. He found it there. She watched him eagerly, as he took it out.

"I must gif it to him," he said, reading her face.

"Hur knows," she said with a bitter sigh of disappointment. "But it is hur right to keep it."

His right! The word struck him. Doctor May had used the same. He washed himself, and went out to find this man Mitchell. His right! Why did this chance word cling to him so obstinately? Do you hear the fierce devils whisper in his ear, as he went slowly down the darkening street?

The evening came on, slow and calm. He seated himself at the end of an alley leading into one of the larger streets. His brain was clear to-night, keen, intent, mastering. It would not start back, cowardly, from any hellish temptation, but meet it face to face. Therefore the great temptation of his life came to him veiled by no sophistry, but bold, defiant, owning its own vile name, trusting to one bold blow for victory.

He did not deceive himself. Theft! That was it. At first the word sickened him; then he grappled with it. Sitting there on a broken cart-wheel, the fading day, the noisy groups, the church-bells' tolling passed before him like a panorama, while the sharp struggle went on within. This money! He took it out, and looked at it. If he gave it back, what then? He was going to be cool about it.

People going by to church saw only a sickly mill-boy watching them quietly at the alley's mouth. They did not know that he was mad, or they would not have gone by so quietly: mad with hunger; stretching out his hands to the world, that had given so much to them, for leave to live the life God meant him to live. His soul within him was smothering to death; he wanted so much, thought so much, and *knew*—nothing. There was nothing of which he was certain, except the mill and things there. Of God and heaven he had heard so little, that they were to him what fairy-land is to a child: something real, but not here; very far off. His brain, greedy, dwarfed, full of thwarted energy and unused powers, questioned these men and women going by, coldly, bitterly, that night. Was it not his right to live as they,—a pure life, a good, true-hearted life, full of beauty and kind words? He only wanted to know how to use the strength within him. His heart warmed, as he thought of it. He suffered himself to think of it longer. If he took the money?

Then he saw himself as he might be, strong, helpful, kindly. The night crept on, as this one image slowly evolved itself from the crowd of other thoughts and stood triumphant. He looked at it. As he might be! What wonder, if it blinded him to delirium,—the madness that underlies all revolution, all progress, and all fall?

You laugh at the shallow temptation? You see the error underlying its argument so clearly,—that to him a true life was one of full development rather than self-restraint? that he was deaf to the higher tone in a cry of voluntary suffering for truth's sake than in the fullest flow of spontaneous harmony? I do not plead his cause. I only want to show you the mote in my brother's eye: then you can see clearly to take it out.

The money,—there it lay on his knee, a little blotted slip of paper, nothing in itself; used to raise him out of the pit; something straight from God's hand. A thief! Well, what was it to be a thief? He met the question at last, face to face, wiping the clammy drops of sweat from his forehead. God made this money—the fresh air, too—for his children's use. He never made the difference between poor and rich. The Something who looked down on him that moment through the cool gray sky had a kindly face, he knew,— loved his children alike. Oh, he knew that!

There were times when the soft floods of color in the crimson and purple flames, or the clear depth of amber in the water below the bridge, had somehow given him a glimpse of another world than this,—of an infinite depth of beauty and of quiet somewhere,—somewhere,—a depth of quiet and rest and love. Looking up now, it became strangely real. The sun had sunk quite below the hills, but his last rays struck upward, touching the zenith. The fog had risen, and the town and river were steeped in its thick, gray damp; but overhead, the sun-touched smoke-clouds opened like a cleft ocean,—shifting, rolling seas of crimson mist, waves of billowy silver veined with blood-scarlet, inner depths unfathomable of glancing light. Wolfe's artist-eye grew drunk with color. The gates of that other world! Fading, flashing before him now! What, in that world of Beauty, Content, and Right, were the petty laws, the mine and thine, of mill-owners and mill-hands?

A consciousness of power stirred within him. He stood up. A man,—he thought, stretching out his hands,—free to work, to live, to love! Free! His right! He folded the scrap of paper in his hand. As his nervous fingers took it in, limp and blotted, so his soul took in the mean temptation, lapped it in fancied rights, in dreams of improved existences, drifting and endless as the cloud-seas of color. Clutching it, as if the tightness of his hold would strengthen his sense of possession, he went aimlessly down the street. It was his watch at the mill. He need not go, need never go again, thank God!—shaking off the thought with unspeakable loathing.

Shall I go over the history of the hours of that night? how the man wandered from one to another of his old haunts, with a half-consciousness of bidding them farewell,—lanes and alleys and back-yards where the mill-hands lodged,—noting, with a new eagerness, the filth and drunkenness, the pig-pens, the ash-heaps covered with potato-skins, the bloated, pimpled women at the doors,—with a new disgust, a new sense of sudden triumph, and, under all, a new, vague dread, unknown before, smothered down, kept under, but still there? It left him but once during the night, when, for the second time in his life, he entered a church. It was a sombre Gothic pile, where the stained light lost itself in far-retreating arches; built to meet the requirements and sympathies of a far other class than Wolfe's. Yet it touched, moved him uncontrollably. The distances, the shadows, the still, marble figures, the mass of silent kneeling worshippers, the mysterious music, thrilled, lifted his soul with a wonderful pain. Wolfe forgot himself, forgot the new life he was going to live, the mean terror gnawing underneath. The voice of the speaker strengthened the charm; it was clear, feeling, full, strong. An old man, who had lived much, suffered much; whose brain was keenly alive, dominant; whose heart was summer-warm with charity. He taught it to-night. He held up Humanity in its grand total; showed the great world-cancer to his people. Who could show it better? He was a Christian reformer; he had studied the age thoroughly; his outlook at man had been free, world-wide, over all time. His faith stood sublime upon the Rock of Ages; his fiery zeal guided vast schemes by which the gospel was to be preached to all nations. How did he preach it to-night? In burning, light-laden words he painted the incarnate Life, Love, the universal Man: words that became reality in the lives of these people,—that lived again in beautiful words and actions, trifling, but heroic. Sin, as he defined it, was a real foe to them; their trials, temptations, were his. His words passed far over the furnace-tender's grasp, toned to suit another class of culture; they sounded in his ears a very pleasant song in an unknown tongue. He meant to cure this world-cancer with a steady eye that had never glared with hunger, and a hand that neither poverty nor strychnine-whiskey had taught to shake. In this morbid, distorted heart of the Welsh puddler he had failed.

Wolfe rose at last, and turned from the church down the street. He looked up; the night had come on foggy, damp; the golden mists had vanished, and the sky lay dull and ash-colored. He wandered again aimlessly down the street, idly wondering what had become of the cloud-sea of crimson and scarlet. The trial-day of this man's life was over, and he had lost the victory. What followed was mere drifting circumstance,—a quicker walking over the path,—that was all. Do you want to hear the end of it? You wish me to make a tragic story out of it? Why, in the police-reports of the morning paper you can find a dozen such tragedies: hints of shipwrecks unlike any that ever befell on the high seas; hints that here a power was lost to heaven,—that there a soul went down where no tide can ebb or flow. Commonplace enough the hints are,—jocose sometimes, done up in rhyme.

Doctor May, a month after the night I have told you of, was reading to his wife at breakfast from this fourth column of the morning-paper: an unusual thing,—these police-reports not being, in general, choice reading for ladies; but it was only one item he read.

"Oh, my dear! You remember that man I told you of, that we saw at Kirby's mill?—that was arrested for robbing Mitchell? Here he is; just listen:—'Circuit Court. Judge Day. Hugh Wolfe, operative in Kirby & John's Loudon Mills. Charge, grand larceny. Sentence, nineteen years hard labor in penitentiary.'—Scoundrel! Serves him right! After all our kindness that night! Picking Mitchell's pocket at the very time!"

His wife said something about the ingratitude of that kind of people, and then they began to talk of something else.

Nineteen years! How easy that was to read! What a simple word for Judge Day to utter! Nineteen years! Half a lifetime!

Hugh Wolfe sat on the window-ledge of his cell, looking out. His ankles were ironed. Not usual in such cases; but he had made two desperate efforts to escape. "Well," as Haley, the jailer, said, "small blame to him! Nineteen years' imprisonment was not a pleasant thing to look forward to." Haley was very good-natured about it, though Wolfe had fought him savagely.

"When he was first caught," the jailer said afterwards, in telling the story, "before the trial, the fellow was cut down at once,—laid there on that pallet like a dead man, with his hands over his eyes. Never saw a man so cut down in my life. Time of the trial, too, came the queerest dodge of any customer I ever had. Would choose no lawyer. Judge gave him one, of course. Gibson it was. He tried to prove the fellow crazy; but it wouldn't go. Thing was plain as day-light: money found on him. 'Twas a hard sentence,—all the law allows; but it was for 'xample's sake. These mill-hands are gettin' onbearable. When the sentence was read, he just looked up, and said the money was his by rights, and that all the world had gone wrong. That night, after the trial, a gentleman came to see him here, name of Mitchell,—him as he stole from. Talked to him for an hour. Thought he came for curiosity, like. After he was gone, thought Wolfe was remarkable quiet, and went into his cell. Found him very low; bed all bloody. Doctor said he had been bleeding at the lungs. He was as weak as a cat; yet, if ye'll b'lieve me, he tried to get a-past me and get out. I just carried him like a baby, and threw him on the pallet. Three days after, he tried it again: that time reached the wall. Lord help you! he fought like a tiger,— giv' some terrible blows. Fightin' for life, you see; for he can't live long, shut up in the stone crib down yonder. Got a death-cough now. 'T took two of us to bring him down that day; so I just put the irons on his feet. There he sits, in there. Goin' to-morrow, with a batch more of 'em. That woman, hunchback, tried with him,—you remember?—she's only got three years. 'Complice. But *she's* a woman, you know. He's been quiet ever since I put on irons: giv' up, I suppose. Looks white, sick-lookin'. It acts different on 'em, bein' sentenced. Most of 'em gets reckless, devilish-like. Some prays awful, and sings them vile songs of the mills, all in a breath. That woman, now, she's desper't'. Been beggin' to see Hugh, as she calls him, for three days. I'm a-goin' to let her in. She don't go with him. Here she is in this next cell. I'm a-goin' now to let her in."

He let her in. Wolfe did not see her. She crept into a corner of the cell, and stood watching him. He was scratching the iron bars of the window with a piece of tin which he had picked up, with an idle, uncertain, vacant stare, just as a child or idiot would do.

"Tryin' to get out, old boy?" laughed Haley. "Them irons will need a crow-bar beside your tin, before you can open 'em."

Wolfe laughed, too, in a senseless way.

"I think I'll get out," he said.

"I believe his brain's touched," said Haley, when he came out.

The puddler scraped away with the tin for half an hour. Still Deborah did not speak. At last she ventured nearer, and touched his arm.

"Blood?" she said, looking at some spots on his coat with a shudder.

He looked up at her. "Why, Deb!" he said, smiling,—such a bright, boyish smile, that it went to poor Deborah's heart directly, and she sobbed and cried out loud.

"Oh, Hugh, lad! Hugh! dunnot look at me, when it wur my fault! To think I brought hur to it! And I loved hur so! Oh, lad, I dud!"

The confession, even in this wretch, came with the woman's blush through the sharp cry.

He did not seem to hear her,—scraping away diligently at the bars with the bit of tin.

Was he going mad? She peered closely into his face. Something she saw there made her draw suddenly back,—something which Haley had not seen, that lay beneath the pinched, vacant look it had caught since the trial, or the curious gray shadow that rested on it. That gray shadow,—yes, she knew what that meant. She had often seen it creeping over women's faces for months, who died at last of slow hunger or consumption. That meant death, distant, lingering: but this—Whatever it was the woman saw, or thought she saw, used as she was to crime and misery, seemed to make her sick with a new horror. Forgetting her fear of him, she caught his shoulders, and looked keenly, steadily, into his eyes.

"Hugh!" she cried, in a desperate whisper,—"oh, boy, not that! for God's sake, not *that!*"

The vacant laugh went off his face, and he answered her in a muttered word or two that drove her away. Yet the words were kindly enough. Sitting there on his pallet, she cried silently a hopeless sort of tears, but did not speak again. The man looked up furtively at her now and then. Whatever his own trouble was, her distress vexed him with a momentary sting.

It was market-day. The narrow window of the jail looked down directly on the carts and wagons drawn up in a long line, where they had unloaded. He could see, too, and hear distinctly the clink of money as it changed hands, the busy crowd of whites and blacks shoving, pushing one another, and the chaffering and swearing at the stalls. Somehow, the sound, more than anything else had done, wakened him up,—made the whole real to him. He was done with the world and the business of it. He let the tin fall, and looked out, pressing his face close to the rusty bars. How they crowded and pushed! And he,—he should never walk that pavement again! There came Neff Sanders, one of the feeders at the mill, with a basket on his arm. Sure enough, Neff was married the other week. He whistled, hoping he would look up; but he did not. He wondered if Neff remembered he was there,—if any of the boys thought of him up there, and thought that he never was to go down that old cinder-road again. Never again! He had not quite understood it before; but now he did. Not for days or years, but never!— that was it.

How clear the light fell on that stall in front of the market! and how like a picture it was, the dark-green heaps of corn, and the crimson beets, and golden melons! There was another with game: how the light flickered on that pheasant's breast, with the purplish blood dripping over the brown feathers! He could see the red shining of the drops, it was so near. In one minute he could be down there. It was just a step. So easy, as it seemed, so natural to go! Yet it could never be—not in all the thousands of years to come—that he should put his foot on that street again! He thought of himself with a sorrowful pity, as of some one else. There was a dog down in the market, walking after his master with such a stately, grave look!—only a dog, yet he could go backwards and forwards just as he pleased: he had good luck! Why, the very vilest cur, yelping there in the gutter, had not lived his life, had been free to act out whatever thought God had put into his brain; while he—No, he would not think of that! He tried to put the thought away, and to listen to a dispute between a countryman and a woman about some meat; but it would come back. He, what had he done to bear this?

Then came the sudden picture of what might have been, and now. He knew what it was to be in the penitentiary,—how it went with men there. He knew how in these long years he should slowly die, but not until soul and body had become corrupt and rotten,—how, when he came out, if he lived to come, even the lowest of the mill-hands would jeer him,—how his hands would be weak, and his brain senseless and stupid. He believed he was almost that now. He put his hand to his head, with a puzzled, weary look. It ached, his head, with thinking. He tried to quiet himself. It was only right, perhaps; he had done wrong. But was there right or wrong for such as he? What was right? And who had ever taught him? He thrust the whole matter away. A dark, cold quiet crept through his brain. It was all wrong; but let it be! It was nothing to him more than the others. Let it be!

The door grated, as Haley opened it.

"Come, my woman! Must lock up for t' night. Come, stir yerself!"

She went up and took Hugh's hand.

"Good-night, Deb," he said, carelessly.

She had not hoped he would say more; but the tired pain on her mouth just then was bitterer than death. She took his passive hand and kissed it.

"Hur'll never see Deb again!" she ventured, her lips growing colder and more bloodless.

What did she say that for? Did he not know it? Yet he would not be impatient with poor old Deb. She had trouble of her own, as well as he.

"No, never again," he said, trying to be cheerful.

She stood just a moment, looking at him. Do you laugh at her, standing there, with her hunchback, her rags, her bleared, withered face, and the great despised love tugging at her heart?

"Come, you!" called Haley, impatiently.

She did not move.

"Hugh!" she whispered.

It was to be her last word. What was it?

"Hugh, boy not *THAT!*"

He did not answer. She wrung her hands, trying to be silent, looking in his face in an agony of entreaty. He smiled again, kindly.

"It is best, Deb. I cannot bear to be hurted any more."

"Hur knows," she said, humbly.

"Tell my father good-bye; and—and kiss little Janey."

She nodded, saying nothing, looked in his face again, and went out of the door. As she went, she staggered.

"Drinkin' to-day?" broke out Haley, pushing her before him. "Where the Devil did you get it? Here, in with ye!" and he shoved her into her cell, next to Wolfe's, and shut the door.

Along the wall of her cell there was a crack low down by the floor, through which she could see the light from Wolfe's. She had discovered it days before. She hurried in now, and, kneeling down by it, listened, hoping to hear some sound. Nothing but the rasping of the tin on the bars. He was at his old amusement again. Something in the noise jarred on her ear, for she shivered as she heard it. Hugh rasped away at the bars. A dull old bit of tin, not fit to cut korl with.

He looked out of the window again. People were leaving the market now. A tall mulatto girl, following her mistress, her basket on her head, crossed the street just below, and looked up. She was laughing; but, when she caught sight of the haggard face peering out through the bars, suddenly grew grave, and hurried by. A free, firm step, a clear-cut olive face, with a scarlet turban tied on one side, dark, shining eyes, and on the head the basket poised, filled with fruit and flowers, under which the scarlet turban and bright eyes looked out half-shadowed. The picture caught his eye. It was good to see a face like that. He would try to-morrow, and cut one like it. *To-morrow!* He threw down the tin, trembling, and covered his face with his hands. When he looked up again, the daylight was gone.

Deborah, crouching near by on the other side of the wall, heard no noise. He sat on the side of the low pallet, thinking. Whatever was the mystery which the woman had seen on his face, it came out now slowly, in the dark there, and became fixed,—a something never seen on his face before. The evening was darkening fast. The market had been over for an hour; the rumbling of the carts over the pavement grew more infrequent: he listened to each, as it passed, because he thought it was to be for the last time. For the same reason, it was, I suppose, that he strained his eyes to catch a glimpse of each passer-by, wondering who they were, what kind of homes they were going to, if they had children,— listening eagerly to every chance word in the street, as if—(God be merciful to the man! what strange fancy was this?)—as if he never should hear human voices again.

It was quite dark at last. The street was a lonely one. The last passenger, he thought, was gone. No,—there was a quick step: Joe Hill, lighting the lamps. Joe was a good old chap; never passed a fellow without some joke or other. He remembered once seeing the place where he lived with his wife. "Granny Hill" the boys called her. Bedridden she was; but so kind as Joe was to her! kept the room so clean!—and the old woman, when he was there, was laughing at "some of t' lad's foolishness." The step was far down the street; but he could see him place the ladder, run up, and light the gas. A longing seized him to be spoken to once more.

"Joe!" he called, out of the grating. "Good-bye, Joe!"

The old man stopped a moment, listening uncertainly; then hurried on. The prisoner thrust his hand out of the window, and called again, louder; but Joe was too far down the street. It was a little thing; but it hurt him,—this disappointment.

"Good-bye, Joe!" he called, sorrowfully enough.

"Be quiet!" said one of the jailers, passing the door, striking on it with his club.

Oh, that was the last, was it?

There was an inexpressible bitterness on his face, as he lay down on the bed, taking the bit of tin, which he had rasped to a tolerable degree of sharpness, in his hand,—to play with, it may be. He bared his arms, looking intently at their corded veins and sinews. Deborah, listening in the next cell, heard a slight clicking sound, often repeated. She shut her lips tightly, that she might not scream, the cold drops of sweat broke over her, in her dumb agony.

"Hur knows best," she muttered at last, fiercely clutching the boards where she lay.

If she could have seen Wolfe, there was nothing about him to frighten her. He lay quite still, his arms outstretched, looking at the pearly stream of moonlight coming into the window. I think in that one hour that came then he lived over all the years that had gone before. I think that all the low, vile life, all his wrongs, all his starved hopes, came then, and stung him with a farewell poison that made him sick unto death. He made neither moan nor cry, only turned his worn face now and then to the pure light, that seemed so far off, as one that said, "How long, O Lord? how long?"

The hour was over at last. The moon, passing over her nightly path, slowly came nearer, and threw the light across his bed on his feet. He watched it steadily, as it crept up, inch by inch, slowly. It seemed to him to carry with it a great silence. He had been so hot and tired there always in the mills! The years had been so fierce and cruel! There was coming now quiet and coolness and sleep. His tense limbs relaxed, and settled in a calm languor. The blood ran fainter and slow from his heart. He did not think now with a savage anger of what might be and was not; he was conscious only of deep stillness creeping over him. At first he saw a sea of faces: the mill-men,—women he had known, drunken and bloated,—Janeys timid and pitiful,—poor old Debs: then they floated together like a mist, and faded away, leaving only the clear, pearly moonlight.

Whether, as the pure light crept up the stretched-out figure, it brought with it calm and peace, who shall say? His dumb soul was alone with God in judgment. A Voice may have spoken for it from far-off Calvary, "Father, forgive them, for they know not what they do!" Who dare say? Fainter and fainter the heart rose and fell, slower and slower the moon floated from behind a cloud, until, when at last its full tide of white splendor swept over the cell, it seemed to wrap and fold into a deeper stillness the dead figure that never should move again. Silence deeper than the Night! Nothing that moved, save the black nauseous stream of blood dripping slowly from the pallet to the floor!

There was outcry and crowd enough in the cell the next day. The coroner and his jury, the local editors, Kirby himself, and boys with their hands thrust knowingly into their pockets and heads on one side, jammed into the corners. Coming and going all day. Only one woman. She came late, and outstayed them all. A Quaker, or Friend, as they call themselves. I think this woman was known by that name in heaven. A homely body, coarsely dressed in gray and white. Deborah (for Haley had let her in) took notice of her. She watched them all—sitting on the end of the pallet, holding his head in her arms—with the ferocity of a watch-dog, if any of them touched the body. There was no meekness, or sorrow, in her face; the stuff out of which murderers are made, instead. All the time Haley and the woman were laying straight the limbs and cleaning the cell, Deborah sat still, keenly watching the Quaker's face. Of all the crowd there that day, this woman alone had not spoken to her,—only once or twice had put some cordial to her lips. After they all were gone, the woman, in the same still, gentle way, brought a vase of wood-leaves and berries, and placed it by the pallet, then opened the narrow window. The fresh air blew in, and swept the woody fragrance over the dead face. Deborah looked up with a quick wonder.

"Did hur know my boy wud like it? Did hur know Hugh?"

"I know Hugh now."

The white fingers passed in a slow, pitiful way over the dead, worn face. There was a heavy shadow in the quiet eyes.

"Did hur know where they'll bury Hugh?" said Deborah in a shrill tone, catching her arm.

This had been the question hanging on her lips all day.

"In t' town-yard? Under t' mud and ash? T' lad'll smother, woman! He wur born on t' lane moor, where t' air is frick and strong. Take hur out, for God's sake, take hur out where t' air blows!"

The Quaker hesitated, but only for a moment. She put her strong arm around Deborah and led her to the window.

"Thee sees the hills, friend, over the river? Thee sees how the light lies warm there, and the winds of God blow all the day? I live there,—where the blue smoke is, by the trees. Look at me." She turned Deborah's face to her own, clear and earnest. "Thee will believe me? I will take Hugh and bury him there to-morrow."

Deborah did not doubt her. As the evening wore on, she leaned against the iron bars, looking at the hills that rose far off, through the thick sodden clouds, like a bright, unattainable calm. As she looked, a shadow of their solemn repose fell on her face: its fierce discontent faded into a pitiful, humble quiet. Slow, solemn tears gathered in her eyes: the poor weak eyes turned so hopelessly to the place where Hugh was to rest, the grave heights looking higher and brighter and more solemn than ever before. The Quaker watched her keenly. She came to her at last, and touched her arm.

"When thee comes back," she said, in a low, sorrowful tone, like one who speaks from a strong heart deeply moved with remorse or pity, "thee shall begin thy life again,—there on the hills. I came too late; but not for thee,—by God's help, it may be."

Not too late. Three years after, the Quaker began her work. I

end my story here. At evening-time it was light. There is no need
to tire you with the long years of sunshine, and fresh air, and slow,
patient Christ-love, needed to make healthy and hopeful this impure body and soul. There is a homely pine house, on one of these
hills, whose windows overlook broad, wooded slopes and clover-
crimsoned meadows,—niched into the very place where the light
is warmest, the air freest. It is the Friends' meeting-house. Once
a week they sit there, in their grave, earnest way, waiting for the
Spirit of Love to speak, opening their simple hearts to receive His
words. There is a woman, old, deformed, who takes a humble place
among them: waiting like them: in her gray dress, her worn face,
pure and meek, turned now and then to the sky. A woman much
loved by these silent, restful people; more silent than they, more
humble, more loving. Waiting: with her eyes turned to hills higher
and purer than these on which she lives,—dim and far off now,
but to be reached some day. There may be in her heart some latent
hope to meet there the love denied her here,—that she shall find
him whom she lost, and that then she will not be all-unworthy.
Who blames her? Something is lost in the passage of every soul
from one eternity to the other,—something pure and beautiful,
which might have been and was not: a hope, a talent, a love, over
which the soul mourns, like Esau deprived of his birthright. What
blame to the meek Quaker, if she took her lost hope to make the
hills of heaven more fair?

Nothing remains to tell that the poor Welsh puddler once lived,
but this figure of the mill-woman cut in korl. I have it here in a
corner of my library. I keep it hid behind a curtain,—it is such a
rough, ungainly thing. Yet there are about it touches, grand sweeps
of outline, that show a master's hand. Sometimes,—to-night, for
instance,—the curtain is accidentally drawn back, and I see a bare
arm stretched out imploringly in the darkness, and an eager, wolfish
face watching mine: a wan, woful face, through which the spirit of
the dead korl-cutter looks out, with its thwarted life, its mighty
hunger, its unfinished work. Its pale, vague lips seem to tremble
with a terrible question. "Is this the End?" they say,—"nothing
beyond?—no more?" Why, you tell me you have seen that look
in the eyes of dumb brutes,—horses dying under the lash. I know.

The deep of the night is passing while I write. The gas-light
wakens from the shadows here and there the objects which lie

scattered through the room: only faintly, though; for they belong to the open sunlight. As I glance at them, they each recall some task or pleasure of the coming day. A half-moulded child's head; Aphrodite; a bough of forest-leaves; music; work; homely fragments, in which lie the secrets of all eternal truth and beauty. Prophetic all! Only this dumb, woful face seems to belong to and end with the night. I turn to look at it. Has the power of its desperate need commanded the darkness away? While the room is yet steeped in heavy shadow, a cool, gray light suddenly touches its head like a blessing hand, and its groping arm points through the broken cloud to the far East, where, in the flickering, nebulous crimson, God has set the promise of the Dawn.

The Yellow Wallpaper
by Charlotte Perkins Gilman

It is very seldom that mere ordinary people like John and myself secure ancestral halls for the summer.

A colonial mansion, a hereditary estate, I would say a haunted house and reach the height of romantic felicity—but that would be asking too much of fate!

Still I will proudly declare that there is something queer about it.

Else, why should it be let so cheaply? And why have stood so long untenanted?

John laughs at me, of course, but one expects that.

John is practical in the extreme. He has no patience with faith, an intense horror of superstition, and he scoffs openly at any talk of things not to be felt and seen and put down in figures.

John is a physician, and *perhaps*—(I would not say it to a living soul, of course, but this is dead paper and a great relief to my mind)—*perhaps* that is one reason I do not get well faster.

You see, he does not believe I am sick! And what can one do?

If a physician of high standing, and one's own husband, assures friends and relatives that there is really nothing the matter with one but temporary nervous depression—a slight hysterical tendency—what is one to do?

My brother is also a physician, and also of high standing, and he says the same thing.

So I take phosphates or phosphites—whichever it is—and tonics, and air and exercise, and journeys, and am absolutely forbidden to "work" until I am well again.

Personally, I disagree with their ideas.

Personally, I believe that congenial work, with excitement and change, would do me good.

But what is one to do?

I did write for a while in spite of them; but it *does* exhaust me a good deal—having to be so sly about it, or else meet with heavy opposition.

I sometimes fancy that in my condition, if I had less opposition and more society and stimulus—but John says the very worst thing I can do is to think about my condition, and I confess it always makes me feel bad.

So I will let it alone and talk about the house.

The most beautiful place! It is quite alone, standing well back from the road, quite three miles from the village. It makes me think of English places that you read about, for there are hedges and walls and gates that lock, and lots of separate little houses for the gardeners and people.

There is a *delicious* garden! I never saw such a garden—large and shady, full of box-bordered paths, and lined with long grape-covered arbors with seats under them.

There were greenhouses, but they are all broken now.

There was some legal trouble, I believe, something about the heirs and co-heirs; anyhow, the place has been empty for years.

That spoils my ghostliness, I am afraid, but I don't care—there is something strange about the house—I can feel it.

I even said so to John one moonlight evening, but he said what I felt was a draught, and shut the window.

I get unreasonably angry with John sometimes. I'm sure I never used to be so sensitive. I think it is due to this nervous condition.

But John says if I feel so I shall neglect proper self-control; so I take pains to control myself—before him, at least, and that makes me very tired.

I don't like our room a bit. I wanted one downstairs that opened onto the piazza and had roses all over the window, and such pretty old-fashioned chintz hangings! But John would not hear of it.

He said there was only one window and not room for two beds, and no near room for him if he took another.

He is very careful and loving, and hardly lets me stir without special direction.

I have a schedule prescription for each hour in the day; he takes all care from me, and so I feel basely ungrateful not to value it more.

He said he came here solely on my account, that I was to have perfect rest and all the air I could get. "Your exercise depends on your strength, my dear," said he, "and your food somewhat on your appetite; but air you can absorb all the time." So we took the nursery at the top of the house.

It is a big, airy room, the whole floor nearly, with windows that look all ways, and air and sunshine galore. It was nursery first, and then playroom and gymnasium, I should judge, for the windows are barred for little children, and there are rings and things in the walls.

The paint and paper look as if a boys' school had used it. It is stripped off—the paper—in great patches all around the head of my bed, about as far as I can reach, and in a great place on the other side of the room low down. I never saw a worse paper in my life. One of those sprawling, flamboyant patterns committing every artistic sin.

It is dull enough to confuse the eye in following, pronounced enough constantly to irritate and provoke study, and when you follow the lame uncertain curves for a little distance they suddenly commit suicide—plunge off at outrageous angles, destroy themselves in unheard-of contradictions.

The color is repellent, almost revolting; a smouldering unclean yellow, strangely faded by the slow-turning sunlight. It is a dull yet lurid orange in some places, a sickly sulphur tint in others.

No wonder the children hated it! I should hate it myself if I had to live in this room long.

There comes John, and I must put this away—he hates to have me write a word.

We have been here two weeks, and I haven't felt like writing before, since the first day.

I am sitting by the window now, up in this atrocious nursery, and there is nothing to hinder my writing as much as I please, save lack of strength.

John is away all day, and even some nights when his cases are serious.

I am glad my case is not serious!

But these nervous troubles are dreadfully depressing.

John does not know how much I really suffer. He knows there is no reason to suffer, and that satisfies him.

Of course it is only nervousness. It does weigh on me so not to do my duty in any way!

I meant to be such a help to John, such a real rest and comfort, and here I am a comparative burden already!

Nobody would believe what an effort it is to do what little I am able—to dress and entertain, and order things.

It is fortunate Mary is so good with the baby. Such a dear baby!

And yet I *cannot* be with him, it makes me so nervous.

I suppose John never was nervous in his life. He laughs at me so about this wallpaper!

At first he meant to repaper the room, but afterward he said that I was letting it get the better of me, and that nothing was worse for a nervous patient than to give way to such fancies.

He said that after the wallpaper was changed it would be the heavy bedstead, and then the barred windows, and then that gate at the head of the stairs, and so on.

"You know the place is doing you good," he said, "and really, dear, I don't care to renovate the house just for a three months' rental."

"Then do let us go downstairs," I said. "There are such pretty rooms there."

Then he took me in his arms and called me a blessed little goose, and said he would go down cellar, if I wished, and have it white-washed into the bargain.

But he is right enough about the beds and windows and things.

It is as airy and comfortable a room as anyone need wish, and, of course, I would not be so silly as to make him uncomfortable just for a whim.

I'm really getting quite fond of the big room, all but that horrid paper.

Out of one window I can see the garden—those mysterious deep-shaded arbors, the riotous old-fashioned flowers, and bushes and gnarly trees.

Out of another I get a lovely view of the bay and a little private wharf belonging to the estate. There is a beautiful shaded lane that runs down there from the house. I always fancy I see people walking in these numerous paths and arbors, but John has cautioned me not to give way to fancy in the least. He says that with my imaginative power and habit of story-making, a nervous weakness like mine is sure to lead to all manner of excited fancies, and that I ought to use my will and good sense to check the tendency. So I try.

I think sometimes that if I were only well enough to write a little it would relieve the press of ideas and rest me.

But I find I get pretty tired when I try.

It is so discouraging not to have any advice and companionship about my work. When I get really well, John says we will ask Cousin Henry and Julia down for a long visit; but he says he would as soon put fireworks in my pillow-case as to let me have those stimulating people about now.

I wish I could get well faster.

But I must not think about that. This paper looks to me as if it *knew* what a vicious influence it had!

There is a recurrent spot where the pattern lolls like a broken neck and two bulbous eyes stare at you upside down.

I get positively angry with the impertinence of it and the everlastingness. Up and down and sideways they crawl, and those absurd unblinking eyes are everywhere. There is one place where two breadths didn't match, and the eyes go all up and down the line, one a little higher than the other.

I never saw so much expression in an inanimate thing before, and we all know how much expression they have! I used to lie awake as a child and get more entertainment and terror out of blank walls and plain furniture than most children could find in a toy-store.

I remember what a kindly wink the knobs of our big old bureau used to have, and there was one chair that always seemed like a strong friend.

I used to feel that if any of the other things looked too fierce I could always hop into that chair and be safe.

The furniture in this room is no worse than inharmonious, however, for we had to bring it all from downstairs. I suppose when this was used as a playroom they had to take the nursery things out, and no wonder! I never saw such ravages as the children have made here.

The wallpaper, as I said before, is torn off in spots, and it sticketh closer than a brother—they must have had perseverance as well as hatred.

Then the floor is scratched and gouged and splintered, the plaster itself is dug out here and there, and this great heavy bed, which is all we found in the room, looks as if it had been through the wars.

But I don't mind it a bit—only the paper.

There comes John's sister. Such a dear girl as she is, and so careful of me! I must not let her find me writing.

She is a perfect and enthusiastic housekeeper, and hopes for no better profession. I verily believe she thinks it is the writing which made me sick!

But I can write when she is out, and see her a long way off from these windows.

There is one that commands the road, a lovely shaded winding road, and one that just looks off over the country. A lovely country, too, full of great elms and velvet meadows.

This wallpaper has a kind of sub-pattern in a different shade, a particularly irritating one, for you can only see it in certain lights, and not clearly then.

But in the places where it isn't faded and where the sun is just so—I can see a strange, provoking, formless sort of figure that seems to skulk about behind that silly and conspicuous front design.

There's sister on the stairs!

Well, the Fourth of July is over! The people are all gone, and I am tired out. John thought it might do me good to see a little company, so we just had Mother and Nellie and the children down for a week.

Of course I didn't do a thing. Jennie sees to everything now.

But it tired me all the same.

John says if I don't pick up faster he shall send me to Weir Mitchell in the fall.

But I don't want to go there at all. I had a friend who was in his hands once, and she says he is just like John and my brother, only more so!

Besides, it is such an undertaking to go so far.

I don't feel as if it was worthwhile to turn my hand over for anything, and I'm getting dreadfully fretful and querulous.

I cry at nothing, and cry most of the time.

Of course I don't when John is here, or anybody else, but when I am alone.

And I am alone a good deal just now. John is kept in town very often by serious cases, and Jennie is good and lets me alone when I want her to.

So I walk a little in the garden or down that lovely lane, sit on the porch under the roses, and lie down up here a good deal.

I'm getting really fond of the room in spite of the wallpaper. Perhaps *because* of the wallpaper.

It dwells in my mind so!

I lie here on this great immovable bed—it is nailed down, I believe—and follow that pattern about by the hour. It is as good as gymnastics, I assure you. I start, we'll say, at the bottom, down in the corner over there where it has not been touched, and I determine for the thousandth time that I *will* follow that pointless pattern to some sort of a conclusion.

I know a little of the principle of design, and I know this thing was not arranged on any laws of radiation, or alternation, or repetition, or symmetry, or anything else that I ever heard of.

It is repeated, of course, by the breadths, but not otherwise.

Looked at in one way, each breadth stands alone; the bloated curves and flourishes—a kind of "debased Romanesque" with delirium tremens—go waddling up and down in isolated columns of fatuity.

But, on the other hand, they connect diagonally, and the sprawling outlines run off in great slanting waves of optic horror, like a lot of wallowing sea-weeds in full chase.

The whole thing goes horizontally, too, at least it seems so, and I exhaust myself trying to distinguish the order of its going in that direction.

They have used a horizontal breadth for a frieze, and that adds wonderfully to the confusion.

There is one end of the room where it is almost intact, and there, when the crosslights fade and the low sun shines directly upon it, I can almost fancy radiation after all—the interminable grotesque seems to form around a common center and rush off in headlong plunges of equal distraction.

It makes me tired to follow it. I will take a nap, I guess.

I don't know why I should write this.

I don't want to.

I don't feel able.

And I know John would think it absurd. But I *must* say what I feel and think in some way—it is such a relief!

But the effort is getting to be greater than the relief.

Half the time now I am awfully lazy, and lie down ever so much. John says I mustn't lose my strength, and has me take cod liver oil and lots of tonics and things, to say nothing of ale and wine and rare meat.

Dear John! He loves me very dearly, and hates to have me sick. I tried to have a real earnest reasonable talk with him the other day, and tell him how I wish he would let me go and make a visit to Cousin Henry and Julia.

But he said I wasn't able to go, nor able to stand it after I got there; and I did not make out a very good case for myself, for I was crying before I had finished.

It is getting to be a great effort for me to think straight. Just this nervous weakness, I suppose.

And dear John gathered me up in his arms, and just carried me upstairs and laid me on the bed, and sat by me and read to me till it tired my head.

He said I was his darling and his comfort and all he had, and that I must take care of myself for his sake, and keep well.

He says no one but myself can help me out of it, that I must use my will and self-control and not let any silly fancies run away with me.

There's one comfort—the baby is well and happy, and does not have to occupy this nursery with the horrid wallpaper.

If we had not used it, that blessed child would have! What a fortunate escape! Why, I wouldn't have a child of mine, an impressionable little thing, live in such a room for worlds.

I never thought of it before, but it is lucky that John kept me here after all; I can stand it so much easier than a baby, you see.

Of course I never mention it to them any more—I am too wise— but I keep watch for it all the same.

There are things in that wallpaper that nobody knows about but me, or ever will.

Behind the outside pattern the dim shapes get clearer every day. It is always the same shape, only very numerous.

And it is like a woman stooping down and creeping about behind that pattern. I don't like it a bit. I wonder—I begin to think—I wish John would take me away from here!

It is so hard to talk with John about my case, because he is so wise, and because he loves me so.

But I tried it last night.

It was moonlight. The moon shines in all around just as the sun does.

I hate to see it sometimes, it creeps so slowly, and always comes in by one window or another.

John was asleep and I hated to waken him, so I kept still and watched the moonlight on that undulating wallpaper till I felt creepy.

The faint figure behind seemed to shake the pattern, just as if she wanted to get out.

I got up softly and went to feel and see if the paper *did* move, and when I came back John was awake.

"What is it, little girl?" he said. "Don't go walking about like that—you'll get cold."

I thought it was a good time to talk, so I told him that I really was not gaining here, and that I wished he would take me away.

"Why, darling!" said he. "Our lease will be up in three weeks, and I can't see how to leave before.

"The repairs are not done at home, and I cannot possibly leave town just now. Of course, if you were in any danger, I could and would, but you really are better, dear, whether you can see it or not. I am a doctor, dear, and I know. You are gaining flesh and color, your appetite is better, I feel really much easier about you."

"I don't weigh a bit more," said I, "nor as much; and my appetite may be better in the evening when you are here but it is worse in the morning when you are away!"

"Bless her little heart!" said he with a big hug. "She shall be as sick as she pleases! But now let's improve the shining hours by going to sleep, and talk about it in the morning!"

"And you won't go away?" I asked gloomily.

"Why, how can I, dear? It is only three weeks more and then we will take a nice little trip of a few days while Jennie is getting the house ready. Really, dear, you are better!"

"Better in body perhaps—" I began, and stopped short, for he sat up straight and looked at me with such a stern, reproachful look that I could not say another word.

"My darling," said he, "I beg of you, for my sake and for our child's sake, as well as for your own, that you will never for one instant let that idea enter your mind! There is nothing so dangerous, so fascinating, to a temperament like yours. It is a false and foolish fancy. Can you not trust me as a physician when I tell you so?"

So of course I said no more on that score, and we went to sleep before long. He thought I was asleep first, but I wasn't, and lay there for hours trying to decide whether that front pattern and the back pattern really did move together or separately.

On a pattern like this, by daylight, there is a lack of sequence, a defiance of law, that is a constant irritant to a normal mind.

The color is hideous enough, but the pattern is torturing.

You think you have mastered it, but just as you get well under way in following, it turns a back-somersault and there you are. It slaps you in the face, knocks you down, and tramples upon you. It is like a bad dream.

The outside pattern is a florid arabesque, reminding one of a fungus. If you can imagine a toadstool in joints, an interminable string of toadstools, budding and sprouting in endless convolutions—why, that is something like it.

That is, sometimes!

There is one marked peculiarity about this paper, a thing nobody seems to notice but myself, and that is that it changes as the light changes.

When the sun shoots in through the east window—I always watch for that first long, straight ray—it changes so quickly that I never can quite believe it.

That is why I watch it always.

By moonlight—the moon shines in all night when there is a moon—I wouldn't know it was the same paper.

At night in any kind of light, in twilight, candlelight, lamplight, and worst of all by moonlight, it becomes bars! The outside pattern, I mean, and the woman behind it is as plain as can be.

I didn't realize for a long time what the thing was that showed behind, that dim sub-pattern, but now I am quite sure it is a woman.

By daylight she is subdued, quiet. I fancy it is the pattern that keeps her so still. It is so puzzling. It keeps me quiet by the hour.

I lie down ever so much now. John says it is good for me, and to sleep all I can.

Indeed he started the habit by making me lie down for an hour after each meal.

It is a very bad habit, I am convinced, for you see, I don't sleep.

And that cultivates deceit, for I don't tell them I'm awake—oh, no!

The fact is I am getting a little afraid of John.

He seems very queer sometimes, and even Jennie has an inexplicable look.

It strikes me occasionally, just as a scientific hypothesis, that perhaps it is the paper!

I have watched John when he did not know I was looking, and come into the room suddenly on the most innocent excuses, and I've caught him several times *looking at the paper!* And Jennie too. I caught Jennie with her hand on it once.

She didn't know I was in the room, and when I asked her in a quiet, a very quiet voice, with the most restrained manner possible, what she was doing with the paper, she turned around as if she had been caught stealing, and looked quite angry—asked me why I should frighten her so!

Then she said that the paper stained everything it touched, that she had found yellow smooches on all my clothes and John's and she wished we would be more careful!

Did not that sound innocent? But I know she was studying that pattern, and I am determined that nobody shall find it out but myself!

———

Life is very much more exciting now than it used to be. You see, I have something more to expect, to look forward to, to watch. I really do eat better, and am more quiet than I was.

John is so pleased to see me improve! He laughed a little the other day, and said I seemed to be flourishing in spite of my wallpaper.

I turned it off with a laugh. I had no intention of telling him it was *because* of the wallpaper—he would make fun of me. He might even want to take me away.

I don't want to leave now until I have found it out. There is a week more, and I think that will be enough.

I'm feeling so much better!

I don't sleep much at night, for it is so interesting to watch developments; but I sleep a good deal during the daytime.

In the daytime it is tiresome and perplexing.

There are always new shoots on the fungus, and new shades of yellow all over it. I cannot keep count of them, though I have tried conscientiously.

It is the strangest yellow, that wallpaper! It makes me think of all the yellow things I ever saw—not beautiful ones like buttercups, but old, foul, bad yellow things.

But there is something else about that paper—the smell! I noticed it the moment we came into the room, but with so much air and sun it was not bad. Now we have had a week of fog and rain, and whether the windows are open or not, the smell is here.

It creeps all over the house.

I find it hovering in the dining-room, skulking in the parlor, hiding in the hall, lying in wait for me on the stairs.

It gets into my hair.

Even when I go to ride, if I turn my head suddenly and surprise it—there is that smell!

Such a peculiar odor, too! I have spent hours in trying to analyze it, to find what it smelled like.

It is not bad—at first—and very gentle, but quite the subtlest, most enduring odor I ever met.

In this damp weather it is awful. I wake up in the night and find it hanging over me.

It used to disturb me at first. I thought seriously of burning the house—to reach the smell.

But now I am used to it. The only thing I can think of that it is like is the *color* of the paper! A yellow smell.

There is a very funny mark on this wall, low down, near the mopboard. A streak that runs round the room. It goes behind every piece of furniture, except the bed, a long, straight, even *smooch,* as if it had been rubbed over and over.

I wonder how it was done and who did it, and what they did it for. Round and round and round—round and round and round— it makes me dizzy!

I really have discovered something at last.

Through watching so much at night, when it changes so, I have finally found out.

The front pattern *does* move—and no wonder! The woman behind shakes it!

Sometimes I think there are a great many women behind, and sometimes only one, and she crawls around fast, and her crawling shakes it all over.

Then in the very bright spots she keeps still, and in the very shady spots she just takes hold of the bars and shakes them hard.

And she is all the time trying to climb through. But nobody could climb through that pattern—it strangles so; I think that is why it has so many heads.

They get through, and then the pattern strangles them off and turns them upside down, and makes their eyes white!

If those heads were covered or taken off it would not be half so bad.

I think that woman gets out in the daytime!

And I'll tell you why—privately—I've seen her!

I can see her out of every one of my windows!

It is the same woman, I know, for she is always creeping, and most women do not creep by daylight.

I see her in that long shaded lane, creeping up and down. I see her in those dark grape arbors, creeping all around the garden.

I see her on that long road under the trees, creeping along, and when a carriage comes she hides under the blackberry vines.

I don't blame her a bit. It must be very humiliating to be caught creeping by daylight!

I always lock the door when I creep by daylight. I can't do it at night, for I know John would suspect something at once.

And John is so queer now that I don't want to irritate him. I wish he would take another room! Besides, I don't want anybody to get that woman out at night but myself.

I often wonder if I could see her out of all the windows at once.

But, turn as fast as I can, I can only see out of one at one time.

And though I always see her, she *may* be able to creep faster than I can turn! I have watched her sometimes away off in the open country, creeping as fast as a cloud shadow in a wind.

If only that top pattern could be gotten off from the under one! I mean to try it, little by little.

I have found out another funny thing, but I shan't tell it this time! It does not do to trust people too much.

There are only two more days to get this paper off, and I believe John is beginning to notice. I don't like the look in his eyes.

And I heard him ask Jennie a lot of professional questions about me. She had a very good report to give.

She said I slept a good deal in the daytime.

John knows I don't sleep very well at night, for all I'm so quiet!

He asked me all sorts of questions, too, and pretended to be very loving and kind.

As if I couldn't see through him!

Still, I don't wonder he acts so, sleeping under this paper for three months.

It only interests me, but I feel sure John and Jennie are affected by it.

Hurrah! This is the last day, but it is enough. John is to stay in town over night, and won't be out until this evening.

Jennie wanted to sleep with me—the sly thing; but I told her I should undoubtedly rest better for a night all alone.

That was clever, for really I wasn't alone a bit! As soon as it was moonlight and that poor thing began to crawl and shake the pattern, I got up and ran to help her.

I pulled and she shook. I shook and she pulled, and before morning we had peeled off yards of that paper.

A strip about as high as my head and half around the room.

And then when the sun came and that awful pattern began to laugh at me, I declared I would finish it today!

We go away tomorrow, and they are moving all my furniture down again to leave things as they were before.

Jennie looked at the wall in amazement, but I told her merrily that I did it out of pure spite at the vicious thing.

She laughed and said she wouldn't mind doing it herself, but I must not get tired.

How she betrayed herself that time!

But I am here, and no person touches this paper but Me—not *alive!*

She tried to get me out of the room—it was too patent! But I said it was so quiet and empty and clean now that I believed I would lie down again and sleep all I could, and not to wake me even for dinner—I would call when I woke.

So now she is gone, and the servants are gone, and the things are gone, and there is nothing left but that great bedstead nailed down, with the canvas mattress we found on it.

We shall sleep downstairs tonight, and take the boat home tomorrow.

I quite enjoy the room, now it is bare again.

How those children did tear about here!

This bedstead is fairly gnawed!

But I must get to work.

I have locked the door and thrown the key down into the front path.

I don't want to go out, and I don't want to have anybody come in, till John comes.

I want to astonish him!

I've got a rope up here that even Jennie did not find. If that woman does get out, and tries to get away, I can tie her!

But I forgot I could not reach far without anything to stand on! This bed will *not* move!

I tried to lift and push it until I was lame, and then I got so angry I bit off a little piece at one corner—but it hurt my teeth.

↑suicide of self

what defines insanity?

Then I peeled off all the paper I could reach standing on the floor. It sticks horribly and the pattern just enjoys it! All those strangled heads and bulbous eyes and waddling fungus growths just shriek with derision!

I am getting angry enough to do something desperate. To jump out of the window would be admirable exercise, but the bars are too strong even to try.

Besides I wouldn't do it. Of course not. I know well enough that a step like that is improper and might be misconstrued.

I don't like to *look* out of the windows even—there are so many of those creeping women, and they creep so fast.

I wonder if they all come out of that wallpaper as I did?

But I am securely fastened now by my well-hidden rope—you don't get *me* out in the road there!

I suppose I shall have to get back behind the pattern when it comes night, and that is hard!

It is so pleasant to be out in this great room and creep around as I please!

I don't want to go outside. I won't, even if Jennie asks me to.

For outside you have to creep on the ground, and everything is green instead of yellow.

But here I can creep smoothly on the floor, and my shoulder just fits in that long smooch around the wall, so I cannot lose my way.

Why, there's John at the door!

It is no use, young man, you can't open it!

How he does call and pound!

Now he's crying to Jennie for an axe.

It would be a shame to break down that beautiful door!

"John, dear!" said I in the gentlest voice. "The key is down by the front steps, under a plantain leaf!"

That silenced him for a few moments.

Then he said, very quietly indeed, "Open the door, my darling!"

"I can't," said I. "The key is down by the front door under a plantain leaf!" And then I said it again, several times, very gently and slowly, and said it so often that he had to go and see, and he got it of course, and came in. He stopped short by the door.

"What is the matter?" he cried. "For God's sake, what are you doing!"

still wants him to see transformation

Conformity?

I kept on creeping just the same, but I looked at him over my shoulder.

"I've got out at last," said I, "in spite of you and Jane. And I've pulled off most of the paper, so you can't put me back!"

Now why should that man have fainted? But he did, and right across my path by the wall, so that I had to creep over him every time! *← woman in power now*

didn't make the ending nice b/c battle still going on?

Why I Wrote "The Yellow Wallpaper"?*

Many and many a reader has asked that. When the story first came out, in the *New England Magazine* about 1891, a Boston physician made protest in *The Transcript*. Such a story ought not to be written, he said; it was enough to drive anyone mad to read it.

Another physician, in Kansas I think, wrote to say that it was the best description of incipient insanity he had ever seen, and— begging my pardon—had I been there?

Now the story of the story is this:

For many years I suffered from a severe and continuous nervous breakdown tending to melancholia—and beyond. During about the third year of this trouble I went, in devout faith and some faint stir of hope, to a noted specialist in nervous diseases, the best known in the country. This wise man put me to bed and applied the rest cure, to which a still-good physique responded so promptly that he concluded there was nothing much the matter with me, and sent me home with solemn advice to "live as domestic a life as far as possible," to "have but two hours' intellectual life a day," and "never to touch pen, brush, or pencil again" as long as I lived. This was in 1887.

I went home and obeyed those directions for some three months, and came so near the borderline of utter mental ruin that I could see over.

Then, using the remnants of intelligence that remained, and helped by a wise friend, I cast the noted specialist's advice to the winds and went to work again—work, the normal life of every human being; work, in which is joy and growth and service, without

wallpaper is representation of women

*"Why I Wrote 'The Yellow Wallpaper'?" appeared in the October 1913 issue of *The Forerunner*. *← ugly, tear it down, "mirror"*

which one is a pauper and a parasite—ultimately recovering some measure of power.

Being naturally moved to rejoicing by this narrow escape, I wrote "The Yellow Wallpaper," with its embellishments and additions, to carry out the ideal (I never had hallucinations or objections to my mural decorations) and sent a copy to the physician who so nearly drove me mad. He never acknowledged it.

The little book is valued by alienists and as a good specimen of one kind of literature. It has, to my knowledge, saved one woman from a similar fate—so terrifying her family that they let her out into normal activity and she recovered.

But the best result is this. Many years later I was told that the great specialist had admitted to friends of his that he had altered his treatment of neurasthenia since reading "The Yellow Wallpaper."

It was not intended to drive people crazy, but to save people from being driven crazy, and it worked.

The Country of the Pointed Firs
by Sarah Orne Jewett

1 _The Return_

There was something about the coast town of Dunnet which made it seem more attractive than other maritime villages of eastern Maine. Perhaps it was the simple fact of acquaintance with that neighborhood which made it so attaching, and gave such interest to the rocky shore and dark woods, and the few houses which seemed to be securely wedged and tree-nailed in among the ledges by the Landing. These houses made the most of their seaward view, and there was a gayety and determined floweriness in their bits of garden ground; the small-paned high windows in the peaks of their steep gables were like knowing eyes that watched the harbor and the far sea-line beyond, or looked northward all along the shore and its background of spruces and balsam firs. When one really knows a village like this and its surroundings, it is like becoming acquainted with a single person. The process of falling in love at first sight is as final as it is swift in such a case, but the growth of true friendship may be a lifelong affair.

After a first brief visit made two or three summers before in the course of a yachting cruise, a lover of Dunnet Landing returned to find the unchanged shores of the pointed firs, the same quaintness of the village with its elaborate conventionalities; all that mixture of remoteness, and childish certainty of being the centre of civilization of which her affectionate dreams had told. One evening in June, a single passenger landed upon the steamboat wharf. The tide was high, there was a fine crowd of spectators, and the younger portion of the company followed her with subdued excitement up the narrow street of the salt-aired, white-clapboarded little town.

2   Mrs. Todd

Later, there was only one fault to find with this choice of a summer
lodging-place, and that was its complete lack of seclusion. At first
the tiny house of Mrs. Almira Todd, which stood with its end to
the street, appeared to be retired and sheltered enough from the
busy world, behind its bushy bit of a green garden, in which all
the blooming things, two or three gay hollyhocks and some London-pride, were pushed back against the gray-shingled wall. It was
a queer little garden and puzzling to a stranger, the few flowers
being put at a disadvantage by so much greenery; but the discovery
was soon made that Mrs. Todd was an ardent lover of herbs, both
wild and tame, and the sea-breezes blew into the low end-window
of the house laden with not only sweet-brier and sweet-mary, but
balm and sage and borage and mint, wormwood and southernwood.
If Mrs. Todd had occasion to step into the far corner of her herb
plot, she trod heavily upon thyme, and made its fragrant presence
known with all the rest. Being a very large person, her full skirts
brushed and bent almost every slender stalk that her feet missed.
You could always tell when she was stepping about there, even
when you were half awake in the morning, and learned to know,
in the course of a few weeks' experience, in exactly which corner
of the garden she might be.

At one side of this herb plot were other growths of a rustic
pharmacopœia, great treasures and rarities among the commoner
herbs. There were some strange and pungent odors that roused a
dim sense and remembrance of something in the forgotten past.
Some of these might once have belonged to sacred and mystic
rites, and have had some occult knowledge handed with them down
the centuries; but now they pertained only to humble compounds
brewed at intervals with molasses or vinegar or spirits in a small
caldron on Mrs. Todd's kitchen stove. They were dispensed to
suffering neighbors, who usually came at night as if by stealth,
bringing their own ancient-looking vials to be filled. One nostrum
was called the Indian remedy, and its price was but fifteen cents;
the whispered directions could be heard as customers passed the
windows. With most remedies the purchaser was allowed to depart
unadmonished from the kitchen, Mrs. Todd being a wise saver of
steps; but with certain vials she gave cautions, standing in the

doorway, and there were other doses which had to be accompanied on their healing way as far as the gate, while she muttered long chapters of directions, and kept up an air of secrecy and importance to the last. It may not have been only the common ails of humanity with which she tried to cope; it seemed sometimes as if love and hate and jealousy and adverse winds at sea might also find their proper remedies among the curious wild-looking plants in Mrs. Todd's garden.

The village doctor and this learned herbalist were upon the best of terms. The good man may have counted upon the unfavorable effect of certain potions which he should find his opportunity in counteracting; at any rate, he now and then stopped and exchanged greetings with Mrs. Todd over the picket fence. The conversation became at once professional after the briefest preliminaries, and he would stand twirling a sweet-scented sprig in his fingers, and make suggestive jokes, perhaps about her faith in a too persistent course of thoroughwort elixir, in which my landlady professed such firm belief as sometimes to endanger the life and usefulness of worthy neighbors.

To arrive at this quietest of seaside villages late in June, when the busy herb-gathering season was just beginning, was also to arrive in the early prime of Mrs. Todd's activity in the brewing of old-fashioned spruce beer. This cooling and refreshing drink had been brought to wonderful perfection through a long series of experiments; it had won immense local fame, and the supplies for its manufacture were always giving out and having to be replenished. For various reasons, the seclusion and uninterrupted days which had been looked forward to proved to be very rare in this otherwise delightful corner of the world. My hostess and I had made our shrewd business agreement on the basis of a simple cold luncheon at noon, and liberal restitution in the matter of hot suppers, to provide for which the lodger might sometimes be seen hurrying down the road, late in the day, with cunner line in hand. It was soon found that this arrangement made large allowance for Mrs. Todd's slow herb-gathering progresses through woods and pastures. The spruce-beer customers were pretty steady in hot weather, and there were many demands for different soothing syrups and elixirs with which the unwise curiosity of my early residence had made me acquainted. Knowing Mrs. Todd to be a widow, who had little beside this slender business and the income from one hungry lodger to maintain her, one's energies and even interest were quickly bestowed, until it became a matter of course that she should go afield every pleasant day, and that the lodger should answer all peremptory knocks at the side door.

In taking an occasional wisdom-giving stroll in Mrs. Todd's company, and in acting as business partner during her frequent absences, I found the July days fly fast, and it was not until I felt myself confronted with too great pride and pleasure in the display, one night, of two dollars and twenty-seven cents which I had taken in during the day, that I remembered a long piece of writing, sadly belated now, which I was bound to do. To have been patted kindly on the shoulder and called "darlin'," to have been offered a surprise of early mushrooms for supper, to have had all the glory of making two dollars and twenty-seven cents in a single day, and then to renounce it all and withdraw from these pleasant successes, needed much resolution. Literary employments are so vexed with uncertainties at best, and it was not until the voice of conscience sounded louder in my ears than the sea on the nearest pebble beach that I said unkind words of withdrawal to Mrs. Todd. She only became more wistfully affectionate than ever in her expressions, and looked as disappointed as I expected when I frankly told her that I could no longer enjoy the pleasure of what we called "seein' folks." I felt that I was cruel to a whole neighborhood in curtailing her liberty in this most important season for harvesting the different wild herbs that were so much counted upon to ease their winter ails.

"Well, dear," she said sorrowfully, "I've took great advantage o' your bein' here. I ain't had such a season for years, but I have never had nobody I could so trust. All you lack is a few qualities, but with time you'd gain judgment an' experience, an' be very able in the business. I'd stand right here an' say it to anybody."

Mrs. Todd and I were not separated or estranged by the change in our business relations; on the contrary, a deeper intimacy seemed to begin. I do not know what herb of the night it was that used sometimes to send out a penetrating odor late in the evening, after the dew had fallen, and the moon was high, and the cool air came up from the sea. Then Mrs. Todd would feel that she must talk to somebody, and I was only too glad to listen. We both fell under the spell, and she either stood outside the window, or made an errand to my sitting-room, and told, it might be very commonplace news of the day, or, as happened one misty summer night, all that lay deepest in her heart. It was in this way that I came to know that she had loved one who was far above her.

"No, dear, him I speak of could never think of me," she said. "When we was young together his mother didn't favor the match, an' done everything she could to part us; and folks thought we both married well, but 't wa'n't what either one of us wanted most; an' now we're left alone again, an' might have had each other all the time. He was above bein' a seafarin' man, an' prospered more than most; he come of a high family, an' my lot was plain an' hard-workin'. I ain't seen him for some years; he's forgot our youthful feelin's, I expect, but a woman's heart is different; them feelin's comes back when you think you've done with 'em, as sure as spring comes with the year. An' I've always had ways of hearin' about him."

She stood in the centre of a braided rug, and its rings of black and gray seemed to circle about her feet in the dim light. Her height and massiveness in the low room gave her the look of a huge sibyl, while the strange fragrance of the mysterious herb blew in from the little garden.

3   *The Schoolhouse*

For some days after this, Mrs. Todd's customers came and went past my windows, and, haying-time being nearly over, strangers began to arrive from the inland country, such was her widespread reputation. Sometimes I saw a pale young creature like a white windflower left over into midsummer, upon whose face consumption had set its bright and wistful mark; but oftener two stout, hard-worked women from the farms came together, and detailed their symptoms to Mrs. Todd in loud and cheerful voices, combining the satisfactions of a friendly gossip with the medical opportunity. They seemed to give much from their own store of therapeutic learning. I became aware of the school in which my landlady had strengthened her natural gift; but hers was always the governing mind, and the final command, "Take of hy'sop one hand-

ful" (or whatever herb it was), was received in respectful silence.
One afternoon, when I had listened,—it was impossible not to
listen, with cottonless ears,—and then laughed and listened again,
with an idle pen in my hand, during a particularly spirited and
personal conversation, I reached for my hat, and taking blotting-
book and all under my arm, I resolutely fled further temptation,
and walked out past the fragrant green garden and up the dusty
road. The way went straight uphill, and presently I stopped and
turned to look back.

The tide was in, the wide harbor was surrounded by its dark
woods, and the small wooden houses stood as near as they could
get to the landing. Mrs. Todd's was the last house on the way
inland. The gray ledges of the rocky shore were well covered with
sod in most places, and the pasture bayberry and wild roses grew
thick among them. I could see the higher inland country and the
scattered farms. On the brink of the hill stood a little white schoolhouse, much wind-blown and weather-beaten, which was a landmark to seagoing folk; from its door there was a most beautiful
view of sea and shore. The summer vacation now prevailed, and
after finding the door unfastened, and taking a long look through
one of the seaward windows, and reflecting afterward for some
time in a shady place near by among the bayberry bushes, I returned
to the chief place of business in the village, and, to the amusement
of two of the selectmen, brothers and autocrats of Dunnet Landing,
I hired the schoolhouse for the rest of the vacation for fifty cents
a week.

Selfish as it may appear, the retired situation seemed to possess
great advantages, and I spent many days there quite undisturbed,
with the sea-breeze blowing through the small, high windows and
swaying the heavy outside shutters to and fro. I hung my hat and
luncheon-basket on an entry nail as if I were a small scholar, but
I sat at the teacher's desk as if I were that great authority, with all
the timid empty benches in rows before me. Now and then an idle
sheep came and stood for a long time looking in at the door. At
sundown I went back, feeling most businesslike, down toward the
village again, and usually met the flavor, not of the herb garden,
but of Mrs. Todd's hot supper, halfway up the hill. On the nights
when there were evening meetings or other public exercises that

demanded her presence we had tea very early, and I was welcomed back as if from a long absence.

Once or twice I feigned excuses for staying at home, while Mrs. Todd made distant excursions, and came home late with both hands full and a heavily laden apron. This was in pennyroyal time, and when the rare lobelia was in its prime and the elecampane was coming on. One day she appeared at the schoolhouse itself, partly out of amused curiosity about my industries; but she explained that there was no tansy in the neighborhood with such snap to it as some that grew about the schoolhouse lot. Being scuffed down all the spring made it grow so much the better, like some folks that had it hard in their youth, and were bound to make the most of themselves before they died.

4   At the Schoolhouse Window

One day I reached the schoolhouse very late, owing to attendance upon the funeral of an acquaintance and neighbor, with whose sad decline in health I had been familiar, and whose last days both the doctor and Mrs. Todd had tried in vain to ease. The services had taken place at one o'clock, and now, at quarter past two, I stood at the schoolhouse window, looking down at the procession as it went along the lower road close to the shore. It was a walking funeral, and even at that distance I could recognize most of the mourners as they went their solemn way. Mrs. Begg had been very much respected, and there was a large company of friends following to her grave. She had been brought up on one of the neighboring farms, and each of the few times that I had seen her she professed great dissatisfaction with town life. The people lived too close together for her liking, at the Landing, and she could not get used to the constant sound of the sea. She had lived to lament three seafaring husbands, and her house was decorated with West Indian curiosities, specimens of conch shells and fine coral which they had brought home from their voyages in lumber-laden ships. Mrs. Todd had told me all our neighbor's history. They had been girls together, and, to use her own phrase, had "both seen trouble till they knew the best and worst on 't." I could see the sorrowful, large figure of Mrs. Todd as I stood at the window. She made a break in the procession by walking slowly and keeping the after-part of it back. She held a handkerchief to her eyes, and I knew, with a pang of sympathy, that hers was not affected grief.

Beside her, after much difficulty, I recognized the one strange and unrelated person in all the company, an old man who had always been mysterious to me. I could see his thin, bending figure. He wore a narrow, long-tailed coat and walked with a stick, and had the same "cant to leeward" as the wind-bent trees on the height above.

This was Captain Littlepage, whom I had seen only once or twice before, sitting pale and old behind a closed window; never out of doors until now. Mrs. Todd always shook her head gravely when I asked a question, and said that he wasn't what he had been once, and seemed to class him with her other secrets. He might have belonged with a simple which grew in a certain slug-haunted corner of the garden, whose use she could never be betrayed into telling me, though I saw her cutting the tops by moonlight once, as if it were a charm, and not a medicine, like the great fading bloodroot leaves.

I could see that she was trying to keep pace with the old captain's lighter steps. He looked like an aged grasshopper of some strange human variety. Behind this pair was a short, impatient, little person, who kept the captain's house, and gave it what Mrs. Todd and others believed to be no proper sort of care. She was usually called "that Mari' Harris" in subdued conversation between intimates, but they treated her with anxious civility when they met her face to face.

The bay-sheltered islands and the great sea beyond stretched away to the far horizon southward and eastward; the little procession in the foreground looked futile and helpless on the edge of the rocky shore. It was a glorious day early in July, with a clear, high sky; there were no clouds, there was no noise of the sea. The song sparrows sang and sang, as if with joyous knowledge of immortality, and contempt for those who could so pettily concern themselves with death. I stood watching until the funeral procession had crept round a shoulder of the slope below and disappeared from the great landscape as if it had gone into a cave.

An hour later I was busy at my work. Now and then a bee blundered in and took me for an enemy; but there was a useful stick upon the teacher's desk, and I rapped to call the bees to order as if they were unruly scholars, or waved them away from their riots over the ink, which I had bought at the Landing store, and discovered too late to be scented with bergamot, as if to refresh the labors of anxious scribes. One anxious scribe felt very dull that day; a sheep-bell tinkled near by, and called her wandering wits after it. The sentences failed to catch these lovely summer cadences. For the first time I began to wish for a companion and for news from the outer world, which had been, half unconsciously, forgotten. Watching the funeral gave one a sort of pain. I began to wonder if I ought not to have walked with the rest, instead of hurrying away at the end of the services. Perhaps the Sunday gown I had put on for the occasion was making this disastrous change of feeling, but I had now made myself and my friends remember that I did not really belong to Dunnet Landing.

I sighed, and turned to the half-written page again.

5 Captain Littlepage

It was a long time after this; an hour was very long in that coast town where nothing stole away the shortest minute. I had lost myself completely in work, when I heard footsteps outside. There was a steep footpath between the upper and the lower road, which I climbed to shorten the way, as the children had taught me, but I believed that Mrs. Todd would find it inaccessible, unless she had occasion to seek me in great haste. I wrote on, feeling like a besieged miser of time, while the footsteps came nearer, and the sheep-bell tinkled away in haste as if some one had shaken a stick in its wearer's face. Then I looked, and saw Captain Littlepage passing the nearest window; the next moment he tapped politely at the door.

"Come in, sir," I said, rising to meet him; and he entered, bowing with much courtesy. I stepped down from the desk and offered him a chair by the window, where he seated himself at once, being sadly spent by his climb. I returned to my fixed seat behind the teacher's desk, which gave him the lower place of a scholar.

"You ought to have the place of honor, Captain Littlepage," I said.

"A happy, rural seat of various views," he quoted, as he gazed out into the sunshine and up the long wooded shore. Then he glanced at me, and looked all about him as pleased as a child.

"My quotation was from Paradise Lost: the greatest of poems, I suppose you know?" and I nodded. "There's nothing that ranks, to my mind, with Paradise Lost; it's all lofty, all lofty," he continued. "Shakespeare was a great poet; he copied life, but you have to put up with a great deal of low talk."

I now remembered that Mrs. Todd had told me one day that Captain Littlepage had overset his mind with too much reading; she had also made dark reference to his having "spells" of some unexplainable nature. I could not help wondering what errand had brought him out in search of me. There was something quite charming in his appearance: it was a face thin and delicate with refinement, but worn into appealing lines, as if he had suffered from loneliness and misapprehension. He looked, with his careful precision of dress, as if he were the object of cherishing care on the part of elderly unmarried sisters, but I knew Mari' Harris to be a very commonplace, inelegant person, who would have no such standards; it was plain that the captain was his own attentive valet. He sat looking at me expectantly. I could not help thinking that, with his queer head and length of thinness, he was made to hop along the road of life rather than to walk. The captain was very grave indeed, and I bade my inward spirit keep close to discretion.

"Poor Mrs. Begg has gone," I ventured to say. I still wore my Sunday gown by way of showing respect.

"She has gone," said the captain,—"very easy at the last, I was informed; she slipped away as if she were glad of the opportunity."

I thought of the Countess of Carberry and felt that history repeated itself.

"She was one of the old stock," continued Captain Littlepage, with touching sincerity. "She was very much looked up to in this town, and will be missed."

I wondered, as I looked at him, if he had sprung from a line of ministers; he had the refinement of look and air of command which are the heritage of the old ecclesiastical families of New England. But as Darwin says in his autobiography, "there is no such king as a sea-captain; he is greater even than a king or a schoolmaster!"

Captain Littlepage moved his chair out of the wake of the sunshine, and still sat looking at me. I began to be very eager to know upon what errand he had come.

"It may be found out some o' these days," he said earnestly. "We may know it all, the next step; where Mrs. Begg is now, for instance. Certainty, not conjecture, is what we all desire."

"I suppose we shall know it all some day," said I.

"We shall know it while yet below," insisted the captain, with a flush of impatience on his thin cheeks. "We have not looked for truth in the right direction. I know what I speak of; those who have laughed at me little know how much reason my ideas are based upon." He waved his hand toward the village below. "In that handful of houses they fancy that they comprehend the universe."

I smiled, and waited for him to go on.

"I am an old man, as you can see," he continued, "and I have been a shipmaster the greater part of my life,—forty-three years in all. You may not think it, but I am above eighty years of age."

He did not look so old, and I hastened to say so.

"You must have left the sea a good many years ago, then, Captain Littlepage?" I said.

"I should have been serviceable at least five or six years more," he answered. "My acquaintance with certain—my experience upon a certain occasion, I might say, gave rise to prejudice. I do not mind telling you that I chanced to learn of one of the greatest discoveries that man has ever made."

Now we were approaching dangerous ground, but a sudden sense of his suffering at the hands of the ignorant came to my help, and I asked to hear more with all the deference I really felt. A swallow flew into the schoolhouse at this moment as if a kingbird were after it, and beat itself against the walls for a minute, and escaped again to the open air; but Captain Littlepage took no notice whatever of the flurry.

"I had a valuable cargo of general merchandise from the London docks to Fort Churchill, a station of the old company on Hudson's Bay," said the captain earnestly. "We were delayed in lading, and baffled by head winds and a heavy tumbling sea all the way north-about and across. Then the fog kept us off the coast; and when I made port at last, it was too late to delay in those northern waters with such a vessel and such a crew as I had. They cared for nothing, and idled me into a fit of sickness; but my first mate was a good, excellent man, with no more idea of being frozen in there until spring than I had, so we made what speed we could to get clear of Hudson's Bay and off the coast. I owned an eighth of the vessel, and he owned a sixteenth of her. She was a full-rigged ship, called the Minerva, but she was getting old and leaky. I meant it should be my last v'y'ge in her, and so it proved. She had been an excellent vessel in her day. Of the cowards aboard her I can't say so much."

"Then you were wrecked?" I asked, as he made a long pause.

"I wa'n't caught astern o' the lighter by any fault of mine," said the captain gloomily. "We left Fort Churchill and run out into the Bay with a light pair o' heels; but I had been vexed to death with their red-tape rigging at the company's office, and chilled with stayin' on deck an' tryin' to hurry up things, and when we were well out o' sight o' land, headin' for Hudson's Straits, I had a bad turn o' some sort o' fever, and had to stay below. The days were getting short, and we made good runs, all well on board but me, and the crew done their work by dint of hard driving."

I began to find this unexpected narrative a little dull. Captain Littlepage spoke with a kind of slow correctness that lacked the longshore high flavor to which I had grown used; but I listened respectfully while he explained the winds having become contrary, and talked on in a dreary sort of way about his voyage, the bad weather, and the disadvantages he was under in the lightness of his ship, which bounced about like a chip in a bucket, and would not answer the rudder or properly respond to the most careful setting of sails.

"So there we were blowin' along anyways," he complained; but looking at me at this moment, and seeing that my thoughts were unkindly wandering, he ceased to speak.

"It was a hard life at sea in those days, I am sure," said I, with redoubled interest.

"It was a dog's life," said the poor old gentleman, quite reassured, "but it made men of those who followed it. I see a change for the worse even in our own town here; full of loafers now, small and poor as 't is, who once would have followed the sea, every lazy soul of 'em. There is no occupation so fit for just that class o' men who never get beyond the fo'cas'le. I view it, in addition, that a community narrows down and grows dreadful ignorant when it is shut up to its own affairs, and gets no knowledge of the outside world except from a cheap, unprincipled newspaper. In the old days, a good part o' the best men here knew a hundred ports and something of the way folks lived in them. They saw the world for themselves, and like's not their wives and children saw it with them. They may not have had the best of knowledge to carry with 'em sight-seein', but they were some acquainted with foreign lands an' their laws, an' could see outside the battle for town clerk here in Dunnet; they got some sense o' proportion. Yes, they lived more dignified, and their houses were better within an' without. Shipping's a terrible loss to this part o' New England from a social point o' view, ma'am."

"I have thought of that myself," I returned, with my interest quite awakened. "It accounts for the change in a great many things,—the sad disappearance of sea-captains,—doesn't it?"

"A shipmaster was apt to get the habit of reading," said my companion, brightening still more, and taking on a most touching air of unreserve. "A captain is not expected to be familiar with his crew, and for company's sake in dull days and nights he turns to his book. Most of us old shipmasters came to know 'most everything about something; one would take to readin' on farming topics, and some were great on medicine,—but Lord help their poor crews!—or some were all for history, and now and then there'd be one like me that gave his time to the poets. I was well acquainted with a shipmaster that was all for bees an' bee-keepin'; and if you met him in port and went aboard, he'd sit and talk a terrible while about their havin' so much information, and the money that could be made out of keepin' 'em. He was one of the smartest captains that ever sailed the seas, but they used to call the Newcastle, a great bark he commanded for many years, Tuttle's beehive. There was old Cap'n Jameson: he had notions of Solomon's Temple, and made a very handsome little model of the same, right from the Scripture measurements, same's other sailors make little ships and design new tricks of rigging and all that. No, there's nothing to take the place of shipping in a place like ours. These bicycles offend me dreadfully; they don't afford no real opportunities of experience such as a man gained on a voyage. No: when folks left home in the old days they left it to some purpose, and when they got home they stayed there and had some pride in it. There's no largeminded way of thinking now: the worst have got to be best and rule every-thing; we're all turned upside down and going back year by year."

"Oh no, Captain Littlepage, I hope not," said I, trying to soothe his feelings.

There was a silence in the schoolhouse, but we could hear the noise of the water on a beach below. It sounded like the strange warning wave that gives notice of the turn of the tide. A late golden robin, with the most joyful and eager of voices, was singing close by in a thicket of wild roses.

6 *The Waiting Place*

"How did you manage with the rest of that rough voyage on the Minerva?" I asked.

"I shall be glad to explain to you," said Captain Littlepage, for-getting his grievances for the moment. "If I had a map at hand I could explain better. We were driven to and fro 'way up toward what we used to call Parry's Discoveries, and lost our bearings. It was thick and foggy, and at last I lost my ship; she drove on a rock, and we managed to get ashore on what I took to be a barren island, the few of us that were left alive. When she first struck, the sea was somewhat calmer than it had been, and most of the crew, against orders, manned the long-boat and put off in a hurry, and were never heard of more. Our own boat upset, but the carpenter kept himself and me above water, and we drifted in. I had no strength to call upon after my recent fever, and laid down to die; but he found the tracks of a man and dog the second day, and got along the shore to one of those far missionary stations that the Moravians support. They were very poor themselves, and in dis-tress; 't was a useless place. There were but few Esquimaux left in that region. There we remained for some time, and I became acquainted with strange events."

The captain lifted his head and gave me a questioning glance. I could not help noticing that the dulled look in his eyes had gone, and there was instead a clear intentness that made them seem dark and piercing.

"There was a supply ship expected, and the pastor, an excellent Christian man, made no doubt that we should get passage in her.

He was hoping that orders would come to break up the station; but everything was uncertain, and we got on the best we could for a while. We fished, and helped the people in other ways; there was no other way of paying our debts. I was taken to the pastor's house until I got better; but they were crowded, and I felt myself in the way, and made excuse to join with an old seaman, a Scotchman, who had built him a warm cabin, and had room in it for another. He was looked upon with regard, and had stood by the pastor in some troubles with the people. He had been on one of those English exploring parties that found one end of the road to the north pole, but never could find the other. We lived like dogs in a kennel, or so you'd thought if you had seen the hut from the outside; but the main thing was to keep warm; there were piles of birdskins to lie on, and he'd made him a good bunk, and there was another for me. 'T was dreadful dreary waitin' there; we begun to think the supply steamer was lost, and my poor ship broke up and strewed herself all along the shore. We got to watching on the headlands; my men and me knew the people were short of supplies and had to pinch themselves. It ought to read in the Bible, 'Man cannot live by fish alone,' if they'd told the truth of things; 'tain't bread that wears the worst on you! First part of the time, old Gaffett, that I lived with, seemed speechless, and I didn't know what to make of him, nor he of me, I dare say; but as we got acquainted, I found he'd been through more disasters than I had, and had troubles that wa'n't going to let him live a great while. It used to ease his mind to talk to an understanding person, so we used to sit and talk together all day, if it rained or blew so that we couldn't get out. I'd got a bad blow on the back of my head at the time we came ashore, and it pained me at times, and my strength was broken, anyway; I've never been so able since."

Captain Littlepage fell into a reverie.

"Then I had the good of my reading," he explained presently. "I had no books; the pastor spoke but little English, and all his books were foreign; but I used to say over all I could remember. The old poets little knew what comfort they could be to a man. I was well acquainted with the works of Milton, but up there it did seem to me as if Shakespeare was the king; he has his sea terms very accurate, and some beautiful passages were calming to the mind. I could say them over until I shed tears; there was nothing beautiful to me in that place but the stars above and those passages of verse.

"Gaffett was always brooding and brooding, and talking to himself; he was afraid he should never get away, and it preyed upon his mind. He thought when I got home I could interest the scientific men in his discovery: but they're all taken up with their own notions; some didn't even take pains to answer the letters I wrote. You observe that I said this crippled man Gaffett had been shipped on a voyage of discovery. I now tell you that the ship was lost on its return, and only Gaffett and two officers were saved off the Greenland coast, and he had knowledge later that those men never got back to England; the brig they shipped on was run down in the night. So no other living soul had the facts, and he gave them to me. There is a strange sort of a country 'way up north beyond the ice, and strange folks living in it. Gaffett believed it was the next world to this."

"What do you mean, Captain Littlepage?" I exclaimed. The old man was bending forward and whispering; he looked over his shoulder before he spoke the last sentence.

"To hear old Gaffett tell about it was something awful," he said, going on with his story quite steadily after the moment of excitement had passed. " 'T was first a tale of dogs and sledges, and cold and wind and snow. Then they begun to find the ice grow rotten; they had been frozen in, and got into a current flowing north, far up beyond Fox Channel, and they took to their boats when the ship got crushed, and this warm current took them out of sight of the ice, and into a great open sea; and they still followed it due north, just the very way they had planned to go. Then they struck a coast that wasn't laid down or charted, but the cliffs were such that no boat could land until they found a bay and struck across under sail to the other side where the shore looked lower; they were scant of provisions and out of water, but they got sight of something that looked like a great town. 'For God's sake, Gaffett!' said I, the first time he told me. 'You don't mean a town two degrees farther north than ships had ever been?' for he'd got their course marked on an old chart that he'd pieced out at the top; but he insisted upon it, and told it over and over again, to be sure I had it straight to carry to those who would be interested. There was no snow and ice, he said, after they had sailed some days with that warm current, which seemed to come right from under the ice that they'd been pinched up in and had been crossing on foot for weeks."

"But what about the town?" I asked. "Did they get to the town?"

"They did," said the captain, "and found inhabitants; 't was an awful condition of things. It appeared, as near as Gaffett could express it, like a place where there was neither living nor dead. They could see the place when they were approaching it by sea pretty near like any town, and thick with habitations; but all at once they lost sight of it altogether, and when they got close inshore they could see the shapes of folks, but they never could get near them,—all blowing gray figures that would pass along alone, or sometimes gathered in companies as if they were watching. The men were frightened at first, but the shapes never came near them,—it was as if they blew back; and at last they all got bold and went ashore, and found birds' eggs and sea fowl, like any wild northern spot where creatures were tame and folks had never been, and there was good water. Gaffett said that he and another man came near one o' the fog-shaped men that was going along slow with the look of a pack on his back, among the rocks, an' they chased him; but, Lord! he flittered away out o' sight like a leaf the wind takes with it, or a piece of cobweb. They would make as if they talked together, but there was no sound of voices, and 'they acted as if they didn't see us, but only felt us coming towards them,' says Gaffett one day, trying to tell the particulars. They couldn't see the town when they were ashore. One day the captain and the doctor were gone till night up across the high land where the town had seemed to be, and they came back at night beat out and white as ashes, and wrote and wrote all next day in their notebooks, and whispered together full of excitement, and they were sharp-spoken with the men when they offered to ask any questions.

"Then there came a day," said Captain Littlepage, leaning toward me with a strange look in his eyes, and whispering quickly. "The men all swore they wouldn't stay any longer; the man on watch early in the morning gave the alarm, and they all put off in the boat and got a little way out to sea. Those folks, or whatever they were, come about 'em like bats; all at once they raised incessant armies, and come as if to drive 'em back to sea. They stood thick

at the edge o' the water like the ridges o' grim war; no thought o'
flight, none of retreat. Sometimes a standing fight, then soaring on
main wing tormented all the air. And when they'd got the boat
out o' reach o' danger, Gaffett said they looked back, and there
was the town again, standing up just as they'd seen it first, comin'
on the coast. Say what you might, they all believed 't was a kind
of waiting-place between this world an' the next."

The captain had sprung to his feet in his excitement, and made
excited gestures, but he still whispered huskily.

"Sit down, sir," I said as quietly as I could, and he sank into his
chair quite spent.

"Gaffett thought the officers were hurrying home to report and
to fit out a new expedition when they were all lost. At the time,
the men got orders not to talk over what they had seen," the old
man explained presently in a more natural tone.

"Weren't they all starving, and wasn't it a mirage or something
of that sort?" I ventured to ask. But he looked at me blankly.

"Gaffett had got so that his mind ran on nothing else," he went
on. "The ship's surgeon let fall an opinion to the captain, one day,
that 't was some condition o' the light and the magnetic currents
that let them see those folks. 'T wa'n't a right-feeling part of the
world, anyway; they had to battle with the compass to make it
serve, an' everything seemed to go wrong. Gaffett had worked it
out in his own mind that they was all common ghosts, but the
conditions were unusual favorable for seeing them. He was always
talking about the Ge'graphical Society, but he never took proper
steps, as I view it now, and stayed right there at the mission. He
was a good deal crippled, and thought they'd confine him in some
jail of a hospital. He said he was waiting to find the right men to
tell, somebody bound north. Once in a while they stopped there
to leave a mail or something. He was set in his notions, and let
two or three proper explorin' expeditions go by him because he
didn't like their looks; but when I was there he had got restless,
fearin' he might be taken away or something. He had all his directions written out straight as a string to give the right ones. I
wanted him to trust 'em to me, so I might have something to show,
but he wouldn't. I suppose he's dead now. I wrote to him, an' I
done all I could. 'T will be a great exploit some o' these days."

I assented absent-mindedly, thinking more just then of my companion's alert, determined look and the seafaring, ready aspect that had come to his face; but at this moment there fell a sudden change, and the old, pathetic, scholarly look returned. Behind me hung a map of North America, and I saw, as I turned a little, that his eyes were fixed upon the northernmost regions and their careful recent outlines with a look of bewilderment.

7   *The Outer Island*

Gaffett with his good bunk and the birdskins, the story of the wreck of the Minerva, the human-shaped creatures of fog and cobweb, the great words of Milton with which he described their onslaught upon the crew, all this moving tale had such an air of truth that I could not argue with Captain Littlepage. The old man looked away from the map as if it had vaguely troubled him, and regarded me appealingly.

"We were just speaking of"—and he stopped. I saw that he had suddenly forgotten his subject.

"There were a great many persons at the funeral," I hastened to say.

"Oh yes," the captain answered, with satisfaction. "All showed respect who could. The sad circumstances had for a moment slipped my mind. Yes, Mrs. Begg will be very much missed. She was a capital manager for her husband when he was at sea. Oh yes, shipping is a very great loss." And he sighed heavily. "There was hardly a man of any standing who didn't interest himself in some way in navigation. It always gave credit to a town. I call it low-water mark now here in Dunnet."

He rose with dignity to take leave, and asked me to stop at his house some day, when he would show me some outlandish things that he had brought home from sea. I was familiar with the subject of the decadence of shipping interests in all its affecting branches, having been already some time in Dunnet, and I felt sure that Captain Littlepage's mind had now returned to a safe level.

As we came down the hill toward the village our ways divided, and when I had seen the old captain well started on a smooth piece of sidewalk which would lead him to his own door, we parted, the best of friends. "Step in some afternoon," he said, as affectionately as if I were a fellow-shipmaster wrecked on the lee shore of age like himself. I turned toward home, and presently met Mrs. Todd coming toward me with an anxious expression.

"I see you sleevin' the old gentleman down the hill," she suggested.

"Yes. I've had a very interesting afternoon with him," I answered; and her face brightened.

"Oh, then he's all right. I was afraid 't was one o' his flighty spells, an' Mari' Harris wouldn't"—

"Yes," I returned, smiling, "he has been telling me some old stories, but we talked about Mrs. Begg and the funeral beside, and Paradise Lost."

"I expect he got tellin' of you some o' his great narratives," she answered, looking at me shrewdly. "Funerals always sets him goin'. Some o' them tales hangs together toler'ble well," she added, with a sharper look than before. "An' he's been a great reader all his seafarin' days. Some thinks he overdid, and affected his head, but for a man o' his years he's amazin' now when he's at his best. Oh, he used to be a beautiful man!"

We were standing where there was a fine view of the harbor and its long stretches of shore all covered by the great army of the pointed firs, darkly cloaked and standing as if they waited to embark. As we looked far seaward among the outer islands, the trees seemed to march seaward still, going steadily over the heights and down to the water's edge.

It had been growing gray and cloudy, like the first evening of autumn, and a shadow had fallen on the darkening shore. Suddenly, as we looked, a gleam of golden sunshine struck the outer islands, and one of them shone out clear in the light, and revealed itself in a compelling way to our eyes. Mrs. Todd was looking off across the bay with a face full of affection and interest. The sunburst upon that outermost island made it seem like a sudden revelation of the world beyond this which some believe to be so near.

"That's where mother lives," said Mrs. Todd. "Can't we see it plain? I was brought up out there on Green Island. I know every rock an' bush on it."

"Your mother!" I exclaimed, with great interest.

"Yes, dear, cert'in; I've got her yet, old's I be. She's one of them spry, light-footed little women; always was, an' light-hearted, too," answered Mrs. Todd, with satisfaction. "She's seen all the trouble folks can see, without it's her last sickness; an' she's got a word of courage for everybody. Life ain't spoilt her a mite. She's eighty-six an' I'm sixty-seven, and I've seen the time I've felt a good sight the oldest. 'Land sakes alive!' says she, last time I was out to see her. 'How you do lurch about steppin' into a bo't!' I laughed so I liked to have gone right over into the water; an' we pushed off, an' left her laughin' there on the shore."

The light had faded as we watched. Mrs. Todd had mounted a gray rock, and stood there grand and architectural, like a *caryatide*. Presently she stepped down, and we continued our way homeward.

"You an' me, we'll take a bo't an' go out some day and see mother," she promised me. " 'T would please her very much, an' there's one or two sca'ce herbs grows better on the island than anywheres else. I ain't seen their like nowheres here on the main.

"Now I'm goin' right down to get us each a mug o' my beer," she announced as we entered the house, "an' I believe I'll sneak in a little mite o' camomile. Goin' to the funeral an' all, I feel to have had a very wearin' afternoon."

I heard her going down into the cool little cellar, and then there was considerable delay. When she returned, mug in hand, I noticed the taste of camomile, in spite of my protest; but its flavor was disguised by some other herb that I did not know, and she stood over me until I drank it all and said that I liked it.

"I don't give that to everybody," said Mrs. Todd kindly; and I felt for a moment as if it were part of a spell and incantation, and as if my enchantress would now begin to look like the cobweb shapes of the arctic town. Nothing happened but a quiet evening and some delightful plans that we made about going to Green Island, and on the morrow there was the clear sunshine and blue sky of another day.

8   *Green Island*

One morning, very early, I heard Mrs. Todd in the garden outside my window. By the unusual loudness of her remarks to a passer-by, and the notes of a familiar hymn which she sang as she worked among the herbs, and which came as if directed purposely to the

sleepy ears of my consciousness, I knew that she wished I would
wake up and come and speak to her.

In a few minutes she responded to a morning voice from behind
the blinds. "I expect you're goin' up to your schoolhouse to pass
all this pleasant day; yes, I expect you're goin' to be dreadful busy,"
she said despairingly.

"Perhaps not," said I. "Why, what's going to be the matter with
you, Mrs. Todd?" For I supposed that she was tempted by the fine
weather to take one of her favorite expeditions along the shore
pastures to gather herbs and simples, and would like to have me
keep the house.

"No, I don't want to go nowhere by land," she answered gayly,—
"no, not by land; but I don't know's we shall have a better day all
the rest of the summer to go out to Green Island an' see mother.
I waked up early thinkin' of her. The wind's light northeast,—
't will take us right straight out; an' this time o' year it's liable to
change round southwest an' fetch us home pretty, 'long late in the
afternoon. Yes, it's goin' to be a good day."

"Speak to the captain and the Bowden boy, if you see anybody
going by toward the landing," said I. "We'll take the big boat."

"Oh, my sakes! now you let me do things my way," said Mrs.
Todd scornfully. "No, dear, we won't take no big bo't. I'll just git
a handy dory, an' Johnny Bowden an' me, we'll man her ourselves.
I don't want no abler bo't than a good dory, an' a nice light breeze
ain't goin' to make no sea; an' Johnny's my cousin's son,—mother'll
like to have him come; an' he'll be down to the herrin' weirs all
the time we're there, anyway; we don't want to carry no men folks
havin' to be considered every minute an' takin' up all our time.
No, you let me do; we'll just slip out an' see mother by ourselves.
I guess what breakfast you'll want's about ready now."

I had become well acquainted with Mrs. Todd as landlady, herb-
gatherer, and rustic philosopher; we had been discreet fellow-
passengers once or twice when I had sailed up the coast to a larger
town than Dunnet Landing to do some shopping; but I was yet to
become acquainted with her as a mariner. An hour later we pushed
off from the landing in the desired dory. The tide was just on the
turn, beginning to fall, and several friends and acquaintances stood
along the side of the dilapidated wharf and cheered us by their
words and evident interest. Johnny Bowden and I were both rowing

in haste to get out where we could catch the breeze and put up the small sail which lay clumsily furled along the gunwale. Mrs. Todd sat aft, a stern and unbending lawgiver.

"You better let her drift; we'll get there 'bout as quick; the tide 'll take her right out from under these old buildin's; there's plenty wind outside."

"Your bo't ain't trimmed proper, Mis' Todd!" exclaimed a voice from shore. "You're lo'ded so the bo't'll drag; you can't git her before the wind, ma'am. You set 'midships, Mis' Todd, an' let the boy hold the sheet 'n' steer after he gits the sail up; you won't never git out to Green Island that way. She's lo'ded bad, your bo't is,—she's heavy behind 's she is now!"

Mrs. Todd turned with some difficulty and regarded the anxious adviser, my right oar flew out of water, and we seemed about to capsize. "That you, Asa? Good-mornin'," she said politely. "I al'ays liked the starn seat best. When'd you git back from up country?"

This allusion to Asa's origin was not lost upon the rest of the company. We were some little distance from shore, but we could hear a chuckle of laughter, and Asa, a person who was too ready with his criticism and advice on every possible subject, turned and walked indignantly away.

When we caught the wind we were soon on our seaward course, and only stopped to underrun a trawl, for the floats of which Mrs. Todd looked earnestly, explaining that her mother might not be prepared for three extra to dinner; it was her brother's trawl, and she meant to just run her eye along for the right sort of a little haddock. I leaned over the boat's side with great interest and excitement, while she skillfully handled the long line of hooks, and made scornful remarks upon worthless, bait-consuming creatures of the sea as she reviewed them and left them on the trawl or shook them off into the waves. At last we came to what she pronounced a proper haddock, and having taken him on board and ended his life resolutely, we went our way.

As we sailed along I listened to an increasingly delightful commentary upon the islands, some of them barren rocks, or at best giving sparse pasturage for sheep in the early summer. On one of these an eager little flock ran to the water's edge and bleated at us so affectingly that I would willingly have stopped; but Mrs. Todd steered away from the rocks, and scolded at the sheep's mean owner, an acquaintance of hers, who grudged the little salt and still less care which the patient creatures needed. The hot midsummer sun makes prisons of these small islands that are a paradise in early June, with their cool springs and short thick-growing grass. On a larger island, farther out to sea, my entertaining companion showed me with glee the small houses of two farmers who shared the island between them, and declared that for three generations the people had not spoken to each other even in times of sickness or death or birth. "When the news come that the war was over, one of 'em knew it a week, and never stepped across his wall to tell the others," she said. "There, they enjoy it: they've got to have somethin' to interest 'em in such a place; 't is a good deal more tryin' to be tied to folks you don't like than 't is to be alone. Each of 'em tells the neighbors their wrongs; plenty likes to hear and tell again; them as fetch a bone 'll carry one, an' so they keep the fight a-goin'. I must say I like variety myself; some folks washes Monday an' irons Tuesday the whole year round, even if the circus is goin' by!"

A long time before we landed at Green Island we could see the small white house, standing high like a beacon, where Mrs. Todd was born and where her mother lived, on a green slope above the water, with dark spruce woods still higher. There were crops in the fields, which we presently distinguished from one another. Mrs. Todd examined them while we were still far at sea. "Mother's late potatoes looks backward; ain't had rain enough so far," she pronounced her opinion. "They look weedier than what they call Front Street down to Cowper Centre. I expect brother William is so occupied with his herrin' weirs an' servin' out bait to the schooners that he don't think once a day of the land."

"What's the flag for, up above the spruces there behind the house?" I inquired with eagerness.

"Oh, that's the sign for herrin' ," she explained kindly, while Johnny Bowden regarded me with contemptuous surprise. "When they get enough for schooners they raise that flag; an' when 't is a poor catch in the weir pocket they just fly a little signal down by the shore, an' then the small bo'ts comes and get enough an' over for their trawls. There, look! there she is: mother sees us; she's wavin' somethin' out o' the fore door! She'll be to the landin'-place quick's we are."

I looked, and could see a tiny flutter in the doorway, but a quicker signal had made its way from the heart on shore to the heart on the sea.

"How do you suppose she knows it's me?" said Mrs. Todd, with a tender smile on her broad face. "There, you never get over bein' a child long's you have a mother to go to. Look at the chimney, now; she's gone right in an' brightened up the fire. Well, there, I'm glad mother's well; you'll enjoy seein' her very much."

Mrs. Todd leaned back into her proper position, and the boat trimmed again. She took a firmer grasp of the sheet, and gave an impatient look up at the gaff and the leech of the little sail, and twitched the sheet as if she urged the wind like a horse. There came at once a fresh gust, and we seemed at once to have doubled our speed. Soon we were near enough to see a tiny figure with handkerchiefed head come down across the field and stand waiting for us at the cove above a curve of pebble beach.

Presently the dory grated on the pebbles, and Johnny Bowden, who had been kept in abeyance during the voyage, sprang out and used manful exertions to haul us up with the next wave, so that Mrs. Todd could make a dry landing.

"You done that very well," she said, mounting to her feet, and coming ashore somewhat stiffly, but with great dignity, refusing our outstretched hands, and returning to possess herself of a bag which had lain at her feet.

"Well, mother, here I be!" she announced with indifference; but they stood and beamed in each other's faces.

"Lookin' pretty well for an old lady, ain't she?" said Mrs. Todd's mother, turning away from her daughter to speak to me. She was a delightful little person herself, with bright eyes and an affectionate air of expectation like a child on a holiday. You felt as if Mrs. Blackett were an old and dear friend before you let go her cordial hand. We all started together up the hill.

"Now don't you haste too fast, mother," said Mrs. Todd warningly; " 't is a far reach o' risin' ground to the fore door, and you won't set an' get your breath when you're once there, but go trotting about. Now don't you go a mite faster than we proceed with this bag an' basket. Johnny, there, 'll fetch up the haddock. I just made one stop to underrun William's trawl till I come to jes' such a fish 's I thought you'd want to make one o' your nice chowders of. I've brought an onion with me that was layin' about on the window-sill at home."

"That's just what I was wantin'," said the hostess. "I give a sigh when you spoke o' chowder, knowin' my onions was out. William forgot to replenish us last time he was to the Landin'. Don't you haste so yourself, Almiry, up this risin' ground. I hear you commencin' to wheeze a'ready."

This mild revenge seemed to afford great pleasure to both giver and receiver. They laughed a little, and looked at each other affectionately, and then at me. Mrs. Todd considerately paused, and faced about to regard the wide sea view. I was glad to stop, being more out of breath than either of my companions, and I prolonged the halt by asking the names of the neighboring islands. There was a fine breeze blowing, which we felt more there on the high land than when we were running before it in the dory.

"Why, this ain't that kitten I saw when I was out last, the one that I said didn't appear likely?" exclaimed Mrs. Todd as we went our way.

"That's the one, Almiry," said her mother. "She always had a likely look to me, an' she's right after her business. I never see such a mouser for one of her age. If 't wan't for William, I never should have housed that other dronin' old thing so long; but he sets by her on account of her havin' a bob tail. I don't deem it advisable to maintain cats just on account of their havin' bob tails; they're like all other curiosities, good for them that wants to see 'em twice. This kitten catches mice for both, an' keeps me respectable as I ain't been for a year. She's a real understandin' little help, this kitten is. I picked her from among five Miss Augusta Pennell had over to Burnt Island," said the old woman, trudging along with the kitten close at her skirts. "Augusta, she says to me, 'Why, Mis' Blackett, you've took the homeliest;' an' says I, 'I've got the smartest; I'm satisfied.'"

"I'd trust nobody sooner'n you to pick out a kitten, mother," said the daughter handsomely, and we went on in peace and harmony.

The house was just before us now, on a green level that looked as if a huge hand had scooped it out of the long green field we had been ascending. A little way above, the dark spruce woods began to climb the top of the hill and cover the seaward slopes of the island. There was just room for the small farm and the forest; we looked down at the fish-house and its rough sheds, and the weirs stretching far out into the water. As we looked upward, the tops of the firs came sharp against the blue sky. There was a great stretch of rough pasture-land round the shoulder of the island to the eastward, and here were all the thick-scattered gray rocks that kept their places, and the gray backs of many sheep that forever wandered and fed on the thin sweet pasturage that fringed the ledges and made soft hollows and strips of green turf like growing velvet. I could see the rich green of bayberry bushes here and there, where the rocks made room. The air was very sweet; one could not help wishing to be a citizen of such a complete and tiny continent and home of fisherfolk.

The house was broad and clean, with a roof that looked heavy on its low walls. It was one of the houses that seem firm-rooted in the ground, as if they were two-thirds below the surface, like icebergs. The front door stood hospitably open in expectation of company, and an orderly vine grew at each side; but our path led to the kitchen door at the house-end, and there grew a mass of gay flowers and greenery, as if they had been swept together by some diligent garden broom into a tangled heap: there were portulacas all along under the lower step and straggling off into the grass, and clustering mallows that crept as near as they dared, like poor relations. I saw the bright eyes and brainless little heads of two half-grown chickens who were snuggled down among the mallows as if they had been chased away from the door more than once, and expected to be again.

"It seems kind o' formal comin' in this way," said Mrs. Todd impulsively, as we passed the flowers and came to the front doorstep; but she was mindful of the proprieties, and walked before us into the best room on the left.

"Why, mother, if you haven't gone an' turned the carpet!" she exclaimed, with something in her voice that spoke of awe and admiration. "When'd you get to it? I s'pose Mis' Addicks come over an' helped you, from White Island Landing?"

"No, she didn't," answered the old woman, standing proudly erect, and making the most of a great moment. "I done it all myself with William's help. He had a spare day, an' took right holt with me; an' 't was all well beat on the grass, an' turned, an' put down

again afore we went to bed. I ripped an' sewed over two o' them
long breadths. I ain't had such a good night's sleep for two years."

"There, what do you think o' havin' such a mother as that for
eighty-six year old?" said Mrs. Todd, standing before us like a large
figure of Victory.

As for the mother, she took on a sudden look of youth; you felt
as if she promised a great future, and was beginning, not ending,
her summers and their happy toils.

"My, my!" exclaimed Mrs. Todd. "I couldn't ha' done it myself,
I've got to own it."

"I was much pleased to have it off my mind," said Mrs. Blackett,
humbly; "the more so because along at the first of the next week
I wasn't very well. I suppose it may have been the change of
weather."

Mrs. Todd could not resist a significant glance at me, but, with
charming sympathy, she forbore to point the lesson or to connect
this illness with its apparent cause. She loomed larger than ever in
the little old-fashioned best room, with its few pieces of good
furniture and pictures of national interest. The green paper curtains
were stamped with conventional landscapes of a foreign order,—
castles on inaccessible crags, and lovely lakes with steep wooded
shores; under-foot the treasured carpet was covered thick with
home-made rugs. There were empty glass lamps and crystallized
bouquets of grass and some fine shells on the narrow mantelpiece.

"I was married in this room," said Mrs. Todd unexpectedly; and
I heard her give a sigh after she had spoken, as if she could not
help the touch of regret that would forever come with all her
thoughts of happiness.

"We stood right there between the windows," she added, "and
the minister stood here. William wouldn't come in. He was always
odd about seein' folks, just 's he is now. I run to meet 'em from
a child, an' William, he'd take an' run away."

"I've been the gainer," said the old mother cheerfully. "William
has been son an' daughter both since you was married off the island.
He's been 'most too satisfied to stop at home 'long o' his old
mother, but I always tell 'em I'm the gainer."

We were all moving toward the kitchen as if by common instinct. The best room was too suggestive of serious occasions, and
the shades were all pulled down to shut out the summer light

and air. It was indeed a tribute to Society to find a room set apart
for her behests out there on so apparently neighborless and remote
an island. Afternoon visits and evening festivals must be few in
such a bleak situation at certain seasons of the year, but Mrs.
Blackett was of those who do not live to themselves, and who have
long since passed the line that divides mere self-concern from a
valued share in whatever Society can give and take. There were
those of her neighbors who never had taken the trouble to furnish
a best room, but Mrs. Blackett was one who knew the uses of a
parlor.

"Yes, do come right out into the old kitchen; I shan't make any
stranger of you," she invited us pleasantly, after we had been properly received in the room appointed to formality. "I expect Almiry,
here, 'll be driftin' out 'mongst the pasture-weeds quick's she can
find a good excuse. 'T is hot now. You'd better content yourselves
till you get nice an' rested, an' 'long after dinner the seabreeze'll
spring up, an' then you can take your walks, an' go up an' see the
prospect from the big ledge. Almiry'll want to show off everything
there is. Then I'll get you a good cup o' tea before you start to go
home. The days are plenty long now."

While we were talking in the best room the selected fish had
been mysteriously brought up from the shore, and lay all cleaned
and ready in an earthen crock on the table.

"I think William might have stopped an' said a word," remarked
Mrs. Todd, pouting with high affront as she caught sight of it.
"He's friendly enough when he comes ashore, an' was remarkable
social the last time, for him."

"He ain't disposed to be very social with the ladies," explained
William's mother, with a delightful glance at me, as if she counted
upon my friendship and tolerance. "He's very particular, and he's
all in his old fishin'-clothes to-day. He'll want me to tell him everything you said and done, after you've gone. William has very deep
affections. He'll want to see you, Almiry. Yes, I guess he'll be in
by an' by."

"I'll search for him by 'n' by, if he don't," proclaimed Mrs. Todd,
with an air of unalterable resolution. "I know all of his burrows
down 'long the shore. I'll catch him by hand 'fore he knows it. I've
got some business with William, anyway. I brought forty-two cents
with me that was due him for them last lobsters he brought in."

"You can leave it with me," suggested the little old mother, who was already stepping about among her pots and pans in the pantry, and preparing to make the chowder.

I became possessed of a sudden unwonted curiosity in regard to William, and felt that half the pleasure of my visit would be lost if I could not make his interesting acquaintance.

9 *William*

Mrs. Todd had taken the onion out of her basket and laid it down upon the kitchen table. "There's Johnny Bowden come with us, you know," she reminded her mother. "He'll be hungry enough to eat his size."

"I've got new doughnuts, dear," said the little old lady. "You don't often catch William 'n' me out o' provisions. I expect you might have chose a somewhat larger fish, but I'll try an' make it do. I shall have to have a few extra potatoes, but there's a field full out there, an' the hoe's leanin' against the well-house, in 'mongst the climbin'-beans." She smiled, and gave her daughter a commanding nod.

"Land sakes alive! Le' 's blow the horn for William," insisted Mrs. Todd, with some excitement. "He needn't break his spirit so far's to come in. He'll know you need him for something particular, an' then we can call to him as he comes up the path. I won't put him to no pain."

Mrs. Blackett's old face, for the first time, wore a look of trouble, and I found it necessary to counteract the teasing spirit of Almira. It was too pleasant to stay indoors altogether, even in such rewarding companionship; besides, I might meet William; and, straying out presently, I found the hoe by the well-house and an old splint basket at the woodshed door, and also found my way down to the field where there was a great square patch of rough, weedy potato-tops and tall ragweed. One corner was already dug, and I chose a fat-looking hill where the tops were well withered. There is all the pleasure that one can have in gold-digging in finding one's hopes satisfied in the riches of a good hill of potatoes. I longed to go on; but it did not seem frugal to dig any longer after my basket was full, and at last I took my hoe by the middle and lifted the basket to go back up the hill. I was sure that Mrs. Blackett must be waiting impatiently to slice the potatoes into the chowder, layer after layer, with the fish.

"You let me take holt o' that basket, ma'am," said a pleasant, anxious voice behind me.

I turned, startled in the silence of the wide field, and saw an elderly man, bent in the shoulders as fishermen often are, gray-headed and clean-shaven, and with a timid air. It was William. He looked just like his mother, and I had been imagining that he was large and stout like his sister, Almira Todd; and, strange to say, my fancy had led me to picture him not far from thirty and a little loutish. It was necessary instead to pay William the respect due to age.

I accustomed myself to plain facts on the instant, and we said good-morning like old friends. The basket was really heavy, and I put the hoe through its handle and offered him one end; then we moved easily toward the house together, speaking of the fine weather and of mackerel which were reported to be striking in all about the bay. William had been out since three o'clock, and had taken an extra fare of fish. I could feel that Mrs. Todd's eyes were upon us as we approached the house, and although I fell behind in the narrow path, and let William take the basket alone and precede me at some little distance the rest of the way, I could plainly hear her greet him.

"Got round to comin' in, didn't you?" she inquired, with amusement. "Well, now, that's clever. Didn't know 's I should see you to-day, William, an' I wanted to settle an account."

I felt somewhat disturbed and responsible, but when I joined them they were on most simple and friendly terms. It became evident that, with William, it was the first step that cost, and that, having once joined in social interests, he was able to pursue them with more or less pleasure. He was about sixty, and not young-looking for his years, yet so undying is the spirit of youth, and bashfulness has such a power of survival, that I felt all the time as if one must try to make the occasion easy for some one who was young and new to the affairs of social life. He asked politely if I would like to go up to the great ledge while dinner was getting ready; so, not without a deep sense of pleasure, and a delighted look of surprise from the two hostesses, we started, William and I, as if both of us felt much younger than we looked. Such was the innocence and simplicity of the moment that when I heard Mrs. Todd laughing behind us in the kitchen I laughed too, but William did not even blush. I think he was a little deaf, and he stepped along before me most businesslike and intent upon his errand.

We went from the upper edge of the field above the house into a smooth, brown path among the dark spruces. The hot sun brought out the fragrance of the pitchy bark, and the shade was pleasant as we climbed the hill. William stopped once or twice to show me a great wasps'-nest close by, or some fishhawks'-nests below in a bit of swamp. He picked a few sprigs of late-blooming linnæa as we came out upon an open bit of pasture at the top of the island, and gave them to me without speaking, but he knew as well as I that one could not say half he wished about linnæa. Through this piece of rough pasture ran a huge shape of stone like the great backbone of an enormous creature. At the end, near the woods, we could climb up on it and walk along to the highest point; there above the circle of pointed firs we could look down over all the island, and could see the ocean that circled this and a hundred other bits of island-ground, the mainland shore and all the far horizons. It gave a sudden sense of space, for nothing stopped the eye or hedged one in,—that sense of liberty in space and time which great prospects always give.

"There ain't no such view in the world, I expect," said William proudly, and I hastened to speak my heartfelt tribute of praise: it was impossible not to feel as if an untraveled boy had spoken, and yet one loved to have him value his native heath.

10   *Where Pennyroyal Grew*

We were a little late to dinner, but Mrs. Blackett and Mrs. Todd were lenient, and we all took our places after William had paused to wash his hands, like a pious Brahmin, at the well, and put on a neat blue coat which he took from a peg behind the kitchen door. Then he resolutely asked a blessing in words that I could not hear, and we ate the chowder and were thankful. The kitten went round and round the table, quite erect, and, holding on by her fierce young claws, she stopped to mew with pathos at each elbow, or darted off to the open door when a song sparrow forgot himself and lit in the grass too near. William did not talk much, but his sister Todd occupied the time and told all the news there was to tell of Dunnet Landing and its coasts, while the old mother listened with delight. Her hospitality was something exquisite; she had the gift which so many women lack, of being able to make themselves and their houses belong entirely to a guest's pleasure,—that charming surrender for the moment of themselves and whatever belongs to them, so that they make a part of one's own life that can never be forgotten. Tact is after all a kind of mindreading, and my hostess held the golden gift. Sympathy is of the mind as well as the heart, and Mrs. Blackett's world and mine were one from the moment we met. Besides, she had that final, that highest gift of heaven, a perfect self-forgetfulness. Sometimes, as I watched her eager, sweet old face, I wondered why she had been set to shine on this lonely island of the northern coast. It must have been to keep the balance true, and make up to all her scattered and depending neighbors for other things which they may have lacked.

When we had finished clearing away the old blue plates, and the kitten had taken care of her share of the fresh haddock, just as we were putting back the kitchen chairs in their places, Mrs. Todd said briskly that she must go up into the pasture now to gather the desired herbs.

"You can stop here an' rest, or you can accompany me," she announced. "Mother ought to have her nap, and when we come back she an' William'll sing for you. She admires music," said Mrs. Todd, turning to speak to her mother.

But Mrs. Blackett tried to say that she couldn't sing as she used, and perhaps William wouldn't feel like it. She looked tired, the good old soul, or I should have liked to sit in the peaceful little house while she slept; I had had much pleasant experience of pastures already in her daughter's company. But it seemed best to go with Mrs. Todd, and off we went.

Mrs. Todd carried the gingham bag which she had brought from home, and a small heavy burden in the bottom made it hang straight and slender from her hand. The way was steep, and she soon grew breathless, so that we sat down to rest awhile on a convenient large stone among the bayberry.

"There, I wanted you to see this,—'t is mother's picture," said Mrs. Todd; "'t was taken once when she was up to Portland, soon after she was married. That's me," she added, opening another worn case, and displaying the full face of the cheerful child she looked like still in spite of being past sixty. "And here's William an' father together. I take after father, large and heavy, an' William is like mother's folks, short an' thin. He ought to have made something o' himself, bein' a man an' so like mother; but though he's been very steady to work, an' kept up the farm, an' done his fishin' too right along, he never had mother's snap an' power o' seein' things just as they be. He's got excellent judgment, too," meditated William's sister, but she could not arrive at any satisfactory decision upon what she evidently thought his failure in life. "I think it is well to see any one so happy an' makin' the most of life just as it falls to hand," she said as she began to put the daguerreotypes away again; but I reached out my hand to see her mother's once more, a most flower-like face of a lovely young woman in quaint dress. There was in the eyes a look of anticipation and joy, a far-off look that sought the horizon; one often sees it in seafaring families, inherited by girls and boys alike from men who spend their lives at sea, and are always watching for distant sails or the first loom of the land. At sea there is nothing to be seen close by, and this has its counterpart in a sailor's character, in the large and brave and patient traits that are developed, the hopeful pleasantness that one loves so in a seafarer.

When the family pictures were wrapped again in a big handkerchief, we set forward in a narrow footpath and made our way to a lonely place that faced northward, where there was more pasturage and fewer bushes, and we went down to the edge of short grass above some rocky cliffs where the deep sea broke with a great noise, though the wind was down and the water looked quiet a little way from shore. Among the grass grew such pennyroyal as the rest of the world could not provide. There was a fine fragrance in the air as we gathered it sprig by sprig and stepped along carefully, and Mrs. Todd pressed her aromatic nosegay between her hands and offered it to me again and again.

"There's nothin' like it," she said; "oh no, there's no such pennyr'yal as this in the State of Maine. It's the right pattern of the plant, and all the rest I ever see is but an imitation. Don't it do you good?" And I answered with enthusiasm.

"There, dear, I never showed nobody else but mother where to find this place; 't is kind of sainted to me. Nathan, my husband, an' I used to love this place when we was courtin', and"—she hesitated, and then spoke softly—"when he was lost, 't was just off shore tryin' to get in by the short channel out there between Squaw Islands, right in sight o' this headland where we'd set an' made our plans all summer long."

I had never heard her speak of her husband before, but I felt that we were friends now since she had brought me to this place.

" 'T was but a dream with us," Mrs. Todd said. "I knew it when he was gone. I knew it"—and she whispered as if she were at confession—"I knew it afore he started to go to sea. My heart was gone out o' my keepin' before I ever saw Nathan; but he loved me well, and he made me real happy, and he died before he ever knew what he'd had to know if we'd lived long together. 'T is very strange about love. No, Nathan never found out, but my heart was troubled when I knew him first. There's more women likes to be loved than there is of those that loves. I spent some happy hours right here. I always liked Nathan, and he never knew. But this pennyr'yal always reminded me, as I'd sit and gather it and hear him talkin'—it always would remind me of—the other one."

She looked away from me, and presently rose and went on by herself. There was something lonely and solitary about her great determined shape. She might have been Antigone alone on the Theban plain. It is not often given in a noisy world to come to the places of great grief and silence. An absolute, archaic grief possessed this countrywoman; she seemed like a renewal of some historic soul, with her sorrows and the remoteness of a daily life busied with rustic simplicities and the scents of primeval herbs.

I was not incompetent at herb-gathering, and after a while, when I had sat long enough waking myself to new thoughts, and reading a page of remembrance with new pleasure, I gathered some bunches, as I was bound to do, and at last we met again higher up the shore, in the plain every-day world we had left behind when we went down to the pennyroyal plot. As we walked together along the high edge of the field we saw a hundred sails about the bay and farther seaward; it was mid-afternoon or after, and the day was coming to an end.

"Yes, they're all makin' towards the shore,—the small craft an' the lobster smacks an' all," said my companion. "We must spend a little time with mother now, just to have our tea, an' then put for home."

"No matter if we lose the wind at sundown; I can row in with Johnny," said I; and Mrs. Todd nodded reassuringly and kept to her steady plod, not quickening her gait even when we saw William come round the corner of the house as if to look for us, and wave his hand and disappear.

"Why, William's right on deck; I didn't know's we should see any more of him!" exclaimed Mrs. Todd. "Now mother'll put the kettle right on; she's got a good fire goin'." I too could see the blue smoke thicken, and then we both walked a little faster, while Mrs. Todd groped in her full bag of herbs to find the daguerreotypes and be ready to put them in their places.

11   *The Old Singers*

William was sitting on the side door step, and the old mother was busy making her tea; she gave into my hand an old flowered-glass tea-caddy.

"William thought you'd like to see this, when he was settin' the table. My father brought it to my mother from the island of Tobago; an' here's a pair of beautiful mugs that came with it." She opened the glass door of a little cupboard beside the chimney. "These I call my best things, dear," she said. "You'd laugh to see how we enjoy 'em Sunday nights in winter: we have a real company tea 'stead o' livin' right along just the same, an' I make somethin' good for a s'prise an' put on some o' my preserves, an' we get a-talkin' together an' have real pleasant times."

Mrs. Todd laughed indulgently, and looked to see what I thought of such childishness.

"I wish I could be here some Sunday evening," said I.

"William an' me'll be talkin' about you an' thinkin' o' this nice day," said Mrs. Blackett affectionately, and she glanced at William, and he looked up bravely and nodded. I began to discover that he and his sister could not speak their deeper feelings before each other.

"Now I want you an' mother to sing," said Mrs. Todd abruptly, with an air of command, and I gave William much sympathy in his evident distress.

"After I've had my cup o' tea, dear," answered the old hostess cheerfully; and so we sat down and took our cups and made merry while they lasted. It was impossible not to wish to stay on forever at Green Island, and I could not help saying so.

"I'm very happy here, both winter an' summer," said old Mrs. Blackett. "William an' I never wish for any other home, do we, William? I'm glad you find it pleasant; I wish you'd come an' stay, dear, whenever you feel inclined. But here's Almiry; I always think Providence was kind to plot an' have her husband leave her a good house where she really belonged. She'd been very restless if she'd had to continue here on Green Island. You wanted more scope, didn't you, Almiry, an' to live in a large place where more things grew? Sometimes folks wonders that we don't live together; perhaps we shall some time," and a shadow of sadness and apprehension flitted across her face. "The time o' sickness an' failin' has got to come to all. But Almiry's got an herb that's good for everything." She smiled as she spoke, and looked bright again.

"There's some herb that's good for everybody, except for them that thinks they're sick when they ain't," announced Mrs. Todd, with a truly professional air of finality. "Come, William, let's have Sweet Home, an' then mother'll sing Cupid an' the Bee for us."

Then followed a most charming surprise. William mastered his timidity and began to sing. His voice was a little faint and frail, like the family daguerreotypes, but it was a tenor voice, and perfectly true and sweet. I have never heard Home, Sweet Home sung as touchingly and seriously as he sang it; he seemed to make it quite new; and when he paused for a moment at the end of the first line and began the next, the old mother joined him and they sang together, she missing only the higher notes, where he seemed to lend his voice to hers for the moment and carry on her very note and air. It was the silent man's real and only means of expression, and one could have listened forever, and have asked for more and more songs of old Scotch and English inheritance and the best that have lived from the ballad music of the war. Mrs. Todd kept time visibly, and sometimes audibly, with her ample foot. I saw the tears in her eyes sometimes, when I could see beyond the tears in mine. But at last the songs ended and the time came to say good-by; it was the end of a great pleasure.

Mrs. Blackett, the dear old lady, opened the door of her bedroom while Mrs. Todd was tying up the herb bag, and William had gone down to get the boat ready and to blow the horn for Johnny Bowden, who had joined a roving boat party who were off the shore lobstering.

I went to the door of the bedroom, and thought how pleasant it looked, with its pink-and-white patchwork quilt and the brown unpainted paneling of its woodwork.

"Come right in, dear," she said. "I want you to set down in my old quilted rockin'-chair there by the window; you'll say it's the prettiest view in the house. I set there a good deal to rest me and when I want to read."

There was a worn red Bible on the lightstand, and Mrs. Blackett's heavy silver-bowed glasses; her thimble was on the narrow window-ledge, and folded carefully on the table was a thick striped-cotton shirt that she was making for her son. Those dear old fingers and their loving stitches, that heart which had made the most of everything that needed love! Here was the real home, the heart of the old house on Green Island! I sat in the rocking-chair, and felt that it was a place of peace, the little brown bedroom, and the quiet outlook upon field and sea and sky.

I looked up, and we understood each other without speaking. "I shall like to think o' your settin' here to-day," said Mrs. Blackett. "I want you to come again. It has been so pleasant for William."

The wind served us all the way home, and did not fall or let the sail slacken until we were close to the shore. We had a generous freight of lobsters in the boat, and new potatoes which William had put aboard, and what Mrs. Todd proudly called a full "kag" of prime number one salted mackerel; and when we landed we had to make business arrangements to have these conveyed to her house in a wheelbarrow.

I never shall forget the day at Green Island. The town of Dunnet Landing seemed large and noisy and oppressive as we came ashore. Such is the power of contrast; for the village was so still that I could hear the shy whippoorwills singing that night as I lay awake in my downstairs bedroom, and the scent of Mrs. Todd's herb garden under the window blew in again and again with every gentle rising of the sea-breeze.

12   *A Strange Sail*

Except for a few stray guests, islanders or from the inland country, to whom Mrs. Todd offered the hospitalities of a single meal, we were quite by ourselves all summer; and when there were signs of invasion, late in July, and a certain Mrs. Fosdick appeared like a strange sail on the far horizon, I suffered much from apprehension. I had been living in the quaint little house with as much comfort and unconsciousness as if it were a larger body, or a double shell, in whose simple convolutions Mrs. Todd and I had secreted ourselves, until some wandering hermit crab of a visitor marked the little spare room for her own. Perhaps now and then a castaway on a lonely desert island dreads the thought of being rescued. I heard of Mrs. Fosdick for the first time with a selfish sense of objection; but after all, I was still vacation-tenant of the schoolhouse, where I could always be alone, and it was impossible not to sympathize with Mrs. Todd, who, in spite of some preliminary grumbling, was really delighted with the prospect of entertaining an old friend.

For nearly a month we received occasional news of Mrs. Fosdick, who seemed to be making a royal progress from house to house in the inland neighborhood, after the fashion of Queen Elizabeth. One Sunday after another came and went, disappointing Mrs. Todd in the hope of seeing her guest at church and fixing the day for the great visit to begin; but Mrs. Fosdick was not ready to commit herself to a date. An assurance of "some time this week" was not sufficiently definite from a free-footed housekeeper's point of view, and Mrs. Todd put aside all herb-gathering plans, and went through the various stages of expectation, provocation, and despair. At last she was ready to believe that Mrs. Fosdick must have forgotten her promise and returned to her home, which was vaguely said to be over Thomaston way. But one evening, just as the supper-table was cleared and "readied up," and Mrs. Todd had put her large apron over her head and stepped forth for an evening stroll in the garden, the unexpected happened. She heard the sound of wheels, and gave an excited cry to me, as I sat by the window, that Mrs. Fosdick was coming right up the street.

"She may not be considerate, but she's dreadful good company," said Mrs. Todd hastily, coming back a few steps from the neighborhood of the gate. "No, she ain't a mite considerate, but there's a small lobster left over from your tea; yes, it's a real mercy there's a lobster. Susan Fosdick might just as well have passed the compliment o' comin' an hour ago."

"Perhaps she has had her supper," I ventured to suggest, sharing the housekeeper's anxiety, and meekly conscious of an inconsiderate appetite for my own supper after a long expedition up the bay. There were so few emergencies of any sort at Dunnet Landing that this one appeared overwhelming.

"No, she's rode 'way over from Nahum Brayton's place. I expect they were busy on the farm, and couldn't spare the horse in proper season. You just sly out an' set the tea-kittle on again, dear, an' drop in a good han'ful o' chips; the fire's all alive. I'll take her right up to lay off her things, an' she'll be occupied with explanations an' gettin' her bunnit off, so you'll have plenty o' time. She's one I shouldn't like to have find me unprepared."

Mrs. Fosdick was already at the gate, and Mrs. Todd now turned with an air of complete surprise and delight to welcome her.

"Why, Susan Fosdick," I heard her exclaim in a fine unhindered voice, as if she were calling across a field, "I come near giving of you up! I was afraid you'd gone an' 'portioned out my visit to somebody else. I s'pose you've been to supper?"

"Lor', no, I ain't, Almiry Todd," said Mrs. Fosdick cheerfully, as she turned, laden with bags and bundles, from making her adieux to the boy driver. "I ain't had a mite o' supper, dear. I've been lottin' all the way on a cup o' that best tea o' yourn,—some o' that Oolong you keep in the little chist. I don't want none o' your useful herbs."

"I keep that tea for ministers' folks," gayly responded Mrs. Todd. "Come right along in, Susan Fosdick. I declare if you ain't the same old sixpence!"

As they came up the walk together, laughing like girls, I fled, full of cares, to the kitchen, to brighten the fire and be sure that the lobster, sole dependence of a late supper, was well out of reach of the cat. There proved to be fine reserves of wild raspberries and bread and butter, so that I regained my composure, and waited impatiently for my own share of this illustrious visit to begin. There was an instant sense of high festivity in the evening air from the moment when our guest had so frankly demanded the Oolong tea.

The great moment arrived. I was formally presented at the stair-foot, and the two friends passed on to the kitchen, where I soon heard a hospitable clink of crockery and the brisk stirring of a tea-cup. I sat in my high-backed rocking-chair by the window in the front room with an unreasonable feeling of being left out, like the child who stood at the gate in Hans Andersen's story. Mrs. Fosdick did not look, at first sight, like a person of great social gifts. She was a serious-looking little bit of an old woman, with a birdlike nod of the head. I had often been told that she was the "best hand in the world to make a visit,"—as if to visit were the highest of vocations; that everybody wished for her, while few could get her; and I saw that Mrs. Todd felt a comfortable sense of distinction in being favored with the company of this eminent person who "knew just how." It was certainly true that Mrs. Fosdick gave both her hostess and me a warm feeling of enjoyment and expectation, as if she had the power of social suggestion to all neighboring minds.

The two friends did not reappear for at least an hour. I could hear their busy voices, loud and low by turns, as they ranged from public to confidential topics. At last Mrs. Todd kindly remembered me and returned, giving my door a ceremonious knock before she stepped in, with the small visitor in her wake. She reached behind her and took Mrs. Fosdick's hand as if she were young and bashful, and gave her a gentle pull forward.

"There, I don't know whether you're goin' to take to each other or not; no, nobody can't tell whether you'll suit each other, but I expect you'll get along some way, both having seen the world," said our affectionate hostess. "You can inform Mis' Fosdick how we found the folks out to Green Island the other day. She's always been well acquainted with mother. I'll slip out now an' put away the supper things an' set my bread to rise, if you'll both excuse me. You can come out an' keep me company when you get ready, either or both." And Mrs. Todd, large and amiable, disappeared and left us.

Being furnished not only with a subject of conversation, but with a safe refuge in the kitchen in case of incompatibility, Mrs. Fosdick and I sat down, prepared to make the best of each other. I soon discovered that she, like many of the elder women of that coast, had spent a part of her life at sea, and was full of a good traveler's curiosity and enlightenment. By the time we thought it discreet to join our hostess we were already sincere friends.

You may speak of a visit's setting in as well as a tide's, and it was impossible, as Mrs. Todd whispered to me, not to be pleased at the way this visit was setting in; a new impulse and refreshing of the social currents and seldom visited bays of memory appeared to have begun. Mrs. Fosdick had been the mother of a large family of sons and daughters,—sailors and sailors' wives,—and most of them had died before her. I soon grew more or less acquainted with the histories of all their fortunes and misfortunes, and subjects of an intimate nature were no more withheld from my ears than if I had been a shell on the mantelpiece. Mrs. Fosdick was not without a touch of dignity and elegance; she was fashionable in her dress, but it was a curiously well-preserved provincial fashion of some years back. In a wider sphere one might have called her a woman of the world, with her unexpected bits of modern knowledge, but Mrs. Todd's wisdom was an intimation of truth itself. She might belong to any age, like an idyl of Theocritus; but while she always understood Mrs. Fosdick, that entertaining pilgrim could not always understand Mrs. Todd.

That very first evening my friends plunged into a borderless sea of reminiscences and personal news. Mrs. Fosdick had been staying with a family who owned the farm where she was born, and she had visited every sunny knoll and shady field corner; but when she said that it might be for the last time, I detected in her tone something expectant of the contradiction which Mrs. Todd promptly offered.

"Almiry," said Mrs. Fosdick, with sadness, "you may say what you like, but I am one of nine brothers and sisters brought up on the old place, and we're all dead but me."

"Your sister Dailey ain't gone, is she? Why, no, Louisa ain't gone!" exclaimed Mrs. Todd, with surprise. "Why, I never heard of that occurrence!"

"Yes'm; she passed away last October, in Lynn. She had made her distant home in Vermont State, but she was making a visit to her youngest daughter. Louisa was the only one of my family whose funeral I wasn't able to attend, but 't was a mere accident. All the rest of us were settled right about home. I thought it was very slack of 'em in Lynn not to fetch her to the old place; but when I came to hear about it, I learned that they'd recently put up a very elegant monument, and my sister Dailey was always great for show. She'd just been out to see the monument the week before she was taken down, and admired it so much that they felt sure of her wishes."

"So she's really gone, and the funeral was up to Lynn!" repeated Mrs. Todd, as if to impress the sad fact upon her mind. "She was some years younger than we be, too. I recollect the first day she ever came to school; 't was that first year mother sent me inshore to stay with aunt Topham's folks and get my schooling. You fetched little Louisa to school one Monday mornin' in a pink dress an' her long curls, and she set between you an' me, and got cryin' after a while, so the teacher sent us home with her at recess."

"She was scared of seeing so many children about her; there was only her and me and brother John at home then; the older boys were to sea with father, an' the rest of us wa'n't born," explained Mrs. Fosdick. "That next fall we all went to sea together. Mother was uncertain till the last minute, as one may say. The ship was waiting orders, but the baby that then was, was born just in time, and there was a long spell of extra bad weather, so mother got about again before they had to sail, an' we all went. I remember my clothes were all left ashore in the east chamber in a basket where mother'd took them out o' my chist o' drawers an' left 'em ready to carry aboard. She didn't have nothing aboard, of her own, that she wanted to cut up for me, so when my dress wore out she just put me into a spare suit o' John's, jacket and trousers. I wasn't but eight years old an' he was most seven and large of his age. Quick as we made a port she went right ashore an' fitted me out pretty, but we was bound for the East Indies and didn't put in anywhere for a good while. So I had quite a spell o' freedom. Mother made my new skirt long because I was growing, and I poked about the deck after that, real discouraged, feeling the hem at my heels every minute, and as if youth was past and gone. I liked the trousers best; I used to climb the riggin' with 'em and frighten mother till she said an' vowed she'd never take me to sea again."

I thought by the polite absent-minded smile on Mrs. Todd's face this was no new story.

"Little Louisa was a beautiful child; yes, I always thought Louisa was very pretty," Mrs. Todd said. "She was a dear little girl in those days. She favored your mother; the rest of you took after your father's folks."

"We did certain," agreed Mrs. Fosdick, rocking steadily. "There, it does seem so pleasant to talk with an old acquaintance that knows what you know. I see so many of these new folks nowadays, that seem to have neither past nor future. Conversation's got to have some root in the past, or else you've got to explain every remark you make, an' it wears a person out."

Mrs. Todd gave a funny little laugh. "Yes'm, old friends is always best, 'less you can catch a new one that's fit to make an old one out of," she said, and we gave an affectionate glance at each other which Mrs. Fosdick could not have understood, being the latest comer to the house.

13   *Poor Joanna*

One evening my ears caught a mysterious allusion which Mrs. Todd made to Shell-heap Island. It was a chilly night of cold northeasterly rain, and I made a fire for the first time in the Franklin stove in my room, and begged my two housemates to come in and keep me company. The weather had convinced Mrs. Todd that it was time to make a supply of cough-drops, and she had been bringing forth herbs from dark and dry hiding-places, until now the pungent dust and odor of them had resolved themselves into one mighty flavor of spearmint that came from a simmering caldron of syrup in the kitchen. She called it done, and well done, and had ostentatiously left it to cool, and taken her knitting-work because Mrs. Fosdick was busy with hers. They sat in the two rocking-chairs, the small woman and the large one, but now and then I could see that Mrs. Todd's thoughts remained with the cough-drops. The time of gathering herbs was nearly over, but the time of syrups and cordials had begun.

The heat of the open fire made us a little drowsy, but something in the way Mrs. Todd spoke of Shell-heap Island waked my interest. I waited to see if she would say any more, and then took a roundabout way back to the subject by saying what was first in my mind: that I wished the Green Island family were there to spend the evening with us,—Mrs. Todd's mother and her brother William.

Mrs. Todd smiled, and drummed on the arm of the rocking-chair. "Might scare William to death," she warned me; and Mrs. Fosdick mentioned her intention of going out to Green Island to stay two or three days, if this wind didn't make too much sea.

"Where is Shell-heap Island?" I ventured to ask, seizing the opportunity.

"Bears nor'east somewheres about three miles from Green Island; right off-shore, I should call it about eight miles out," said Mrs. Todd. "You never was there, dear; 't is off the thoroughfares, and a very bad place to land at best."

"I should think 't was," agreed Mrs. Fosdick, smoothing down her black silk apron. " 'T is a place worth visitin' when you once get there. Some o' the old folks was kind o' fearful about it. 'T was 'counted a great place in old Indian times; you can pick up their stone tools 'most any time if you hunt about. There's a beautiful spring o' water, too. Yes, I remember when they used to tell queer stories about Shell-heap Island. Some said 't was a great bangeing-place for the Indians, and an old chief resided there once that ruled the winds; and others said they'd always heard that once the Indians come down from up country an' left a captive there without any bo't, an' 't was too far to swim across to Black Island, so called, an' he lived there till he perished."

"I've heard say he walked the island after that, and sharp-sighted folks could see him an' lose him like one o' them citizens Cap'n Littlepage was acquainted with up to the north pole," announced Mrs. Todd grimly. "Anyway, there was Indians,—you can see their shell-heap that named the island; and I've heard myself that 't was one o' their cannibal places, but I never could believe it. There never was no cannibals on the coast o' Maine. All the Indians o' these regions are tame-looking folks."

"Sakes alive, yes!" exclaimed Mrs. Fosdick. "Ought to see them painted savages I've seen when I was young out in the South Sea Islands! That was the time for folks to travel, 'way back in the old whalin' days!"

"Whalin' must have been dull for a lady, hardly ever makin' a lively port, and not takin' in any mixed cargoes," said Mrs. Todd. "I never desired to go a whalin' v'y'ge myself."

"I used to return feelin' very slack an' behind the times, 't is

true," explained Mrs. Fosdick, "but 't was excitin', an' we always
done extra well, and felt rich when we did get ashore. I liked the
variety. There, how times have changed; how few seafarin' families
there are left! What a lot o' queer folks there used to be about
here, anyway, when we was young, Almiry. Everybody's just like
everybody else, now; nobody to laugh about, and nobody to cry
about."

It seemed to me that there were peculiarities of character in the
region of Dunnet Landing yet, but I did not like to interrupt.

"Yes," said Mrs. Todd after a moment of meditation, "there was
certain a good many curiosities of human natur' in this neighborhood years ago. There was more energy then, and in some the
energy took a singular turn. In these days the young folks is all
copy-cats, 'fraid to death they won't be all just alike; as for the old
folks, they pray for the advantage o' bein' a little different."

"I ain't heard of a copy-cat this great many years," said Mrs.
Fosdick, laughing; " 't was a favorite term o' my grandmother's.
No, I wa'n't thinking o' those things, but of them strange straying
creatur's that used to rove the country. You don't see them now,
or the ones that used to hive away in their own houses with some
strange notion or other."

I thought again of Captain Littlepage, but my companions were
not reminded of his name; and there was brother William at Green
Island, whom we all three knew.

"I was talking o' poor Joanna the other day. I hadn't thought of
her for a great while," said Mrs. Fosdick abruptly. "Mis' Brayton
an' I recalled her as we sat together sewing. She was one o' your
peculiar persons, wa'n't she? Speaking of such persons," she turned
to explain to me, "there was a sort of a nun or hermit person lived
out there for years all alone on Shell-heap Island. Miss Joanna
Todd, her name was,—a cousin o' Almiry's late husband."

I expressed my interest, but as I glanced at Mrs. Todd I saw that
she was confused by sudden affectionate feeling and unmistakable
desire for reticence.

"I never want to hear Joanna laughed about," she said anxiously.

"Nor I," answered Mrs. Fosdick reassuringly. "She was crossed
in love,—that was all the matter to begin with; but as I look back,
I can see that Joanna was one doomed from the first to fall into a
melancholy. She retired from the world for good an' all, though

she was a well-off woman. All she wanted was to get away from folks; she thought she wasn't fit to live with anybody, and wanted to be free. Shell-heap Island come to her from her father, and first thing folks knew she'd gone off out there to live, and left word she didn't want no company. 'T was a bad place to get to, unless the wind an' tide were just right; 't was hard work to make a landing."

"What time of year was this?" I asked.

"Very late in the summer," said Mrs. Fosdick. "No, I never could laugh at Joanna, as some did. She set everything by the young man, an' they were going to marry in about a month, when he got bewitched with a girl 'way up the bay, and married her, and went off to Massachusetts. He wasn't well thought of,—there were those who thought Joanna's money was what had tempted him; but she'd given him her whole heart, an' she wa'n't so young as she had been. All her hopes were built on marryin', an' havin' a real home and somebody to look to; she acted just like a bird when its nest is spoilt. The day after she heard the news she was in dreadful woe, but the next she came to herself very quiet, and took the horse and wagon, and drove fourteen miles to the lawyer's, and signed a paper givin' her half of the farm to her brother. They never had got along very well together, but he didn't want to sign it, till she acted so distressed that he gave in. Edward Todd's wife was a good woman, who felt very bad indeed, and used every argument with Joanna; but Joanna took a poor old boat that had been her father's and lo'ded in a few things, and off she put all alone, with a good land breeze, right out to sea. Edward Todd ran down to the beach, an' stood there cryin' like a boy to see her go, but she was out o' hearin'. She never stepped foot on the mainland again long as she lived."

"How large an island is it? How did she manage in winter?" I asked.

"Perhaps thirty acres, rocks and all," answered Mrs. Todd, taking up the story gravely. "There can't be much of it that the salt spray don't fly over in storms. No, 't is a dreadful small place to make a world of; it has a different look from any of the other islands, but there's a sheltered cove on the south side, with mud-flats across one end of it at low water where there's excellent clams, and the big shell-heap keeps some o' the wind off a little house her father took the trouble to build when he was a young man. They said there was an old house built o' logs there before that, with a kind of natural cellar in the rock under it. He used to stay out there days to a time, and anchor a little sloop he had, and dig clams to fill it, and sail up to Portland. They said the dealers always gave him an extra price, the clams were so noted. Joanna used to go out and stay with him. They were always great companions, so she knew just what 't was out there. There was a few sheep that belonged to her brother an' her, but she bargained for him to come and get them on the edge o' cold weather. Yes, she desired him to come for the sheep; an' his wife thought perhaps Joanna'd return, but he said no, an' lo'ded the bo't with warm things an' what he thought she'd need through the winter. He come home with the sheep an' left the other things by the house, but she never so much as looked out o' the window. She done it for a penance. She must have wanted to see Edward by that time."

Mrs. Fosdick was fidgeting with eagerness to speak.

"Some thought the first cold snap would set her ashore, but she always remained," concluded Mrs. Todd soberly.

"Talk about the men not having any curiosity!" exclaimed Mrs. Fosdick scornfully. "Why, the waters round Shell-heap Island were white with sails all that fall. 'T was never called no great of a fishin'-ground before. Many of 'em made excuse to go ashore to get water at the spring; but at last she spoke to a bo't-load, very dignified and calm, and said that she'd like it better if they'd make a practice of getting water to Black Island or somewheres else and leave her alone, except in case of accident or trouble. But there was one man who had always set everything by her from a boy. He'd have married her if the other hadn't come about an' spoilt his chance, and he used to get close to the island, before light, on his way out fishin', and throw a little bundle 'way up the green slope front o' the house. His sister told me she happened to see, the first time, what a pretty choice he made o' useful things that a woman would feel lost without. He stood off fishin', and could see them in the grass all day, though sometimes she'd come out and walk right by them. There was other bo'ts near, out after mackerel. But early next morning his present was gone. He didn't presume too much, but once he took her a nice firkin o' things he got up to Portland, and when spring come he landed her a hen and chickens in a nice little coop. There was a good many old friends had Joanna on their minds."

"Yes," said Mrs. Todd, losing her sad reserve in the growing sympathy of these reminiscences. "How everybody used to notice whether there was smoke out of the chimney! The Black Island folks could see her with their spy-glass, and if they'd ever missed getting some sign o' life they'd have sent notice to her folks. But after the first year or two Joanna was more and more forgotten as an every-day charge. Folks lived very simple in those days, you know," she continued, as Mrs. Fosdick's knitting was taking much thought at the moment. "I expect there was always plenty of drift-wood thrown up, and a poor failin' patch of spruces covered all the north side of the island, so she always had something to burn. She was very fond of workin' in the garden ashore, and that first summer she began to till the little field out there, and raised a nice parcel o' potatoes. She could fish, o' course, and there was all her clams an' lobsters. You can always live well in any wild place by the sea when you'd starve to death up country, except 't was berry time. Joanna had berries out there, blackberries at least, and there was a few herbs in case she needed them. Mullein in great quantities and a plant o' wormwood I remember seeing once when I stayed there, long before she fled out to Shell-heap. Yes, I recall the wormwood, which is always a planted herb, so there must have been folks there before the Todds' day. A growin' bush makes the best gravestone; I expect that wormwood always stood for some-body's solemn monument. Catnip, too, is a very endurin' herb about an old place."

"But what I want to know is what she did for other things," interrupted Mrs. Fosdick. "Almiry, what did she do for clothin' when she needed to replenish, or risin' for her bread, or the piece-bag that no woman can live long without?"

"Or company," suggested Mrs. Todd. "Joanna was one that loved her friends. There must have been a terrible sight o' long winter evenin's that first year."

"There was her hens," suggested Mrs. Fosdick, after reviewing the melancholy situation. "She never wanted the sheep after that first season. There wa'n't no proper pasture for sheep after the June grass was past, and she ascertained the fact and couldn't bear to see them suffer; but the chickens done well. I remember sailin' by one spring afternoon, an' seein' the coops out front o' the house in the sun. How long was it before you went out with the minister? You were the first ones that ever really got ashore to see Joanna."

I had been reflecting upon a state of society which admitted such personal freedom and a voluntary hermitage. There was something mediæval in the behavior of poor Joanna Todd under a disappointment of the heart. The two women had drawn closer together, and were talking on, quite unconscious of a listener.

"Poor Joanna!" said Mrs. Todd again, and sadly shook her head as if there were things one could not speak about.

"I called her a great fool," declared Mrs. Fosdick, with spirit, "but I pitied her then, and I pity her far more now. Some other minister would have been a great help to her,—one that preached self-forgetfulness and doin' for others to cure our own ills; but Parson Dimmick was a vague person, well meanin', but very numb in his feelin's. I don't suppose at that troubled time Joanna could think of any way to mend her troubles except to run off and hide."

"Mother used to say she didn't see how Joanna lived without having nobody to do for, getting her own meals and tending her own poor self day in an' day out," said Mrs. Todd sorrowfully.

"There was the hens," repeated Mrs. Fosdick kindly. "I expect she soon came to makin' folks o' them. No, I never went to work to blame Joanna, as some did. She was full o' feeling, and her troubles hurt her more than she could bear. I see it all now as I couldn't when I was young."

"I suppose in old times they had their shut-up convents for just such folks," said Mrs. Todd, as if she and her friend had disagreed about Joanna once, and were now in happy harmony. She seemed to speak with new openness and freedom. "Oh yes, I was only too pleased when the Reverend Mr. Dimmick invited me to go out with him. He hadn't been very long in the place when Joanna left home and friends. 'T was one day that next summer after she went, and I had been married early in the spring. He felt that he ought to go out and visit her. She was a member of the church, and might wish to have him consider her spiritual state. I wa'n't so sure o' that, but I always liked Joanna, and I'd come to be her cousin by marriage. Nathan an' I had conversed about goin' out to pay her a visit, but he got his chance to sail sooner'n he expected. He always thought everything of her, and last time he come home, knowing nothing of her change, he brought her a beautiful coral pin from a port he'd touched at somewheres up the Mediterranean. So I wrapped the little box in a nice piece of paper and put it in my pocket, and picked her a bunch of fresh lemon balm, and off we started."

Mrs. Fosdick laughed. "I remember hearin' about your trials on the v'y'ge," she said.

"Why, yes," continued Mrs. Todd in her company manner. "I picked her the balm, an' we started. Why, yes, Susan, the minister liked to have cost me my life that day. He would fasten the sheet, though I advised against it. He said the rope was rough an' cut his hand. There was a fresh breeze, an' he went on talking rather high flown, an' I felt some interested. All of a sudden there come up a gust, and he give a screech and stood right up and called for help, 'way out there to sea. I knocked him right over into the bottom o' the bo't, getting by to catch hold of the sheet an' untie it. He wasn't but a little man; I helped him right up after the squall passed, and made a handsome apology to him, but he did act kind o' offended."

"I do think they ought not to settle them landlocked folks in parishes where they're liable to be on the water," insisted Mrs. Fosdick. "Think of the families in our parish that was scattered all about the bay, and what a sight o' sails you used to see, in Mr. Dimmick's day, standing across to the mainland on a pleasant Sunday morning, filled with church-going folks, all sure to want him some time or other! You couldn't find no doctor that would stand up in the boat and screech if a flaw struck her."

"Old Dr. Bennett had a beautiful sailboat, didn't he?" responded Mrs. Todd. "And how well he used to brave the weather! Mother always said that in time o' trouble that tall white sail used to look like an angel's wing comin' over the sea to them that was in pain. Well, there's a difference in gifts. Mr. Dimmick was not without light."

"'T was light o' the moon, then," snapped Mrs. Fosdick; "he was pompous enough, but I never could remember a single word he said. There, go on, Mis' Todd; I forget a great deal about that day you went to see poor Joanna."

"I felt she saw us coming, and knew us a great way off; yes, I seemed to feel it within me," said our friend, laying down her

knitting. "I kept my seat, and took the bo't in shore without saying
a word; there was a short channel that I was sure Mr. Dimmick
wasn't acquainted with, and the tide was very low. She never came
out to warn us off nor anything, and I thought, as I hauled the bo't
up on a wave and let the Reverend Mr. Dimmick step out, that it
was somethin' gained to be safe ashore. There was a little smoke
out o' the chimney o' Joanna's house, and it did look sort of homelike and pleasant with wild mornin'-glory vines trained up; an' there
was a plot o' flowers under the front window, portulacas and things.
I believe she'd made a garden once, when she was stopping there
with her father, and some things must have seeded in. It looked
as if she might have gone over to the other side of the island. 'T
was neat and pretty all about the house, and a lovely day in July.
We walked up from the beach together very sedate, and I felt for
poor Nathan's little pin to see if 't was safe in my dress pocket.
All of a sudden Joanna come right to the fore door and stood there,
not sayin' a word."

14   The Hermitage

My companions and I had been so intent upon the subject of the
conversation that we had not heard any one open the gate, but at
this moment, above the noise of the rain, we heard a loud knocking.
We were all startled as we sat by the fire, and Mrs. Todd rose
hastily and went to answer the call, leaving her rocking-chair in
violent motion. Mrs. Fosdick and I heard an anxious voice at the
door speaking of a sick child, and Mrs. Todd's kind, motherly voice
inviting the messenger in: then we waited in silence. There was a
sound of heavy dropping of rain from the eaves, and the distant
roar and undertone of the sea. My thoughts flew back to the lonely
woman on her outer island; what separation from humankind she
must have felt, what terror and sadness, even in a summer storm
like this!

"You send right after the doctor if she ain't better in half an
hour," said Mrs. Todd to her worried customer as they parted; and
I felt a warm sense of comfort in the evident resources of even so
small a neighborhood, but for the poor hermit Joanna there was
no neighbor on a winter night.

"How did she look?" demanded Mrs. Fosdick, without preface, as our large hostess returned to the little room with a mist about her from standing long in the wet doorway, and the sudden draught of her coming beat out the smoke and flame from the Franklin stove. "How did poor Joanna look?"

"She was the same as ever, except I thought she looked smaller," answered Mrs. Todd after thinking a moment; perhaps it was only a last considering thought about her patient. "Yes, she was just the same, and looked very nice, Joanna did. I had been married since she left home, an' she treated me like her own folks. I expected she'd look strange, with her hair turned gray in a night or somethin', but she wore a pretty gingham dress I'd often seen her wear before she went away; she must have kept it nice for best in the afternoons. She always had beautiful, quiet manners. I remember she waited till we were close to her, and then kissed me real affectionate, and inquired for Nathan before she shook hands with the minister, and then she invited us both in. 'T was the same little house her father had built him when he was a bachelor, with one livin'-room, and a little mite of a bedroom out of it where she slept, but 't was neat as a ship's cabin. There was some old chairs, an' a seat made of a long box that might have held boat tackle an' things to lock up in his fishin' days, and a good enough stove so anybody could cook and keep warm in cold weather. I went over once from home and stayed 'most a week with Joanna when we was girls, and those young happy days rose up before me. Her father was busy all day fishin' or clammin'; he was one o' the pleasantest men in the world, but Joanna's mother had the grim streak, and never knew what 't was to be happy. The first minute my eyes fell upon Joanna's face that day I saw how she had grown to look like Mis' Todd. 'T was the mother right over again."

"Oh dear me!" said Mrs. Fosdick.

"Joanna had done one thing very pretty. There was a little piece o' swamp on the island where good rushes grew plenty, and she'd gathered 'em, and braided some beautiful mats for the floor and a thick cushion for the long bunk. She'd showed a good deal of invention; you see there was a nice chance to pick up pieces o' wood and boards that drove ashore, and she'd made good use o' what she found. There wasn't no clock, but she had a few dishes on a shelf, and flowers set about in shells fixed to the walls, so it did look sort of homelike, though so lonely and poor. I couldn't keep the tears out o' my eyes, I felt so sad. I said to myself, I must get mother to come over an' see Joanna; the love in mother's heart would warm her, an' she might be able to advise."

"Oh no, Joanna was dreadful stern," said Mrs. Fosdick.

"We were all settin' down very proper, but Joanna would keep stealin' glances at me as if she was glad I come. She had but little to say; she was real polite an' gentle, and yet forbiddin'. The minister found it hard," confessed Mrs. Todd; "he got embarrassed, an' when he put on his authority and asked her if she felt to enjoy religion in her present situation, an' she replied that she must be excused from answerin', I thought I should fly. She might have made it easier for him; after all, he was the minister and had taken some trouble to come out, though 't was kind of cold an' unfeelin' the way he inquired. I thought he might have seen the little old Bible a-layin' on the shelf close by him, an' I wished he knew enough to just lay his hand on it an' read somethin' kind an' fatherly 'stead of accusin' her, an' then given poor Joanna his blessin' with the hope she might be led to comfort. He did offer prayer, but 't was all about hearin' the voice o' God out o' the whirlwind; and I thought while he was goin' on that anybody that had spent the long cold winter all alone out on Shell-heap Island knew a good deal more about those things than he did. I got so provoked I opened my eyes and stared right at him.

"She didn't take no notice, she kep' a nice respectful manner towards him, and when there come a pause she asked if he had any interest about the old Indian remains, and took down some queer stone gouges and hammers off of one of her shelves and showed them to him same's if he was a boy. He remarked that he'd like to walk over an' see the shell-heap; so she went right to the door and pointed him the way. I see then that she'd made her some kind o' sandal-shoes out o' the fine rushes to wear on her feet; she stepped light an' nice in 'em as shoes."

Mrs. Fosdick leaned back in her rocking-chair and gave a heavy sigh.

"I didn't move at first, but I'd held out just as long as I could," said Mrs. Todd, whose voice trembled a little. "When Joanna returned from the door, an' I could see that man's stupid back departin' among the wild rose bushes, I just ran to her an' caught her in my arms. I wasn't so big as I be now, and she was older than me, but I hugged her tight, just as if she was a child. 'Oh, Joanna dear,' I says, 'won't you come ashore an' live 'long o' me at the Landin', or go over to Green Island to mother's when winter comes? Nobody shall trouble you, an' mother finds it hard bein' alone. I can't bear to leave you here'—and I burst right out crying. I'd had my own trials, young as I was, an' she knew it. Oh, I did entreat her; yes, I entreated Joanna."

"What did she say then?" asked Mrs. Fosdick, much moved.

"She looked the same way, sad an' remote through it all," said Mrs. Todd mournfully. "She took hold of my hand, and we sat down close together; 't was as if she turned round an' made a child of me. 'I haven't got no right to live with folks no more,' she said. 'You must never ask me again, Almiry: I've done the only thing I could do, and I've made my choice. I feel a great comfort in your kindness, but I don't deserve it. I have committed the unpardonable sin; you don't understand,' says she humbly. 'I was in great wrath and trouble, and my thoughts was so wicked towards God that I can't expect ever to be forgiven. I have come to know what it is to have patience, but I have lost my hope. You must tell those that ask how 't is with me,' she said, 'an' tell them I want to be alone.' I couldn't speak; no, there wa'n't anything I could say, she seemed so above everything common. I was a good deal younger then than I be now, and I got Nathan's little coral pin out o' my pocket and put it into her hand; and when she saw it and I told her where it come from, her face did really light up for a minute, sort of bright an' pleasant. 'Nathan an' I was always good friends; I'm glad he don't think hard of me,' says she. 'I want you to have it, Almiry, an' wear it for love o' both o' us,' and she handed it back to me. 'You give my love to Nathan,—he's a dear good man,' she said; 'an' tell your mother, if I should be sick she mustn't wish I could get well, but I want her to be the one to come.' Then she seemed to have said all she wanted to, as if she was done with the world, and we sat there a few minutes longer together. It was real sweet and quiet except for a good many birds and the sea rollin' up on the beach; but at last she rose, an' I did too, and she kissed me and held my hand in hers a minute, as if to say good-by; then she turned and went right away out o' the door and disappeared.

"The minister come back pretty soon, and I told him I was all ready, and we started down to the bo't. He had picked up some round stones and things and was carrying them in his pocket-handkerchief; an' he sat down amidships without making any question, and let me take the rudder an' work the bo't, an' made no remarks for some time, until we sort of eased it off speaking of the weather, an' subjects that arose as we skirted Black Island, where two or three families lived belongin' to the parish. He preached next Sabbath as usual, somethin' high soundin' about the creation, and I couldn't help thinkin' he might never get no further; he seemed to know no remedies, but he had a great use of words."

Mrs. Fosdick sighed again. "Hearin' you tell about Joanna brings the time right back as if 't was yesterday," she said. "Yes, she was one o' them poor things that talked about the great sin; we don't seem to hear nothing about the unpardonable sin now, but you may say 't was not uncommon then."

"I expect that if it had been in these days, such a person would be plagued to death with idle folks," continued Mrs. Todd, after a long pause. "As it was, nobody trespassed on her; all the folks about the bay respected her an' her feelings; but as time wore on, after you left here, one after another ventured to make occasion to put somethin' ashore for her if they went that way. I know mother used to go to see her sometimes, and send William over now and then with something fresh an' nice from the farm. There is a point on the sheltered side where you can lay a boat close to shore an' land anything safe on the turf out o' reach o' the water. There were one or two others, old folks, that she would see, and now an' then she'd hail a passin' boat an' ask for somethin'; and mother got her to promise that she would make some sign to the Black Island folks if she wanted help. I never saw her myself to speak to after that day."

"I expect nowadays, if such a thing happened, she'd have gone out West to her uncle's folks or up to Massachusetts and had a change, an' come home good as new. The world's bigger an' freer than it used to be," urged Mrs. Fosdick.

"No," said her friend. " 'T is like bad eyesight, the mind of such a person: if your eyes don't see right there may be a remedy, but there's no kind of glasses to remedy the mind. No, Joanna was Joanna, and there she lays on her island where she lived and did her poor penance. She told mother the day she was dyin' that she always used to want to be fetched inshore when it come to the last; but she'd thought it over, and desired to be laid on the island, if 't was thought right. So the funeral was out there, a Saturday afternoon in September. 'T was a pretty day, and there wa'n't hardly a boat on the coast within twenty miles that didn't head for Shell-heap cram-full o' folks, an' all real respectful, same's if she'd always stayed ashore and held her friends. Some went out o' mere curiosity, I don't doubt,—there's always such to every funeral; but most had real feelin', and went purpose to show it. She'd got most o' the wild sparrows as tame as could be, livin' out there so long among 'em, and one flew right in and lit on the coffin an' begun to sing while Mr. Dimmick was speakin'. He was put out by it, an' acted as if he didn't know whether to stop or go on. I may have been prejudiced, but I wa'n't the only one thought the poor little bird done the best of the two."

"What became o' the man that treated her so, did you ever hear?" asked Mrs. Fosdick. "I know he lived up to Massachusetts for a while. Somebody who came from the same place told me that he was in trade there an' doin' very well, but that was years ago."

"I never heard anything more than that; he went to the war in one o' the early rigiments. No, I never heard any more of him," answered Mrs. Todd. "Joanna was another sort of person, and perhaps he showed good judgment in marryin' somebody else, if only he'd behaved straightforward and manly. He was a shifty-eyed, coaxin' sort of man, that got what he wanted out o' folks, an' only gave when he wanted to buy, made friends easy and lost 'em without knowin' the difference. She'd had a piece o' work tryin' to make him walk accordin' to her right ideas, but she'd have had too much variety ever to fall into a melancholy. Some is meant to be the Joannas in this world, an' 't was her poor lot."

15   On Shell-heap Island

Some time after Mrs. Fosdick's visit was over and we had returned to our former quietness, I was out sailing alone with Captain Bowden in his large boat. We were taking the crooked northeasterly channel seaward, and were well out from shore while it was still early in the afternoon. I found myself presently among some un-

familiar islands, and suddenly remembered the story of poor
Joanna. There is something in the fact of a hermitage that cannot
fail to touch the imagination; the recluses are a sad kindred, but
they are never commonplace. Mrs. Todd had truly said that Joanna
was like one of the saints in the desert; the loneliness of sorrow
will forever keep alive their sad succession.

"Where is Shell-heap Island!" I asked eagerly.

"You see Shell-heap now, layin' 'way out beyond Black Island
there," answered the captain, pointing with outstretched arm as he
stood, and holding the rudder with his knee.

"I should like very much to go there," said I, and the captain,
without comment, changed his course a little more to the eastward
and let the reef out of his mainsail.

"I don't know's we can make an easy landin' for ye," he remarked
doubtfully. "May get your feet wet; bad place to land. Trouble is
I ought to have brought a tagboat; but they clutch on to the water
so, an' I do love to sail free. This gre't boat gets easy bothered
with anything trailin'. 'T ain't breakin' much on the meetin'-house
ledges; guess I can fetch in to Shell-heap."

"How long is it since Miss Joanna Todd died?" I asked, partly
by way of explanation.

"Twenty-two years come September," answered the captain,
after reflection. "She died the same year my oldest boy was born,
an' the town house was burnt over to the Port. I didn't know but
you merely wanted to hunt for some o' them Indian relics. Long
's you want to see where Joanna lived—No, 't aint' breakin' over
the ledges; we'll manage to fetch across the shoals somehow, 't is
such a distance to go 'way round, and tide's a-risin'," he ended
hopefully, and we sailed steadily on, the captain speechless with
intent watching of a difficult course, until the small island with its
low whitish promontory lay in full view before us under the bright
afternoon sun.

The month was August, and I had seen the color of the islands
change from the fresh green of June to a sunburnt brown that made
them look like stone, except where the dark green of the spruces
and fir balsam kept the tint that even winter storms might deepen,
but not fade. The few wind-bent trees on Shell-heap Island were
mostly dead and gray, but there were some low-growing bushes,
and a stripe of light green ran along just above the shore, which I

knew to be wild morning-glories. As we came close I could see
the high stone walls of a small square field, though there were no
sheep left to assail it; and below, there was a little harbor-like cove
where Captain Bowden was boldly running the great boat in to
seek a landing-place. There was a crooked channel of deep water
which led close up against the shore.

"There, you hold fast for'ard there, an' wait for her to lift on
the wave. You'll make a good landin' if you're smart; right on the
port-hand side!" the captain called excitedly; and I, standing ready
with high ambition, seized my chance and leaped over to the grassy
bank.

"I'm beat if I ain't aground after all!" mourned the captain de-
spondently.

But I could reach the bowsprit, and he pushed with the boat-
hook, while the wind veered round a little as if on purpose and
helped with the sail; so presently the boat was free and began to
drift out from shore.

"Used to call this p'int Joanna's wharf privilege, but 't has worn
away in the weather since her time. I thought one or two bumps
wouldn't hurt us none,—paint's got to be renewed, anyway,—but
I never thought she'd tetch. I figured on shyin' by," the captain
apologized. "She's too gre't a boat to handle well in here; but I
used to sort of shy by in Joanna's day, an' cast a little somethin'
ashore—some apples or a couple o' pears if I had 'em—on the
grass, where she'd be sure to see."

I stood watching while Captain Bowden cleverly found his way
back to deeper water. "You needn't make no haste," he called to
me; "I'll keep within call. Joanna lays right up there in the far
corner o' the field. There used to be a path led to the place. I
always knew her well. I was out here to the funeral."

I found the path; it was touching to discover that this lonely spot
was not without its pilgrims. Later generations will know less and
less of Joanna herself, but there are paths trodden to the shrines
of solitude the world over,—the world cannot forget them, try as
it may; the feet of the young find them out because of curiosity
and dim foreboding, while the old bring hearts full of remembrance. This plain anchorite had been one of those whom sorrow
made too lonely to brave the sight of men, too timid to front the
simple world she knew, yet valiant enough to live alone with her

poor insistent human nature and the calms and passions of the sea and sky.

The birds were flying all about the field; they fluttered up out of the grass at my feet as I walked along, so tame that I liked to think they kept some happy tradition from summer to summer of the safety of nests and good fellowship of mankind. Poor Joanna's house was gone except the stones of its foundations, and there was little trace of her flower garden except a single faded sprig of much-enduring French pinks, which a great bee and a yellow butterfly were befriending together. I drank at the spring, and thought that now and then some one would follow me from the busy, hard-worked, and simple-thoughted countryside of the mainland, which lay dim and dreamlike in the August haze, as Joanna must have watched it many a day. There was the world, and here was she with eternity well begun. In the life of each of us, I said to myself, there is a place remote and islanded, and given to endless regret or secret happiness; we are each the uncompanioned hermit and recluse of an hour or a day; we understand our fellows of the cell to whatever age of history they may belong.

But as I stood alone on the island, in the sea-breeze, suddenly there came a sound of distant voices; gay voices and laughter from a pleasure-boat that was going seaward full of boys and girls. I knew, as if she had told me, that poor Joanna must have heard the like on many and many a summer afternoon, and must have welcomed the good cheer in spite of hopelessness and winter weather, and all the sorrow and disappointment in the world.

16   *The Great Expedition*

Mrs. Todd never by any chance gave warning over night of her great projects and adventures by sea and land. She first came to an understanding with the primal forces of nature, and never trusted to any preliminary promise of good weather, but examined the day for herself in its infancy. Then, if the stars were propitious, and the wind blew from a quarter of good inheritance whence no surprises of sea-turns or southwest sultriness might be feared, long before I was fairly awake I used to hear a rustle and knocking like a great mouse in the walls, and an impatient tread on the steep garret stairs that led to Mrs. Todd's chief place of storage. She went and came as if she had already started on her expedition with utmost haste and kept returning for something that was forgotten. When I appeared in quest of my breakfast, she would be absent-minded and sparing of speech, as if I had displeased her, and she was now, by main force of principle, holding herself back from altercation and strife of tongues.

These signs of a change became familiar to me in the course of time, and Mrs. Todd hardly noticed some plain proofs of divination one August morning when I said, without preface, that I had just seen the Beggs' best chaise go by, and that we should have to take the grocery. Mrs. Todd was alert in a moment.

"There! I might have known!" she exclaimed. "It's the 15th of August, when he goes and gets his money. He heired an annuity from an uncle o' his on his mother's side. I understood the uncle said none o' Sam Begg's wife's folks should make free with it, so after Sam's gone it'll all be past an' spent, like last summer. That's what Sam prospers on now, if you can call it prosperin'. Yes, I might have known. 'T is the 15th o' August with him, an' he gener'ly stops to dinner with a cousin's widow on the way home. Feb'uary an' August is the times. Takes him 'bout all day to go an' come."

I heard this explanation with interest. The tone of Mrs. Todd's voice was complaining at the last.

"I like the grocery just as well as the chaise," I hastened to say, referring to a long-bodied high wagon with a canopy-top, like an attenuated four-posted bedstead on wheels, in which we sometimes journeyed. "We can put things in behind—roots and flowers and raspberries, or anything you are going after—much better than if we had the chaise."

Mrs. Todd looked stony and unwilling. "I counted upon the chaise," she said, turning her back to me, and roughly pushing back all the quiet tumblers on the cupboard shelf as if they had been impertinent. "Yes, I desired the chaise for once. I ain't goin' berryin' nor to fetch home no more wilted vegetation this year. Season's about past, except for a poor few o' late things," she added in a milder tone. "I'm goin' up country. No, I ain't intendin' to go berryin'. I've been plottin' for it the past fortnight and hopin' for a good day."

"Would you like to have me go too?" I asked frankly, but not without a humble fear that I might have mistaken the purpose of this latest plan.

"Oh certain, dear!" answered my friend affectionately. "Oh no, I never thought o' any one else for comp'ny, if it's convenient for you, long's poor mother ain't come. I ain't nothin' like so handy with a conveyance as I be with a good bo't. Comes o' my early bringing-up. I expect we've got to make that great high wagon do. The tires want settin' and 't is all loose-jointed, so I can hear it shackle the other side o' the ridge. We'll put the basket in front. I ain't goin' to have it bouncin' an' twirlin' all the way. Why, I've been makin' some nice hearts and rounds to carry."

These were signs of high festivity, and my interest deepened moment by moment.

"I'll go down to the Beggs' and get the horse just as soon as I finish my breakfast," said I. "Then we can start whenever you are ready."

Mrs. Todd looked cloudy again. "I don't know but you look nice enough to go just as you be," she suggested doubtfully. "No, you wouldn't want to wear that pretty blue dress o' yourn 'way up country. 'T ain't dusty now, but it may be comin' home. No, I expect you'd rather not wear that and the other hat."

"Oh yes, I shouldn't think of wearing these clothes," said I, with sudden illumination. "Why, if we're going up country and are likely to see some of your friends, I'll put on my blue dress, and you must wear your watch; I am not going at all if you mean to wear the big hat."

"Now you're behavin' pretty," responded Mrs. Todd, with a gay toss of her head and a cheerful smile, as she came across the room, bringing a saucerful of wild raspberries, a pretty piece of salvage from supper-time. "I was cast down when I see you come to breakfast. I didn't think 't was just what you'd select to wear to the reunion, where you're goin' to meet everybody."

"What reunion do you mean?" I asked, not without amazement. "Not the Bowden Family's? I thought that was going to take place in September."

"To-day's the day. They sent word the middle o' the week. I thought you might have heard of it. Yes, they changed the day. I been thinkin' we'd talk it over, but you never can tell beforehand how it's goin' to be, and 't ain't worth while to wear a day all out before it comes." Mrs. Todd gave no place to the pleasures of anticipation, but she spoke like the oracle that she was. "I wish mother was here to go," she continued sadly. "I did look for her last night, and I couldn't keep back the tears when the dark really fell and she wa'n't here, she does so enjoy a great occasion. If William had a mite o' snap an' ambition, he'd take the lead at such a time. Mother likes variety, and there ain't but a few nice opportunities 'round here, an' them she has to miss 'less she contrives to get ashore to me. I do re'lly hate to go to the reunion without mother, an' 't is a beautiful day; everybody'll be asking where she is. Once she'd have got here anyway. Poor mother's beginnin' to feel her age."

"Why, there's your mother now!" I exlaimed with joy, I was so glad to see the dear old soul again. "I hear her voice at the gate." But Mrs. Todd was out of the door before me.

There, sure enough, stood Mrs. Blackett, who must have left Green Island before daylight. She had climbed the steep road from the water-side so eagerly that she was out of breath, and was standing by the garden fence to rest. She held an old-fashioned brown wicker cap-basket in her hand, as if visiting were a thing of every day, and looked up at us as pleased and triumphant as a child.

"Oh, what a poor, plain garden! Hardly a flower in it except your bush o' balm!" she said. "But you do keep your garden neat, Almiry. Are you both well, an' goin' up country with me?" She came a step or two closer to meet us, with quaint politeness and quite as delightful as if she were at home. She dropped a quick little curtsey before Mrs. Todd.

"There, mother, what a girl you be! I am so pleased! I was just bewailin' you," said the daughter, with unwonted feeling. "I was just bewailin' you, I was so disappointed, an' I kep' myself awake a good piece o' the night scoldin' poor William. I watched for the boat till I was ready to shed tears yisterday, and when 't was comin' dark I kep' making errands out to the gate an' down the road to see if you wa'n't in the doldrums somewhere down the bay."

"There was a head wind, as you know," said Mrs. Blackett, giving me the cap-basket, and holding my hand affectionately as we walked up the clean-swept path to the door. "I was partly ready to come, but dear William said I should be all tired out and might get cold, havin' to beat all the way in. So we give it up, and set down and spent the evenin' together. It was a little rough and windy outside, and I guess 't was better judgment; we went to bed very early and made a good start just at daylight. It's been a lovely mornin' on the water. William thought he'd better fetch across beyond Bird Rocks, rowin' the greater part o' the way; then we sailed from there right over to the Landin', makin' only one tack. William'll be in again for me to-morrow, so I can come back here an' rest me over night, an' go to meetin' to-morrow, and have a nice, good visit."

"She was just havin' her breakfast," said Mrs. Todd, who had listened eagerly to the long explanation without a word of disapproval, while her face shone more and more with joy. "You just sit right down an' have a cup of tea and rest you while we make our preparations. Oh, I am so gratified to think you've come! Yes, she was just havin' her breakfast, and we were speakin' of you. Where's William?"

"He went right back; he said he expected some schooners in about noon after bait, but he'll come an' have his dinner with us to-morrow, unless it rains; then next day. I laid his best things out all ready," explained Mrs. Blackett, a little anxiously. "This wind will serve him nice all the way home. Yes, I will take a cup of tea, dear,—a cup of tea is always good; and then I'll rest a minute and be all ready to start."

"I do feel condemned for havin' such hard thoughts o' William," openly confessed Mrs. Todd. She stood before us so large and serious that we both laughed and could not find it in our hearts to convict so rueful a culprit. "He shall have a good dinner to-morrow, if it can be got, and I shall be real glad to see William," the confession ended handsomely, while Mrs. Blackett smiled approval and made haste to praise the tea. Then I hurried away to make sure of the grocery wagon. Whatever might be the good of the reunion, I was going to have the pleasure and delight of a day in Mrs. Blackett's company, not to speak of Mrs. Todd's.

The early morning breeze was still blowing, and the warm, sunshiny air was of some ethereal northern sort, with a cool freshness as if it came over new-fallen snow. The world was filled with a fragrance of fir-balsam and the faintest flavor of seaweed from the ledges, bare and brown at low tide in the little harbor. It was so

still and so early that the village was but half awake. I could hear
no voices but those of the birds, small and great,—the constant
song sparrows, the clink of a yellow-hammer over in the woods,
and the far conversation of some deliberate crows. I saw William
Blackett's escaping sail already far from land, and Captain Littlepage was sitting behind his closed window as I passed by, watching
for some one who never came. I tried to speak to him, but he did
not see me. There was a patient look on the old man's face, as if
the world were a great mistake and he had nobody with whom to
speak his own language or find companionship.

17 *A Country Road*

Whatever doubts and anxieties I may have had about the incon-
venience of Beggs' high wagon for a person of Mrs. Blackett's age
and shortness, they were happily overcome by the aid of a chair
and her own valiant spirit. Mrs. Todd bestowed great care upon
seating us as if we were taking passage by boat, but she finally
pronounced that we were properly trimmed. When we had gone
only a little way up the hill she remembered that she had left the
house door wide open, though the large key was safe in her pocket.
I offered to run back, but my offer was met with lofty scorn, and
we lightly dismissed the matter from our minds, until two or three
miles further on we met the doctor, and Mrs. Todd asked him to
stop and ask her nearest neighbor to step over and close the door
if the dust seemed to blow in the afternoon.

"She'll be there in her kitchen; she'll hear you the minute you
call; 't won't give you no delay," said Mrs. Todd to the doctor.
"Yes, Mis' Dennett's right there, with the windows all open. It
isn't as if my fore door opened right on the road, anyway." At
which proof of composure Mrs. Blackett smiled wisely at me.

The doctor seemed delighted to see our guest; they were evidently the warmest friends, and I saw a look of affectionate confidence in their eyes. The good man left his carriage to speak to
us, but as he took Mrs. Blackett's hand he held it a moment, and,
as if merely from force of habit, felt her pulse as they talked; then
to my delight he gave the firm old wrist a commending pat.

"You're wearing well: good for another ten years at this rate,"
he assured her cheerfully, and she smiled back. "I like to keep a

strict account of my old stand-bys," and he turned to me. "Don't you let Mrs. Todd overdo to-day,—old folks like her are apt to be thoughtless;" and then we all laughed, and, parting, went our ways gayly.

"I suppose he puts up with your rivalry the same as ever?" asked Mrs. Blackett. "You and he are as friendly as ever, I see, Almiry," and Almira sagely nodded.

"He's got too many long routes now to stop to 'tend to all his door patients," she said, "especially them that takes pleasure in talkin' themselves over. The doctor and me have got to be kind of partners; he's gone a good deal, far an' wide. Looked tired, didn't he? I shall have to advise with him an' get him off for a good rest. He'll take the big boat from Rockland an' go off up to Boston an' mouse round among the other doctors, once in two or three years, and come home fresh as a boy. I guess they think consider'ble of him up there." Mrs. Todd shook the reins and reached determinedly for the whip, as if she were compelling public opinion.

Whatever energy and spirit the white horse had to begin with were soon exhausted by the steep hills and his discernment of a long expedition ahead. We toiled slowly along. Mrs. Blackett and I sat together, and Mrs. Todd sat alone in front with much majesty and the large basket of provisions. Part of the way the road was shaded by thick woods, but we also passed one farmhouse after another on the high uplands, which we all three regarded with deep interest, the house itself and the barns and garden-spots and poultry all having to suffer an inspection of the shrewdest sort. This was a highway quite new to me; in fact, most of my journeys with Mrs. Todd had been made afoot and between the roads, in open pasturelands. My friends stopped several times for brief dooryard visits, and made so many promises of stopping again on the way home that I began to wonder how long the expedition would last. I had often noticed how warmly Mrs. Todd was greeted by her friends, but it was hardly to be compared to the feeling now shown toward Mrs. Blackett. A look of delight came to the faces of those who recognized the plain, dear old figure beside me; one revelation after another was made of the constant interest and intercourse that had linked the far island and these scattered farms into a golden chain of love and dependence.

"Now, we mustn't stop again if we can help it," insisted Mrs.

Todd at last. "You'll get tired, mother, and you'll think the less o' reunions. We can visit along here any day. There, if they ain't frying doughnuts in this next house, too! These are new folks, you know, from over St. George way; they took this old Talcot farm last year. 'T is the best water on the road, and the check-rein's come undone—yes, we'd best delay a little and water the horse."

We stopped, and seeing a party of pleasure-seekers in holiday attire, the thin, anxious mistress of the farmhouse came out with wistful sympathy to hear what news we might have to give. Mrs. Blackett first spied her at the half-closed door, and asked with such cheerful directness if we were trespassing that, after a few words, she went back to her kitchen and reappeared with a plateful of doughnuts.

"Entertainment for man and beast," announced Mrs. Todd with satisfaction. "Why, we've perceived there was new doughnuts all along the road, but you're the first that has treated us."

Our new acquaintance flushed with pleasure, but said nothing.

"They're very nice; you've had good luck with 'em," pronounced Mrs. Todd. "Yes, we've observed there was doughnuts all the way along; if one house is frying all the rest is; 't is so with a great many things."

"I don't suppose likely you're goin' up to the Bowden reunion?" asked the hostess as the white horse lifted his head and we were saying good-by.

"Why, yes," said Mrs. Blackett and Mrs. Todd and I, all together.

"I am connected with the family. Yes, I expect to be there this afternoon. I've been lookin' forward to it," she told us eagerly.

"We shall see you there. Come and sit with us if it's convenient," said dear Mrs. Blackett, and we drove away.

"I wonder who she was before she was married?" said Mrs. Todd, who was usually unerring in matters of genealogy. "She must have been one of that remote branch that lived down beyond Thomaston. We can find out this afternoon. I expect that the families'll march together, or be sorted out some way. I'm willing to own a relation that has such proper ideas of doughnuts."

"I seem to see the family looks," said Mrs. Blackett. "I wish we'd asked her name. She's a stranger, and I want to help make it pleasant for all such."

"She resembles Cousin Pa'lina Bowden about the forehead," said Mrs. Todd with decision.

We had just passed a piece of woodland that shaded the road, and come out to some open fields beyond, when Mrs. Todd suddenly reined in the horse as if somebody had stood on the roadside and stopped her. She even gave that quick reassuring nod of her head which was usually made to answer for a bow, but I discovered that she was looking eagerly at a tall ash-tree that grew just inside the field fence.

"I thought 't was goin' to do well," she said complacently as we went on again. "Last time I was up this way that tree was kind of drooping and discouraged. Grown trees act that way sometimes, same's folks; then they'll put right to it and strike their roots off into new ground and start all over again with real good courage. Ash-trees is very likely to have poor spells; they ain't got the resolution of other trees."

I listened hopefully for more; it was this peculiar wisdom that made one value Mrs. Todd's pleasant company.

"There's sometimes a good hearty tree growin' right out of the bare rock, out o' some crack that just holds the roots;" she went on to say, "right on the pitch o' one o' them bare stony hills where you can't seem to see a wheel-barrowful o' good earth in a place, but that tree'll keep a green top in the driest summer. You lay your ear down to the ground an' you'll hear a little stream runnin'. Every such tree has got its own livin' spring; there's folks made to match 'em."

I could not help turning to look at Mrs. Blackett, close beside me. Her hands were clasped placidly in their thin black woolen gloves, and she was looking at the flowery wayside as we went slowly along, with a pleased, expectant smile. I do not think she had heard a word about the trees.

"I just saw a nice plant o' elecampane growin' back there," she said presently to her daughter.

"I haven't got my mind on herbs today," responded Mrs. Todd, in the most matter-of-fact way. "I'm bent on seeing folks," and she shook the reins again.

I for one had no wish to hurry, it was so pleasant in the shady roads. The woods stood close to the road on the right; on the left were narrow fields and pastures where there were as many acres of spruces and pines as there were acres of bay and juniper and huckleberry, with a little turf between. When I thought we were in the heart of the inland country, we reached the top of a hill, and suddenly there lay spread out before us a wonderful great view of well-cleared fields that swept down to the wide water of a bay. Beyond this were distant shores like another country in the midday haze which half hid the hills beyond, and the far-away pale blue mountains on the northern horizon. There was a schooner with all sails set coming down the bay from a white village that was sprinkled on the shore, and there were many sailboats flitting about. It was a noble landscape, and my eyes, which had grown used to the narrow inspection of a shaded roadside, could hardly take it in.

"Why, it's the upper bay," said Mrs. Todd. "You can see 'way over into the town of Fessenden. Those farms 'way over there are all in Fessenden. Mother used to have a sister that lived up that shore. If we started as early's we could on a summer mornin', we couldn't get to her place from Green Island till late afternoon, even with a fair, steady breeze, and you had to strike the time just right so as to fetch up 'long o' the tide and land near the flood. 'T was ticklish business, an' we didn't visit back an' forth as much as mother desired. You have to go 'way down the co'st to Cold Spring Light an' round that long point,—up here's what they call the Back Shore."

"No, we were 'most always separated, my dear sister and me, after the first year she was married," said Mrs. Blackett. "We had our little families an' plenty o' cares. We were always lookin' forward to the time we could see each other more. Now and then she'd get out to the island for a few days while her husband'd go fishin'; and once he stopped with her an' two children, and made him some flakes right there and cured all his fish for winter. We did have a beautiful time together, sister an' me; she used to look back to it long's she lived.

"I do love to look over there where she used to live," Mrs. Blackett went on as we began to go down the hill. "It seems as if she must still be there, though she's long been gone. She loved their farm,—she didn't see how I got so used to our island; but somehow I was always happy from the first."

"Yes, it's very dull to me up among those slow farms," declared Mrs. Todd. "The snow troubles 'em in winter. They're all besieged

by winter, as you may say; 't is far better by the shore than up
among such places. I never thought I should like to live up
country."

"Why, just see the carriages ahead of us on the next rise!" exclaimed Mrs. Blackett. "There's going to be a great gathering, don't
you believe there is, Almiry? It hasn't seemed up to now as if
anybody was going but us. An' 't is such a beautiful day, with
yesterday cool and pleasant to work an' get ready, I shouldn't
wonder if everybody was there, even the slow ones like Phebe
Ann Brock."

Mrs. Blackett's eyes were bright with excitement, and even Mrs.
Todd showed remarkable enthusiasm. She hurried the horse and
caught up with the holiday-makers ahead. "There's all the Dep'-
fords goin', six in the wagon," she told us joyfully; "an Mis' Alva
Tilley's folks are now risin' the hill in their new carryall."

Mrs. Blackett pulled at the neat bow of her black bonnet-strings,
and tied them again with careful precision. "I believe your bonnet's
on a little sideways, dear," she advised Mrs. Todd as if she were
a child; but Mrs. Todd was too much occupied to pay proper heed.
We began to feel a new sense of gayety and of taking part in the
great occasion as we joined the little train.

18   The Bowden Reunion

It is very rare in country life, where high days and holidays are
few, that any occasion of general interest proves to be less than
great. Such is the hidden fire of enthusiasm in the New England
nature that, once given an outlet, it shines forth with almost vol-
canic light and heat. In quiet neighborhoods such inward force
does not waste itself upon those petty excitements of every day
that belong to cities, but when, at long intervals, the altars to
patriotism, to friendship, to the ties of kindred, are reared in our
familiar fields, then the fires glow, the flames come up as if from
the inexhaustible burning heart of the earth; the primal fires break
through the granite dust in which our souls are set. Each heart is
warm and every face shines with the ancient light. Such a day as
this has transfiguring powers, and easily makes friends of those
who have been cold-hearted, and gives to those who are dumb
their chance to speak, and lends some beauty to the plainest face.

"Oh, I expect I shall meet friends today that I haven't seen in a long while," said Mrs. Blackett with deep satisfaction. " 'T will bring out a good many of the old folks, 't is such a lovely day. I'm always glad not to have them disappointed."

"I guess likely the best of 'em'll be there," answered Mrs. Todd with gentle humor, stealing a glance at me. "There's one thing certain: there's nothing takes in this whole neighborhood like anything related to the Bowdens. Yes, I do feel that when you call upon the Bowdens you may expect most families to rise up between the Landing and the far end of the Back Cove. Those that aren't kin by blood are kin by marriage."

"There used to be an old story goin' about when I was a girl," said Mrs. Blackett, with much amusement. "There was a great many more Bowdens then than there are now, and the folks was all setting in meeting a dreadful hot Sunday afternoon, and a scatter-witted little bound girl came running to the meetin'-house door all out o' breath from somewheres in the neighborhood. 'Mis' Bowden, Mis' Bowden!' says she. 'Your baby's in a fit!' They used to tell that the whole congregation was up on its feet in a minute and right out into the aisles. All the Mis' Bowdens was setting right out for home; the minister stood there in the pulpit tryin' to keep sober, an' all at once he burst right out laughin'. He was a very nice man, they said, and he said he'd better give 'em the benediction, and they could hear the sermon next Sunday, so he kept it over. My mother was there, and she thought certain 't was me."

"None of our family was ever subject to fits," interrupted Mrs. Todd severely. "No, we never had fits, none of us, and 't was lucky we didn't 'way out there to Green Island. Now these folks right in front: dear sakes knows the bunches o' soothing catnip an' yarrow I've had to favor old Mis' Evins with dryin'! You can see it right in their expressions, all them Evins folks. There, just you look up to the crossroads, mother," she suddenly exclaimed. "See all the teams ahead of us. And oh, look down on the bay; yes, look down on the bay! See what a sight o' boats, all headin' for the Bowden place cove!"

"Oh, ain't it beautiful!" said Mrs. Blackett, with all the delight of a girl. She stood up in the high wagon to see everything, and when she sat down again she took fast hold of my hand.

"Hadn't you better urge the horse a little, Almiry?" she asked.

"He's had it easy as we came along, and he can rest when we get there. The others are some little ways ahead, and I don't want to lose a minute."

We watched the boats drop their sails one by one in the cove as we drove along the high land. The old Bowden house stood, low-storied and broad-roofed, in its green fields as if it were a motherly brown hen waiting for the flock that came straying toward it from every direction. The first Bowden settler had made his home there, and it was still the Bowden farm; five generations of sailors and farmers and soldiers had been its children. And presently Mrs. Blackett showed me the stone-walled burying-ground that stood like a little fort on a knoll overlooking the bay, but, as she said, there were plenty of scattered Bowdens who were not laid there,—some lost at sea, and some out West, and some who died in the war; most of the home graves were those of women.

We could see now that there were different footpaths from along shore and across country. In all these there were straggling processions walking in single file, like old illustrations of the Pilgrim's Progress. There was a crowd about the house as if huge bees were swarming in the lilac bushes. Beyond the fields and cove a higher point of land ran out into the bay, covered with woods which must have kept away much of the northwest wind in winter. Now there was a pleasant look of shade and shelter there for the great family meeting.

We hurried on our way, beginning to feel as if we were very late, and it was a great satisfaction at last to turn out of the stony highroad into a green lane shaded with old apple-trees. Mrs. Todd encouraged the horse until he fairly pranced with gayety as we drove round to the front of the house on the soft turf. There was an instant cry of rejoicing, and two or three persons ran toward us from the busy group.

"Why, dear Mis' Blackett!—here's Mis' Blackett!" I heard them say, as if it were pleasure enough for one day to have a sight of her. Mrs. Todd turned to me with a lovely look of triumph and self-forgetfulness. An elderly man who wore the look of a prosperous sea-captain put up both arms and lifted Mrs. Blackett down from the high wagon like a child, and kissed her with hearty affection. "I was master afraid she wouldn't be here," he said, looking at Mrs. Todd with a face like a happy sunburnt schoolboy, while everybody crowded round to give their welcome.

"Mother's always the queen," said Mrs. Todd. "Yes, they'll all make everything of mother; she'll have a lovely time to-day. I wouldn't have had her miss it, and there won't be a thing she'll ever regret, except to mourn because William wa'n't here."

Mrs. Blackett having been properly escorted to the house, Mrs. Todd received her own full share of honor, and some of the men, with a simple kindness that was the soul of chivalry, waited upon us and our baskets and led away the white horse. I already knew some of Mrs. Todd's friends and kindred, and felt like an adopted Bowden in this happy moment. It seemed to be enough for any one to have arrived by the same conveyance as Mrs. Blackett, who presently had her court inside the house, while Mrs. Todd, large, hospitable, and pre-eminent, was the centre of a rapidly increasing crowd about the lilac bushes. Small companies were continually coming up the long green slope from the water, and nearly all the boats had come to shore. I counted three or four that were baffled by the light breeze, but before long all the Bowdens, small and great, seemed to have assembled, and we started to go up to the grove across the field.

Out of the chattering crowd of noisy children, and large-waisted women whose best black dresses fell straight to the ground in generous folds, and sunburnt men who looked as serious as if it were town-meeting day, there suddenly came silence and order. I saw the straight, soldierly little figure of a man who bore a fine resemblance to Mrs. Blackett, and who appeared to marshal us with perfect ease. He was imperative enough, but with a grand military sort of courtesy, and bore himself with solemn dignity of importance. We were sorted out according to some clear design of his own, and stood as speechless as a troop to await his orders. Even the children were ready to march together, a pretty flock, and at the last moment Mrs. Blackett and a few distinguished companions, the ministers and those who were very old, came out of the house together and took their places. We ranked by fours, and even then we made a long procession.

There was a wide path mowed for us across the field, and, as we moved along, the birds flew up out of the thick second crop of clover, and the bees hummed as if it still were June. There was a flashing of white gulls over the water where the fleet of boats rode the low waves together in the cove, swaying their small masts as if they kept time to our steps. The plash of water could be heard faintly, yet still be heard; we might have been a company of ancient Greeks going to celebrate a victory, or to worship the god of harvests in the grove above. It was strangely moving to see this and to make part of it. The sky, the sea, have watched poor humanity at its rites so long; we were no more a New England family celebrating its own existence and simple progress; we carried the tokens and inheritance of all such households from which this had descended, and were only the latest of our line. We possessed the instincts of a far, forgotten childhood; I found myself thinking that we ought to be carrying green branches and singing as we went. So we came to the thick shaded grove still silent, and were set in our places by the straight trees that swayed together and let sunshine through here and there like a single golden leaf that flickered down, vanishing in the cool shade.

The grove was so large that the great family looked far smaller than it had in the open field; there was a thick growth of dark pines and firs with an occasional maple or oak that gave a gleam of color like a bright window in the great roof. On three sides we could see the water, shining behind the tree-trunks, and feel the cool salt breeze that began to come up with the tide just as the day reached its highest point of heat. We could see the green sunlit field we had just crossed as if we looked out at it from a dark room, and the old house and its lilacs standing placidly in the sun, and the great barn with a stockade of carriages from which two or three care-taking men who had lingered were coming across the field together. Mrs. Todd had taken off her warm gloves and looked the picture of content.

"There!" she exclaimed. "I've always meant to have you see this place, but I never looked for such a beautiful opportunity— weather an' occasion both made to match. Yes, it suits me: I don't ask no more. I want to know if you saw mother walkin' at the head! It choked me right up to see mother at the head, walkin' with the ministers," and Mrs. Todd turned away to hide the feelings she could not instantly control.

"Who was the marshal?" I hastened to ask. "Was he an old soldier?"

"Don't he do well?" answered Mrs. Todd with satisfaction.

"He don't often have such a chance to show off his gifts," said Mrs. Caplin, a friend from the Landing who had joined us. "That's Sant Bowden; he always takes the lead, such days. Good for nothing else most o' his time; trouble is, he"—

I turned with interest to hear the worst. Mrs. Caplin's tone was both zealous and impressive.

"Stim'lates," she explained scornfully.

"No, Santin never was in the war," said Mrs. Todd with lofty indifference. "It was a cause of real distress to him. He kep' enlistin', and traveled far an' wide about here, an' even took the bo't and went to Boston to volunteer: but he ain't a sound man, an' they wouldn't have him. They say he knows all their tactics, an' can tell all about the battle o' Waterloo well's he can Bunker Hill. I told him once the country'd lost a great general, an' I meant it, too."

"I expect you're near right," said Mrs. Caplin, a little crestfallen and apologetic.

"I be right," insisted Mrs. Todd with much amiability. " 'T was most too bad to cramp him down to his peaceful trade, but he's a most excellent shoemaker at his best, an' he always says it's a trade that gives him time to think an' plan his manœuvres. Over to the Port they always invite him to march Decoration Day, same as the rest, an' he does look noble; he comes of soldier stock."

I had been noticing with great interest the curiously French type of face which prevailed in this rustic company. I had said to myself before that Mrs. Blackett was plainly of French descent, in both her appearance and her charming gifts, but this is not surprising when one has learned how large a proportion of the early settlers on this northern coast of New England were of Huguenot blood, and that it is the Norman Englishman, not the Saxon, who goes adventuring to a new world.

"They used to say in old times," said Mrs. Todd modestly, "that our family came of very high folks in France, and one of 'em was a great general in some o' the old wars. I sometimes think that Santin's ability has come 'way down from then. 'T ain't nothin' he's ever acquired; 't was born in him. I don't know's he ever saw a fine parade, or met with those that studied up such things. He's figured it all out an' got his papers so he knows how to aim a cannon right for William's fish-house five miles out on Green Island, or up there on Burnt Island where the signal is. He had it all over to me one day, an' I tried hard to appear interested. His life's all in it, but he will have those poor gloomy spells come over him now an' then, an' then he has to drink."

Mrs. Caplin gave a heavy sigh.

"There's a great many such strayaway folks, just as there is plants," continued Mrs. Todd, who was nothing if not botanical. "I know of just one sprig of laurel that grows over back here in a wild spot, an' I never could hear of no other on this coast. I had a large bunch brought me once from Massachusetts way, so I know it. This piece grows in an open spot where you'd think 't would do well, but it's sort o' poor-lookin'. I've visited it time an' again, just to notice its poor blooms. 'T is a real Sant Bowden, out of its own place."

Mrs. Caplin looked bewildered and blank. "Well, all I know is, last year he worked out some kind of a plan so's to parade the county conference in platoons, and got 'em all flustered up tryin' to sense his ideas of a holler square," she burst forth. "They was holler enough anyway after ridin' 'way down from up country into the salt air, and they'd been treated to a sermon on faith an' works from old Fayther Harlow that never knows when to cease. 'T wa'n't no time for tactics then,—they wa'n't a-thinkin' of the church military. Sant, he couldn't do nothin' with 'em. All he thinks of, when he sees a crowd, is how to march 'em. 'T is all very well when he don't 'tempt too much. He never did act like other folks."

"Ain't I just been maintainin' that he ain't like 'em?" urged Mrs. Todd decidedly. "Strange folks has got to have strange ways for what I see."

"Somebody observed once that you could pick out the likeness of 'most every sort of a foreigner when you looked about you in our parish," said Sister Caplin, her face brightening with sudden illumination. "I didn't see the bearin' of it then quite so plain. I always did think Mari' Harris resembled a Chinee."

"Mari' Harris was pretty as a child, I remember," said the pleasant voice of Mrs. Blackett, who, after receiving the affectionate greetings of nearly the whole company, came to join us,—to see, as she insisted, that we were out of mischief.

"Yes, Mari' was one o' them pretty little lambs that make dreadful homely old sheep," replied Mrs. Todd with energy. "Cap'n Little-page never'd look so disconsolate if she was any sort of a proper person to direct things. She might divert him; yes, she might divert the old gentleman, an' let him think he had his own way, 'stead o' arguing everything down to the bare bone. 'T wouldn't hurt her to sit down an' hear his great stories once in a while."

"The stories are very interesting," I ventured to say.

"Yes, you always catch yourself a-thinkin' what if they was all true, and he had the right of it," answered Mrs. Todd. "He's a good sight better company, though dreamy, than such sordid crea-tur's as Mari' Harris."

"Live and let live," said dear old Mrs. Blackett gently. "I haven't seen the captain for a good while, now that I ain't so constant to meetin'," she added wistfully. "We always have known each other."

"Why, if it is a good pleasant day tomorrow, I'll get William to call an' invite the capt'in to dinner. William'll be in early so's to pass up the street without meetin' anybody."

"There, they're callin' out it's time to set the tables," said Mrs. Caplin, with great excitement.

"Here's Cousin Sarah Jane Blackett! Well, I am pleased, certain!" exclaimed Mrs. Todd, with unaffected delight; and these kindred spirits met and parted with the promise of a good talk later on. After this there was no more time for conversation until we were seated in order at the long tables.

"I'm one that always dreads seeing some o' the folks that I don't like, at such a time as this," announced Mrs. Todd privately to me after a season of reflection. We were just waiting for the feast to begin. "You wouldn't think such a great creatur' 's I be could feel all over pins an' needles. I remember, the day I promised to Na-than, how it come over me, just 's I was feelin' happy 's I could, that I'd got to have an own cousin o' his for my near relation all the rest o' my life, an' it seemed as if die I should. Poor Nathan saw somethin' had crossed me,—he had very nice feelings,—and when he asked me what 't was, I told him. 'I never could like her myself,' said he. 'You sha'n't be bothered, dear,' he says; an' 't was one o' the things that made me set a good deal by Nathan, he didn't make a habit of always opposin', like some men. 'Yes,' says I, 'but think o' Thanksgivin' times an' funerals; she's our relation, an' we've got to own her.' Young folks don't think o' those things. There she goes now, do let's pray her by!" said Mrs. Todd, with an alarming transition from general opinions to particular animosities. "I hate her just the same as I always did; but she's got on a real pretty dress. I do try to remember that she's Nathan's cousin. Oh dear, well; she's gone by after all, an' ain't seen me. I expected she'd come pleasantin' round just to show off an' say afterwards she was acquainted."

This was so different from Mrs. Todd's usual largeness of mind that I had a moment's uneasiness; but the cloud passed quickly over her spirit, and was gone with the offender.

There never was a more generous out-of-door feast along the coast than the Bowden family set forth that day. To call it a picnic would make it seem trivial. The great tables were edged with pretty oak-leaf trimming, which the boys and girls made. We brought flowers from the fence-thickets of the great field; and out of the disorder of flowers and provisions suddenly appeared as orderly a scheme for the feast as the marshal had shaped for the procession. I began to respect the Bowdens for their inheritance of good taste and skill and a certain pleasing gift of formality. Something made them do all these things in a finer way than most country people would have done them. As I looked up and down the tables there was a good cheer, a grave soberness that shone with pleasure, a humble dignity of bearing. There were some who should have sat below the salt for lack of this good breeding; but they were not many. So, I said to myself, their ancestors may have sat in the great hall of some old French house in the Middle Ages, when battles and sieges and processions and feasts were familiar things. The ministers and Mrs. Blackett, with a few of their rank and age, were put in places of honor, and for once that I looked any other way I looked twice at Mrs. Blackett's face, serene and mindful of privilege and responsibility, the mistress by simple fitness of this great day.

Mrs. Todd looked up at the roof of green trees, and then carefully surveyed the company. "I see 'em better now they're all settin' down," she said with satisfaction. "There's old Mr. Gilbraith and his sister. I wish they were settin' with us; they're not among folks they can parley with, an' they look disappointed."

As the feast went on, the spirits of my companion steadily rose. The excitement of an unexpectedly great occasion was a subtle stimulant to her disposition, and I could see that sometimes when Mrs. Todd had seemed limited and heavily domestic, she had simply grown sluggish for lack of proper surroundings. She was not so much reminiscent now as expectant, and as alert and gay as a girl. We who were her neighbors were full of gayety, which was but the reflected light from her beaming countenance. It was not the first time that I was full of wonder at the waste of human ability in this world, as a botanist wonders at the wastefulness of nature, the thousand seeds that die, the unused provision of every sort. The reserve force of society grows more and more amazing to one's thought. More than one face among the Bowdens showed that only opportunity and stimulus were lacking,—a narrow set of circumstances had caged a fine able character and held it captive. One sees exactly the same types in a country gathering as in the most brilliant city company. You are safe to be understood if the spirit of your speech is the same for one neighbor as for the other.

19   The Feast's End

The feast was a noble feast, as has already been said. There was an elegant ingenuity displayed in the form of pies which delighted my heart. Once acknowledge that an American pie is far to be preferred to its humble ancestor, the English tart, and it is joyful to be reassured at a Bowden reunion that invention has not yet failed. Beside a delightful variety of material, the decorations went beyond all my former experience; dates and names were wrought in lines of pastry and frosting on the tops. There was even more elaborate reading matter on an excellent early-apple pie which we began to share and eat, precept upon precept. Mrs. Todd helped me generously to the whole word *Bowden*, and consumed *Reunion* herself, save an undecipherable fragment; but the most renowned essay in cookery on the tables was a model of the old Bowden house made of durable gingerbread, with all the windows and doors in the right places, and sprigs of genuine lilac set at the front. It must have been baked in sections, in one of the last of the great brick ovens, and fastened together on the morning of the day. There was a general sigh when this fell into ruin at the feast's end, and it was shared by a great part of the assembly, not without seriousness, and as if it were a pledge and token of loyalty. I met the maker of the gingerbread house, which had called up lively remembrances of a childish story. She had the gleaming eye of an enthusiast and a look of high ideals.

"I could just as well have made it all of frosted cake," she said, "but 't wouldn't have been the right shade; the old house as you observe, was never painted, and I concluded that plain gingerbread would represent it best. It wasn't all I expected it would be," she said sadly, as many an artist had said before her of his work.

There were speeches by the ministers; and there proved to be a historian among the Bowdens, who gave some fine anecdotes of the family history; and then appeared a poetess, whom Mrs. Todd regarded with wistful compassion and indulgence, and when the long faded garland of verses came to an appealing end, she turned to me with words of praise.

"Sounded pretty," said the generous listener. "Yes, I thought she did very well. We went to school together, an' Mary Anna had a very hard time; trouble was, her mother thought she'd given birth to a genius an' Mary Anna's come to believe it herself. There, I don't know what we should have done without her; there ain't nobody else that can write poetry between here and 'way up to-wards Rockland; it adds a great deal at such a time. When she speaks o' those that are gone, she feels it all, and so does everybody else, but she harps too much. I'd laid half of that away for next time, if I was Mary Anna. There comes mother to speak to her, an' old Mr. Gilbraith's sister; now she'll be heartened right up. Mother'll say just the right thing."

The leave-takings were as affecting as the meetings of these old friends had been. There were enough young persons at the reunion, but it is the old who really value such opportunities; as for the young, it is the habit of every day to meet their comrades,—the time of separation has not come. To see the joy with which these elder kinsfolk and acquaintances had looked in one another's faces, and the lingering touch of their friendly hands; to see these affec-tionate meetings and then the reluctant partings, gave one a new idea of the isolation in which it was possible to live in that after all thinly settled region. They did not expect to see one another again very soon; the steady, hard work on the farms, the difficulty of getting from place to place, especially in winter when boats were laid up, gave double value to any occasion which could bring a large number of families together. Even funerals in this country of the pointed firs were not without their social advantages and satisfactions. I heard the words "next summer" repeated many times, though summer was still ours and all the leaves were green.

The boats began to put out from shore, and the wagons to drive away. Mrs. Blackett took me into the old house when we came back from the grove: it was her father's birthplace and early home, and she had spent much of her own childhood there with her grandmother. She spoke of those days as if they had but lately passed; in fact, I could imagine that the house looked almost exactly the same to her. I could see the brown rafters of the unfinished roof as I looked up the steep staircase, though the best room was as handsome with its good wainscoting and touch of ornament on the cornice as any old room of its day in a town.

Some of the guests who came from a distance were still sitting in the best room when we went in to take leave of the master and mistress of the house. We all said eagerly what a pleasant day it had been, and how swiftly the time had passed. Perhaps it is the great national anniversaries which our country has lately kept, and the soldiers' meetings that take place everywhere, which have made reunions of every sort the fashion. This one, at least, had been very interesting. I fancied that old feuds had been overlooked, and the old saying that blood is thicker than water had again proved itself true, though from the variety of names one argued a certain adulteration of the Bowden traits and belongings. Clannishness is an instinct of the heart,—it is more than a birthright, or a custom; and lesser rights were forgotten in the claim to a common inheritance.

We were among the very last to return to our proper lives and lodgings. I came near to feeling like a true Bowden, and parted from certain new friends as if they were old friends; we were rich with the treasure of a new remembrance.

At last we were in the high wagon again; the old white horse had been well fed in the Bowden barn, and we drove away and soon began to climb the long hill toward the wooded ridge. The road was new to me, as roads always are, going back. Most of our companions had been full of anxious thoughts of home,—of the cows, or of young children likely to fall into disaster,—but we had no reasons for haste, and drove slowly along, talking and resting by the way. Mrs. Todd said once that she really hoped her front door had been shut on account of the dust blowing in, but added that nothing made any weight on her mind except not to forget to turn a few late mullein leaves that were drying on a newspaper in the little loft. Mrs. Blackett and I gave our word of honor that we would remind her of this heavy responsibility. The way seemed short, we had so much to talk about. We climbed hills where we could see the great bay and the islands, and then went down into shady valleys where the air began to feel like evening, cool and damp with a fragrance of wet ferns. Mrs. Todd alighted once or twice, refusing all assistance in securing some boughs of a rare shrub which she valued for its bark, though she proved incommunicative as to her reasons. We passed the house where we had been so kindly entertained with doughnuts earlier in the day, and found it closed and deserted, which was a disappointment.

"They must have stopped to tea somewheres and thought they'd finish up the day," said Mrs. Todd. "Those that enjoyed it best'll want to get right home so's to think it over."

"I didn't see the woman there after all, did you?" asked Mrs. Blackett as the horse stopped to drink at the trough.

"Oh yes, I spoke with her," answered Mrs. Todd, with but scant interest or approval. "She ain't a member o' our family."

"I thought you said she resembled Cousin Pa'lina Bowden about the forehead," suggested Mrs. Blackett.

"Well, she don't," answered Mrs. Todd impatiently. "I ain't one that's ord'narily mistaken about family likenesses, and she didn't seem to meet with friends, so I went square up to her. 'I expect you're a Bowden by your looks,' says I. 'Yes, I take it you're one o' the Bowdens.' 'Lor', no,' says she. 'Dennett was my maiden name, but I married a Bowden for my first husband. I thought I'd come an' just see what was a-goin' on'!"

Mrs. Blackett laughed heartily. "I'm goin' to remember to tell William o' that," she said. "There, Almiry, the only thing that's troubled me all this day is to think how William would have enjoyed it. I do so wish William had been there."

"I sort of wish he had, myself," said Mrs. Todd frankly.

"There wa'n't many old folks there, somehow," said Mrs. Blackett, with a touch of sadness in her voice. "There ain't so many to come as there used to be, I'm aware, but I expected to see more."

"I thought they turned out pretty well, when you come to think of it; why, everybody was sayin' so an' feelin' gratified," answered Mrs. Todd hastily with pleasing unconsciousness; then I saw the quick color flash into her cheek, and presently she made some excuse to turn and steal an anxious look at her mother. Mrs. Blackett was smiling and thinking about her happy day, though she began to look a little tired. Neither of my companions was troubled by her burden of years. I hoped in my heart that I might be like them as I lived on into age, and then smiled to think that I too was no longer very young. So we always keep the same hearts, though our outer framework fails and shows the touch of time.

" 'T was pretty when they sang the hymn, wasn't it?" asked Mrs. Blackett at suppertime, with real enthusiasm. "There was such a plenty o' men's voices; where I sat it did sound beautiful. I had to stop and listen when they came to the last verse."

I saw that Mrs. Todd's broad shoulders began to shake. "There was good singers there; yes, there was excellent singers," she agreed heartily, putting down her teacup, "but I chanced to drift alongside Mis' Peter Bowden o' Great Bay, an' I couldn't help thinkin' if she was as far out o' town as she was out o' tune, she wouldn't get back in a day."

20 *Along Shore*

One day as I went along the shore beyond the old wharves and the newer, high-stepped fabric of the steamer landing, I saw that all the boats were beached, and the slack water period of the early afternoon prevailed. Nothing was going on, not even the most leisurely of occupations, like baiting trawls or mending nets, or repairing lobster pots; the very boats seemed to be taking an afternoon nap in the sun. I could hardly discover a distant sail as I looked seaward, except a weather-beaten lobster smack, which seemed to have been taken for a plaything by the light airs that blew about the bay. It drifted and turned about so aimlessly in the wide reach off Burnt Island, that I suspected there was nobody at the wheel, or that she might have parted her rusty anchor chain while all the crew were asleep.

I watched her for a minute or two; she was the old Miranda, owned by some of the Caplins, and I knew her by an odd shaped patch of newish duck that was set into the peak of her dingy mainsail. Her vagaries offered such an exciting subject for conversation that my heart rejoiced at the sound of a hoarse voice behind me. At that moment, before I had time to answer, I saw something large and shapeless flung from the Miranda's deck that splashed the water high against her black side, and my companion gave a satisfied chuckle. The old lobster smack's sail caught the breeze again at this moment, and she moved off down the bay. Turning, I found old Elijah Tilley, who had come softly out of his dark fish house, as if it were a burrow.

"Boy got kind o' drowsy steerin' of her; Monroe he hove him right overboard; 'wake now fast enough," explained Mr. Tilley, and we laughed together.

I was delighted, for my part, that the vicissitudes and dangers of the Miranda, in a rocky channel, should have given me this opportunity to make acquaintance with an old fisherman to whom I had never spoken. At first he had seemed to be one of those evasive and uncomfortable persons who are so suspicious of you that they make you almost suspicious of yourself. Mr. Elijah Tilley appeared to regard a stranger with scornful indifference. You might see him standing on the pebble beach or in a fish-house doorway, but when you came nearer he was gone. He was one of the small company of elderly, gaunt-shaped great fishermen whom I used to like to see leading up a deep-laden boat by the head, as if it were a horse, from the water's edge to the steep slope of the pebble beach. There were four of these large old men at the Landing, who were the survivors of an earlier and more vigorous generation. There was an alliance and understanding between them, so close that it was apparently speechless. They gave much time to watching one another's boats go out or come in; they lent a ready hand at tending one another's lobster traps in rough weather; they helped to clean the fish, or to sliver porgies for the trawls, as if they were in close partnership; and when a boat came in from deep-sea fishing they were never far out of the way, and hastened to help carry it ashore, two by two, splashing alongside, or holding its steady head, as if it were a willful sea colt. As a matter of fact no boat could help being steady and way-wise under their instant direction and companionship. Abel's boat and Jonathan Bowden's boat were as distinct and experienced personalities as the men themselves, and as inexpressive. Arguments and opinions were unknown to the conversation of these ancient friends; you would as soon have expected to hear small talk in a company of elephants as to hear old Mr. Bowden or Elijah Tilley and their two mates waste breath upon any form of trivial gossip. They made brief statements to one another from time to time. As you came to know them you wondered more and more that they should talk at all. Speech seemed to be a light and elegant accomplishment, and their unexpected acquaintance with its arts made them of new value to the listener. You felt almost as if a landmark pine should suddenly address you in regard to the weather, or a lofty-minded old camel make a remark as you stood respectfully near him under the circus tent.

I often wondered a great deal about the inner life and thought of these self-contained old fishermen; their minds seemed to be fixed upon nature and the elements rather than upon any contrivances of man, like politics or theology. My friend, Captain Bowden, who was the nephew of the eldest of this group, regarded them with deference; but he did not belong to their secret companionship, though he was neither young nor talkative.

"They've gone together ever since they were boys, they know most everything about the sea amon'st them," he told me once. "They was always just as you see 'em now since the memory of man."

These ancient seafarers had houses and lands not outwardly different from other Dunnet Landing dwellings, and two of them were fathers of families, but their true dwelling places were the sea, and the stony beach that edged its familiar shore, and the fishhouses, where much salt brine from the mackerel kits had soaked the very timbers into a state of brown permanence and petrifaction. It had also affected the old fishermen's hard complexions, until one fancied that when Death claimed them it could only be with the aid, not of any slender modern dart, but the good serviceable harpoon of a seventeenth century woodcut.

Elijah Tilley was such an evasive, discouraged-looking person, heavy-headed, and stooping so that one could never look him in the face, that even after his friendly exclamation about Monroe Pennell, the lobster smack's skipper, and the sleepy boy, I did not venture at once to speak again. Mr. Tilley was carrying a small haddock in one hand, and presently shifted it to the other hand lest it might touch my skirt. I knew that my company was accepted, and we walked together a little way.

"You mean to have a good supper," I ventured to say, by way of friendliness.

"Goin' to have this 'ere haddock an' some o' my good baked potatoes; must eat to live," responded my companion with great pleasantness and open approval. I found that I had suddenly left the forbidding coast and come into a smooth little harbor of friendship.

"You ain't never been up to my place," said the old man. "Folks don't come now as they used to; no, 't ain't no use to ask folks now. My poor dear she was a great hand to draw young company."

I remembered that Mrs. Todd had once said that this old fisherman had been sore stricken and unconsoled at the death of his wife.

"I should like very much to come," said I. "Perhaps you are going to be at home later on?"

Mr. Tilley agreed, by a sober nod, and went his way bent-shouldered and with a rolling gait. There was a new patch high on the shoulder of his old waistcoat, which corresponded to the renewing of the Miranda's mainsail down the bay, and I wondered if his own fingers, clumsy with much deep-sea fishing, had set it in.

"Was there a good catch to-day?" I asked, stopping a moment. "I didn't happen to be on the shore when the boats came in."

"No; all come in pretty light," answered Mr. Tilley. "Addicks an' Bowden they done the best; Abel an' me we had but a slim fare. We went out 'arly, but not so 'arly as sometimes; looked like a poor mornin'. I got nine haddick, all small, and seven fish; the rest on 'em got more fish than haddick. Well, I don't expect they feel like bitin' every day; we l'arn to humor 'em a little, an' let 'em have their way 'bout it. These plaguey dog-fish kind of worry 'em." Mr. Tilley pronounced the last sentence with much sympathy, as if he looked upon himself as a true friend of all the haddock and codfish that lived on the fishing grounds, and so we parted.

Later in the afternoon I went along the beach again until I came to the foot of Mr. Tilley's land, and found his rough track across the cobble-stones and rocks to the field edge, where there was a heavy piece of old wreck timber, like a ship's bone, full of treenails. From this a little footpath, narrow with one man's treading, led up across the small green field that made Mr. Tilley's whole estate, except a straggling pasture that tilted on edge up the steep hillside beyond the house and road. I could hear the tinkle-tankle of a cow-bell somewhere among the spruces by which the pasture was being walked over and forested from every side; it was likely to be called the wood lot before long, but the field was unmolested. I could not see a bush or a brier anywhere within its walls, and hardly a stray pebble showed itself. This was most surprising in that country of firm ledges, and scattered stones which all the walls that industry could devise had hardly begun to clear away off the land. In the narrow field I noticed some stout stakes, apparently planted at random in the grass and among the hills of potatoes, but carefully painted yellow and white to match the house, a neat sharp-edged little dwelling, which looked strangely modern for its owner. I should have much sooner believed that the smart young wholesale egg merchant of the Landing was its occupant than Mr. Tilley, since a man's house is really but his larger body, and expresses in a way his nature and character.

I went up the field, following the smooth little path to the side door. As for using the front door, that was a matter of great ceremony; the long grass grew close against the high stone step, and a snowberry bush leaned over it, top-heavy with the weight of a morning-glory vine that had managed to take what the fishermen might call a half hitch about the door-knob. Elijah Tilley came to the side door to receive me; he was knitting a blue yarn stocking without looking on, and was warmly dressed for the season in a thick blue flannel shirt with white crockery buttons, a faded waistcoat and trousers heavily patched at the knees. These were not his fishing clothes. There was something delightful in the grasp of his hand, warm and clean, as if it never touched anything but the comfortable woolen yarn, instead of cold sea water and slippery fish.

"What are the painted stakes for, down in the field?" I hastened to ask, and he came out a step or two along the path to see; and looked at the stakes as if his attention were called to them for the first time.

"Folks laughed at me when I first bought this place an' come here to live," he explained. "They said 't wa'n't no kind of a field privilege at all; no place to raise anything, all full o' stones. I was aware 't was good land, an' I worked some on it—odd times when I didn't have nothin' else on hand—till I cleared them loose stones all out. You never see a prettier piece than 't is now; now did ye? Well, as for them painted marks, them 's my buoys. I struck on to some heavy rocks that didn't show none, but a plow'd be liable to ground on 'em, an' so I ketched holt an' buoyed 'em same's you see. They don't trouble me no more 'n if they wa'n't there."

"You haven't been to sea for nothing," I said laughing.

"One trade helps another," said Elijah with an amiable smile. "Come right in an' set down. Come in an' rest ye," he exclaimed, and led the way into his comfortable kitchen. The sunshine poured in at the two further windows, and a cat was curled up sound asleep on the table that stood between them. There was a new-looking light oilcloth of a tiled pattern on the floor, and a crockery teapot, large for a household of only one person, stood on the bright stove. I ventured to say that somebody must be a very good housekeeper.

"That's me," acknowledged the old fisherman with frankness. "There ain't nobody here but me. I try to keep things looking right, same's poor dear left 'em. You set down here in this chair, then you can look off an' see the water. None on 'em thought I was goin' to get along alone, no way, but I wa'n't goin' to have my house turned upsi' down an' all changed about; no, not to please nobody. I was the only one knew just how she liked to have things set, poor dear, an' I said I was goin' to make shift, and I have made shift. I'd rather tough it out alone." And he sighed heavily, as if to sigh were his familiar consolation.

We were both silent for a minute; the old man looked out of the window, as if he had forgotten I was there.

"You must miss her very much?" I said at last.

"I do miss her," he answered, and sighed again. "Folks all kep' repeatin' that time would ease me, but I can't find it does. No, I miss her just the same every day."

"How long is it since she died?" I asked.

"Eight year now, come the first of October. It don't seem near so long. I've got a sister that comes and stops 'long o' me a little spell, spring an' fall, an' odd times if I send after her. I ain't near so good a hand to sew as I be to knit, and she's very quick to set everything to rights. She's a married woman with a family; her son's folks lives at home, an' I can't make no great claim on her time. But it makes me a kind o' good excuse, when I do send, to help her a little; she ain't none too well off. Poor dear always liked her, and we used to contrive our ways together. 'T is full as easy to be alone. I set here an' think it all over, an' think considerable when the weather's bad to go outside. I get so some days it feels as if poor dear might step right back into this kitchen. I keep a-watchin' them doors as if she might step in to ary one. Yes, ma'am, I keep a-lookin' off an' droppin' o' my stitches; that's just how it seems. I can't git over losin' of her no way nor no how. Yes, ma'am, that's just how it seems to me."

I did not say anything, and he did not look up.

"I git feelin' so sometimes I have to lay everything by an' go out door. She was a sweet pretty creatur' long 's she lived," the old man added mournfully. "There's that little rockin' chair o' her'n, I set an' notice it an' think how strange 't is a creatur' like her should be gone an' that chair be here right in its old place."

"I wish I had known her; Mrs. Todd told me about your wife one day," I said.

"You'd have liked to come and see her; all the folks did," said poor Elijah. "She'd been so pleased to hear everything and see somebody new that took such an int'rest. She had a kind o' gift to make it pleasant for folks. I guess likely Almiry Todd told you she was a pretty woman, especially in her young days; late years, too, she kep' her looks and come to be so pleasant lookin'. There, 't ain't so much matter, I shall be done afore a great while. No; I sha'n't trouble the fish a great sight more."

The old widower sat with his head bowed over his knitting, as if he were hastily shortening the very thread of time. The minutes went slowly by. He stopped his work and clasped his hands firmly together. I saw he had forgotten his guest, and I kept the afternoon watch with him. At last he looked up as if but a moment had passed of his continual loneliness.

"Yes, ma'am, I'm one that has seen trouble," he said, and began to knit again.

The visible tribute of his careful housekeeping, and the clean bright room which had once enshrined his wife, and now enshrined her memory, was very moving to me; he had no thought for any one else or for any other place. I began to see her myself in her home,—a delicate-looking, faded little woman, who leaned upon his rough strength and affectionate heart, who was always watching for his boat out of this very window, and who always opened the door and welcomed him when he came home.

"I used to laugh at her, poor dear," said Elijah, as if he read my thought. "I used to make light of her timid notions. She used to be fearful when I was out in bad weather or baffled about gettin' ashore. She used to say the time seemed long to her, but I've found out all about it now. I used to be dreadful thoughtless when I was a young man and the fish was bitin' well. I'd stay out late some o' them days, an' I expect she'd watch an' watch an' lose heart a-waitin'. My heart alive! what a supper she'd git, an' be right there watchin' from the door, with somethin' over her head if 't was cold, waitin' to hear all about it as I come up the field. Lord, how I think o' all them little things!

"This was what she called the best room; in this way," he said presently, laying his knitting on the table, and leading the way across the front entry and unlocking a door, which he threw open with an air of pride. The best room seemed to me a much sadder and more empty place than the kitchen; its conventionalities lacked the simple perfection of the humbler room and failed on the side of poor ambition; it was only when one remembered what patient saving, and what high respect for society in the abstract go to such furnishing that the little parlor was interesting at all. I could imagine the great day of certain purchases, the bewildering shops of the next large town, the aspiring anxious woman, the clumsy sea-tanned man in his best clothes, so eager to be pleased, but at ease only when they were safe back in the sail-boat again, going down the bay with their precious freight, the hoarded money all spent and nothing to think of but tiller and sail. I looked at the unworn carpet, the glass vases on the mantelpiece with their prim bunches of bleached swamp grass and dusty marsh rosemary, and I could read the history of Mrs. Tilley's best room from its very beginning.

"You see for yourself what beautiful rugs she could make; now I'm going to show you her best tea things she thought so much of," said the master of the house, opening the door of a shallow cupboard. "That's real chiny, all of it on those two shelves," he told me proudly. "I bought it all myself, when we was first married, in the port of Bordeaux. There never was one single piece of it broke until—Well, I used to say, long as she lived, there never was a piece broke, but long at the last I noticed she'd looked kind o' distressed, an' I thought 't was 'count o' me boastin'. When they asked if they should use it when the folks was here to supper, time o' her funeral, I knew she'd want to have everything nice, and I said 'certain.' Some o' the women they come runnin' to me an' called me, while they was takin' of the chiny down, an' showed me there was one o' the cups broke an' the pieces wropped in paper and pushed way back here, corner o' the shelf. They didn't want me to go an' think they done it. Poor dear! I had to put right out o' the house when I see that. I knowed in one minute how 't was. We'd got so used to sayin' 't was all there just 's I fetched it home, an' so when she broke that cup somehow or 'nother she couldn't frame no words to come an' tell me. She couldn't think 't would vex me, 't was her own hurt pride. I guess there wa'n't no other secret ever lay between us."

The French cups with their gay sprigs of pink and blue, the best tumblers, an old flowered bowl and tea caddy, and a japanned waiter or two adorned the shelves. These, with a few daguerreotypes in a little square pile, had the closet to themselves, and I was conscious of much pleasure in seeing them. One is shown over many a house in these days where the interest may be more complex, but not more definite.

"Those were her best things, poor dear," said Elijah as he locked the door again. "She told me that last summer before she was taken away that she couldn't think o' anything more she wanted, there was everything in the house, an' all her rooms was furnished pretty. I was goin' over to the Port, an' inquired for errands. I used to ask her to say what she wanted, cost or no cost—she was a very reasonable woman, an' 't was the place where she done all but her extra shopping. It kind o' chilled me up when she spoke so satisfied."

"You don't go out fishing after Christmas?" I asked, as we came back to the bright kitchen.

"No; I take stiddy to my knitting after January sets in," said the old seafarer. " 'T ain't worth while, fish make off into deeper water an' you can't stand no such perishin' for the sake o' what you get. I leave out a few traps in sheltered coves an' do a little lobsterin' on fair days. The young fellows braves it out, some on 'em; but, for me, I lay in my winter's yarn an' set here where 't is warm, an' knit an' take my comfort. Mother learnt me once when I was a lad; she was a beautiful knitter herself. I was laid up with a bad knee, an' she said 't would take up my time an' help her; we was a large family. They'll buy all the folks can do down here to Addicks' store. They say our Dunnet stockin's is gettin' to be celebrated up to Boston,—good quality o' wool an' even knittin' or somethin'. I've always been called a pretty hand to do nettin', but seines is master cheap to what they used to be when they was all hand worked. I change off to nettin' long towards spring, and I piece up my trawls and lines and get my fishin' stuff to rights. Lobster pots they require attention, but I make 'em up in spring weather when it's warm there in the barn. No; I ain't one o' them that likes to set an' do nothin'.

"You see the rugs, poor dear did them; she wa'n't very partial to knittin'," old Elijah went on, after he had counted his stitches. "Our rugs is beginnin' to show wear, but I can't master none o' them womanish tricks. My sister, she tinkers 'em up. She said last time she was here that she guessed they'd last my time."

"The old ones are always the prettiest," I said.

"You ain't referrin' to the braided ones now?" answered Mr. Tilley. "You see ours is braided for the most part, an' their good looks is all in the beginnin'. Poor dear used to say they made an easier floor. I go shufflin' round the house same 's if 't was a bo't, and I always used to be stubbin' up the corners o' the hooked kind. Her an' me was always havin' our jokes together same 's a boy an' girl. Outsiders never'd know nothin' about it to see us. She had nice manners with all, but to me there was nobody so entertainin'. She'd take off anybody's natural talk winter evenin's when we set here alone, so you'd think 't was them a-speakin'. There, there!"

I saw that he had dropped a stitch again, and was snarling the blue yarn round his clumsy fingers. He handled it and threw it off at arm's length as if it were a cod line; and frowned impatiently, but I saw a tear shining on his cheek.

I said that I must be going, it was growing late, and asked if I might come again, and if he would take me out to the fishing grounds some day.

"Yes, come any time you want to," said my host, "'t ain't so pleasant as when poor dear was here. Oh, I didn't want to lose her an' she didn't want to go, but it had to be. Such things ain't for us to say; there's no yes an' no to it."

"You find Almiry Todd one o' the best o' women?" said Mr. Tilley as we parted. He was standing in the doorway and I had started off down the narrow green field. "No, there ain't a better hearted woman in the State o' Maine. I've known her from a girl. She's had the best o' mothers. You tell her I'm liable to fetch her up a couple or three nice good mackerel early tomorrow," he said. "Now don't let it slip your mind. Poor dear, she always thought a sight o' Almiry, and she used to remind me there was nobody to fish for her; but I don't rec'lect it as I ought to. I see you drop a line yourself very handy now an' then."

We laughed together like the best of friends, and I spoke again about the fishing grounds, and confessed that I had no fancy for a southerly breeze and a ground swell.

"Nor me neither," said the old fisherman. "Nobody likes 'em, say what they may. Poor dear was disobliged by the mere sight of a bo't. Almiry's got the best o' mothers, I expect you know; Mis' Blackett out to Green Island; and we was always plannin' to go out when summer come; but there, I couldn't pick no day's weather that seemed to suit her just right. I never set out to worry her neither, 't wa'n't no kind o' use; she was so pleasant we couldn't have no fret nor trouble. 'T was never 'you dear an' you darlin'' afore folks, an' 'you divil' behind the door!"

As I looked back from the lower end of the field I saw him still standing, a lonely figure in the doorway. "Poor dear," I repeated to myself half aloud; "I wonder where she is and what she knows of the little world she left. I wonder what she has been doing these eight years!"

I gave the message about the mackerel to Mrs. Todd.

"Been visitin' with 'Lijah?" she asked with interest. "I expect you had kind of a dull session; he ain't the talkin' kind; dwellin' so much long o' fish seems to make 'em lose the gift o' speech." But when I told her that Mr. Tilley had been talking to me that day, she interrupted me quickly.

"Then 't was all about his wife, an' he can't say nothin' too pleasant neither. She was modest with strangers, but there ain't one o' her old friends can ever make up her loss. For me, I don't want to go there no more. There's some folks you miss and some folks you don't, when they're gone, but there ain't hardly a day I don't think o' dear Sarah Tilley. She was always right there; yes, you knew just where to find her like a plain flower. 'Lijah's worthy enough; I do esteem 'Lijah, but he's a ploddin' man."

21 *A Dunnet Shepherdess*

I

Early one morning at Dunnet Landing, as if it were still night, I waked, suddenly startled by a spirited conversation beneath my window. It was not one of Mrs. Todd's morning soliloquies; she was not addressing her plants and flowers in words of either praise or blame. Her voice was declamatory though perfectly good-humored, while the second voice, a man's, was of lower pitch and somewhat deprecating.

The sun was just above the sea, and struck straight across my room through a crack in the blind. It was a strange hour for the arrival of a guest, and still too soon for the general run of business, even in that tiny eastern haven where daybreak fisheries and early tides must often rule the day.

The man's voice suddenly declared itself to my sleepy ears. It was Mr. William Blackett's.

"Why, sister Almiry," he protested gently, "I don't need none o' your nostrums!"

"Pick me a small han'ful," she commanded. "No, no, a *small* han'ful, I said,—o' them large pennyr'yal sprigs! I go to all the trouble an' cossetin' of 'em just so as to have you ready to meet such occasions, an' last year, you may remember, you never stopped here at all the day you went up country. An' the frost come at last an' blacked it. I never saw any herb that so objected to gardin ground; might as well try to flourish mayflowers in a common front yard. There, you can come in now, an' set and eat what breakfast you've got patience for. I've found everything I want, an' I'll mash 'em up an' be all ready to put 'em on."

I heard such a pleading note of appeal as the speakers went round the corner of the house, and my curiosity was so demanding, that I dressed in haste, and joined my friends a little later, with two unnoticed excuses of the beauty of the morning, and the early mail boat. William's breakfast had been slighted; he had taken his cup of tea and merely pushed back the rest on the kitchen table. He was now sitting in a helpless condition by the side window, with one of his sister's purple calico aprons pinned close about his neck. Poor William was meekly submitting to being smeared, as to his countenance, with a most pungent and unattractive lotion of pennyroyal and other green herbs which had been hastily pounded and mixed with cream in the little white stone mortar.

I had to cast two or three straightforward looks at William to reassure myself that he really looked happy and expectant in spite of his melancholy circumstances, and was not being overtaken by retribution. The brother and sister seemed to be on delightful terms with each other for once, and there was something of cheerful anticipation in their morning talk. I was reminded of Medea's anointing Jason before the great episode of the iron bulls, but to-day William really could not be going up country to see a railroad for the first time. I knew this to be one of his great schemes, but he was not fitted to appear in public, or to front an observing world of strangers. As I appeared he essayed to rise, but Mrs. Todd pushed him back into the chair.

"Set where you be till it dries on," she insisted. "Land sakes, you'd think he'd get over bein' a boy some time or 'nother, gettin' along in years as he is. An' you'd think he'd seen full enough o' fish, but once a year he has to break loose like this, an' travel off way up back o' the Bowden place—far out o' my beat, 't is—an' go a trout fishin'!"

Her tone of amused scorn was so full of challenge that William changed color even under the green streaks.

"I want some change," he said, looking at me and not at her. " 'T is the prettiest little shady brook you ever saw."

"If he ever fetched home more'n a couple o' minnies, 't would seem worth while," Mrs. Todd concluded, putting a last dab of the mysterious compound so perilously near her brother's mouth that William flushed again and was silent.

A little later I witnessed his escape, when Mrs. Todd had taken the foolish risk of going down cellar. There was a horse and wagon outside the garden fence, and presently we stood where we could see him driving up the hill with thoughtless speed. Mrs. Todd said nothing, but watched him affectionately out of sight.

"It serves to keep the mosquitoes off," she said, and a moment later it occurred to my slow mind that she spoke of the pennyroyal lotion. "I don't know sometimes but William's kind of poetical," she continued, in her gentlest voice. "You'd think if anything could cure him of it, 't would be the fish business."

It was only twenty minutes past six on a summer morning, but we both sat down to rest as if the activities of the day were over. Mrs. Todd rocked gently for a time, and seemed to be lost, though not poorly, like Macbeth, in her thoughts. At last she resumed relations with her actual surroundings. "I shall now put my lobsters on. They'll make us a good supper," she announced. "Then I can let the fire out for all day; give it a holiday, same's William. You can have a little one now, nice an' hot, if you ain't got all the breakfast you want. Yes, I'll put the lobsters on. William was very thoughtful to bring 'em over; William *is* thoughtful; if he only had a spark o' ambition, there be few could match him."

This unusual concession was afforded a sympathetic listener from the depths of the kitchen closet. Mrs. Todd was getting out her old iron lobster pot, and began to speak of prosaic affairs. I hoped that I should hear something more about her brother and their island life, and sat idly by the kitchen window looking at the morning glories that shaded it, believing that some flaw of wind might set Mrs. Todd's mind on its former course. Then it occurred to me that she had spoken about our supper rather than our dinner, and I guessed that she might have some great scheme before her for the day.

When I had loitered for some time and there was no further word about William, and at last I was conscious of receiving no attention whatever, I went away. It was something of a disappointment to find that she put no hindrance in the way of my usual morning affairs, of going up to the empty little white schoolhouse

on the hill where I did my task of writing. I had been almost sure
of a holiday when I discovered that Mrs. Todd was likely to take
one herself; we had not been far afield to gather herbs and pleasures for many days now, but a little later she had silently vanished.
I found my luncheon ready on the table in the little entry, wrapped
in its shining old homespun napkin, and as if by way of special
consolation, there was a stone bottle of Mrs. Todd's best spruce
beer, with a long piece of cod line wound round it by which it
could be lowered for coolness into the deep schoolhouse well.

I walked away with a dull supply of writing-paper and these
provisions, feeling like a reluctant child who hopes to be called
back at every step. There was no relenting voice to be heard, and
when I reached the schoolhouse, I found that I had left an open
window and a swinging shutter the day before, and the sea wind
that blew at evening had fluttered my poor sheaf of papers all about
the room.

So the day did not begin very well, and I began to recognize
that it was one of the days when nothing could be done without
company. The truth was that my heart had gone trouting with
William, but it would have been too selfish to say a word even to
one's self about spoiling his day. If there is one way above another
of getting so close to nature that one simply is a piece of nature,
following a primeval instinct with perfect self-forgetfulness and
forgetting everything except the dreamy consciousness of pleasant
freedom, it is to take the course of a shady trout brook. The dark
pools and the sunny shallows beckon one on; the wedge of sky
between the trees on either bank, the speaking, companioning
noise of the water, the amazing importance of what one is doing,
and the constant sense of life and beauty make a strange transformation of the quick hours. I had a sudden memory of all this, and
another, and another. I could not get myself free from "fishing and
wishing."

At that moment I heard the unusual sound of wheels, and I
looked past the high-growing thicket of wild-roses and straggling
sumach to see the white nose and meagre shape of the Caplin
horse; then I saw William sitting in the open wagon, with a small
expectant smile upon his face.

"I've got two lines," he said. "I was quite apiece up the road. I
thought perhaps 't was so you'd feel like going."

There was enough excitement for most occasions in hearing William speak three sentences at once. Words seemed but vain to me at that bright moment. I stepped back from the schoolhouse window with a beating heart. The spruce-beer bottle was not yet in the well, and with that and my luncheon, and Pleasure at the helm, I went out into the happy world. The land breeze was blowing, and, as we turned away, I saw a flutter of white go past the window as I left the schoolhouse and my morning's work to their neglected fate.

II

One seldom gave way to a cruel impulse to look at an ancient seafaring William, but one felt as if he were a growing boy; I only hope that he felt much the same about me. He did not wear the fishing clothes that belonged to his sea-going life, but a strangely shaped old suit of tea-colored linen garments that might have been brought home years ago from Canton or Bombay. William had a peculiar way of giving silent assent when one spoke, but of answering your unspoken thoughts as if they reached him better than words. "I find them very easy," he said, frankly referring to the clothes. "Father had them in his old sea-chest."

The antique fashion, a quaint touch of foreign grace and even imagination about the cut were very pleasing; if ever Mr. William Blackett had faintly resembled an old beau, it was upon that day. He now appeared to feel as if everything had been explained between us, as if everything were quite understood; and we drove for some distance without finding it necessary to speak again about anything. At last, when it must have been a little past nine o'clock, he stopped the horse beside a small farmhouse, and nodded when I asked if I should get down from the wagon. "You can steer about northeast right across the pasture," he said, looking from under the eaves of his hat with an expectant smile. "I always leave the team here."

I helped to unfasten the harness, and William led the horse away to the barn. It was a poor-looking little place, and a forlorn woman looked at us through the window before she appeared at the door. I told her that Mr. Blackett and I came up from the Landing to go fishing. "He keeps a-comin', don't he?" she answered, with a funny little laugh, to which I was at a loss to find answer. When he joined us, I could not see that he took notice of her presence in any way, except to take an armful of dried salt fish from a corded stack in the back of the wagon which had been carefully covered with a piece of old sail. We had left a wake of their pungent flavor behind us all the way. I wondered what was going to become of the rest of them and some fresh lobsters which were also disclosed to view, but he laid the present gift on the doorstep without a word, and a few minutes later, when I looked back as we crossed the pasture, the fish were being carried into the house.

I could not see any signs of a trout brook until I came close upon it in the bushy pasture, and presently we struck into the low woods of straggling spruce and fir mixed into a tangle of swamp maples and alders which stretched away on either hand up and down stream. We found an open place in the pasture where some taller trees seemed to have been overlooked rather than spared. The sun was bright and hot by this time, and I sat down in the shade while William produced his lines and cut and trimmed us each a slender rod. I wondered where Mrs. Todd was spending the morning, and if later she would think that pirates had landed and captured me from the schoolhouse.

III

The brook was giving that live, persistent call to a listener that trout brooks always make; it ran with a free, swift current even here, where it crossed an apparently level piece of land. I saw two unpromising, quick barbel chase each other upstream from bank to bank as we solemnly arranged our hooks and sinkers. I felt that William's glances changed from anxiety to relief when he found that I was used to such gear; perhaps he felt that we must stay together if I could not bait my own hook, but we parted happily, full of a pleasing sense of companionship.

William had pointed me up the brook, but I chose to go down, which was only fair because it was his day, though one likes as well to follow and see where a brook goes as to find one's way to the places it comes from, and its tiny springs and headwaters, and in this case trout were not to be considered. William's only real anxiety was lest I might suffer from mosquitoes. His own complexion was still strangely impaired by its defenses, but I kept forgetting it, and looking to see if we were treading fresh pennyroyal un-

derfoot, so efficient was Mrs. Todd's remedy. I was conscious, after
we parted, and I turned to see if he were already fishing, and saw
him wave his hand gallantly as he went away, that our friendship
had made a great gain.

The moment that I began to fish the brook, I had a sense of its
emptiness; when my bait first touched the water and went lightly
down the quick stream, I knew that there was nothing to lie in
wait for it. It is the same certainty that comes when one knocks
at the door of an empty house, a lack of answering consciousness
and of possible response; it is quite different if there is any life
within. But it was a lovely brook, and I went a long way through
woods and breezy open pastures, and found a forsaken house and
overgrown farm, and laid up many pleasures for future joy and
remembrance. At the end of the morning I came back to our
meeting-place hungry and without any fish. William was already
waiting, and we did not mention the matter of trout. We ate our
luncheons with good appetites, and William brought our two stone
bottles of spruce beer from the deep place in the brook where he
had left them to cool. Then we sat awhile longer in peace and
quietness on the green banks.

As for William, he looked more boyish than ever, and kept a
more remote and juvenile sort of silence. Once I wondered how
he had come to be so curiously wrinkled, forgetting, absent-mindedly, to recognize the effects of time. He did not expect any one
else to keep up a vain show of conversation, and so I was silent as
well as he. I glanced at him now and then, but I watched the leaves
tossing against the sky and the red cattle moving in the pasture.
"I don't know's we need head for home. It's early yet," he said at
last, and I was as startled as if one of the gray firs had spoken.

"I guess I'll go up-along and ask after Thankful Hight's folks,"
he continued. "Mother'd like to get word;" and I nodded a pleased
assent.

IV

William led the way across the pasture, and I followed with a deep
sense of pleased anticipation. I do not believe that my companion
had expected me to make any objection, but I knew that he was
gratified by the easy way that his plans for the day were being
seconded. He gave a look at the sky to see if there were any

portents, but the sky was frankly blue; even the doubtful morning haze had disappeared.

We went northward along a rough, clayey road, across a bare-looking, sunburnt country full of tiresome long slopes where the sun was hot and bright, and I could not help observing the forlorn look of the farms. There was a great deal of pasture, but it looked deserted, and I wondered afresh why the people did not raise more sheep when that seemed the only possible use to make of their land. I said so to Mr. Blackett, who gave me a look of pleased surprise.

"That's what She always maintains," he said eagerly. "She's right about it, too; well, you'll see!" I was glad to find myself approved, but I had not the least idea whom he meant, and waited until he felt like speaking again.

A few minutes later we drove down a steep hill and entered a large tract of dark spruce woods. It was delightful to be sheltered from the afternoon sun, and when we had gone some distance in the shade, to my great pleasure William turned the horse's head toward some bars, which he let down, and I drove through into one of those narrow, still, sweet-scented by-ways which seem to be paths rather than roads. Often we had to put aside the heavy drooping branches which barred the way, and once, when a sharp twig struck William in the face, he announced with such spirit that somebody ought to go through there with an axe, that I felt un-expectedly guilty. So far as I now remember, this was William's only remark all the way through the woods to Thankful Hight's folks, but from time to time he pointed or nodded at something which I might have missed: a sleepy little owl snuggled into the bend of a branch, or a tall stalk of cardinal flowers where the sunlight came down at the edge of a small, bright piece of marsh. Many times, being used to the company of Mrs. Todd and other friends who were in the habit of talking, I came near making an idle remark to William, but I was for the most part happily pre-served; to be with him only for a short time was to live on a different level, where thoughts served best because they were thoughts in common; the primary effect upon our minds of the simple things and beauties that we saw. Once when I caught sight of a lovely gay pigeon-woodpecker eyeing us curiously from a dead branch, and instinctively turned toward William, he gave an indulgent, comprehending nod which silenced me all the rest of the way. The wood-road was not a place for common noisy conversation; one would interrupt the birds and all the still little beasts that belonged there. But it was mortifying to find how strong the habit of idle speech may become in one's self. One need not always be saying something in this noisy world. I grew conscious of the difference between William's usual fashion of life and mine; for him there were long days of silence in a sea-going boat, and I could believe that he and his mother usually spoke very little because they so perfectly understood each other. There was something peculiarly unresponding about their quiet island in the sea, solidly fixed into the still foundations of the world, against whose rocky shores the sea beats and calls and is unanswered.

We were quite half an hour going through the woods; the horse's feet made no sound on the brown, soft track under the dark evergreens. I thought that we should come out at last into more pastures, but there was no half-wooded strip of land at the end; the high woods grew squarely against an old stone wall and a sunshiny open field, and we came out suddenly into broad daylight that startled us and even startled the horse, who might have been napping as he walked, like an old soldier. The field sloped up to a low unpainted house that faced the east. Behind it were long, frost-whitened ledges that made the hill, with strips of green turf and bushes between. It was the wildest, most Titanic sort of pasture country up there; there was a sort of daring in putting a frail wooden house before it, though it might have the homely field and honest woods to front against. You thought of the elements and even of possible volcanoes as you looked up the stony heights. Suddenly I saw that a region of what I had thought gray stones was slowly moving, as if the sun was making my eyesight unsteady.

"There's the sheep!" exclaimed William, pointing eagerly. "You see the sheep?" and sure enough, it was a great company of woolly backs, which seemed to have taken a mysterious protective resemblance to the ledges themselves. I could discover but little chance for pasturage on that high sunburnt ridge, but the sheep were moving steadily in a satisfied way as they fed along the slopes and hollows.

"I never have seen half so many sheep as these, all summer long!" I cried with admiration.

"There ain't so many," answered William soberly. "It's a great sight. They do so well because they're shepherded, but you can't beat sense into some folks."

"You mean that somebody stays and watches them?" I asked.

"She observed years ago in her readin' that they don't turn out their flocks without protection anywhere but in the State o' Maine," returned William. "First thing that put it into her mind was a little old book mother's got; she read it one time when she come out to the Island. They call it the 'Shepherd o' Salisbury Plain.' 'T wasn't the purpose o' the book to most, but when she read it, 'There, Mis' Blackett!' she said, 'that's where we've all lacked sense; our Bibles ought to have taught us that what sheep need is a shepherd.' You see most folks about here gave up sheep-raisin' years ago 'count o' the dogs. So she gave up school-teachin' and went out to tend her flock, and has shepherded ever since, an' done well."

For William, this approached an oration. He spoke with enthusiasm, and I shared the triumph of the moment. "There she is now!" he exclaimed, in a different tone, as the tall figure of a woman came following the flock and stood still on the ridge, looking toward us as if her eyes had been quick to see a strange object in the familiar emptiness of the field. William stood up in the wagon, and I thought he was going to call or wave his hand to her, but he sat down again more clumsily than if the wagon had made the familiar motion of a boat, and we drove on toward the house.

It was a most solitary place to live,—a place where one might think that a life could hide itself. The thick woods were between the farm and the main road, and as one looked up and down the country, there was no other house in sight.

"Potatoes look well," announced William. "The old folks used to say that there wa'n't no better land outdoors than the Hight field."

I found myself possessed of a surprising interest in the shepherdess, who stood far away in the hill pasture with her great flock, like a figure of Millet's, high against the sky.

V

Everything about the old farmhouse was clean and orderly, as if the green dooryard were not only swept, but dusted. I saw a flock of turkeys stepping off carefully at a distance, but there was not the usual untidy flock of hens about the place to make everything look in disarray. William helped me out of the wagon as carefully as if I had been his mother, and nodded toward the open door with a reassuring look at me; but I waited until he had tied the horse and could lead the way, himself. He took off his hat just as we were going in, and stopped for a moment to smooth his thin gray hair with his hand, by which I saw that we had an affair of some ceremony. We entered an old-fashioned country kitchen, the floor scrubbed into unevenness, and the doors well polished by the touch of hands. In a large chair facing the window there sat a masterful-looking old woman with features of a warlike Roman emperor, emphasized by a bonnet-like black cap with a band of green ribbon. Her sceptre was a palm-leaf fan.

William crossed the room toward her, and bent his head close to her ear.

"Feelin' pretty well to-day, Mis' Hight?" he asked, with all the voice his narrow chest could muster.

"No, I ain't, William. Here I have to set," she answered coldly, but she gave an inquiring glance over his shoulder at me.

"This is the young lady who is stopping with Almiry this summer," he explained, and I approached as if to give the countersign. She offered her left hand with considerable dignity, but her expression never seemed to change for the better. A moment later she said that she was pleased to meet me, and I felt as if the worst were over. William must have felt some apprehension, while I was only ignorant, as we had come across the field. Our hostess was more than disapproving, she was forbidding; but I was not long in suspecting that she felt the natural resentment of a strong energy that has been defeated by illness and made the spoil of captivity.

"Mother well as usual since you was up last year?" and William replied by a series of cheerful nods. The mention of dear Mrs. Blackett was a help to any conversation.

"Been fishin', ashore," he explained, in a somewhat conciliatory voice. "Thought you'd like a few for winter," which explained at once the generous freight we had brought in the back of the wagon. I could see that the offering was no surprise, and that Mrs. Hight was interested.

"Well, I expect they're good as the last," she said, but did not even approach a smile. She kept a straight, discerning eye upon me.

"Give the lady a cheer," she admonished William, who hastened to place close by her side one of the straight-backed chairs that stood against the kitchen wall. Then he lingered for a moment like a timid boy. I could see that he wore a look of resolve, but he did not ask the permission for which he evidently waited.

"You can go search for Esther," she said, at the end of a long pause that became anxious for both her guests. "Esther'd like to see her;" and William in his pale nankeens disappeared with one light step and was off.

VI

"Don't speak too loud, it jars a person's head," directed Mrs. Hight plainly. "Clear an' distinct is what reaches me best. Any news to the Landin'?"

I was happily furnished with the particulars of a sudden death, and an engagement of marriage between a Caplin, a seafaring widower home from his voyage, and one of the younger Harrises; and now Mrs. Hight really smiled and settled herself in her chair. We exhausted one subject completely before we turned to the other. One of the returning turkeys took an unwarrantable liberty, and, mounting the doorstep, came in and walked about the kitchen without being observed by its strict owner; and the tin dipper slipped off its nail behind us and made an astonishing noise, and jar enough to reach Mrs. Hight's inner ear and make her turn her head to look at it; but we talked straight on. We came at last to understand each other upon such terms of friendship that she unbent her majestic port and complained to me as any poor old woman might of the hardships of her illness. She had already fixed various dates upon the sad certainty of the year when she had the shock, which had left her perfectly helpless except for a clumsy left hand which fanned and gestured, and settled and resettled the folds of her dress, but could do no comfortable time-shortening work.

"Yes'm, you can feel sure I use it what I can," she said severely. " 'T was a long spell before I could let Esther go forth in the mornin' till she'd got me up an' dressed me, but now she leaves things ready overnight and I get 'em as I want 'em with my light pair o' tongs, and I feel very able about helpin' myself to what I once did. Then when Esther returns, all she has to do is to push me out here into the kitchen. Some parts o' the year Esther stays out all night, them moonlight nights when the dogs are apt to be after the sheep, but she don't use herself as hard as she once had to. She's well able to hire somebody, Esther is, but there, you can't find no hired man that wants to git up before five o'clock nowadays; 't ain't as 't was in my time. They're liable to fall asleep, too, and them moonlight nights she's so anxious she can't sleep, and out she goes. There's a kind of a fold, she calls it, up there in a sheltered spot, and she sleeps up in a little shed she's got,—built it herself for lambin' time and when the poor foolish creatur's gets hurt or anything. I've never seen it, but she says it's in a lovely spot and always pleasant in any weather. You see off, other side of the ridge, to the south'ard, where there's houses. I used to think some time I'd get up to see it again, and all them spots she lives in, but I sha'n't now. I'm beginnin' to go back; an' 't ain't surprisin'. I've kind of got used to disappointments," and the poor soul drew a deep sigh.

VII

It was long before we noticed the lapse of time; I not only told every circumstance known to me of recent events among the households of Mrs. Todd's neighborhood at the shore, but Mrs. Hight became more and more communicative on her part, and went carefully into the genealogical descent and personal experience of many acquaintances, until between us we had pretty nearly circumnavigated the globe and reached Dunnet Landing from an opposite direction to that in which we had started. It was long before my own interest began to flag; there was a flavor of the best sort in her definite and descriptive fashion of speech. It may be only a fancy of my own that in the sound and value of many words, with their lengthened vowels and doubled cadences, there is some faint survival on the Maine coast of the sound of English speech of Chaucer's time.

At last Mrs. Thankful Hight gave a suspicious look through the window.

"Where do you suppose they be?" she asked me. "Esther must ha' been off to the far edge o' everything. I doubt William ain't been able to find her; can't he hear their bells? His hearin' all right?"

William had heard some herons that morning which were beyond the reach of my own ears, and almost beyond eyesight in the upper skies, and I told her so. I was luckily preserved by some unconscious instinct from saying that we had seen the shepherdess so near as we crossed the field. Unless she had fled faster than Atalanta, William must have been but a few minutes in reaching her immediate neighborhood. I now discovered with a quick leap of amusement and delight in my heart that I had fallen upon a serious chapter of romance. The old woman looked suspiciously at me, and I made a dash to cover with a new piece of information; but she listened with lofty indifference, and soon interrupted my eager statements.

"Ain't William been gone some considerable time?" she demanded, and then in a milder tone: "The time has re'lly flown; I do enjoy havin' company. I set here alone a sight o' long days. Sheep is dreadful fools; I expect they heard a strange step, and set right off through bush an' brier, spite of all she could do. But William might have the sense to return, 'stead o' searchin' about. I want to inquire of him about his mother. What was you goin' to say? I guess you'll have time to relate it."

My powers of entertainment were on the ebb, but I doubled my diligence and we went on for another half-hour at least with banners flying, but still William did not reappear. Mrs. Hight frankly began to show fatigue.

"Somethin' 's happened, an' he's stopped to help her," groaned the old lady, in the middle of what I had found to tell her about a rumor of disaffection with the minister of a town I merely knew by name in the weekly newspaper to which Mrs. Todd subscribed. "You step to the door, dear, an' look if you can't see 'em." I promptly stepped, and once outside the house I looked anxiously in the direction which William had taken.

To my astonishment I saw all the sheep so near that I wonder we had not been aware in the house of every bleat and tinkle. And there, within a stone's-throw, on the first long gray ledge that showed above the juniper, were William and the shepherdess engaged in pleasant conversation. At first I was provoked and then amused, and a thrill of sympathy warmed my whole heart. They

had seen me and risen as if by magic; I had a sense of being the
messenger of Fate. One could almost hear their sighs of regret as
I appeared; they must have passed a lovely afternoon. I hurried
into the house with the reassuring news that they were not only
in sight but perfectly safe, with all the sheep.

VIII

Mrs. Hight, like myself, was spent with conversation, and had
ceased even the one activity of fanning herself. I brought a desired
drink of water, and happily rememberd some fruit that was left
from my luncheon. She revived with splendid vigor, and told me
the simple history of her later years since she had been smitten in
the prime of her life by the stroke of paralysis, and her husband
had died and left her alone with Esther and a mortgage on their
farm. There was only one field of good land, but they owned a
great region of sheep pasture and a little woodland. Esther had
always been laughed at for her belief in sheep-raising when one
by one their neighbors were giving up their flocks, and when everything had come to the point of despair she had raised all the money
and bought all the sheep she could, insisting that Maine lambs were
as good as any, and that there was a straight path by sea to Boston
market. And by tending her flock herself she had managed to
succeed; she had made money enough to pay off the mortgage five
years ago, and now what they did not spend was safe in the bank.
"It has been stubborn work, day and night, summer and winter,
an' now she's beginnin' to get along in years," said the old mother
sadly. "She's tended me 'long o' the sheep, an' she's been a good
girl right along, but she ought to have been a teacher;" and Mrs.
Hight sighed heavily and plied the fan again.

We heard voices, and William and Esther entered; they did not
know that it was so late in the afternoon. William looked almost
bold, and oddly like a happy young man rather than an ancient
boy. As for Esther, she might have been Jeanne d'Arc returned to
her sheep, touched with age and gray with the ashes of a great
remembrance. She wore the simple look of sainthood and un-
feigned devotion. My heart was moved by the sight of her plain
sweet face, weatherworn and gentle in its looks, her thin figure in
its close dress, and the strong hand that clasped a shepherd's staff,
and I could only hold William in new reverence; this silent farmer-

fisherman who knew, and he alone, the noble and patient heart that beat within her breast. I am not sure that they acknowledged even to themselves that they had always been lovers; they could not consent to anything so definite or pronounced but they were happy in being together in the world. Esther was untouched by the fret and fury of life; she had lived in sunshine and rain among her silly sheep, and been refined instead of coarsened, while her touching patience with a ramping old mother, stung by the sense of defeat and mourning her lost activities, had given back a lovely self-possession, and habit of sweet temper. I had seen enough of old Mrs. Hight to know that nothing a sheep might do could vex a person who was used to the uncertainties and severities of her companionship.

IX

Mrs. Hight told her daughter at once that she had enjoyed a beautiful call, and got a great many new things to think of. This was said so frankly in my hearing that it gave a consciousness of high reward, and I was indeed recompensed by the grateful look in Esther's eyes. We did not speak much together, but we understood each other. For the poor old woman did not read, and could not sew or knit with her helpless hand, and they were far from any neighbors, while her spirit was as eager in age as in youth, and expected even more from a disappointing world. She had lived to see the mortgage paid and money in the bank, and Esther's success acknowledged on every hand, and there were still a few pleasures left in life. William had his mother, and Esther had hers, and they had not seen each other for a year, though Mrs. Hight had spoken of a year's making no change in William even at his age. She must have been in the far eighties herself, but of a noble courage and persistence in the world she ruled from her stiff-backed rocking-chair.

William unloaded his gift of dried fish, each one chosen with perfect care, and Esther stood by, watching him, and then she walked across the field with us beside the wagon. I believed that I was the only one who knew their happy secret, and she blushed a little as we said good-by.

"I hope you ain't goin' to feel too tired, mother's so deaf; no, I hope you won't be tired," she said kindly, speaking as if she well knew what tiredness was. We could hear the neglected sheep bleating on the hill in the next moment's silence. Then she smiled at me, a smile of noble patience, of uncomprehended sacrifice, which I can never forget. There was all the remembrance of disappointed hopes, the hardships of winter, the loneliness of single-handedness in her look, but I understood, and I love to remember her worn face and her young blue eyes.

"Good-by, William," she said gently, and William said good-by, and gave her a quick glance, but he did not turn to look back, though I did, and waved my hand as she was putting up the bars behind us. Nor did he speak again until we had passed through the dark woods and were on our way homeward by the main road. The grave yearly visit had been changed from a hope into a happy memory.

"You can see the sea from the top of her pasture hill," said William at last.

"Can you?" I asked, with surprise.

"Yes, it's very high land; the ledges up there show very plain in clear weather from the top of our island, and there's a high up-standin' tree that makes a landmark for the fishin' grounds." And William gave a happy sigh.

When we had nearly reached the Landing, my companion looked over into the back of the wagon and saw that the piece of sailcloth was safe, with which he had covered the dried fish. "I wish we had got some trout," he said wistfully. "They always appease Almiry, and make her feel 't was worth while to go."

I stole a glance at William Blackett. We had not seen a solitary mosquito, but there was a dark stripe across his mild face, which might have been an old scar won long ago in battle.

22 *The Queen's Twin*

I

The coast of Maine was in former years brought so near to foreign shores by its busy fleet of ships that among the older men and women one still finds a surprising proportion of travelers. Each seaward-stretching headland with its high-set houses, each island of a single farm, has sent its spies to view many a Land of Eshcol; one may see plain, contented old faces at the windows, whose eyes have looked at far-away ports and known the splendors of the Eastern world. They shame the easy voyager of the North Atlantic and the Mediterranean; they have rounded the Cape of Good Hope and braved the angry seas of Cape Horn in small wooden ships; they have brought up their hardy boys and girls on narrow decks; they were among the last of the Northmen's children to go adventuring to unknown shores. More than this one cannot give to a young State for its enlightenment; the sea captains and the captains' wives of Maine knew something of the wide world, and never mistook their native parishes for the whole instead of a part thereof; they knew not only Thomaston and Castine and Portland, but London and Bristol and Bordeaux, and the strange-mannered harbors of the China Sea.

One September day, when I was nearly at the end of my summer at Dunnet Landing, Mrs. Todd came home from a long, solitary stroll in the wild pastures, with an eager look as if she were just starting on a hopeful quest instead of returning. She brought a little basket with blackberries enough for supper, and held it towards me so that I could see that there were also some late and surprising raspberries sprinkled on top, but she made no comment upon her wayfaring. I could tell plainly that she had something very important to say.

"You haven't brought home a leaf of anything," I ventured to this practiced herb-gatherer. "You were saying yesterday that the witch hazel might be in bloom."

"I dare say, dear," she answered in a lofty manner; "I ain't goin' to say it wasn't; I ain't much concerned either way 'bout the facts o' witch hazel. Truth is, I've been off visitin'; there's an old Indian footpath leadin' over towards the Back Shore through the great heron swamp that anybody can't travel over all summer. You have to seize your time some day just now, while the low ground's summer-dried as it is to-day, and before the fall rains set in. I never thought of it till I was out o' sight o' home, and I says to myself, 'To-day's the day, certain!' and stepped along smart as I could. Yes, I've been visitin'. I did get into one spot that was wet underfoot before I noticed; you wait till I get me a pair o' dry woolen stockings, in case of cold, and I'll come an' tell ye."

Mrs. Todd disappeared. I could see that something had deeply interested her. She might have fallen in with either the sea-serpent or the lost tribes of Israel, such was her air of mystery and satisfaction. She had been away since just before mid-morning, and as I sat waiting by my window I saw the last red glow of autumn sunshine flare along the gray rocks of the shore and leave them cold again, and touch the far sails of some coastwise schooners so that they stood like golden houses on the sea.

I was left to wonder longer than I liked. Mrs. Todd was making an evening fire and putting things in train for supper; presently she returned, still looking warm and cheerful after her long walk.

"There's a beautiful view from a hill over where I've been," she told me; "yes, there's a beautiful prospect of land and sea. You wouldn't discern the hill from any distance, but 't is the pretty situation of it that counts. I sat there a long spell, and I did wish for you. No, I didn't know a word about goin' when I set out this morning" (as if I had openly reproached her!); "I only felt one o' them travelin' fits comin' on, an' I ketched up my little basket; I didn't know but I might turn and come back time for dinner. I thought it wise to set out your luncheon for you in case I didn't. Hope you had all you wanted; yes, I hope you had enough."

"Oh, yes, indeed," said I. My landlady was always peculiarly bountiful in her supplies when she left me to fare for myself, as if she made a sort of peace-offering or affectionate apology.

"You know that hill with the old house right on top, over beyond the heron swamp? You'll excuse me for explainin'," Mrs. Todd began, "but you ain't so apt to strike inland as you be to go right along shore. You know that hill; there's a path leadin' right over to it that you have to look sharp to find nowadays; it belonged to the up-country Indians when they had to make a carry to the landing here to get to the out' islands. I've heard the old folks say that there used to be a place across a ledge where they'd worn a deep track with their moccasin feet, but I never could find it. 'T is so overgrown in some places that you keep losin' the path in the bushes and findin' it as you can; but it runs pretty straight considerin' the lay o' the land, and I keep my eye on the sun and the moss that grows one side o' the tree trunks. Some brook's been choked up and the swamp's bigger than it used to be. Yes; I did get in deep enough, one place!"

I showed the solicitude that I felt. Mrs. Todd was no longer young, and in spite of her strong, great frame and spirited behavior,

I knew that certain ills were apt to seize upon her, and would end some day by leaving her lame and ailing.

"Don't you go to worryin' about me," she insisted, "settin' still's the only way the Evil One'll ever get the upper hand o' me. Keep me movin' enough, an' I'm twenty year old summer an' winter both. I don't know why 't is, but I've never happened to mention the one I've been to see. I don't know why I never happened to speak the name of Abby Martin, for I often give her a thought, but 't is a dreadful out-o'-the-way place where she lives, and I haven't seen her myself for three or four years. She's a real good interesting woman, and we're well acquainted; she's nigher mother's age than mine, but she's very young feeling. She made me a nice cup o' tea, and I don't know but I should have stopped all night if I could have got word to you not to worry."

Then there was a serious silence before Mrs. Todd spoke again to make a formal announcement.

"She is the Queen's Twin," and Mrs. Todd looked steadily to see how I might bear the great surprise.

"The Queen's Twin?" I repeated.

"Yes, she's come to feel a real interest in the Queen, and anybody can see how natural 't is. They were born the very same day, and you would be astonished to see what a number o' other things have corresponded. She was speaking o' some o' the facts to me to-day, an' you'd think she'd never done nothing but read history. I see how earnest she was about it as I never did before. I've often and often heard her allude to the facts, but now she's got to be old and the hurry's over with her work, she's come to live a good deal in her thoughts, as folks often do, and I tell you 't is a sight o' company for her. If you want to hear about Queen Victoria, why Mis' Abby Martin'll tell you everything. And the prospect from that hill I spoke of is as beautiful as anything in this world; 't is worth while your goin' over to see her just for that."

"When can you go again?" I demanded eagerly.

"I should say to-morrow," answered Mrs. Todd; "yes, I should say to-morrow; but I expect 't would be better to take one day to rest, in between. I considered that question as I was comin' home, but I hurried so that there wa'n't much time to think. It's a dreadful long way to go with a horse; you have to go 'most as far as the old Bowden place an' turn off to the left, a master long, rough road, and then you have to turn right round as soon as you get there if you mean to get home before nine o'clock at night. But to strike across country from here, there's plenty o' time in the shortest day, and you can have a good hour or two's visit beside; 't ain't but a very few miles, and it's pretty all the way along. There used to be a few good families over there, but they've died and scattered, so now she's far from neighbors. There, she really cried, she was so glad to see anybody comin'. You'll be amused to hear her talk about the Queen, but I thought twice or three times as I set there 't was about all the company she'd got."

"Could we go day after to-morrow?" I asked eagerly.

" 'T would suit me exactly," said Mrs. Todd.

II

One can never be so certain of good New England weather as in the days when a long easterly storm has blown away the warm late-summer mists, and cooled the air so that however bright the sunshine is by day, the nights come nearer and nearer to frostiness. There was a cold freshness in the morning air when Mrs. Todd and I locked the house-door behind us; we took the key of the fields into our own hands that day, and put out across country as one puts out to sea. When we reached the top of the ridge behind the town it seemed as if we had anxiously passed the harbor bar and were comfortably in open sea at last.

"There, now!" proclaimed Mrs. Todd, taking a long breath, "now I do feel safe. It's just the weather that's liable to bring somebody to spend the day; I've had a feeling of Mis' Elder Caplin from North Point bein' close upon me ever since I waked up this mornin', an' I didn't want to be hampered with our present plans. She's a great hand to visit; she'll be spendin' the day somewhere from now till Thanksgivin', but there's plenty o' places at the Landin' where she goes, an' if I ain't there she'll just select another. I thought mother might be in, too, 't is so pleasant; but I run up the road to look off this mornin' before you was awake, and there was no sign o' the boat. If they hadn't started by that time they wouldn't start, just as the tide is now; besides, I see a lot o' mackerel-men headin' Green Island way, and they'll detain William. No, we're safe now, an' if mother should be comin' in to-morrow we'll have all this to tell her. She an' Mis' Abby Martin's very old friends."

We were walking down the long pasture slopes towards the dark woods and thickets of the low ground. They stretched away northward like an unbroken wilderness; the early mists still dulled much of the color and made the uplands beyond look like a very far-off country.

"It ain't so far as it looks from here," said my companion reassuringly, "but we've got no time to spare either," and she hurried on, leading the way with a fine sort of spirit in her step; and presently we struck into the old Indian footpath, which could be plainly seen across the long-unploughed turf of the pastures, and followed it among the thick, low-growing spruces. There the ground was smooth and brown under foot, and the thin-stemmed trees held a dark and shadowy roof overhead. We walked a long way without speaking; sometimes we had to push aside the branches, and sometimes we walked in a broad aisle where the trees were larger. It was a solitary wood, birdless and beastless; there was not even a rabbit to be seen, or a crow high in air to break the silence.

"I don't believe the Queen ever saw such a lonesome trail as this," said Mrs. Todd, as if she followed the thoughts that were in my mind. Our visit to Mrs. Abby Martin seemed in some strange way to concern the high affairs of royalty. I had just been thinking of English landscapes, and of the solemn hills of Scotland with their lonely cottages and stone-walled sheepfolds, and the wandering flocks on high cloudy pastures. I had often been struck by the quick interest and familiar allusion to certain members of the royal house which one found in distant neighborhoods of New England; whether some old instincts of personal loyalty have survived all changes of time and national vicissitudes, or whether it is only that the Queen's own character and disposition have won friends for her so far away, it is impossible to tell. But to hear of a twin sister was the most surprising proof of intimacy of all, and I must confess that there was something remarkably exciting to the imagination in my morning walk. To think of being presented at Court in the usual way was for the moment quite commonplace.

III

Mrs. Todd was swinging her basket to and fro like a schoolgirl as she walked, and at this moment it slipped from her hand and rolled lightly along the ground as if there were nothing in it. I picked it up and gave it to her, whereupon she lifted the cover and looked in with anxiety.

" 'T is only a few little things, but I don't want to lose 'em," she explained humbly. " 'T was lucky you took the other basket if I was goin' to roll it round. Mis' Abby Martin complained o' lacking some pretty pink silk to finish one o' her little frames, an' I thought I'd carry her some, and I had a bunch o' gold thread that had been in a box o' mine this twenty year. I never was one to do much fancy work, but we're all liable to be swept away by fashion. And then there's a small packet o' very choice herbs that I gave a good deal of attention to; they'll smarten her up and give her the best of appetites, come spring. She was tellin' me that spring weather is very wiltin' an' tryin' to her, and she was beginnin' to dread it already. Mother's just the same way; if I could prevail on mother to take some o' these remedies in good season 't would make a world o' difference, but she gets all down hill before I have a chance to hear of it, and then William comes in to tell me, sighin' and bewailin', how feeble mother is. 'Why can't you remember 'bout them good herbs that I never let her be without?' I say to him— he does provoke me so; and then off he goes, sulky enough, down to his boat. Next thing I know, she comes in to go to meetin', wantin' to speak to everybody and feelin' like a girl. Mis' Martin's case is very much the same; but she's nobody to watch her. William's kind o' slow-moulded; but there, any William's better than none when you get to be Mis' Martin's age."

"Hadn't she any children?" I asked.

"Quite a number," replied Mrs. Todd grandly, "but some are gone and the rest are married and settled. She never was a great hand to go about visitin'. I don't know but Mis' Martin might be called a little peculiar. Even her own folks has to make company of her; she never slips in and lives right along with the rest as if 't was at home, even in her own children's houses. I heard one o' her sons' wives say once she'd much rather have the Queen to spend the day if she could choose between the two, but I never thought Abby was so difficult as that. I used to love to have her come; she may have been sort o' ceremonious, but very pleasant and sprightly if you had sense enough to treat her her own way. I always think she'd know just how to live with great folks, and feel easier 'long of them an' their ways. Her son's wife's a great driver with farm-work, boards a great tableful o' men in hayin' time, an' feels right in her element. I don't say but she's a good woman an' smart, but sort o' rough. Anybody that's gentle-mannered an' precise like Mis' Martin would be a sort o' restraint.

"There's all sorts o' folks in the country, same's there is in the city," concluded Mrs. Todd gravely, and I as gravely agreed. The thick woods were behind us now, and the sun was shining clear overhead, the morning mists were gone, and a faint blue haze softened the distance; as we climbed the hill where we were to see the view, it seemed like a summer day. There was an old house on the height, facing southward,—a mere forsaken shell of an old house, with empty windows that looked like blind eyes. The frost-bitten grass grew close about it like brown fur, and there was a single crooked bough of lilac holding its green leaves close by the door.

"We'll just have a good piece of bread-an'-butter now," said the commander of the expedition, "and then we'll hang up the basket on some peg inside the house out o' the way o' the sheep, and have a han'some entertainment as we're comin' back. She'll be all through her little dinner when we get there, Mis' Martin will; but she'll want to make us some tea, an' we must have our visit an' be startin' back pretty soon after two. I don't want to cross all that low ground again after it's begun to grow chilly. An' it looks to me as if the clouds might begin to gather late in the afternoon."

Before us lay a splendid world of sea and shore. The autumn colors already brightened the landscape; and here and there at the edge of a dark tract of pointed firs stood a row of bright swamp-maples like scarlet flowers. The blue sea and the great tide inlets were untroubled by the lightest winds.

"Poor land, this is!" sighed Mrs. Todd as we sat down to rest on the worn doorstep. "I've known three good hard-workin' families that come here full o' hope an' pride and tried to make something o' this farm, but it beat 'em all. There's one small field that's excellent for potatoes if you let half of it rest every year; but the land's always hungry. Now, you see them little peakéd-topped spruces an' fir balsams comin' up over the hill all green an' hearty; they've got it all their own way! Seems sometimes as if wild Natur' got jealous over a certain spot, and wanted to do just as she'd a mind to. You'll see here; she'll do her own ploughin' an' harrowin' with frost an' wet, an' plant just what she wants and wait for her own crops. Man can't do nothin' with it, try as he may. I tell you those little trees means business!"

I looked down the slope, and felt as if we ourselves were likely to be surrounded and overcome if we lingered too long. There was a vigor of growth, a persistence and savagery about the sturdy little trees that put weak human nature at complete defiance. One felt a sudden pity for the men and women who had been worsted after a long fight in that lonely place; one felt a sudden fear of the unconquerable, immediate forces of Nature, as in the irresistible moment of a thunderstorm.

"I can recollect the time when folks were shy o' these woods we just come through," said Mrs. Todd seriously. "The men-folks themselves never'd venture into 'em alone; if their cattle got strayed they'd collect whoever they could get, and start off all together. They said a person was liable to get bewildered in there alone, and in old times folks had been lost. I expect there was considerable fear left over from the old Indian times, and the poor days o' witchcraft; anyway, I've seen bold men act kind o' timid. Some women o' the Asa Bowden family went out one afternoon berryin' when I was a girl, and got lost and was out all night; they found 'em middle o' the mornin' next day, not half a mile from home, scared most to death, an' sayin' they'd heard wolves and other beasts sufficient for a caravan. Poor creatur's! they'd strayed at last into a kind of low place amongst some alders, an' one of 'em was so overset she never got over it, an' went off in a sort o' slow decline. 'T was like them victims that drowns in a foot o' water; but their minds did suffer dreadful. Some folks is born afraid of the woods and all wild places, but I must say they've always been like home to me."

I glanced at the resolute, confident face of my companion. Life was very strong in her, as if some force of Nature were personified in this simple-hearted woman and gave her cousinship to the ancient deities. She might have walked the primeval fields of Sicily; her strong gingham skirts might at that very moment bend the slender stalks of asphodel and be fragrant with trodden thyme, instead of the brown wind-brushed grass of New England and frost-bitten goldenrod. She was a great soul, was Mrs. Todd, and I her humble follower, as we went our way to visit the Queen's Twin, leaving the bright view of the sea behind us, and descending to a lower country-side through the dry pastures and fields.

The farms all wore a look of gathering age, though the settlement was, after all, so young. The fences were already fragile, and it seemed as if the first impulse of agriculture had soon spent itself without hope of renewal. The better houses were always those that had some hold upon the riches of the sea; a house that could not harbor a fishingboat in some neighboring inlet was far from being sure of every-day comforts. The land alone was not enough to live upon in that stony region; it belonged by right to the forest, and to the forest it fast returned. From the top of the hill where we had been sitting we had seen prosperity in the dim distance, where the land was good and the sun shone upon fat barns, and where warm-looking houses with three or four chimneys apiece stood high on their solid ridge above the bay.

As we drew nearer to Mrs. Martin's it was sad to see what poor bushy fields, what thin and empty dwelling-places had been left by those who had chosen this disappointing part of the northern country for their home. We crossed the last field and came into a narrow rain-washed road, and Mrs. Todd looked eager and expectant and said that we were almost at our journey's end. "I do hope Mis' Martin'll ask you into her best room where she keeps all the Queen's pictures. Yes, I think likely she will ask you; but 't ain't everybody she deems worthy to visit 'em, I can tell you!" said Mrs. Todd warningly. "She's been collectin' 'em an' cuttin' 'em out o' newspapers an' magazines time out o' mind, and if she heard of anybody sailin' for an English port she'd contrive to get a little money to 'em and ask to have the last likeness there was. She's most covered her best-room wall now; she keeps that room shut up sacred as a meetin'-house! 'I won't say but I have my favorites amongst 'em,' she told me t' other day, 'but they're all beautiful to me as they can be!' And she's made some kind o' pretty little frames for 'em all—you know there's always a new fashion o' frames comin' round; first 't was shell-work, and then 't was pine-cones, and bead-work's had its day, and now she's much concerned with perforated cardboard worked with silk. I tell you that best room's a sight to see! But you mustn't look for anything elegant," continued Mrs. Todd, after a moment's reflection. "Mis' Martin's always been in very poor, strugglin' circumstances. She had ambition for her children, though they took right after their father an' had little for themselves; she wa'n't over an' above well married, however kind she may see fit to speak. She's been patient an' hardworkin' all her life, and always high above makin' mean complaints of other folks. I expect all this business about the Queen has buoyed her over many a shoal place in life. Yes, you might say that Abby'd been a slave, but there ain't any slave but has some freedom."

IV

Presently I saw a low gray house standing on a grassy bank close to the road. The door was at the side, facing us, and a tangle of snowberry bushes and cinnamon roses grew to the level of the window-sills. On the doorstep stood a bent-shouldered, little old woman; there was an air of welcome and of unmistakable dignity about her.

"She sees us coming," exclaimed Mrs. Todd in an excited whisper. "There, I told her I might be over this way again if the weather held good, and if I came I'd bring you. She said right off she'd take great pleasure in havin' a visit from you; I was surprised, she's usually so retirin'."

Even this reassurance did not quell a faint apprehension on our part; there was something distinctly formal in the occasion, and one felt that consciousness of inadequacy which is never easy for the humblest pride to bear. On the way I had torn my dress in an unexpected encounter with a little thornbush, and I could now imagine how it felt to be going to Court and forgetting one's feathers or her Court train.

The Queen's Twin was oblivious of such trifles; she stood waiting with a calm look until we came near enough to take her kind hand. She was a beautiful old woman, with clear eyes and a lovely quietness and genuineness of manner; there was not a trace of anything pretentious about her, or high-flown, as Mrs. Todd would say comprehensively. Beauty in age is rare enough in women who have spent their lives in the hard work of a farmhouse; but autumnlike and withered as this woman may have looked, her features had kept, or rather gained, a great refinement. She led us into her old kitchen and gave us seats, and took one of the little straight-backed chairs herself and sat a short distance away, as if she were giving audience to an ambassador. It seemed as if we should all be standing; you could not help feeling that the habits of her life were more ceremonious, but that for the moment she assumed the simplicities of the occasion.

Mrs. Todd was always Mrs. Todd, too great and self-possessed a soul for any occasion to ruffle. I admired her calmness, and presently the slow current of neighborhood talk carried one easily along; we spoke of the weather and the small adventures of the way, and then, as if I were after all not a stranger, our hostess turned almost affectionately to speak to me.

"The weather will be growing dark in London now. I expect that you've been in London, dear?" she said.

"Oh, yes," I answered. "Only last year."

"It is a great many years since I was there, along in the forties," said Mrs. Martin. " 'T was the only voyage I ever made; most of my neighbors have been great travelers. My brother was master of a vessel, and his wife usually sailed with him; but that year she had a young child more frail than the others, and she dreaded the care of it at sea. It happened that my brother got a chance for my husband to go as supercargo, being a good accountant, and came one day to urge him to take it; he was very ill-disposed to the sea, but he had met with losses, and I saw my own opportunity and persuaded them both to let me go too. In those days they didn't object to a woman's being aboard to wash and mend, the voyages were sometimes very long. And that was the way I come to see the Queen."

Mrs. Martin was looking straight in my eyes to see if I showed any genuine interest in the most interesting person in the world.

"Oh, I am very glad you saw the Queen," I hastened to say. "Mrs. Todd has told me that you and she were born the very same day."

"We were indeed, dear!" said Mrs. Martin, and she leaned back comfortably and smiled as she had not smiled before. Mrs. Todd gave a satisfied nod and glance, as if to say that things were going on as well as possible in this anxious moment.

"Yes," said Mrs. Martin again, drawing her chair a little nearer, " 't was a very remarkable thing; we were born the same day, and at exactly the same hour, after you allowed for all the difference in time. My father figured it out sea-fashion. Her Royal Majesty and I opened our eyes upon this world together; say what you may, 't is a bond between us."

Mrs. Todd assented with an air of triumph, and untied her hat-strings and threw them back over her shoulders with a gallant air.

"And I married a man by the name of Albert, just the same as she did, and all by chance, for I didn't get the news that she had an Albert too till a fortnight afterward; news was slower coming then than it is now. My first baby was a girl, and I called her Victoria after my mate; but the next one was a boy, and my husband wanted the right to name him, and took his own name and his brother Edward's, and pretty soon I saw in the paper that the little Prince o' Wales had been christened just the same. After that I made excuse to wait till I knew what she'd named her children. I didn't want to break the chain, so I had an Alfred, and my darling Alice that I lost long before she lost hers, and there I stopped. If I'd only had a dear daughter to stay at home with me, same's her youngest one, I should have been so thankful! But if only one of us could have a little Beatrice, I'm glad 't was the Queen; we've both seen trouble, but she's had the most care."

I asked Mrs. Martin if she lived alone all the year, and was told that she did except for a visit now and then from one of her grandchildren, "the only one that really likes to come an' stay quiet 'long o' grandma. She always says quick as she's through her schoolin' she's goin' to live with me all the time, but she's very pretty an' has taking ways," said Mrs. Martin, looking both proud and wistful, "so I can tell nothing at all about it! Yes, I've been alone most o' the time since my Albert was taken away, and that's a great many years; he had a long time o' failing and sickness first." (Mrs. Todd's foot gave an impatient scuff on the floor.) "An' I've always lived right here. I ain't like the Queen's Majesty, for this is the only palace I've got," said the dear old thing, smiling again. "I'm glad of it too, I don't like changing about, an' our stations in life are set very different. I don't require what the Queen does, but sometimes I've thought 't was left to me to do the plain things she don't have time for. I expect she's a beautiful housekeeper, nobody couldn't have done better in her high place, and she's been as good a mother as she's been a queen."

"I guess she has, Abby," agreed Mrs. Todd instantly. "How was it you happened to get such a good look at her? I meant to ask you again when I was here t' other day."

"Our ship was layin' in the Thames, right there above Wapping. We was dischargin' cargo, and under orders to clear as quick as we could for Bordeaux to take on an excellent freight o' French goods," explained Mrs. Martin eagerly. "I heard that the Queen was goin' to a great review of her army, and would drive out o' her Buckin'ham Palace about ten o'clock in the mornin', and I run aft to Albert, my husband, and brother Horace where they was standin' together by the hatchway, and told 'em they must one of 'em take me. They laughed, I was in such a hurry, and said they couldn't go; and I found they meant it and got sort of impatient when I began to talk, and I was 'most brokenhearted; 't was all the reason I had for makin' that hard voyage. Albert couldn't help often reproachin' me, for he did so resent the sea, an' I'd known how 't would be before we sailed; but I'd minded nothing all the way till then, and I just crep' back to my cabin an' begun to cry. They was disappointed about their ship's cook, an' I'd cooked for fo'c's'le an' cabin myself all the way over; 't was dreadful hard work, specially in rough weather; we'd had head winds an' a six weeks' voyage. They'd acted sort of ashamed o' me when I pled so to go ashore, an' that hurt my feelin's most of all. But Albert come below pretty soon; I'd never given way so in my life, an' he begun to act frightened, and treated me gentle just as he did when we was goin' to be married, an' when I got over sobbin' he went on deck and saw Horace an' talked it over what they could do; they really had their duty to the vessel, and couldn't be spared that day. Horace was real good when he understood everything, and he come an' told me I'd more than worked my passage an' was goin' to do just as I liked now we was in port. He'd engaged a cook, too, that was comin' aboard that mornin', and he was goin' to send the ship's carpenter with me—a nice fellow from up Thomaston way; he'd gone to put on his ashore clothes as quick's he could. So then I got ready, and we started off in the small boat and rowed up river. I was afraid we were too late, but the tide was setting up very strong, and we landed an' left the boat to a keeper, and I run all the way up those great streets and across a park. 'T was a great day, with sights o' folks everywhere, but 't was just as if they was nothin' but wax images to me. I kep' askin' my way an' runnin' on, with the carpenter comin' after as best he could, and just as I worked to the front o' the crowd by the palace, the gates was flung open and out she came; all prancin' horses and shinin' gold, and in a beautiful carriage there she sat; 't was a moment o' heaven to me. I saw her plain, and she looked right at me so pleasant and happy, just as if she knew there was somethin' different between us from other folks."

There was a moment when the Queen's Twin could not go on and neither of her listeners could ask a question.

"Prince Albert was sitting right beside her in the carriage," she continued. "Oh, he was a beautiful man! Yes, dear, I saw 'em both together just as I see you now, and then she was gone out o' sight in another minute, and the common crowd was all spread over the place pushin' an' cheerin'. 'T was some kind o' holiday, an' the carpenter and I got separated, an' then I found him again after I didn't think I should, an' he was all for makin' a day of it, and goin' to show me all the sights; he'd been in London before, but I didn't want nothin' else, an' we went back through the streets down to the waterside an' took the boat. I remember I mended an old coat o' my Albert's as good as I could, sittin' on the quarter-deck in the sun all that afternoon, and 't was all as if I was livin' in a lovely dream. I don't know how to explain it, but there hasn't been no friend I've felt so near to me ever since."

One could not say much—only listen. Mrs. Todd put in a discerning question now and then, and Mrs. Martin's eyes shone brighter and brighter as she talked. What a lovely gift of imagination and true affection was in this fond old heart! I looked about the plain New England kitchen, with its wood-smoked walls and homely braided rugs on the worn floor, and all its simple furnishings. The loud-ticking clock seemed to encourage us to speak; at the other side of the room was an early newspaper portrait of Her Majesty the Queen of Great Britain and Ireland. On a shelf below were some flowers in a little glass dish, as if they were put before a shrine.

"If I could have had more to read, I should have known 'most everything about her," said Mrs. Martin wistfully. "I've made the most of what I did have, and thought it over and over till it came clear. I sometimes seem to have her all my own, as if we'd lived right together. I've often walked out into the woods alone and told her what my troubles was, and it always seemed as if she told me 't was all right, an' we must have patience. I've got her beautiful book about the Highlands; 't was dear Mis' Todd here that found out about her printing it and got a copy for me, and it's been a treasure to my heart, just as if 't was written right to me. I always read it Sundays now, for my Sunday treat. Before that I used to have to imagine a good deal, but when I come to read her book, I knew what I expected was all true. We do think alike about so many things," said the Queen's Twin with affectionate certainty. "You see, there is something between us, being born just at the same time; 't is what they call a birthright. She's had great tasks put upon her, being the Queen, an' mine has been the humble lot; but she's done the best she could, nobody can say to the contrary, and there's something between us; she's been the great lesson I've had to live by. She's been everything to me. An' when she had her Jubilee, oh, how my heart was with her!

"There, 't wouldn't play the part in her life it has in mine," said Mrs. Martin generously, in answer to something one of her listeners had said. "Sometimes I think, now she's older, she might like to know about us. When I think how few old friends anybody has left at our age, I suppose it may be just the same with her as it is with me; perhaps she would like to know how we came into life together. But I've had a great advantage in seeing her, an' I can always fancy her goin' on, while she don't know nothin' yet about me, except she may feel my love stayin' her heart sometimes an' not know just where it comes from. An' I dream about our being together out in some pretty fields, young as ever we was, and holdin' hands as we walk along. I'd like to know if she ever has that dream too. I used to have days when I made believe she did know, an' was comin' to see me," confessed the speaker shyly, with a little flush on her cheeks; "and I'd plan what I could have nice for supper, and I wasn't goin' to let anybody know she was here havin' a good rest, except I'd wish you, Almira Todd, or dear Mis' Blackett would happen in, for you'd know just how to talk with her. You see, she likes to be up in Scotland, right out in the wild country, better than she does anywhere else."

"I'd really love to take her out to see mother at Green Island," said Mrs. Todd with a sudden impulse.

"Oh, yes! I should love to have you," exclaimed Mrs. Martin, and then she began to speak in a lower tone. "One day I got thinkin' so about my dear Queen," she said, "an' livin' so in my thoughts, that I went to work an' got all ready for her, just as if she was really comin'. I never told this to a livin' soul before, but I feel you'll understand. I put my best fine sheets and blankets I spun an' wove myself on the bed, and I picked some pretty flowers and put 'em all round the house, an' I worked as hard an' happy as I could all day, and had as nice a supper ready as I could get, sort of telling myself a story all the time. She was comin' an' I was goin' to see her again, an' I kep' it up until nightfall; an' when I see the dark an' it come to me I was all alone, the dream left me, an' I sat down on the doorstep an' felt all foolish an' tired. An', if you'll believe it, I heard steps comin', an' an old cousin o' mine come wanderin' along, one I was apt to be shy of. She wasn't all there, as folks used to say, but harmless enough and a kind of poor old talking body. And I went right to meet her when I first heard her call, 'stead o' hidin' as I sometimes did, an' she come in dreadful willin', an' we sat down to supper together; 't was a supper I should have had no heart to eat alone."

"I don't believe she ever had such a splendid time in her life as she did then. I heard her tell all about it afterwards," exclaimed Mrs. Todd compassionately. "There, now I hear all this it seems just as if the Queen might have known and couldn't come herself, so she sent that poor old creatur' that was always in need!"

Mrs. Martin looked timidly at Mrs. Todd and then at me. " 'T was childish o' me to go an' get supper," she confessed.

"I guess you wa'n't the first one to do that," said Mrs. Todd. "No, I guess you wa'n't the first one who's got supper that way, Abby," and then for a moment she could say no more.

Mrs. Todd and Mrs. Martin had moved their chairs a little so that they faced each other, and I, at one side, could see them both.

"No, you never told me o' that before, Abby," said Mrs. Todd gently. "Don't it show that for folks that have any fancy in 'em, such beautiful dreams is the real part o' life? But to most folks the common things that happens outside 'em is all in all."

Mrs. Martin did not appear to understand at first, strange to say, when the secret of her heart was put into words; then a glow of pleasure and comprehension shone upon her face. "Why, I believe you're right, Almira!" she said, and turned to me.

"Wouldn't you like to look at my pictures of the Queen?" she asked, and we rose and went into the best room.

V

The mid-day visit seemed very short. September hours are brief to match the shortening days. The great subject was dismissed for a while after our visit to the Queen's pictures, and my companions spoke much of lesser persons until we drank the cup of tea which Mrs. Todd had foreseen. I happily remembered that the Queen herself is said to like a proper cup of tea, and this at once seemed to make her Majesty kindly join so remote and reverent a company. Mrs. Martin's thin cheeks took on a pretty color like a girl's. "Somehow I always have thought of her when I made it extra good," she said. "I got a real china cup that belonged to my grandmother, and I believe I shall call it hers now."

"Why don't you?" responded Mrs. Todd warmly, with a delightful smile.

Later they spoke of a promised visit which was to be made in the Indian summer to the Landing and Green Island, but I observed that Mrs. Todd presented the little parcel of dried herbs, with full directions, for a cure-all in the spring, as if there were no real chance of their meeting again first. As we looked back from the turn of the road the Queen's Twin was still standing on the doorstep watching us away, and Mrs. Todd stopped, and stood still for a moment before she waved her hand again.

"There's one thing certain, dear," she said to me with great discernment; "it ain't as if we left her all alone!"

Then we set out upon our long way home over the hill, where we lingered in the afternoon sunshine, and through the dark woods across the heron-swamp.

23 *William's Wedding*

I

The hurry of life in a large town, the constant putting aside of preference to yield to a most unsatisfactory activity, began to vex me, and one day I took the train, and only left it for the eastward-bound boat. Carlyle says somewhere that the only happiness a man ought to ask for is happiness enough to get his work done; and against this the complexity and futile ingenuity of social life seems a conspiracy. But the first salt wind from the east, the first sight of a lighthouse set boldly on its outer rock, the flash of a gull, the waiting procession of seaward-bound firs on an island, made me feel solid and definite again, instead of a poor, incoherent being. Life was resumed, and anxious living blew away as if it had not been. I could not breathe deep enough or long enough. It was a return to happiness.

The coast had still a wintry look; it was far on in May, but all the shore looked cold and sterile. One was conscious of going north as well as east, and as the day went on the sea grew colder, and all the warmer air and bracing strength and stimulus of the autumn weather, and storage of the heat of summer, were quite gone. I was very cold and very tired when I came at evening up the lower bay, and saw the white houses of Dunnet Landing climbing the hill. They had a friendly look, these little houses, not as if they were climbing up the shore, but as if they were rather all coming down to meet a fond and weary traveler, and I could hardly wait with patience to step off the boat. It was not the usual eager company on the wharf. The coming-in of the mailboat was the one large public event of a summer day, and I was disappointed at seeing none of my intimate friends but Johnny Bowden, who had evidently done nothing all winter but grow, so that his short sea-smitten clothes gave him a look of poverty.

Johnny's expression did not change as we greeted each other, but I suddenly felt that I had shown indifference and inconvenient delay by not coming sooner; before I could make an apology he took my small portmanteau, and walking before me in his old fashion he made straight up the hilly road toward Mrs. Todd's. Yes, he was much grown—it had never occurred to me the summer before that Johnny was likely, with the help of time and other forces, to grow into a young man; he was such a well-framed and well-settled chunk of a boy that nature seemed to have set him aside as something finished, quite satisfactory, and entirely completed.

The wonderful little green garden had been enchanted away by winter. There were a few frost-bitten twigs and some thin shrubbery against the fence, but it was a most unpromising small piece of ground. My heart was beating like a lover's as I passed it on the way to the door of Mrs. Todd's house, which seemed to have become much smaller under the influence of winter weather.

"She hasn't gone away?" I asked Johnny Bowden with a sudden anxiety just as we reached the doorstep.

"Gone away!" he faced me with blank astonishment,—"I see her settin' by Mis' Caplin's window, the one nighest the road, about four o'clock!" And eager with suppressed news of my coming he made his entrance as if the house were a burrow.

Then on my homesick heart fell the voice of Mrs. Todd. She stopped, through what I knew to be excess of feeling, to rebuke Johnny for bringing in so much mud, and I dallied without for one moment during the ceremony; then we met again face to face.

II

"I dare say you can advise me what shapes they are goin' to wear. My meetin'-bunnit ain't goin' to do me again this year; no! I can't expect 't would do me forever," said Mrs. Todd, as soon as she could say anything. "There! do set down and tell me how you have been! We've got a weddin' in the family, I s'pose you know?"

"A wedding!" said I, still full of excitement.

"Yes; I expect if the tide serves and the line storm don't overtake him they'll come in and appear out on Sunday. I shouldn't have concerned me about the bunnit for a month yet, nobody would notice, but havin' an occasion like this I shall show consider'ble. 'T will be an ordeal for William!"

"For *William!*" I exclaimed. "What do you mean, Mrs. Todd?"

She gave a comfortable little laugh. "Well, the Lord's seen reason at last an' removed Mis' Cap'n Hight up to the farm, an' I don't know but the weddin's goin' to be this week. Esther's had a great deal of business disposin' of her flock, but she's done extra well— the folks that owns the next place goin' up country are well off. 'T is elegant land north side o' that bleak ridge, an' one o' the boys has been Esther's right-hand man of late. She instructed him in all matters, and after she markets the early lambs he's goin' to take the farm on halves, an' she's give the refusal to him to buy her out within two years. She's reserved the buryin'-lot, an' the right o' way in, an'—"

I couldn't stop for details. I demanded reassurance of the central fact.

"William going to be married?" I repeated; whereat Mrs. Todd gave me a searching look that was not without scorn.

"Old Mis' Hight's funeral was a week ago Wednesday, and 't was very well attended," she assured me after a moment's pause.

"Poor thing!" said I, with a sudden vision of her helplessness and angry battle against the fate of illness; "it was very hard for her."

"I thought it was hard for Esther!" said Mrs. Todd without sentiment.

III

I had an odd feeling of strangeness: I missed the garden, and the little rooms, to which I had added a few things of my own the summer before, seemed oddly unfamiliar. It was like the hermit crab in a cold new shell,—and with the windows shut against the raw May air, and a strange silence and grayness of the sea all that first night and day of my visit, I felt as if I had after all lost my hold of that quiet life.

Mrs. Todd made the apt suggestion that city persons were prone to run themselves to death, and advised me to stay and get properly rested now that I had taken the trouble to come. She did not know how long I had been homesick for the conditions of life at the Landing the autumn before—it was natural enough to feel a little unsupported by compelling incidents on my return.

Some one has said that one never leaves a place, or arrives at one, until the next day! But on the second morning I woke with the familiar feeling of interest and ease, and the bright May sun was streaming in, while I could hear Mrs. Todd's heavy footsteps pounding about in the other part of the house as if something were going to happen. There was the first golden robin singing somewhere close to the house, and a lovely aspect of spring now, and I looked at the garden to see that in the warm night some of its treasures had grown a hand's breadth; the determined spikes of yellow daffies stood tall against the doorsteps, and the bloodroot was unfolding leaf and flower. The belated spring which I had left behind farther south had overtaken me on this northern coast. I even saw a presumptuous dandelion in the garden border.

It is difficult to report the great events of New England; expression is so slight, and those few words which escape us in moments of deep feeling look but meagre on the printed page. One has to assume too much of the dramatic fervor as one reads; but as I came out of my room at breakfast-time I met Mrs. Todd face to face, and when she said to me, "This weather'll bring William in after her; 't is their happy day!" I felt something take possession of me which ought to communicate itself to the least sympathetic reader of this cold page. It is written for those who have a Dunnet Landing of their own: who either kindly share this with the writer, or possess another.

"I ain't seen his comin' sail yet; he'll be likely to dodge round among the islands so he'll be the less observed," continued Mrs. Todd. "You can get a dory up the bay, even a clean new painted one, if you know as how, keepin' it against the high land." She stepped to the door and looked off to sea as she spoke. I could see her eye follow the gray shores to and fro, and then a bright light spread over her calm face. "There he comes, and he's strikin' right in across the open bay like a man!" she said with splendid approval. "See, there he comes! Yes, there's William, and he's bent his new sail."

I looked too, and saw the fleck of white no larger than a gull's wing yet, but present to her eager vision.

I was going to France for the whole long summer that year, and the more I thought of such an absence from these simple scenes the more dear and delightful they became. Santa Teresa says that the true proficiency of the soul is not in much thinking, but in much loving, and sometimes I believed that I had never found love in its simplicity as I had found it at Dunnet Landing in the various hearts of Mrs. Blackett and Mrs. Todd and William. It is only because one came to know them, these three, loving and wise and true, in their own habitations. Their counterparts are in every village in the world, thank heaven, and the gift to one's life is only in its discernment. I had only lived in Dunnet until the usual distractions and artifices of the world were no longer in control, and I saw these simple natures clear. "The happiness of life is in its recognitions. It seems that we are not ignorant of these truths, and even that we believe them; but we are so little accustomed to think of them, they are so strange to us—"

"Well now, deary me!" said Mrs. Todd, breaking into exclamation; "I've got to fly round—I thought he'd have to beat; he can't sail far on that tack, and he won't be in for a good hour yet—I expect he's made every arrangement, but he said he shouldn't go up after Esther unless the weather was good, and I declare it did look doubtful this morning."

I remembered Esther's weather-worn face. She was like a Frenchwoman who had spent her life in the fields. I remembered her pleasant look, her childlike eyes, and thought of the astonishment of joy she would feel now in being taken care of and tenderly sheltered from wind and weather after all these years. They were going to be young again now, she and William, to forget work and care in the spring weather. I could hardly wait for the boat to come to land, I was so eager to see his happy face.

"Cake an' wine I'm goin' to set 'em out!" said Mrs. Todd. "They won't stop to set down for an orderly meal, they'll want to get right out home quick's they can. Yes, I'll give 'em some cake an' wine— I've got a rare plum-cake from my best receipt, and a bottle o' wine that the old Cap'n Denton of all give me, one of two, the day I was married, one we had and one we saved, and I've never touched it till now. He said there wa'n't none like it in the State o' Maine."

It was a day of waiting, that day of spring; the May weather was as expectant as our fond hearts, and one could see the grass grow green hour by hour. The warm air was full of birds, there was a glow of light on the sea instead of the cold shining of chilly weather which had lingered late. There was a look on Mrs. Todd's face which I saw once and could not meet again. She was in her highest mood. Then I went out early for a walk, and when I came back we sat in different rooms for the most part. There was such a thrill in the air that our only conversation was in her most abrupt and incisive manner. She was knitting, I believe, and as for me I dallied with a book. I heard her walking to and fro, and, the door being wide open now, she went out and paced the front walk to the gate as if she walked a quarterdeck.

It is very solemn to sit waiting for the great events of life—most of us have done it again and again—to be expectant of life or expectant of death gives one the same feeling.

But at the last Mrs. Todd came quickly back from the gate, and standing in the sunshine at the door, she beckoned me as if she were a sibyl.

"I thought you comprehended everything the day you was up there," she added with a little more patience in her tone, but I felt that she thought I had lost instead of gained since we parted the autumn before.

"William's made this pretext o' goin' fishin' for the last time. 'T wouldn't done to take notice, 't would 'a scared him to death! but there never was nobody took less comfort out o' forty years courtin'. No, he won't have to make no further pretexts," said Mrs. Todd, with an air of triumph.

"Did you know where he was going that day?" I asked, with a sudden burst of admiration at such discernment.

"I did!" replied Mrs. Todd grandly.

"Oh! but that pennyroyal lotion," I indignantly protested, remembering that under pretext of mosquitoes she had besmeared the poor lover in an awful way—why, it was outrageous! Medea could not have been more conscious of high ultimate purposes.

"Darlin'," said Mrs. Todd, in the excitement of my arrival and the great concerns of marriage, "he's got a beautiful shaped face, and they pison him very unusual—you wouldn't have had him present himself to his lady all lopsided with a mosquito-bite? Once when we was young I rode up with him, and they set upon him in concert the minute we entered the woods." She stood before me reproachfully, and I was conscious of deserved rebuke. "Yes, you've come just in the nick of time to advise me about a bunnit. They say large bows on top is liable to be worn."

IV

The period of waiting was one of direct contrast to these high moments of recognition. The very slowness of the morning hours wasted that sense of excitement with which we had begun the day. Mrs. Todd came down from the mount where her face had shone so bright, to the cares of common life, and some acquaintances from Black Island for whom she had little natural preference or liking came, bringing a poor, sickly child to get medical advice. They were noisy women, with harsh, clamorous voices, and they stayed a long time. I heard the clink of teacups, however, and could detect no impatience in the tones of Mrs. Todd's voice; but when they were at last going away, she did not linger unduly over her leave-taking, and returned to me to explain that they were people she had never liked, and they had made an excuse of a friendly visit to save their doctor's bill; but she pitied the poor little child, and knew beside that the doctor was away.

"I had to give 'em the remedies right out," she told me; "they wouldn't have bought a cent's worth o' drugs down to the store for that dwindlin' thing. She needed feedin' up, and I don't expect she gets milk enough; they're great butter-makers down to Black Island, 't is excellent pasturage, but they use no milk themselves, and their butter is heavy laden with salt to make weight, so that you'd think all their ideas come down from Sodom."

She was very indignant and very wistful about the pale little girl. "I wish they'd let me kept her," she said. "I kind of advised it, and her eyes was so wishful in that pinched face when she heard me, so that I could see what was the matter with her, but they said she wa'n't prepared. Prepared!" And Mrs. Todd snuffed like an offended war-horse, and departed; but I could hear her still grumbling and talking to herself in high dudgeon an hour afterward.

At the end of that time her arch enemy, Mari' Harris, appeared at the side-door with a gingham handkerchief over her head. She was always on hand for the news, and made some formal excuse for her presence,—she wished to borrow the weekly paper. Captain Littlepage, whose housekeeper she was, had taken it from the post-office in the morning, but had forgotten, being of failing memory, what he had done with it.

"How is the poor old gentleman?" asked Mrs. Todd with solicitude, ignoring the present errand of Maria and all her concerns.

I had spoken the evening before of intended visits to Captain Littlepage and Elijah Tilley, and I now heard Mrs. Todd repeating my inquiries and intentions, and fending off with unusual volubility of her own the curious questions that were sure to come. But at last Maria Harris secured an opportunity and boldly inquired if she had not seen William ashore early that morning.

"I don't say he wasn't," replied Mrs. Todd; "Thu'sday's a very usual day with him to come ashore."

"He was all dressed up," insisted Maria—she really had no sense of propriety. "I didn't know but they was going to be married?"

Mrs. Todd did not reply. I recognized from the sounds that reached me that she had retired to the fastnesses of the kitchen-closet and was clattering the tins.

"I expect they'll marry soon anyway," continued the visitor.

"I expect they will if they want to," answered Mrs. Todd. "I don't know nothin' 't all about it; that's what folks say." And presently the gingham handkerchief retreated past my window.

"I routed her, horse and foot," said Mrs. Todd proudly, coming at once to stand at my door. "Who's comin' now?" as two figures passed inward bound to the kitchen.

They were Mrs. Begg and Johnny Bowden's mother, who were favorites, and were received with Mrs. Todd's usual civilities. Then one of the Mrs. Caplins came with a cup in hand to borrow yeast. On one pretext or another nearly all our acquaintances came to satisfy themselves of the facts and see what Mrs. Todd would impart about the wedding. But she firmly avoided the subject through the length of every call and errand, and answered the final leading question of each curious guest with her noncommittal phrase, "I don't know nothin' 't all about it; that's what folks say!"

She had just repeated this for the fourth or fifth time and shut the door upon the last comers, when we met in the little front entry. Mrs. Todd was not in a bad temper, but highly amused. "I've been havin' all sorts o' social privileges, you may have observed. They didn't seem to consider that if they could only hold out till afternoon they'd know as much as I did. There wa'n't but one o' the whole sixteen that showed real interest, the rest demeaned themselves to ask out o' cheap curiosity; no, there wa'n't but one showed any real feelin'."

"Miss Maria Harris, you mean?" and Mrs. Todd laughed.

"Certain, dear," she agreed, "how you do understand poor human natur'!"

A short distance down the hilly street stood a narrow house that was newly painted white. It blinded one's eyes to catch the reflection of the sun. It was the house of the minister, and a wagon had just stopped before it; a man was helping a woman to alight, and they stood side by side for a moment, while Johnny Bowden appeared as if by magic, and climbed to the wagon-seat. Then they went into the house and shut the door. Mrs. Todd and I stood close together and watched; the tears were running down her cheeks. I watched Johnny Bowden, who made light of so great a moment by so handling the whip that the old white Caplin horse started up from time to time and was inexorably stopped as if he had some idea of running away. There was something in the back of the wagon which now and then claimed the boy's attention; he leaned over as if there were something very precious left in his charge; perhaps it was only Esther's little trunk going to its new home.

At last the door of the parsonage opened, and two figures came out. The minister followed them and stood in the doorway, delaying them with parting words; he could not have thought it was a time for admonition.

"He's all alone; his wife's up to Portland to her sister's," said Mrs. Todd aloud, in a matter-of-fact voice. "She's a nice woman, but she might ha' talked too much. There! see, they're comin' here. I didn't know how 't would be. Yes, they're comin' up to see us before they go home. I declare, if William ain't lookin' just like a king!"

Mrs. Todd took one step forward, and we stood and waited. The happy pair came walking up the street, Johnny Bowden driving ahead. I heard a plaintive little cry from time to time to which in the excitement of the moment I had not stopped to listen; but when William and Esther had come and shaken hands with Mrs. Todd and then with me, all in silence, Esther stepped quickly to the back of the wagon, and unfastening some cords returned to us carrying a little white lamb. She gave a shy glance at William as she fondled it and held it to her heart, and then, still silent, we went into the house together. The lamb had stopped bleating. It was lovely to see Esther carry it in her arms.

When we got into the house, all the repression of Mrs. Todd's usual manner was swept away by her flood of feeling. She took

Esther's thin figure, lamb and all, to her heart and held her there, kissing her as she might have kissed a child, and then held out her hand to William and they gave each other the kiss of peace. This was so moving, so tender, so free from their usual fetters of self-consciousness, that Esther and I could not help giving each other a happy glance of comprehension. I never saw a young bride half so touching in her happiness as Esther was that day of her wedding. We took the cake and wine of the marriage feast together, always in silence, like a true sacrament, and then to my astonishment I found that sympathy and public interest in so great an occasion were going to have their way. I shrank from the thought of William's possible sufferings, but he welcomed both the first group of neighbors and the last with heartiness; and when at last they had gone, for there were thoughtless loiterers in Dunnet Landing, I made ready with eager zeal and walked with William and Esther to the water-side. It was only a little way, and kind faces nodded reassuringly from the windows, while kind voices spoke from the doors. Esther carried the lamb on one arm; she had found time to tell me that its mother had died that morning and she could not bring herself to the thought of leaving it behind. She kept the other hand on William's arm until we reached the landing. Then he shook hands with me, and looked me full in the face to be sure I understood how happy he was, and stepping into the boat held out his arms to Esther—at last she was his own.

I watched him make a nest for the lamb out of an old sea-cloak at Esther's feet, and then he wrapped her own shawl round her shoulders, and finding a pin in the lapel of his Sunday coat he pinned it for her. She looked at him fondly while he did this, and then glanced up at us, a pretty, girlish color brightening her cheeks.

We stood there together and watched them go far out into the bay. The sunshine of the May day was low now, but there was a steady breeze, and the boat moved well.

"Mother'll be watching for them," said Mrs. Todd. "Yes, mother'll be watching all day, and waiting. She'll be so happy to have Esther come."

We went home together up the hill, and Mrs. Todd said nothing more; but we held each other's hands all the way.

24   *The Backward View*

At last it was the time of late summer, when the house was cool and damp in the morning, and all the light seemed to come through green leaves; but at the first step out of doors the sunshine always laid a warm hand on my shoulder, and the clear, high sky seemed to lift quickly as I looked at it. There was no autumnal mist on the coast, nor any August fog; instead of these, the sea, the sky, all the long shore line and the inland hills, with every bush of bay and every fir-top, gained a deeper color and a sharper clearness. There was something shining in the air, and a kind of lustre on the water and the pasture grass,—a northern look that, except at this moment of the year, one must go far to seek. The sunshine of a northern summer was coming to its lovely end.

The days were few then at Dunnet Landing, and I let each of them slip away unwillingly as a miser spends his coins. I wished to have one of my first weeks back again, with those long hours when nothing happened except the growth of herbs and the course of the sun. Once I had not even known where to go for a walk; now there were many delightful things to be done and done again, as if I were in London. I felt hurried and full of pleasant engagements, and the days flew by like a handful of flowers flung to the sea wind.

At last I had to say good-by to all my Dunnet Landing friends, and my homelike place in the little house, and return to the world in which I feared to find myself a foreigner. There may be restrictions to such a summer's happiness, but the ease that belongs to simplicity is charming enough to make up for whatever a simple life may lack, and the gifts of peace are not for those who live in the thick of battle.

I was to take the small unpunctual steamer that went down the bay in the afternoon, and I sat for a while by my window looking out on the green herb garden, with regret for company. Mrs. Todd had hardly spoken all day except in the briefest and most disapproving way; it was as if we were on the edge of a quarrel. It seemed impossible to take my departure with anything like composure. At last I heard a footstep, and looked up to find that Mrs. Todd was standing at the door.

"I've seen to everything now," she told me in an unusually loud and business-like voice. "Your trunks are on the w'arf by this time. Cap'n Bowden he come and took 'em down himself, an' is going to see that they're safe aboard. Yes, I've seen to all your 'rangements," she repeated in a gentler tone. "These things I've left on the kitchen table you'll want to carry by hand; the basket needn't be returned. I guess I shall walk over towards the Port now an' inquire how old Mis' Edward Caplin is."

I glanced at my friend's face, and saw a look that touched me to the heart. I had been sorry enough before to go away.

"I guess you'll excuse me if I ain't down there to stand round on the w'arf and see you go," she said, still trying to be gruff. "Yes, I ought to go over and inquire for Mis' Edward Caplin; it's her third shock, and if mother gets in on Sunday she'll want to know just how the old lady is." With this last word Mrs. Todd turned and left me as if with sudden thought of something she had forgotten, so that I felt sure she was coming back, but presently I heard her go out of the kitchen door and walk down the path toward the gate. I could not part so; I ran after her to say good-by, but she shook her head and waved her hand without looking back when she heard my hurrying steps, and so went away down the street.

When I went in again the little house had suddenly grown lonely, and my room looked empty as it had the day I came. I and all my belongings had died out of it, and I knew how it would seem when Mrs. Todd came back and found her lodger gone. So we die before our own eyes; so we see some chapters of our lives come to their natural end.

I found the little packages on the kitchen table. There was a quaint West Indian basket which I knew its owner had valued, and which I had once admired; there was an affecting provision laid beside it for my seafaring supper, with a neatly tied bunch of southernwood and a twig of bay, and a little old leather box which held the coral pin that Nathan Todd brought home to give to poor Joanna.

There was still an hour to wait, and I went up to the hill just above the schoolhouse and sat there thinking of things, and looking off to sea, and watching for the boat to come in sight. I could see

Green Island, small and darkly wooded at that distance; below me were the houses of the village with their apple-trees and bits of garden ground. Presently, as I looked at the pastures beyond, I caught a last glimpse of Mrs. Todd herself, walking slowly in the footpath that led along, following the shore toward the Port. At such a distance one can feel the large, positive qualities that control a character. Close at hand, Mrs. Todd seemed able and warm-hearted and quite absorbed in her bustling industries, but her distant figure looked mateless and appealing, with something about it that was strangely self-possessed and mysterious. Now and then she stooped to pick something,—it might have been her favorite pennyroyal,—and at last I lost sight of her as she slowly crossed an open space on one of the higher points of land, and disappeared again behind a dark clump of juniper and the pointed firs.

As I came away on the little coastwise steamer, there was an old sea running which made the surf leap high on all the rocky shores. I stood on deck, looking back, and watched the busy gulls agree and turn, and sway together down the long slopes of air, then separate hastily and plunge into the waves. The tide was setting in, and plenty of small fish were coming with it, unconscious of the silver flashing of the great birds overhead and the quickness of their fierce beaks. The sea was full of life and spirit, the tops of the waves flew back as if they were winged like the gulls themselves, and like them had the freedom of the wind. Out in the main channel we passed a bent-shouldered old fisherman bound for the evening round among his lobster traps. He was toiling along with short oars, and the dory tossed and sank and tossed again with the steamer's waves. I saw that it was old Elijah Tilley, and though we had so long been strangers we had come to be warm friends, and I wished that he had waited for one of his mates, it was such hard work to row along shore through rough seas and tend the traps alone. As we passed I waved my hand and tried to call to him, and he looked up and answered my farewells by a solemn nod. The little town, with the tall masts of its disabled schooners in the inner bay, stood high above the flat sea for a few minutes, then it sank back into the uniformity of the coast, and became indistinguishable from the other towns that looked as if they were crumbled on the furzy-green stoniness of the shore.

The small outer islands of the bay were covered among the ledges with turf that looked as fresh as the early grass; there had been some days of rain the week before, and the darker green of the sweet-fern was scattered on all the pasture heights. It looked like the beginning of summer ashore, though the sheep, round and warm in their winter wool, betrayed the season of the year as they went feeding along the slopes in the low afternoon sunshine. Presently the wind began to blow, and we struck out seaward to double the long sheltering headland of the cape, and when I looked back again, the islands and the headland had run together and Dunnet Landing and all its coasts were lost to sight.

Souls Belated
by Edith Wharton

I

Their railway carriage had been full when the train left Bologna; but at the first station beyond Milan their only remaining companion—a courtly person who ate garlic out of a carpetbag—had left his crumb-strewn seat with a bow.

Lydia's eye regretfully followed the shiny broadcloth of his retreating back till it lost itself in the cloud of touts and cab drivers hanging about the station; then she glanced across at Gannett and caught the same regret in his look. They were both sorry to be alone.

"*Par-ten-za!*" shouted the guard. The train vibrated to a sudden slamming of doors; a waiter ran along the platform with a tray of fossilized sandwiches; a belated porter flung a bundle of shawls and bandboxes into a third-class carriage; the guard snapped out a brief *Partenza!* which indicated the purely ornamental nature of his first shout; and the train swung out of the station.

The direction of the road had changed, and a shaft of sunlight struck across the dusty red-velvet seats into Lydia's corner. Gannet did not notice it. He had returned to his *Revue de Paris,* and she had to rise and lower the shade of the farther window. Against the vast horizon of their leisure such incidents stood out sharply.

Having lowered the shade, Lydia sat down, leaving the length of the carriage between herself and Gannett. At length he missed her and looked up.

"I moved out of the sun," she hastily explained.

He looked at her curiously: the sun was beating on her through the shade.

"Very well," he said pleasantly; adding, "You don't mind?" as he drew a cigarette case from his pocket.

It was a refreshing touch, relieving the tension of her spirit with the suggestion that, after all, if he could *smoke*—! The relief was only momentary. Her experience of smokers was limited (her husband had disapproved of the use of tobacco) but she knew from hearsay that men sometimes smoked to get away from things; that a cigar might be the masculine equivalent of darkened windows and a headache. Gannett, after a puff or two, returned to his review.

It was just as she had foreseen; he feared to speak as much as she did. It was one of the misfortunes of their situation that they were never busy enough to necessitate, or even to justify, the postponement of unpleasant discussions. If they avoided a question it was obviously, unconcealably because the question was disagreeable. They had unlimited leisure and an accumulation of mental energy to devote to any subject that presented itself; new topics were in fact at a premium. Lydia sometimes had premonitions of a famine-stricken period when there would be nothing left to talk about, and she had already caught herself doling out piecemeal what, in the first prodigality of their confidences, she would have flung to him in a breath. Their silence therefore might simply mean that they had nothing to say; but it was another disadvantage of their position that it allowed infinite opportunity for the classification of minute differences. Lydia had learned to distinguish between real and factitious silences; and under Gannett's she now detected a hum of speech to which her own thoughts made breathless answer.

How could it be otherwise, with that thing between them? She glanced up at the rack overhead. The *thing* was there, in her dressing bag, symbolically suspended over her head and his. He was thinking of it now, just as she was; they had been thinking of it in unison ever since they had entered the train. While the carriage had held other travelers they had screened her from his thoughts; but now that he and she were alone she knew exactly what was passing through his mind; she could almost hear him asking himself what he should say to her.

The thing had come that morning, brought up to her in an innocent-looking envelope with the rest of their letters, as they were leaving the hotel at Bologna. As she tore it open, she and Gannett were laughing over some ineptitude of the local guidebook—they had been driven, of late, to make the most of such incidental humors of travel. Even when she had unfolded the document she took it for some unimportant business paper sent abroad for her signature, and her eye traveled inattentively over the curly *Whereases* of the preamble until a word arrested her: Divorce. There it stood, an impassable barrier, between her husband's name and hers.

She had been prepared for it, of course, as healthy people are said to be prepared for death, in the sense of knowing it must come without in the least expecting that it will. She had known from the first that Tillotson meant to divorce her—but what did it matter? Nothing mattered, in those first days of supreme deliverance, but the fact that she was free; and not so much (she had begun to be aware) that freedom had released her from Tillotson as that it had given her to Gannett. This discovery had not been agreeable to her self-esteem. She had preferred to think that Tillotson had himself embodied all her reasons for leaving him; and those he represented had seemed cogent enough to stand in no need of reinforcement. Yet she had not left him till she met Gannett. It was her love for Gannett that had made life with Tillotson so poor and incomplete a business. If she had never, from the first, regarded her marriage as a full canceling of her claims upon life, she had at least, for a number of years, accepted it as a provisional compensation,—she had made it "do." Existence in the commodious Tillotson mansion in Fifth Avenue—with Mrs. Tillotson senior commanding the approaches from the second-story front windows—had been reduced to a series of purely automatic acts. The moral atmosphere of the Tillotson interior was as carefully screened and curtained as the house itself: Mrs. Tillotson senior dreaded ideas as much as a draft in her back. Prudent people liked an even temperature; and to do anything unexpected was as foolish as going out in the rain. One of the chief advantages of being rich was that one need not be exposed to unforeseen contingencies: by

the use of ordinary firmness and common sense one could make
sure of doing exactly the same thing every day at the same hour.
These doctrines, reverentially imbibed with his mother's milk, Tillotson (a model son who had never given his parents an hour's
anxiety) complacently expounded to his wife, testifying to his sense
of their importance by the regularity with which he wore galoshes
on damp days, his punctuality at meals, and his elaborate precau-
tions against burglars and contagious diseases. Lydia, coming from
a smaller town, and entering New York life through the portals
of the Tillotson mansion, had mechanically accepted this point of
view as inseparable from having a front pew in church and a parterre
box at the opera. All the people who came to the house revolved
in the same small circle of prejudices. It was the kind of society
in which, after dinner, the ladies compared the exorbitant charges
of their children's teachers, and agreed that, even with the new
duties on French clothes, it was cheaper in the end to get everything
from Worth; while the husbands, over their cigars, lamented mu-
nicipal corruption, and decided that the men to start a reform were
those who had no private interests at stake.

To Lydia this view of life had become a matter of course, just
as lumbering about in her mother-in-law's landau had come to seem
the only possible means of locomotion, and listening every Sunday
to a fashionable Presbyterian divine the inevitable atonement for
having thought oneself bored on the other six days of the week.
Before she met Gannett her life had seemed merely dull; his coming made it appear like one of those dismal Cruikshank prints in
which the people are all ugly and all engaged in occupations that
are either vulgar or stupid.

It was natural that Tillotson should be the chief sufferer from
this readjustment of focus. Gannett's nearness had made her husband ridiculous, and a part of the ridicule had been reflected on
herself. Her tolerance laid her open to a suspicion of obtuse-
ness from which she must, at all costs, clear herself in Gannett's
eyes.

She did not understand this until afterwards. At the time she
fancied that she had merely reached the limits of endurance. In so
large a charter of liberties as the mere act of leaving Tillotson
seemed to confer, the small question of divorce or no divorce did
not count. It was when she saw that she had left her husband only

to be with Gannett that she perceived the significance of anything affecting their relations. Her husband, in casting her off, had virtually flung her at Gannett: it was thus that the world viewed it. The measure of alacrity with which Gannett would receive her would be the subject of curious speculation over afternoon tea tables and in club corners. She knew what would be said—she had heard it so often of others! The recollection bathed her in misery. The men would probably back Gannett to "do the decent thing"; but the ladies' eyebrows would emphasize the worthlessness of such enforced fidelity; and after all, they would be right. She had put herself in a position where Gannett "owed" her something; where, as a gentleman, he was bound to "stand the damage." The idea of accepting such compensation had never crossed her mind; the so-called rehabilitation of such a marriage had always seemed to her the only real disgrace. What she dreaded was the necessity of having to explain herself; of having to combat his arguments; of calculating, in spite of herself, the exact measure of insistence with which he pressed them. She knew not whether she most shrank from his insisting too much or too little. In such a case the nicest sense of proportion might be at fault; and how easily to fall into the error of taking her resistance for a test of his sincerity! Whichever way she turned, an ironical implication confronted her: she had the exasperated sense of having walked into the trap of some stupid practical joke.

Beneath all these preoccupations lurked the dread of what he was thinking. Sooner or later, of course, he would have to speak; but that, in the meantime, he should think, even for a moment, that there was any use in speaking, seemed to her simply unendurable. Her sensitiveness on this point was aggravated by another fear, as yet barely on the level of consciousness; the fear of unwillingly involving Gannett in the trammels of her dependence. To look upon him as the instrument of her liberation; to resist in herself the least tendency to a wifely taking possession of his future; had seemed to Lydia the one way of maintaining the dignity of their relation. Her view had not changed, but she was aware of a growing inability to keep her thoughts fixed on the essential point—the point of parting with Gannett. It was easy to face as long as she kept it sufficiently far off: but what was this act of mental postponement but a gradual encroachment on his future?

What was needful was the courage to recognize the moment when, by some word or look, their voluntary fellowship should be transformed into a bondage the more wearing that it was based on none of those common obligations which make the most imperfect marriage in some sort a center of gravity.

When the porter, at the next station, threw the door open, Lydia drew back, making way for the hoped-for intruder; but none came, and the train took up its leisurely progress through the spring wheat fields and budding copses. She now began to hope that Gannett would speak before the next station. She watched him furtively, half-disposed to return to the seat opposite his, but there was an artificiality about his absorption that restrained her. She had never before seen him read with so conspicuous an air of warding off interruption. What could he be thinking of? Why should he be afraid to speak? Or was it her answer that he dreaded?

The train paused for the passing of an express, and he put down his book and leaned out of the window. Presently he turned to her with a smile.

"There's a jolly old villa out here," he said.

His easy tone relieved her, and she smiled back at him as she crossed over to his corner.

Beyond the embankment, through the opening in a mossy wall, she caught sight of the villa, with its broken balustrades, its stagnant fountains, and the stone satyr closing the perspective of a dusky grass walk.

"How should you like to live there?" he asked as the train moved on.

"There?"

"In some such place, I mean. One might do worse, don't you think so? There must be at least two centuries of solitude under those yew trees. Shouldn't you like it?"

"I—I don't know," she faltered. She knew now that he meant to speak.

He lit another cigarette. "We shall have to live somewhere, you know," he said as he bent above the match.

Lydia tried to speak carelessly. "*Je n'en vois pas la nécessité!* Why not live everywhere, as we have been doing?"

"But we can't travel forever, can we?"

"Oh, forever's a long word," she objected, picking up the review he had thrown aside.

"For the rest of our lives then," he said, moving nearer.

She made a slight gesture which caused his hand to slip from hers.

"Why should we make plans? I thought you agreed with me that it's pleasanter to drift."

He looked at her hesitatingly. "It's been pleasant, certainly; but I suppose I shall have to get at my work again some day. You know I haven't written a line since—all this time," he hastily amended.

She flamed with sympathy and self-reproach. "Oh, if you mean *that*—if you want to write—of course we must settle down. How stupid of me not to have thought of it sooner! Where shall we go? Where do you think you could work best? We oughtn't to lose any more time."

He hesitated again. "I had thought of a villa in these parts. It's quiet; we shouldn't be bothered. Should you like it?"

"Of course I should like it." She paused and looked away. "But I thought—I remember your telling me once that your best work had been done in a crowd—in big cities. Why should you shut yourself up in a desert?"

Gannett, for a moment, made no reply. At length he said, avoiding her eye as carefully as she avoided his: "It might be different now; I can't tell, of course, till I try. A writer ought not to be dependent on his *milieu;* it's a mistake to humor oneself in that way; and I thought that just at first you might prefer to be—"

She faced him. "To be what?"

"Well—quiet. I mean—"

"What do you mean by 'at first'?" she interrupted.

He paused again. "I mean after we are married."

She thrust up her chin and turned toward the window. "Thank you!" she tossed back at him.

"Lydia!" he exclaimed blankly; and she felt in every fiber of her averted person that he had made the inconceivable, the unpardonable mistake of anticipating her acquiescence.

The train rattled on and he groped for a third cigarette. Lydia remained silent.

"I haven't offended you?" he ventured at length, in the tone of a man who feels his way.

She shook her head with a sigh. "I thought you understood," she moaned. Their eyes met and she moved back to his side.

"Do you want to know how not to offend me? By taking it for granted, once for all, that you've said your say on the odious question and that I've said mine, and that we stand just where we did this morning before that—that hateful paper came to spoil everything between us!"

"To spoil everything between us? What on earth do you mean? Aren't you glad to be free?"

"I was free before."

"Not to marry me," he suggested.

"But I don't *want* to marry you!" she cried.

She saw that he turned pale. "I'm obtuse, I suppose," he said slowly. "I confess I don't see what you're driving at. Are you tired of the whole business? Or was I simply a—an excuse for getting away? Perhaps you didn't care to travel alone? Was that it? And now you want to chuck me?" His voice had grown harsh. "You owe me a straight answer, you know; don't be tenderhearted!"

Her eyes swam as she leaned to him. "Don't you see it's because I care—because I care so much? Oh, Ralph! Can't you see how it would humiliate me? Try to feel it as a woman would! Don't you see the misery of being made your wife in this way? If I'd known you as a girl—that would have been a real marriage! But now—this vulgar fraud upon society—and upon a society we despised and laughed at—this sneaking back into a position that we've voluntarily forfeited: don't you see what a cheap compromise it is? We neither of us believe in the abstract 'sacredness' of marriage; we both know that no ceremony is needed to consecrate our love for each other; what object can we have in marrying, except the secret fear of each that the other may escape, or the secret longing to work our way back gradually—oh, very gradually—into the esteem of the people whose conventional morality we have always ridiculed and hated? And the very fact that, after a decent interval, these same people would come and dine with us—the women who talk about the indissolubility of marriage, and who would let me die in a gutter today because I am 'leading a life of sin'—doesn't that disgust you more than their turning their backs on us now? I can stand being cut by them, but I couldn't stand their coming to call and asking what I meant to do about visiting that unfortunate Mrs. So-and-so!"

She paused, and Gannett maintained a perplexed silence.

"You judge things too theoretically," he said at length, slowly. "Life is made up of compromises."

"The life we ran away from—yes! If we had been willing to accept them"—she flushed—"we might have gone on meeting each other at Mrs. Tillotson's dinners."

He smiled slightly. "I didn't know that we ran away to found a new system of ethics. I supposed it was because we loved each other."

"Life is complex, of course; isn't it the very recognition of that fact that separates us from the people who see it *tout d'une pièce?* If *they* are right—if marriage is sacred in itself and the individual must always be sacrificed to the family—then there can be no real marriage between us, since our—our being together is a protest against the sacrifice of the individual to the family." She interrupted herself with a laugh. "You'll say now that I'm giving you a lecture on sociology! Of course one acts as one can—as one must, perhaps—pulled by all sorts of invisible threads; but at least one needn't pretend, for social advantages, to subscribe to a creed that ignores the complexity of human motives—that classifies people by arbitrary signs, and puts it in everybody's reach to be on Mrs. Tillotson's visiting list. It may be necessary that the world should be ruled by conventions—but if we believed in them, why did we break through them? And if we don't believe in them, is it honest to take advantage of the protection they afford?"

Gannett hesitated. "One may believe in them or not; but as long as they do rule the world it is only by taking advantage of their protection that one can find a *modus vivendi.*"

"Do outlaws need a *modus vivendi?*"

He looked at her hopelessly. Nothing is more perplexing to man than the mental process of a woman who reasons her emotions.

She thought she had scored a point and followed it up passionately. "You do understand, don't you? You see how the very thought of the thing humiliates me! We are together today because we choose to be—don't let us look any farther than that!" She caught his hands. "*Promise* me you'll never speak of it again; promise me you'll never *think* of it even," she implored, with a tearful prodigality of italics.

Through what followed—his protests, his arguments, his final unconvinced submission to her wishes—she had a sense of his but half-discerning all that, for her, had made the moment so tumultuous. They had reached that memorable point in every heart history when, for the first time, the man seems obtuse and the woman irrational. It was the abundance of his intentions that consoled her, on reflection, for what they lacked in quality. After all, it would have been worse, incalculably worse, to have detected any overreadiness to understand her.

II

When the train at nightfall brought them to their journey's end at the edge of one of the lakes, Lydia was glad that they were not, as usual, to pass from one solitude to another. Their wanderings during the year had indeed been like the flight of the outlaws: through Sicily, Dalmatia, Transylvania and Southern Italy they had persisted in their tacit avoidance of their kind. Isolation, at first, had deepened the flavor of their happiness, as night intensifies the scent of certain flowers; but in the new phase on which they were entering, Lydia's chief wish was that they should be less abnormally exposed to the action of each other's thoughts.

She shrank, nevertheless, as the brightly-looming bulk of the fashionable Anglo-American hotel on the water's brink began to radiate toward their advancing boat its vivid suggestion of social order, visitors' lists, Church services, and the bland inquisition of the *table d'hôte.* The mere fact that in a moment or two she must take her place on the hotel register as Mrs. Gannett seemed to weaken the springs of her resistance.

They had meant to stay for a night only, on their way to a lofty village among the glaciers of Monte Rosa; but after the first plunge into publicity, when they entered the dining room, Lydia felt the relief of being lost in a crowd, of ceasing for a moment to be the center of Gannett's scrutiny; and in his face she caught the reflection of her feeling. After dinner, when she went upstairs, he strolled into the smoking room, and an hour or two later, sitting in the darkness of her window, she heard his voice below and saw him walking up and down the terrace with a companion cigar at his side. When he came he told her he had been talking to the hotel chaplain—a very good sort of fellow.

"Queer little microcosms, these hotels! Most of these people live here all summer and then migrate to Italy or the Riviera. The English are the only people who can lead that kind of life with dignity—those soft-voiced old ladies in Shetland shawls somehow carry the British Empire under their caps. *Civis Romanus sum.* It's a curious study—there might be some good things to work up here."

He stood before her with the vivid preoccupied stare of the novelist on the trail of a "subject." With a relief that was half painful she noticed that, for the first time since they had been together, he was hardly aware of her presence.

"Do you think you could write here?"

"Here? I don't know." His stare dropped. "After being out of things so long one's first impressions are bound to be tremendously vivid, you know. I see a dozen threads already that one might follow—"

He broke off with a touch of embarrassment.

"Then follow them. We'll stay," she said with sudden decision.

"Stay here?" He glanced at her in surprise, and then, walking to the window, looked out upon the dusky slumber of the garden.

"Why not?" she said at length, in a tone of veiled irritation.

"The place is full of old cats in caps who gossip with the chaplain. Shall you like—I mean, it would be different if—"

She flamed up.

"Do you suppose I care? It's none of their business."

"Of course not; but you won't get them to think so."

"They may think what they please."

He looked at her doubtfully.

"It's for you to decide."

"We'll stay," she repeated.

Gannett, before they met, had made himself known as a successful writer of short stories and of a novel which had achieved the distinction of being widely discussed. The reviewers called him "promising," and Lydia now accused herself of having too long interfered with the fulfilment of his promise. There was a special irony in the fact, since his passionate assurances that only the

stimulus of her companionship could bring out his latent faculty
had almost given the dignity of a "vocation" to her course: there
had been moments when she had felt unable to assume, before
posterity, the responsibility of thwarting his career. And, after all,
he had not written a line since they had been together: his first
desire to write had come from renewed contact with the world!
Was it all a mistake then? Must the most intelligent choice work
more disastrously than the blundering combinations of chance? Or
was there a still more humiliating answer to her perplexities? His
sudden impulse of activity so exactly coincided with her own wish
to withdraw, for a time, from the range of his observation, that
she wondered if he too were not seeking sanctuary from intolerable
problems.

"You must begin tomorrow!" she cried, hiding a tremor under
the laugh with which she added, "I wonder if there's any ink in
the inkstand?"

Whatever else they had at the Hotel Bellosguardo, they had, as
Miss Pinsent said, "a certain tone." It was to Lady Susan Condit
that they owed this inestimable benefit; an advantage ranking in
Miss Pinsent's opinion above even the lawn tennis courts and the
resident chaplain. It was the fact of Lady Susan's annual visit that
made the hotel what it was. Miss Pinsent was certainly the last to
underrate such a privilege: "It's so important, my dear, forming as
we do a little family, that there should be someone to give *the tone;*
and no one could do it better than Lady Susan—an earl's daughter
and a person of such determination. Dear Mrs. Ainger now—who
really *ought,* you know, when Lady Susan's away—absolutely re-
fuses to assert herself." Miss Pinsent sniffed derisively. "A bishop's
niece!—my dear, I saw her once actually give in to some South
Americans—and before us all. She gave up her seat at table to
oblige them—such a lack of dignity! Lady Susan spoke to her very
plainly about it afterwards."

Miss Pinsent glanced across the lake and adjusted her auburn
front.

"But of course I don't deny that the stand Lady Susan takes is
not always easy to live up to—for the rest of us, I mean. Monsieur
Grossart, our good proprietor, finds it trying at times, I know—
he has said as much, privately, to Mrs. Ainger and me. After all,

the poor man is not to blame for wanting to fill his hotel, is he? And Lady Susan is so difficult—so very difficult—about new people. One might almost say that she disapproves of them beforehand, on principle. And yet she's had warnings—she very nearly made a dreadful mistake once with the Duchess of Levens, who dyed her hair and—well, swore and smoked. One would have thought that might have been a lesson to Lady Susan." Miss Pinsent resumed her knitting with a sigh. "There are exceptions, of course. She took at once to you and Mr. Gannett—it was quite remarkable, really. Oh, I don't mean that either—of course not! It was perfectly natural—we *all* thought you so charming and interesting from the first day—we knew at once that Mr. Gannett was intellectual, by the magazines you took in; but you know what I mean. Lady Susan is so very—well, I won't say prejudiced, as Mrs. Ainger does— but so prepared *not* to like new people, that her taking to you in that way was a surprise to us all, I confess."

Miss Pinsent sent a significant glance down the long laurustinus alley from the other end of which two people—a lady and a gentleman—were strolling toward them through the smiling neglect of the garden.

"In this case, of course, it's very different; that I'm willing to admit. Their looks are against them; but, as Mrs. Ainger says, one can't exactly tell them so."

"She's very handsome," Lydia ventured, with her eyes on the lady, who showed, under the dome of a vivid sunshade, the hourglass figure and superlative coloring of a Christmas chromo.

"That's the worst of it. She's too handsome."

"Well, after all, she can't help that."

"Other people manage to," said Miss Pinsent skeptically.

"But isn't it rather unfair of Lady Susan—considering that nothing is known about them?"

"But, my dear, that's the very thing that's against them. It's infinitely worse than any actual knowledge."

Lydia mentally agreed that, in the case of Mrs. Linton, it possibly might be.

"I wonder why they came here?" she mused.

"That's against them too. It's always a bad sign when loud people come to a quiet place. And they've brought van loads of boxes— her maid told Mrs. Ainger's that they meant to stop indefinitely."

"And Lady Susan actually turned her back on her in the salon?"

"My dear, she said it was for our sakes: that makes it so unanswerable! But poor Grossart *is* in a way! The Lintons have taken his most expensive suite, you know—the yellow damask drawing room above the portico—and they have champagne with every meal!"

They were silent as Mr. and Mrs. Linton sauntered by; the lady with tempestuous brows and challenging chin; the gentleman, a blond stripling, trailing after her, head downward, like a reluctant child dragged by his nurse.

"What does your husband think of them, my dear?" Miss Pinsent whispered as they passed out of earshot.

Lydia stooped to pick a violet in the border.

"He hasn't told me."

"Of your speaking to them, I mean. Would he approve of that? I know how very particular nice Americans are. I think your action might make a difference; it would certainly carry weight with Lady Susan."

"Dear Miss Pinsent, you flatter me!"

Lydia rose and gathered up her book and sunshade.

"Well, if you're asked for an opinion—if Lady Susan asks you for one—I think you ought to be prepared," Miss Pinsent admonished her as she moved away.

III

Lady Susan held her own. She ignored the Lintons, and her little family, as Miss Pinsent phrased it, followed suit. Even Mrs. Ainger agreed that it was obligatory. If Lady Susan owed it to the others not to speak to the Lintons, the others clearly owed it to Lady Susan to back her up. It was generally found expedient, at the Hotel Bellosguardo, to adopt this form of reasoning.

Whatever effect this combined action may have had upon the Lintons, it did not at least have that of driving them away. Monsieur Grossart, after a few days of suspense, had the satisfaction of seeing them settle down in his yellow damask *premier* with what looked like a permanent installation of palm trees and silk cushions, and a gratifying continuance in the consumption of champagne. Mrs. Linton trailed her Doucet draperies up and down the garden with the same challenging air, while her husband, smoking innumerable cigarettes, dragged himself dejectedly in her wake; but neither of them, after the first encounter with Lady Susan, made any attempt to extend their acquaintance. They simply ignored their ignorers. As Miss Pinsent resentfully observed, they behaved exactly as though the hotel were empty.

It was therefore a matter of surprise, as well as of displeasure, to Lydia, to find, on glancing up one day from her seat in the garden, that the shadow which had fallen across her book was that of the enigmatic Mrs. Linton.

"I want to speak to you," that lady said, in a rich hard voice that seemed the audible expression of her gown and her complexion.

Lydia started. She certainly did not want to speak to Mrs. Linton.

"Shall I sit down here?" the latter continued, fixing her intensely-shaded eyes on Lydia's face, "or are you afraid of being seen with me?"

"Afraid?" Lydia colored. "Sit down, please. What is it that you wish to say?"

Mrs. Linton, with a smile, drew up a garden chair and crossed one openwork ankle above the other.

"I want you to tell me what my husband said to your husband last night."

Lydia turned pale.

"My husband—to yours?" she faltered, staring at the other.

"Didn't you know they were closeted together for hours in the smoking room after you went upstairs? My man didn't get to bed until nearly two o'clock and when he did I couldn't get a word out of him. When he wants to be aggravating I'll back him against anybody living!" Her teeth and eyes flashed persuasively upon Lydia. "But you'll tell me what they were talking about, won't you? I know I can trust you—you look so awfully kind. And it's for his own good. He's such a precious donkey and I'm so afraid he's got into some beastly scrape or other. If he'd only trust his own old woman! But they're always writing to him and setting him against me. And I've got nobody to turn to." She laid her hand on Lydia's with a rattle of bracelets. "You'll help me, won't you?"

Lydia drew back from the smiling fierceness of her brows.

"I'm sorry—but I don't think I understand. My husband has said nothing to me of—of yours."

The great black crescents above Mrs. Linton's eyes met angrily.

"I say—is that true?" she demanded.

Lydia rose from her seat.

"Oh, look here, I didn't mean that, you know—you mustn't take one up so! Can't you see how rattled I am?"

Lydia saw that, in fact, her beautiful mouth was quivering beneath softened eyes.

"I'm beside myself!" the splendid creature wailed, dropping into her seat.

"I'm so sorry," Lydia repeated, forcing herself to speak kindly; "but how can I help you?"

Mrs. Linton raised her head sharply.

"By finding out—there's a darling!"

"Finding what out?"

"What Trevenna told him."

"Trevenna—?" Lydia echoed in bewilderment.

Mrs. Linton clapped her hand to her mouth.

"Oh, Lord—there, it's out! What a fool I am! But I supposed of course you knew; I supposed everybody knew." She dried her eyes and bridled. "Didn't you know that he's Lord Trevenna? I'm Mrs. Cope."

Lydia recognized the names. They had figured in a flamboyant elopement which had thrilled fashionable London some six months earlier.

"Now you see how it is—you understand, don't you?" Mrs. Cope continued on a note of appeal. "I knew you would—that's the reason I came to you. I suppose *he* felt the same thing about your husband; he's not spoken to another soul in the place." Her face grew anxious again. "He's awfully sensitive, generally—he feels our position, he says—as if it wasn't *my* place to feel that! But when he does get talking there's no knowing what he'll say. I know he's been brooding over something lately, and I *must* find out what it is—it's to his interest that I should. I always tell him that I think only of his interest; if he'd only trust me! But he's been so odd lately—I can't think what he's plotting. You will help me, dear?"

Lydia, who had remained standing, looked away uncomfortably.

"If you mean by finding out what Lord Trevenna has told my husband, I'm afraid it's impossible."

"Why impossible?"

"Because I infer that it was told in confidence."

Mrs. Cope stared incredulously.

"Well, what of that? Your husband looks such a dear—anyone can see he's awfully gone on you. What's to prevent your getting it out of him?"

Lydia flushed.

"I'm not a spy!" she exclaimed.

"A spy—a spy? How dare you?" Mrs. Cope flamed out. "Oh, I don't mean that either! Don't be angry with me—I'm so miserable." She essayed a softer note. "Do you call that spying—for one woman to help out another? I do need help so dreadfully! I'm at my wits' end with Trevenna, I am indeed. He's such a boy—a mere baby, you know; he's only two-and-twenty." She dropped her orbed lids. "He's younger than me—only fancy, a few months younger. I tell him he ought to listen to me as if I was his mother; oughtn't he now? But he won't, he won't! All his people are at him, you see— oh, I know *their* little game! Trying to get him away from me before I can get my divorce—that's what they're up to. At first he wouldn't listen to them; he used to toss their letters over to me to read; but now he reads them himself, and answers 'em too, I fancy; he's always shut up in his room, writing. If I only knew what his plan is I could stop him fast enough—he's such a simpleton. But he's dreadfully deep too—at times I can't make him out. But I know he's told your husband everything—I knew that last night the minute I laid eyes on him. And I *must* find out—you must help me—I've got no one else to turn to!"

She caught Lydia's fingers in a stormy pressure.

"Say you'll help me—you and your husband."

Lydia tried to free herself.

"What you ask is impossible; you must see that it is. No one could interfere in—in the way you ask."

Mrs. Cope's clutch tightened.

"You won't, then? You won't?"

"Certainly not. Let me go, please."

Mrs. Cope released her with a laugh.

"Oh, go by all means—pray don't let me detain you! Shall you go and tell Lady Susan Condit that there's a pair of us—or shall I save you the trouble of enlightening her?"

Lydia stood still in the middle of the path, seeing her antagonist through a mist of terror. Mrs. Cope was still laughing.

"Oh, I'm not spiteful by nature, my dear; but you're a little more than flesh and blood can stand! It's impossible, is it? Let you go, indeed! You're too good to be mixed up in my affairs, are you? Why, you little fool, the first day I laid eyes on you I saw that you and I were both in the same box—that's the reason I spoke to you."

She stepped nearer, her smile dilating on Lydia like a lamp through a fog.

"You can take your choice, you know; I always play fair. If you'll tell I'll promise not to. Now then, which is it to be?"

Lydia, involuntarily, had begun to move away from the pelting storm of words; but at this she turned and sat down again.

"You may go," she said simply. "I shall stay here."

IV

She stayed there for a long time, in the hypnotized contemplation, not of Mrs. Cope's present, but of her own past. Gannett, early that morning, had gone off on a long walk—he had fallen into the habit of taking these mountain tramps with various fellow lodgers; but even had he been within reach she could not have gone to him just then. She had to deal with herself first. She was surprised to find how, in the last months, she had lost the habit of introspection. Since their coming to the Hotel Bellosguardo she and Gannett had tacitly avoided themselves and each other.

She was aroused by the whistle of the three o'clock steamboat as it neared the landing just beyond the hotel gates. Three o'clock! Then Gannett would soon be back—he had told her to expect him before four. She rose hurriedly, her face averted from the inquisitorial façade of the hotel. She could not see him just yet; she could not go indoors. She slipped through one of the overgrown garden alleys and climbed a steep path to the hills.

It was dark when she opened their sitting-room door. Gannett was sitting on the window ledge smoking a cigarette. Cigarettes were now his chief resource: he had not written a line during the two months they had spent at the Hotel Bellosguardo. In that respect, it had turned out not to be the right *milieu* after all.

He started up at Lydia's entrance.

"Where have you been? I was getting anxious."

She sat down in a chair near the door.

"Up the mountain," she said wearily.

"Alone?"

"Yes."

Gannett threw away his cigarette: the sound of her voice made him want to see her face.

"Shall we have a little light?" he suggested.

She made no answer and he lifted the globe from the lamp and put a match to the wick. Then he looked at her.

"Anything wrong? You look done up."

She sat glancing vaguely about the little sitting room, dimly lit by the pallid-globed lamp, which left in twilight the outlines of the furniture, of his writing table heaped with books and papers, of the tea roses and jasmine drooping on the mantelpiece. How like home it had all grown—how like home!

"Lydia, what is wrong?" he repeated.

She moved away from him, feeling for her hatpins and turning to lay her hat and sunshade on the table.

Suddenly she said: "That woman has been talking to me."

Gannett stared.

"That woman? What woman?"

"Mrs. Linton—Mrs. Cope."

He gave a start of annoyance, still, as she perceived, not grasping the full import of her words.

"The deuce! She told you—?"

"She told me everything."

Gannett looked at her anxiously.

"What impudence! I'm so sorry that you should have been exposed to this, dear."

"Exposed!" Lydia laughed.

Gannett's brow clouded and they looked away from each other.

"Do you know *why* she told me? She had the best of reasons. The first time she laid eyes on me she saw that we were both in the same box."

"Lydia!"

"So it was natural, of course, that she should turn to me in a difficulty."

"What difficulty?"

"It seems she has reason to think that Lord Trevenna's people are trying to get him away from her before she gets her divorce—"

"Well?"

"And she fancied he had been consulting with you last night as to—as to the best way of escaping from her."

Gannett stood up with an angry forehead.

"Well—what concern of yours was all this dirty business? Why should she go to you?"

"Don't you see? It's so simple. I was to wheedle his secret out of you."

"To oblige that woman?"

"Yes; or, if I was unwilling to oblige her, then to protect myself."

"To protect yourself? Against whom?"

"Against her telling everyone in the hotel that she and I are in the same box."

"She threatened that?"

"She left me the choice of telling it myself or of doing it for me."

"The beast!"

There was a long silence. Lydia had seated herself on the sofa, beyond the radius of the lamp, and he leaned against the window. His next question surprised her.

"When did this happen? At what time, I mean?"

She looked at him vaguely.

"I don't know—after luncheon, I think. Yes, I remember; it must have been at about three o'clock."

He stepped into the middle of the room and as he approached the light she saw that his brow had cleared.

"Why do you ask?" she said.

"Because when I came in, at about half-past three, the mail was just being distributed, and Mrs. Cope was waiting as usual to pounce on her letters; you know she was always watching for the postman. She was standing so close to me that I couldn't help seeing a big official-looking envelope that was handed to her. She tore it open, gave one look at the inside, and rushed off upstairs like a whirlwind, with the director shouting after her that she had left all her other letters behind. I don't believe she ever thought of you again after that paper was put into her hand."

"Why?"

"Because she was too busy. I was sitting in the window, watching for you, when the five o'clock boat left, and who should go on board, bag and baggage, valet and maid, dressing bags and poodle, but Mrs. Cope and Trevenna. Just an hour and a half to pack up in! And you should have seen her when they started. She was radiant—shaking hands with everybody—waving her handkerchief from the deck—distributing bows and smiles like an empress. If ever a woman got what she wanted just in the nick of time that woman did. She'll be Lady Trevenna within a week, I'll wager."

"You think she has her divorce?"

"I'm sure of it. And she must have got it just after her talk with you."

Lydia was silent.

At length she said, with a kind of reluctance, "She was horribly angry when she left me. It wouldn't have taken long to tell Lady Susan Condit."

"Lady Susan Condit has not been told."

"How do you know?"

"Because when I went downstairs half an hour ago I met Lady Susan on the way—"

He stopped, half smiling.

"Well?"

"And she stopped to ask if I thought you would act as patroness to a charity concert she is getting up."

In spite of themselves they both broke into a laugh. Lydia's ended in sobs and she sank down with her face hidden. Gannett bent over her, seeking her hands.

"That vile woman—I ought to have warned you to keep away from her; I can't forgive myself! But he spoke to me in confidence; and I never dreamed—well, it's all over now."

Lydia lifted her head.

"Not for me. It's only just beginning."

"What do you mean?"

She put him gently aside and moved in her turn to the window. Then she went on, with her face turned toward the shimmering blackness of the lake, "You see of course that it might happen again at any moment."

"What?"

"This—this risk of being found out. And we could hardly count again on such a lucky combination of chances, could we?"

He sat down with a groan.

Still keeping her face toward the darkness, she said, "I want you to go and tell Lady Susan—and the others."

Gannett, who had moved towards her, paused a few feet off.

"Why do you wish me to do this?" he said at length, with less surprise in his voice than she had been prepared for.

"Because I've behaved basely, abominably, since we came here: letting these people believe we were married—lying with every breath I drew—"

"Yes, I've felt that too," Gannett exclaimed with sudden energy.

The words shook her like a tempest: all her thoughts seemed to fall about her in ruins.

"You—you've felt so?"

"Of course I have." He spoke with low-voiced vehemence. "Do you suppose I like playing the sneak any better than you do? It's damnable."

He had dropped on the arm of a chair, and they stared at each other like blind people who suddenly see.

"But you have liked it here," she faltered.

"Oh, I've liked it—I've liked it." He moved impatiently. "Haven't you?"

"Yes," she burst out; "that's the worst of it—that's what I can't bear. I fancied it was for your sake that I insisted on staying— because you thought you could write here; and perhaps just at first that really was the reason. But afterwards I wanted to stay myself— I loved it." She broke into a laugh. "Oh, do you see the full derision of it? These people—the very prototypes of the bores you took me away from, with the same fenced-in view of life, the same keep-off-the-grass morality, the same little cautious virtues and the same little frightened vices—well, I've clung to them, I've delighted in them, I've done my best to please them. I've toadied Lady Susan, I've gossiped with Miss Pinsent, I've pretended to be shocked with Mrs. Ainger. Respectability! It was the one thing in life that I was sure I didn't care about, and it's grown so precious to me that I've stolen it because I couldn't get it in any other way."

She moved across the room and returned to his side with another laugh.

"I who used to fancy myself unconventional! I must have been born with a cardcase in my hand. You should have seen me with that poor woman in the garden. She came to me for help, poor creature, because she fancied that, having 'sinned,' as they call it, I might feel some pity for others who had been tempted in the same way. Not I! She didn't know me. Lady Susan would have been kinder, because Lady Susan wouldn't have been afraid. I hated the woman—my one thought was not to be seen with her—I could have killed her for guessing my secret. The one thing that mattered to me at that moment was my standing with Lady Susan!"

Gannett did not speak.

"And you—you've felt it too!" she broke out accusingly. "You've enjoyed being with these people as much as I have; you've let the chaplain talk to you by the hour about The Reign of Law and Professor Drummond. When they asked you to hand the plate in church I was watching you—*you wanted to accept.*"

She stepped close, laying her hand on his arm.

"Do you know, I begin to see what marriage is for. It's to keep people away from each other. Sometimes I think that two people who love each other can be saved from madness only by the things that come between them—children, duties, visits, bores, relations—the things that protect married people from each other. We've been too close together—that has been our sin. We've seen the nakedness of each other's souls."

She sank again on the sofa, hiding her face in her hands.

Gannett stood above her perplexedly: he felt as though she were being swept away by some implacable current while he stood helpless on its bank.

At length he said, "Lydia, don't think me a brute—but don't you see yourself that it won't do?"

"Yes, I see it won't do," she said without raising her head.

His face cleared.

"Then we'll go tomorrow."

"Go—where?"

"To Paris; to be married."

For a long time she made no answer; then she asked slowly, "Would they have us here if we were married?"

"Have us here?"

"I mean Lady Susan—and the others."

"Have us here? Of course they would."

"Not if they knew—at least, not unless they could pretend not to know."

He made an impatient gesture.

"We shouldn't come back here, of course; and other people needn't know—no one need know."

She sighed. "Then it's only another form of deception and a meaner one. Don't you see that?"

"I see that we're not accountable to any Lady Susans on earth!"

"Then why are you ashamed of what we are doing here?"

"Because I'm sick of pretending that you're my wife when you're not—when you won't be."

She looked at him sadly.

"If I were your wife you'd have to go on pretending. You'd have to pretend that I'd never been—anything else. And our friends would have to pretend that they believed what you pretended."

Gannett pulled off the sofa tassel and flung it away.

"You're impossible," he groaned.

"It's not I—it's our being together that's impossible. I only want you to see that marriage won't help it."

"What will help it then?"

She raised her head.

"My leaving you."

"Your leaving me?" He sat motionless, staring at the tassel which lay at the other end of the room. At length some impulse of retaliation for the pain she was inflicting made him say deliberately:

"And where would you go if you left me?"

"Oh!" she cried.

He was at her side in an instant.

"Lydia—Lydia—you know I didn't mean it; I couldn't mean it! But you've driven me out of my senses; I don't know what I'm saying. Can't you get out of this labyrinth of self-torture? It's destroying us both."

"That's why I must leave you."

"How easily you say it!" He drew her hands down and made her face him. "You're very scrupulous about yourself—and others. But have you thought of me? You have no right to leave me unless you've ceased to care—"

"It's because I care—"

"Then I have a right to be heard. If you love me you can't leave me."

Her eyes defied him.

"Why not?"

He dropped her hands and rose from her side.

"Can you?" he said sadly.

The hour was late and the lamp flickered and sank. She stood up with a shiver and turned toward the door of her room.

V

At daylight a sound in Lydia's room woke Gannett from a troubled sleep. He sat up and listened. She was moving about softly, as though fearful of disturbing him. He heard her push back one of the creaking shutters; then there was a moment's silence, which seemed to indicate that she was waiting to see if the noise had roused him.

Presently she began to move again. She had spent a sleepless night, probably, and was dressing to go down to the garden for a breath of air. Gannett rose also; but some undefinable instinct made his movements as cautious as hers. He stole to his window and looked out through the slats of the shutter.

It had rained in the night and the dawn was gray and lifeless. The cloud-muffled hills across the lake were reflected in its surface as in a tarnished mirror. In the garden, the birds were beginning to shake the drops from the motionless laurustinus boughs.

An immense pity for Lydia filled Gannett's soul. Her seeming intellectual independence had blinded him for a time to the feminine cast of her mind. He had never thought of her as a woman who wept and clung: there was a lucidity in her intuitions that made them appear to be the result of reasoning. Now he saw the cruelty he had committed in detaching her from the normal conditions of life; he felt, too, the insight with which she had hit upon the real cause of their suffering. Their life was "impossible," as she had said—and its worst penalty was that it had made any other life impossible for them. Even had his love lessened, he was bound to her now by a hundred ties of pity and self-reproach; and she, poor child, must turn back to him as Latude returned to his cell.

A new sound startled him: it was the stealthy closing of Lydia's door. He crept to his own and heard her footsteps passing down the corridor. Then he went back to the window and looked out.

A minute or two later he saw her go down the steps of the porch and enter the garden. From his post of observation her face was invisible, but something about her appearance struck him. She wore a long traveling cloak and under its folds he detected the outline of a bag or bundle. He drew a deep breath and stood watching her.

She walked quickly down the laurustinus alley toward the gate; there she paused a moment, glancing about the little shady square. The stone benches under the trees were empty, and she seemed to gather resolution from the solitude about her, for she crossed the square to the steamboat landing, and he saw her pause before the ticket office at the head of the wharf. Now she was buying her ticket. Gannett turned his head a moment to look at the clock: the boat was due in five minutes. He had time to jump into his clothes and overtake her—

He made no attempt to move; an obscure reluctance restrained him. If any thought emerged from the tumult of his sensations, it was that he must let her go if she wished it. He had spoken last night of his rights: what were they? At the last issue, he and she were two separate beings, not made one by the miracle of common forbearances, duties, abnegations, but bound together in a *noyade* of passion that left them resisting yet clinging as they went down.

After buying her ticket, Lydia had stood for a moment looking out across the lake; then he saw her seat herself on one of the benches near the landing. He and she, at that moment, were both listening for the same sound: the whistle of the boat as it rounded the nearest promontory. Gannett turned again to glance at the clock: the boat was due now.

Where would she go? What would her life be when she had left him? She had no near relations and few friends. There was money enough . . . but she asked so much of life, in ways so complex and immaterial. He thought of her as walking barefooted through a stony waste. No one would understand her—no one would pity her—and he, who did both, was powerless to come to her aid.

He saw that she had risen from the bench and walked toward the edge of the lake. She stood looking in the direction from which the steamboat was to come; then she turned to the ticket office, doubtless to ask the cause of the delay. After that she went back to the bench and sat down with bent head. What was she thinking of?

The whistle sounded; she started up, and Gannett involuntarily made a movement toward the door. But he turned back and continued to watch her. She stood motionless, her eyes on the trail of smoke that preceded the appearance of the boat. Then the little craft rounded the point, a dead white object on the leaden water: a minute later it was puffing and backing at the wharf.

The few passengers who were waiting—two or three peasants and a snuffy priest—were clustered near the ticket office. Lydia stood apart under the trees.

The boat lay alongside now; the gangplank was run out and the peasants went on board with their baskets of vegetables, followed by the priest. Still Lydia did not move. A bell began to ring querulously; there was a shriek of steam, and someone must have called to her that she would be late, for she started forward, as though in answer to a summons. She moved waveringly, and at the edge of the wharf she paused. Gannett saw a sailor beckon to her; the bell rang again and she stepped upon the gangplank.

Halfway down the short incline to the deck she stopped again; then she turned and ran back to the land. The gangplank was drawn in, the bell ceased to ring, and the boat backed out into the lake. Lydia, with slow steps, was walking toward the garden.

As she approached the hotel she looked up furtively and Gannett drew back into the room. He sat down beside a table; a Bradshaw lay at his elbow, and mechanically, without knowing what he did, he began looking out the trains to Paris.

Notes

LIFE IN THE IRON MILLS

3 *Is this the end?*
  O Life, as futile, then, as frail!
  What hope of answer, of redress?
  Probably by Rebecca Harding Davis, modelled after Alfred, Lord
  Tennyson's long poem, "In Memoriam" (1850), XII, verse 4:

  And circle moaning in the air,
  'Is this the end? Is this the end?'
  or "Mariana in the South," verse 6:
  Is this the end, to be left alone,
  To live forgotten, and die forlorn?
  Lynchburg: city not far from Wheeling, West Virginia [but at that
  time still in Virginia]—i.e., local tobacco.
  pig-iron: crude iron cast in molds.

4 *la belle rivière:* the lovely stream; French-Canadian epithet for the
  Ohio River.
  puddler: the man who stirs the molten crude ore to remove imper-
  fections.
  dilettante: amateur.

5 *Egoist:* one who acts, on principle, according to self-interest.
  Pantheist: worshiper of all nature.
  Arminian: one who believes in man's free will versus predestination.
  life of one of these men: thirty-seven was the average life expectancy
  for an American man at mid-nineteenth century; under the conditions described here, it would have been still lower.
  rolling-mills: factory where metal is rolled into sheets or bars.

5 *feeder:* man who shovels ore to the processor.

7 *Milesian:* Irish.

8 *flitch:* salt bacon, cut into strips (flitches).

lager-bier: German-style beer.

12 *Korl:* slag, a calcium aluminium silicate; residue from iron-refining process.

13 *Dante {Alighieri}:* (1265–1321) Italian poet, wrote *The Divine Comedy,* of which the *Inferno* was one part.

Farinata: member of an avaricious Florentine family, mentioned in Dante's *Inferno,* Canto VI, l.79.

14 *sinking-fund:* money accumulated to pay off corporate debt.

blasé: bored, sophisticated.

15 *{Immanuel} Kant:* (1724–1804) German philosopher, known for his *Critique of Pure Reason.*

Novalis: Pseudonym of Friedrich Leopold Von Hardenberg (1772–1801), naturalist, statesman, explorer.

17 *Ce n'est pas mon affaire:* That's no business of mine.

18 *Liberté . . . Égalité:* plus *fraternité* make up the slogan of the French Revolution.

19 *De profundis clamavi:* Out of the depths I cry—first line of Psalm 130 in Latin. "Hungry and thirsty, his soul faints in him" is not a translation of that line.

I am innocent of the blood of this man: New Testament, Matthew 27:24.

Inasmuch as ye did it unto one of the least of these, ye did it unto me: New Testament, Matthew 25:40.

Deist: believer in a Divine Power but adhering to no religion.

n'est ce pas: isn't it.

20 *Saint Simonian:* follower of doctrines of Louis de Rouvroy Saint-Simon (1760–1825), founder of French socialism.

21 *Magdalens:* prostitutes, from Matthew 15:39.

Baconian: Francis Bacon (1561–1626), English philosopher-scientist.

{Johann Wolfgang} Goethe: (1749–1832) German poet-thinker.

Jean Paul Jacques {Rousseau}: (1712–1778) French philosopher.

{Oliver} Cromwell: (1599–1656) English political, military, and religious leader.

35 *Father, forgive them, for they know not what they do:* New Testament, Luke 23:34. Jesus asks forgiveness for the soldiers who crucified him.

36 *frick:* fresh.

37 *Esau deprived:* Old Testament, Genesis 27. Jacob cheats Esau of his blessing.

38 *Aphrodite:* mythical Greek goddess of love.

THE YELLOW WALLPAPER

41 *phosphates:* tonic with phosphoric acid.

43 *paper:* wallpaper, much used in America from colonial times onward; originated in France as a less expensive substitute for costly Italian fabric wall-hangings.

flamboyant patterns: wallpapers imitated the swags and folds of draped silks, brocades, and velvets; later geometric designs, like trellises and checkerboards, were much in demand.

color: yellow—or gold—was a favorite color for French papers.

45 *two bulbous eyes:* may have represented large nailheads fastening the imagined cloth hanging.

46 *sticketh closer than a brother:* Old Testament, Proverbs 24.

sub-pattern in a different shade: sometimes double rollers were used to print two different patterns, one superimposed on the other.

Dr. Weir Mitchell: see Introduction.

47 *debased Romanesque:* a medieval style with heavy, curved arches, which was revived in the nineteenth century.

delirium tremens: acute alcohol poisoning, among whose symptoms are hallucinations.

frieze: wallpaper made in horizontal bands for trimming around the ceiling, in patterns related, but not identical, to those printed on the longer, vertical rolls.

52 *the smell:* wallpaper paste was formerly made with flour, a good medium for damp mildew and mold.

THE COUNTRY OF THE POINTED FIRS

61 *steamboat:* as early as 1815, steamboats ran up and down the Hudson River.

62 *hollyhocks:* tall, bright-flowering plant with medicinal powers (*Althaea rosea*).

London-pride: small pink flowers (*Saxifraga spathularis umbrosa*).

sweet-brier: old-fashioned rose (rose eglantine).

sweet-mary: also sweet-mary-anne, cost-mary (chrysanthemum balsamita); tall flowering perennial; aromatic and medicinal herb. A poultice of leaves heals sores; at bottom of cake-pan, flavors cake.

balm: lemon balm; salad and medicinal herb (*Melissa officinalis*). When infused makes a tonic drink to relieve headaches and an antidote to morning sickness.

sage: culinary and medicinal herb; infused, good against colds, coughs, constipation, and rheumatism (*Salvia officinalis*).

borage: "bee bread," "herb of gladness"; salad and medicinal herb; when infused reduces fever, relieves liver and kidney troubles, and acts as a laxative (*Borago officinalis*).

mint: aromatic leaves for flavoring fruit and drinks; a medicinal herb when infused and drunk for digestion; a poultice for sprains, toothache, headache (*Mentha*).

wormwood: absinthe; also green ginger, old woman (*Artemesia absinthium*).

southernwood: also old man, lad's love (*Artemesia abrotanum*); medicinal herb; when infused a tonic and mild sedative, an antiseptic moth-repellent.

thyme: a culinary and medicinal herb; infused, a drink for headaches, coughs, asthma, and antiseptic rinse for cuts (*Thymus vulgaris*).

Indian remedy: American Ipecac (*Gillenia stipulata*); medicinal herb; induces vomiting.

63 *thoroughwort elixir:* also agueweed, boneset (*Eupatorium*); medicinal herb; reduces fevers and helps mend broken bones.

spruce beer: slightly fermented lightly alcoholic beverage brewed from spruce needles, twigs, and molasses.

cunner: small North Atlantic fish (*Tautogolabrus adspersus*).

64 *mysterious herb of the night with fragrance:* possibly *nicotiana*, tobacco plant; or mignonette (*Roseda odorata*).

65 *sibyl:* woman regarded as oracle or prophetess by ancient Greeks and Romans.

windflower: anemone.

66 *hy'sop:* medicinal herb; in infusion for colds and expectorant for coughs; as compress for aches (*Hyssopus officinalis*).

cottonless ears: reference to Greek hero Odysseus, who blocked the ears of his crew (but not his own) against the sirens' song.

bayberry: native aromatic shrub (*Myrica pennsylvanica*) used to make candles; related to *Laurus mobilis,* the classical laurel used for ceremonial crowns in ancient Greece and Rome.

67 *pennyroyal:* a strongly scented medicinal herb; also run-by-the-ground, lurk in the ditch, pudding grass (*Mentha pulegium*); in infusion for bronchitis and digestion, antiflatulent; formerly grown in pots by sailors for long voyages to purify stale water.

rare lobelia: perhaps the red Cardinal flower.

elecampane: also horseheal, scabwort, velvet dock (*Inula helenium*); medicinal herb; infusion of root for cough; an ointment for muscular aches.

tansy: also buttons (*Tanacetum vulgare*); tonic and insect repellent.

68 *cant to leeward:* tilt in the direction the wind blows (as opposed to windward, leaning into the wind).

69 *bergamot:* also Oswego tea, beebalm (*Monarda didyma*); attracted insects; a medicinal herb; infused, soothes and relaxes cramps. Per-

haps the ink was scented with bergamot; however, sweet-fern (*Comptonia asplendifolia*) is heavily scented and is used to make ink.

69 *A happy, rural seat of various views:* John Milton (1608–1674), *Paradise Lost,* Book IV 1.247. One of the most popular books in early New England.
Countess of Carberry: Carberry in County Midlothian, Scotland.
[Charles Robert] *Darwin:* (1809–1882) English naturalist.

71 *Fort Churchill:* settlement at river's mouth on west shore of Hudson's Bay.
lading: unloading cargo.
head winds: winds directly against course of ship.

72 *Minerva:* Roman goddess of wisdom.
astern o' the lighter: nautical idiom for being in the wrong place (*lit.,* behind a barge).
light pair of heels: without ballast or cargo; riding high in the water.
longshore: seacoast.
fo'cas'le: forecastle; superstructure at bow of ship where crew is housed.

73 *bicycles:* by 1877, mass-produced in Boston.

74 *Parry's Discoveries:* north of magnetic pole.
Moravians: Hussite Protestants from eastern Europe.

75 *English exploring parties:* The disappearance of Sir John Franklin's expedition to the North Pole in 1845 set off a whole series of later expeditions. The arctic was not fully mapped until the twentieth century. The arctic was outer space to the nineteenth century, and their explorers were our astronauts.

77 *incessant armies . . . ridges of grim war . . . no thought of flight . . . soaring on main wing tormented all the air: Paradise Lost,* Book VI 1.242.

79 *lee shore:* shore toward which wind blows.

81 *caryatide:* in classical architecture, a supporting column carved in female shape; priestesses of Artemis.
camomile: a medicinal herb that makes a fragrant tonic tea (*Matricaria chamomilla*).

82 *dory:* a small, double-bowed, flat-bottomed, high-sided seaworthy New England rowboat.
herrin' weirs: fishing net fastened on poles set offshore.

83 *furled:* way to roll sail so it shakes out and hoists quickly.
gunwale: upper edge of boat's side.
trimmed: balanced.
sheet: rope at outer bottom of sail.
underrun a trawl: pull up a fishing line strung offshore with baited hooks.
floats: buoys or corks marking location of hooks along fishing lines.

85 *gaff:* small hook to attach top of sail to top of mast.
   leech: edge of sail.

87 *portulacas:* rose moss annual.
   mallows: pink wild flowers (*Malva moschata*).

88 *Victory:* ancient Greek statue of winged goddess.

91 *it was the first step that cost:* old French proverb, "Ce n'est que le premier pas qui coute."

92 linnæa: honeysuckle (*Linnæa borealis*); also twinflower, pink flower.

95 *Antigone:* In Sophocles's classical Greek tragedy, a sister who defies a royal edict to bury her brother.

97 *war:* American Civil War (1861–1865).

100 *lotting:* counting on.
    Oolong: dark, partly fermented China tea.

101 *child who stood at the gate in Hans Andersen's story: Fairy Tales,* by Hans Christian Andersen (1805–1875).

102 *Theocritus:* third century B.C.; Greek pastoral poet.

104 *spearmint:* flavorful medicinal herb for soothing coughs and aiding digestion (*Mentha spicata*).

105 *bangeing:* term derived from banjo, a musical instrument sacred to American Indians.

108 *sloop:* single-masted ship.

109 *mullein:* medicinal herb (*Verbascum thapsus*); also snapdragon, Aaron's Rod, hag taper, Adam's Flannel, Jacob's Staff, Shepherd's Club; makes a yellow tea that soothes persistent coughs.
    catnip: medicinal herb (*Nopeta cataria*); catmint in poultices, remedy for pain, bruises, and female complaints.

111 *fasten the sheet:* tie the mainsail rope; an unseaworthy act.
    fresh: strong.
    flaw: sudden squall of wind.

113 *Franklin stove:* cast-iron wood stove with front doors that open.

116 *up to Massachusetts:* state-of-Mainers go *up* to Massachusetts and return "down East" to Maine.

118 *reef:* section at bottom of sail tied down to boom to reduce sail area in strong winds.
    tagboat: a small rowing tender, fastened astern.
    clutch: drag.

119 *hold fast for'ard:* stay at bow.

120 *French pinks:* carnations (*dianthus*).

122 *hearts and rounds:* sugar cookies cut into traditional shapes.

123 *in the doldrums:* becalmed.

124 *beat:* sail close-hauled, obliquely, first on one tack and then the other, as near to windward as possible.
    fetch: sail directly toward one point without beating.

tack: sail on one course or in one direction.

schooners: ships with three to five masts.

127 *checkrein:* short rein from horse's bridle to shaft of carriage.

129 *flakes:* fillets of fish for curing.

131 *yarrow:* also nosebleed, milfoil, old man's pepper, devil's nettle, toothache weed (*Achillea millefolium*); medicinal herb used to heal cuts; infused, as diuretic and fever reducer.

132 *Pilgrim's Progress:* by John Bunyan (1628–1688), a religious allegory very popular in New England.

143 *smack:* a sloop-rigged boat.

144 *duck:* heavy cotton for sails.

peak: top corner of sail.

fish-house: where fish are salted and cured.

145 *sliver porgies:* cut bait.

way-wise: following the right course.

mackerel kits: tubs or boxes holding preserved fish.

147 *half-hitch:* a simple knot.

dog-fish: small shark.

151 *japanned waiter:* lacquered tray.

155 *mayflowers:* prefer to hide in woods (*trailing arbutus*).

Medea's anointing Jason: Medea, a mythical oriental sorceress, first seduced Jason (the Greek Argonaut) with a magic herbal potion and then gave him a magic charm which permitted him to tame the wild bulls.

157 *sumach:* small trees bearing large red fruit (*Rhus*).

158 *Pleasure at the helm:* Thomas Gray (1716–1771), *The Bard,* II, 2, 1.

159 *barbel:* (*barbus*) catfish.

162 *Titanic:* an older generation of mythological Greek gods, who were giants.

163 *"The Shepherd of Salisbury Plain":* by Hannah More (1745–1833), a widely read religious tract.

[Jean Francois] *Millet:* (1814–1875) French painter of rural landscapes and farms.

165 *Esther:* (*Haddassah* in Hebrew) a clever and brave Jewish girl who became a Persian queen in the Old Testament Bible.

167 *Atalanta:* a mythical Greek maiden who lost a wager and a running race by stopping to pick up golden apples.

168 *messenger of Fate:* a stock figure in classical Greek tragedy.

Jeanne d'Arc: (1412–1431) a shepherdess who became a heroine in France by leading the French army against the British, was burned as a witch, later sanctified.

170 *Land of Eshcol:* Old Testament, Numbers 12; where Moses sent spies who found fruit.

173 *Queen Victoria:* (1819–1901) Queen of England and Empress of. India.

178 *Sicily:* a major colony of ancient Athens.
asphodel: flower that bloomed in the Elysian Fields of Greek myth; said to be narcissus-like.

188 [Thomas] *Carlyle:* (1795–1891) English essayist.

191 *daffies:* daffodils (*narcissus*) spring bulbs.
bloodroot: white spring woodland flower (*Sanguinaria canadensis*).
bent: sail rigged onto mast and boom for the first time.

193 *down from the mount where her face had shone so bright:* see Old Testament, Exodus 34:29, where Moses' face shines because he had been talking to God.

194 *Sodom:* city filled with wicked men; see Old Testament, Genesis 19.

195 *I routed her, horse and foot:* I defeated an army, including cavalry and infantry.

201 *sweet-fern:* fragrant, very popular plant (*Comptonia asplendifolia*) for indoor growing, drying, in nineteenth century; earlier, used for making ink.

SOULS BELATED

205 *cloud of touts:* a touter is one who solicits custom; one who canvasses for customers or clients—i.e., for hotels.
"Par-ten-za!": leaving; "All aboard!"
Revue de Paris: a mainly literary review, 1829–45 and 1851–89; partly with a view to helping unknown writers; it was the first literary review to serialize novels (like *Madame Bovary*).

208 *a parterre box at the opera:* the part of the ground floor of the auditorium of a theater behind the orchestra; later in the U.S., that part beneath the galleries.
cheaper in the end to get everything from Worth: Charles Frederick Worth (1825–1895); Anglo-French dressmaker; designer of women's clothes in Paris; arbiter of Paris fashions for thirty years.
landau: carriage.
Cruikshank prints: presumably George (1792–1878), caricaturist and political satirist, as well as an illustrator; political and social caricatures of fashionable costume and manners.

210 *Je n'en vois pas las nécessité!:* It is not necessary to me; it does not matter to me.

213 *tout d'une pièce:* all of a piece.
a modus vivendi: a way of being in the world.

214 *table d'hôte:* ordinary people.
Monte Rosa: in Switzerland.

215 *Civis Romanus sum:* I am a Roman citizen.

216 *Hotel Bellosguardo: Bellosguardo* means "good view"—i.e., the hotel

with a good view, but it can also be interpreted as a hotel where the viewing is good—i.e., a good place to watch people.

217 *the laurustrinus alley:* an alley covered with an evergreen, winter-flowering shrub.

218 *premier:* the best suite of rooms in a hotel.

Doucet: an elegant French designer of the mid-1800s.

227 *The Reign of Law and Professor Drummond:* "The Reign of Law in Nature is universal"—James Lawson Drummond, M.D. (1783–1853), professor of anatomy; founded the Belfast Natural History Society and Philosophical Society.

229 *as Latude returned to his cell:* Henri Masers de Latude (1725–1805), French state prisoner.

230 *noyade of passion:* a drowning.

231 *Bradshaw:* colloquial designation of Bradshaw's Railway Guide, a timetable of all railway trains running in Great Britain; in its earliest form issued by George Bradshaw in 1839; ceased in 1961.

FOR THE BEST IN PAPERBACKS, LOOK FOR THE

In every corner of the world, on every subject under the sun, Penguin represents quality and variety—the very best in publishing today.

For complete information about books available from Penguin—including Penguin Classics, Penguin Compass, and Puffins—and how to order them, write to us at the appropriate address below. Please note that for copyright reasons the selection of books varies from country to country.

In the United States: Please write to *Penguin Group (USA), P.O. Box 12289 Dept. B, Newark, New Jersey 07101-5289* or call *1-800-788-6262.*

In the United Kingdom: Please write to *Dept. EP, Penguin Books Ltd, Bath Road, Harmondsworth, West Drayton, Middlesex UB7 0DA.*

In Canada: Please write to *Penguin Books Canada Ltd, 90 Eglinton Avenue East, Suite 700, Toronto, Ontario M4P 2Y3.*

In Australia: Please write to *Penguin Books Australia Ltd, P.O. Box 257, Ringwood, Victoria 3134.*

In New Zealand: Please write to *Penguin Books (NZ) Ltd, Private Bag 102902, North Shore Mail Centre, Auckland 10.*

In India: Please write to *Penguin Books India Pvt Ltd, 11 Panchsheel Shopping Centre, Panchsheel Park, New Delhi 110 017.*

In the Netherlands: Please write to *Penguin Books Netherlands bv, Postbus 3507, NL-1001 AH Amsterdam.*

In Germany: Please write to *Penguin Books Deutschland GmbH, Metzlerstrasse 26, 60594 Frankfurt am Main.*

In Spain: Please write to *Penguin Books S. A., Bravo Murillo 19, 1° B, 28015 Madrid.*

In Italy: Please write to *Penguin Italia s.r.l., Via Benedetto Croce 2, 20094 Corsico, Milano.*

In France: Please write to *Penguin France, Le Carré Wilson, 62 rue Benjamin Baillaud, 31500 Toulouse.*

In Japan: Please write to *Penguin Books Japan Ltd, Kaneko Building, 2-3-25 Koraku, Bunkyo-Ku, Tokyo 112.*

In South Africa: Please write to *Penguin Books South Africa (Pty) Ltd, Private Bag X14, Parkview, 2122 Johannesburg.*